ALISON
dean pa
and Ess
study an
Univers
2006 an
lished in

logy of Glasgow writing, *Outside of a Dog*. In 2007 she was awarded a Scottish Arts Council New Writer's Bursary. *This Road is Red* is her first novel and was developed through her close association with Glasgow Life's Red Road Flats Cultural Project.

She lives in Glasgow with her family.

A Word from the Red Road Flats Cultural Project.

Glasgow Housing Association (GHA) and Glasgow Life created a partnership in 2008 to develop and deliver a range of historical and art programmes for current and former residents of Red Road and the surrounding neighbourhoods to commemorate the end of an era in Glasgow's history.

As much of Red Road's significance is attributed to its size, the programmes undertaken have focused on people's memories, stories and photographs.

The aim of the project is to capture the full story of Red Road's fifty-year life. We hope this book will help keep Red Road alive for years to come.

Details of the full range of projects which have been delivered and are in progress are available at www.redroadflats.org.uk.

This Road is Red

ALISON IRVINE

Luath Press Limited

EDINBURGH

www.luath.co.uk

First published 2011

ISBN : 978-1-906817-81-7

Published by Luath Press in association with

The paper used in this book is neutral sized and recyclable.
It is made from elemental chlorine free pulps sourced from
renewable forests.

Printed and bound by
CPI Bookmarque, Croydon CRO 4TD

Typeset in 10.5 point Sabon
by 3btype.com

For Eddie

In memory of John McNally,
resident of the Red Road Flats 1969–2009

Acknowledgements

THE BOOK WOULD NOT have been possible without the generosity of the people I interviewed. Their time, their enthusiasm for the project and their willingness to go over the tiny details of their experiences gave me such rich material to work with. Thank you so much. You have made writing this book an absolute pleasure:

Beki
June Aird
Matt Barr
Mojgan Behkar
Jim Bonner
Louise Christie
Sara Farrukh
Jahanzeb Farrukh
Derek Fowler
Ruvinbo Gombedza
Aysha Iqbal
Azam Khan
Veronica Low
Willy Maley
Jim McAveety
Helen McDermott
Sharon McDermott
Billy McDonald
Peter McDonald
Jean McGeough
Finlay McKay
John McNally
Frank Miller

Ntombi Ngwenya
Bob Niven
Thomas Plunkett
Marie Quinn
Grant Richmond
Donna Taylor
Iseult Timmermans

And the young people from Impact Arts' Gallery 37: Ibrahim, Christian, Heder, Rahel, Ibrahim and James.

Thank you also to Bash Khan, Johnny McBrier, James Muir, Lindsay Perth, Remzije Sherifi, Eulalia Stewart, Kate Tough, Impact Arts, the Scottish Refugee Council, members of the Red Road Flats Project Steering Group, and Glasgow Life's Martin Wright, Ruth Wright and the rest of the team. Thanks to Glasgow Housing Association for funding the project. Particular thanks to Jonny Howes from Glasgow Life whose support has been invaluable.

Thank you to Gavin MacDougall, Christine Wilson and their colleagues at Luath Press, and to Mitch Miller who illustrated the book.

Lastly, thank you to all my family: especially to Linda, Luke and Sammy Byrne, and of course to Arlene and Isla. To Eddie, thank you for everything. I couldn't have done this without you.

Prologue

1964–1969

A MAN WITH A strong back and muscles thumbs braces over his shoulders, then sits to tie black boots. He stands at the sink and drinks tea with milk and sugar. Tunes the radio to fiddle music. Butters bread, cuts cheese and makes his piece. Finds his silver piece tin and puts his piece inside. Pours boiling water over tea leaves in a flask. Combs Bay Rum through his hair.

A pile of library books on the table. A basin under the table for later, to steep his feet. His wakening household. Children; nine of them, shifting in their shared beds. A son, the youngest, waiting at the kitchen door to make his breakfast and retune the radio. Bunnet. Coat. Piece tin and flask. Out the door. His son takes over the kitchen.

The man walks to Red Road. Mud and cabbage fields. Wet and wind and rain. The steel hanging off cranes. The gangs assembling. A day's work. Years' work. For him and for the trades. Good money.

Eating his piece and a young one sits next to him, tells him he's not happy because he's working overtime and not getting as much as his pal in another gang. You'll get your bonus, don't fash, the man says and takes it upon himself to have a word with the ganger.

Every day, the walk in his hard boots through Possil to Red Road. The steel frame rising, fixed at the joints by men with balance and nerve. The man going up in a hoist. Using muscles honed laying sleepers at Cowlairs. Hup hup hup. They get their bonus.

Twenty floors up. Someone lights a fire to fend off the

freezing cold. Someone else tells him to put it out or they'll all get sent down the road. Men not expecting their legs to sway with fear, looking down at the mud and the kit and the huts.

The man sees Arran on the clearest day yet. Its blue-grey bulk at the far side of the sky. The Clyde and the shipyards. Grit and glitter. It's shipyard steel they're building with. Sand and gold on the Campsie Fells. The men stop work to look, take bunnets off and wipe foreheads.

In summer eight students and their teacher come from Barmulloch College, go up in the hoist, learn about sway in tall buildings. Hold a plumb line and see that the steel structure sways. Can't feel it but see the line move so believe it. The man feels it when they clad the steel, and the wind bullies the blocks, unable to get through anymore. Oh, then they sway.

More disputes. The men hear of another gang on more over-time. They're not trades, he and these men, they're the lowest paid and he will not have them exploited. He's a union man, a fighter for the left. Don't fash he says to the young ones.

They stop work for the opening of Ten Red Road. Thirty floors of four-room apartments. Ceremonies, plaudits, photographs. Ballots and excitement. Firemen doubling up as removal men and pulling up with people's furniture.

Then on with Thirty-three Petershill Drive. Newspapers tell of overspend and high costs. It's work though, for locals and those who move into the area, turning up with skills and strength. Working six or seven days a week, like the man, for his wife and his weans.

Late May 1967 and the boy waits for his father. The street is empty of boys and footballs. Everyone's inside. The man works overtime and checks his watch. He's too high up to hear cheers or roars from television sets. It's on his mind as he works. They stop in time to run to Springburn and stand outside Rediffusion. Black and white televisions in the window show the match in Lisbon. He stands with other labourers and they watch the second half from the pavement, looking in at the televisions. At the final whistle their arms raise above their heads and the man sees the smiles of the fans in the crowd and the smiles of the players and their own smiles reflected in the shop's window. Come for a drink, his workmates say, and he says no, he doesn't care to drink anymore and he walks home happy. He finds his boy celebrating out the back and stands among triumphant neighbours watching wee ones go wild.

His wash at the sink is pleasurable and slow. Champions. All day labouring, all day thinking about the game. He pours water from the kettle into the basin, tops it up with cold. Moves a chair. Sits. His boy watches as he unlaces his hard boots and rolls each sock down an ankle and foot. He puts his feet in the basin and the boy tunes the radio to Sanderson and Crampsey. A plate of food, kept warm, a quick sleep and the next day is work and some of the boys are tired from celebrating.

The man is sixty years old. He labours on all the buildings. Is there till the last in 1969. He builds the concrete castle for the weans and the paths that go from building to building. Low walls. Grass. A place where the shops will be. Full classes and overspills in the primary schools. More schools needing built. The last of the trades come in to do their jobs. Tenants move in and the workers move out. Red Road. He built the highest towers in Europe.

His son views the flats as he walks with his siblings in a line behind his father and he thinks of the Yellow Brick Road. Likes them. Sleek. Space age. Mammoth. Rid Road says his mother. Red Road. His father's last workplace. Red Road. Houses for thousands.

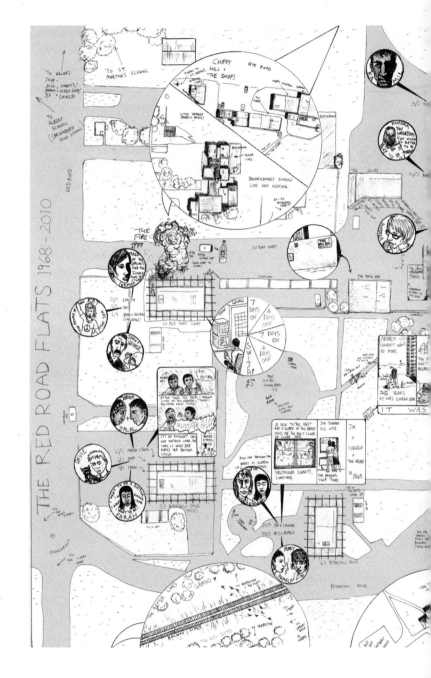

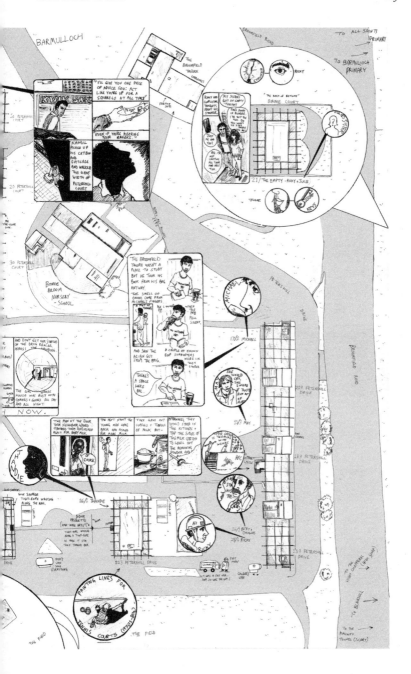

Section One

May 1966

SHE WATCHED AS THE towers grew larger. Her boy played with the frayed seat-top in front of him. The bus slowed at every stop and people took an age to get on and off. She would cry, she swore, if they'd run out of houses and she had to go back to the Calton.

The buildings were shocking. Massive. Some finished, with sleek sides and neat rows of windows, others with their insides exposed, dark as engines. Half-finished cladding. Cranes hanging over the tops. Scaffolding. The noise of the construction was exhilarating.

'Ma, Ma, look up, they're falling!'

May pulled her son's arm and told him they didn't have time to stop but she glanced at the tumbling clouds at the tops of the towers and knew what he meant.

It seemed like the whole of Glasgow was in the foyer of one-eight-three Petershill Drive. Shouts and laughter and hand claps.

'Are they nice?' May said to someone, anyone.

'Brand new.'

'What did you get?'

'Twenty-two floor. Number four.' The woman's face was full and freckled. She smiled.

Her man dangled a key from his thumb and forefinger then snapped his fist around it. He wore a suit. His smile was huge.

'It's something else.' The woman touched May on the shoulder. 'The most beautiful house I've ever seen.'

'Come on, son.'

May didn't care what she got but she had to get something.

The man at the desk sat like Santa. He clicked a pen with his thumb.

'What do I do?'

'Put your hand in and take a piece of paper.'

'Are there any left?'

'Oh, aye, plenty.'

May stopped. It was too much. She couldn't believe it could happen. The police, the Corporation, they said they'd help her get away and here she was about to get her new start. He'll find me. He'll chase me all the way to Red Road. He'll wreck it. She didn't deserve this, one of these immaculate houses.

The man waved his hand over the ballot box and said, 'On you go.'

Yes, she bloody did deserve it.

Eyes closed, she put in her hand and felt for a slip of paper.

'What have we got, what have we got?' Her son jumped up to look at the piece of paper.

'Fifteen/three, that's what we've got,' she said to her son. 'Fifteen/three.'

'Is that a good one?'

'Oh aye, son, that's a good one.'

'Now, some folk have been swapping their houses if they'd prefer something higher up or lower down, and that's fine,' the man said.

'Oh no. I won't be swapping my house.'

She handed the piece of paper to the man who wrote her name and house number in a ledger and gave her a set of keys. An elderly couple leaning on sticks stood behind her. May turned around and held her keys out to them, just as the man in the suit had done to her.

'I've got my house.'

'Well done, hen, that's smashing.'

'On you go up in the lift,' the man behind the desk said.

'Which one?'

'Either. They both go up and they both go down.'

May took her son's hand and stood proudly by the lift,

looking at the painted walls and the sparkling ceiling and floor. She tapped her fingers against his.

'Calm down, Ma,' her son said.

'I can't help it.'

The lift was full of people when the doors opened. They seemed like her kind of people, happy and friendly and the folk that squeezed in with them seemed like her kind of people too, one man taking all the orders for the floors, pressing the buttons and calling out mind the doors.

It was the cleanest, most amazing house she had ever seen, with a view out over the Broomfield. All fields and grass. Gorgeous. A bathroom inside the house with basin, toilet, bath. A kitchen with spotless cupboards, an electric cooker and oven. A living room, two bedrooms, a veranda off one of the bedrooms and another room with no windows but big enough for something – what? – she barely had anything to fill the house with. It opened out, bare and lit and freshly painted, in front of her. She would work to fill the house with furniture and rugs and crockery and toys. She would work to pay the high rent. By God, she would work. She took off her coat. Where to start? And that's when she cried, finally, knowing they were safe.

Jim 1966

Each day as Jim passed he used to see the men at work boring the fields by Red Road. He knew something was going to happen. Each day on their way along the road to the Provan Gasworks he and his wife, who worked at the gasworks too, saw the men and noted the small developments; the ground levelled, the surplus earth pushed into heaps, the concrete mixers, diggers and cranes, the workmen's huts, until eventually it was all steel, steel, steel. Then, Jim and his wife realised that something big was taking place, something mammoth.

Jim worked hard; the gaffer of the labouring squad at the

gasworks. When the industry moved from old coal to oil, the foreign gas, he was there, in charge of his squad. The catalyst squad. The pick and shovel days were away and it was chemicals they used now. Cleaner, safer. Jim took his job seriously.

It was his wife who said to him shall we try for a house in the Red Road Flats and because it would be handy for work, Jim said, aye, why not. The older children married or working away. Just the younger two under the roof. The bairnies.

Twenty-eight/four. Ten Red Road. A view to the west and a glimpse of the Arran hills on the clearest of days. High enough to see whole sunsets spread like syrup across the sky.

Matt Barr

I was nine when we moved there. My first memories were my dad trying to describe an electric fire. It was fitted on the wall in the living room. We came from Springburn, a room and kitchen up a close with an outside toilet on the landing. My mum and dad slept in the kitchen in a wee in-shot where there was a double bed and then you went through a lobby and there was a big front room which was like a general purpose room but we had a big double bed in it and all three brothers slept in the same bed together. It was a godsend to move to a beautiful brand-new house. I remember when we moved in they were still actually building all the other blocks and there was a big fence that ran all the way round the building site. I remember there was nothing to do, no playgrounds, no amenities. So we played in the building works a lot. We were always getting chased by watchmen. We were quite young. We never did anything bad.

Jennifer 1966

They went for a walk. To get to know the area, her father said, and her mother spent a wee while at the mirror fixing her hair. Her father kissed her mother's neck. Jennifer and her brother wore their chapel shoes and their granny's knitted jumpers underneath their winter coats. Their mother tilted their faces to her and patted their heads before they left the house. The lift shook its way to the ground.

'Where are we going?' Jennifer said, because the day felt like an event.

'Where the wind blows,' her father said.

When they walked through the canopy by the foyer doors the wind did blow, swirling construction-site dust and debris at their feet. Jennifer and her mother nearly toppled and their coats flapped open to their bottom buttons. The family stepped out from the canopy where the wind was still cold but less charged.

Around them noise from the construction site was loud. They walked through frozen mud tracks and stood by the perimeter fence of the new long block and listened to the clangs and chips and thuds of the workmen inside.

'What I would like to do is get a loaf of bread,' Jennifer's mother said and they looked for a shop.

'That's where they'll build the shops,' her father said.

'No good to me at the moment.'

'Will we walk to Springburn? Or the ones at the top of the road?'

'We'll have to.'

But they didn't walk yet. Instead they looked up at the building in which they lived and their father told them to count down three rows of windows from the top. Twenty-eight, Ten Red Road Court. Flat four.

'It hurts my neck to look,' Jennifer said.

At the very top of the building strips of cladding met in a pinch, not quite a point, and the windows thinned to black lines.

Her father curved his hands above his eyes. 'What an idea. The audacity of those men. Colleen, did you ever think we'd be living twenty-eight up in a brand-new multi-storey?'

'No, I did not. If they built some shops, this place would be perfect.'

They stood, the family, in the cold wind and waved at the men and women and weans standing at other windows, eager and open and smiling.

'Where can we play?' Jennifer said.

Her mother and father looked about them at the workmen's huts and cranes and scaffolding.

'You can take a skipping rope or your balls and play outside the building,' her mother said and although there were no swings or slides, Jennifer thought that Red Road – the half-built buildings, the fields, the dips and ditches – was the most exciting place she'd ever seen.

'Jim, these weans will bring mud into the house every time they come in,' Jennifer's mother said. 'To think I scrubbed the Possil house from top to bottom to make them let us live here.'

'It worked. You did good. We're here,' Jennifer's father said and he took his wife's hand. 'Handy for work, too.'

Davie 1966

He held onto the cold scaffolding and looked at the pile of sand that rose below him like a great grey wave. One more jump. The highest one yet. They'd given the night watchman the runaround then hidden until he'd walked away, thinking, perhaps, they'd finally gone to their beds. Not so, Mr Watchman. He knew his friends were waiting behind the fence with their booty – scaffolding bolts and wooden boards. He turned and gave them the A-OK finger circle and breathed in before he leapt.

It was supposed to be a silent jump, like the Commandos, but it wasn't. He couldn't.

'Raaaah, oh oh oh rahhhh, ya beauty!'

He hooted and yelled and roared his beautiful drop to the sand. Sand covered him when he landed and he rolled, nothing in his ears but the scuff and rustle of his moving body, and when he lay in the sand, shoulders and head and arse half-buried, and breath coming out in laughs, he looked through the high scaffolding and felt extraordinary. The night fizzed, the clouds hung heavily.

Then he remembered the rats and sat up. Shouts.

'Sorry Davie!'

'Davie! Enemy!'

It was his pals, running away, the fence still jangling. Davie dragged his legs through the sand and was running to leap the fence when the night watchman's torch dazzled him. Before he could bolt, the night watchman's hand grabbed his arm and got him in a head hold. It hurt. He felt knuckles against his forehead.

'Game over, son.'

Torchlight was in his eyes again. Sand in his mouth.

'I'll go quietly.'

'You annoying wee prick.'

'I was training.'

'I've got a job to do.'

'Don't tell my da.'

'Now that's an idea. Right, you, out, and come with me.'

The night watchman straightened Davie up and gripped his neck, marching him to the gate. They walked to Thirty-three Petershill Drive. Davie wondered if his friends were hiding any-where and he did some Commando hand signals in case they were but stopped when the night watchman told him to pack it in, you bammy bastard.

Nobody about. Warm lights in some of the houses. Davie wondered what his da would say. His brothers would laugh. They'd be able to laugh in safety now, because they had their own beds, unlike the other house, with the three of them in one bed and never knowing who was going to get skelped as well when his da came in to administer discipline.

'I'm going to leave you here and watch you get in the lift and you're going to go in your house and get into your bed and give me some peace. If I catch you out here again I promise you, your da will know about this.'

The night watchman pushed Davie through the door. Davie pressed the button for the lift and wiped sand off his knees. He snuck a look at the watchman and saw that he was shorter than he'd thought, and younger, and he looked a bit like his uncle John. He watched him put a cigarette between his lips and light up, flicking the match to the ground.

'On you go,' the night watchman said through smoke, and motioned towards the lift.

Without a word Davie returned to his house.

'Did you do the jump?' his brother asked, lifting his head off the pillow.

'Aye. I flew.'

'Did you get caught?'

Davie undid the catch on the window and leaned right out.

'No way.'

He saw the night watchman down below, patrolling the piles of sand and scaffolding with the unmade tower reaching into the dark sky, and when the night watchman was away over the other side of the site, he saw the rats come out, odd random rats at first, darting and stopping and starting, and then a whole teeming load of them, crawling over everything, getting in about it, reclaiming the place and picking at the workmen's pieces.

Jennifer 1966

Jennifer's mother told the children to go out or stay in but not to play on the landing. Her children chose to go, the back stairs ringing with their heavy footsteps. We want to try these stairs, they said and she shouted after them to take care and mind they didn't bring mud into the house when they returned.

Then Jennifer's mother propped open her front door and collected up her neighbours' doormats and her own. She put hot water in a bucket, added some Flash and took her mop from the cupboard. Downstairs in the foyer she'd seen a sign with the number four on it which meant it was her turn for washing the floor.

Flakes of mud and faint footsteps covered the floor. There was more dust and dirt in the rectangles where the doormats had lain. She swept first with a bristled brush and tipped the sweepings down the chute. Then she ran the mop over the mud, pushing it hard over the bits that had stuck to the tiles.

The woman from number three opened her door and told her to come in for a cup of tea after, if she had time, and Colleen said she would, even though there was the tea to be cooked and she was just in from her work herself. She used fresh water to clean the suds from the floor and then she used a dish towel to dry the floor. And while she had the mop and bucket out she did her own floors too. Then she went next door for a cup of tea and the women stood on the veranda with their cups in their hands and the wind in their faces, looking down at the weans and the workers coming home off the buses below.

Jean McGeogh

Aye, they were all going up, they were all getting built. There was a lot of noise but it was good. I loved the flats, I loved them. Great neighbours. Neighbours in a million they were. Really all working-class folk, you know, good, honest, and you could leave your door opened and anything.

Jennifer 1967

Jennifer's father called the family into the living room. He told them to mind the pasting table and be careful of the dust cloth. Then he cast a hand in front of the red swirls on the wall and said, 'See this, this wallpaper. It will outlast us. Outlive us. Put up by the hands of a master decorator. It'll be up for the next fifty years.'

Jennifer's mother ran her palm over the wall and said, 'It's very red.'

'Do you like it?'

She smiled. 'I love it. It's just how I wanted it.'

Jennifer liked it too. The living room looked like the pages of her mother's magazines. Hot and red and luscious; the swirls on the walls like the swirls on her dress.

'Away and play,' her mother and father said at the same time. Her father put his fingers through his hair and his hair stayed spiked. Jennifer and James grabbed their coats and shut the door behind them.

Outside, they ran across the mud to where the men were building the next tower. Steel and cranes and temporary floors way up the inside of the building. They found a sheet of plastic which James stabbed at with a stick. They saw asbestos. Jennifer picked up a piece then threw it to the ground. She found a better piece, good for drawing lines, and they ran back across the mud to the side of their block. James left her and went to talk to a boy on a bike. Jennifer marked her beds on the ground and threw her peever stone. Girls came along, including the girl from number three with pigtails, Jennifer's neighbour. They played, taking their own stones from their peever tins, bending close to the ground as they drew more beds with more asbestos.

Her brother dragged a piece of wood and stamped on it, telling the girls he was breaking it into pieces for his crossbow. A girl they'd never seen before took two balls from her coat pocket and began to throw them against the wall. The others stopped to watch her as she chanted her rhyme and slapped at the balls and when there was nothing new to see they went back to their beds.

Jennifer's mother at the very top of Ten Red Road with a basket of wet sheets, the wind swaying the washing lines and flicking the sheets into her face when she hangs them up. The sheets shifting and flapping. She's holding pegs in her teeth and clipping a bedspread to the line. Her hair in her face, her dress with the swirls on it flat against her legs. Thick clouds and a white sky. Seagulls sit on the ledge that goes round the building. The ledge is as high as Jennifer's mother's shoulders. The very top of the flats. It's exhilarating.

And Jennifer's mother is proud of her family; her husband who she walks with every day to the gasworks in Provanmill where she cooks and he labours; her children who are well-mannered and doing great at school. The rent is a leap from the house in Possil, yes, ten pounds a month, and more than they paid for a quarter year in their old house. But they won't want to move to Cumbernauld like their neighbours from across the landing. No thank you. They're happy at Red Road.

They're still building the flats. The work goes on and on. She's at the centre of a new era. New housing. New Glasgow. She looks at the half-finished cladding on Ninety-three Petershill Drive. Semi-clothed. A trouser halfway up a leg. To the left of the building a boy crosses the wasteland. He scampers; leaping and veering and running. He wears shorts and a T-shirt with a collar. He carries a bag that hangs from his fist like a cartoon burglar's sack. Strong legs. Windblown hair. She watches him run out of her view, behind the half-built tower. A scan of where he came from – the open ground and the railway – and then she picks up her washing basket and peg bag and goes back down the stair.

The boy ran straight at them, his sandshoes slapping on the concrete. Jennifer and the girls stopped their beds and waited for him to go away. James looked up from where he sat on the ground, nailing his pieces of wood into a cross shape. He stared at the older boy. The older boy stopped and panted, a lick of fringe falling below one eyebrow, his bag hanging from one hand.

'Are you making a crossbow?'

'Aye.'

'For hunting rats?'

'Maybe.'

One of the girls threw her stone and hopped over her beds.

'What's in your bag?' James said.

Something in the bag jerked and scrabbled. The boy held the bag out in front of him, his fist gripped tightly around it.

'Guess,' the boy said.

James stared.

'A ferret,' Jennifer said.

'How did you know?'

'I seen another boy with a ferret in a bag.'

'Who?'

'Kenneth Campbell.'

'I don't know him.'

'Well he had a ferret too. What's your name?'

'Davie. Did you see the ferret?'

'No.'

'Do you want to see this?'

'Aye.'

The girls held their stones, James stood up and the girl with the balls stopped playing. Davie smiled. He had the beginnings of an Adam's apple in his throat and hair that hung loose around his ears and neck. He held the bag in the crook of one elbow and slipped a hand in. His wrist came out first and then he lifted out the ferret. Davie dropped the bag and put his other hand on the ferret, bringing it close to his body. The children stepped in to look and the ferret twitched and struggled, its back and sides moving as it breathed.

'Ah it's so cute!' one of the girls said.

'Does it bite?' said Jennifer.

'Yes.'

The girl with the balls ran away.

'Where did you find it?' James asked.

'By the railway.'

'How did you catch it?'

'Jumped it.'

Eyes raised from the ferret to Davie's face to the ferret again.

'What will you do with it?'

'Play with it, then let it go.'

The children took a turn at stroking the ferret's fur. Its eyes didn't stop moving.

Davie said, 'I'm going to let it go now.'

'You didn't keep it for long,' said one of the girls.

'I can catch another one, easy. Pass me that bag.'

James picked up the bag and held it out to Davie who took it and released the ferret. Then he turned and walked away. James stared after him. The girls stared too.

'He's my big brother's pal,' one of them said.

James picked up his crossbow, left his sister and her pals, and went after Davie.

Davie and some big boys kicked stones as they walked, in no particular hurry and in no particular direction. They grabbed at things they found on the ground, hurling them in the air. One picked up an empty ginger bottle and swung it from a finger. Another pulled his arms out of his jumper, stretched it over his head and tied it around his waist. James watched Davie drag a piece of wood along the side of a wall, then step on the wood and snap it, the bag with the ferret gone. The boy's jumper slipped off his waist and fell on the mud. James was about to shout after them but they ran, suddenly, and James had to run too. He stopped at the jumper, picked it up and followed the boys into the foyer of his own building, Ten Red Road. They got in the lift.

'That's my jumper,' one of the boys said.

'I came to give it to you.' James held out the jumper and the boy took it.

'Cheers wee man.' The boy sniffed like a grown up.

James looked up at the big boys. They chewed sweets with wet lips and leaned against the walls of the lift.

'What will we do?' one of them said. 'Play in the lift or chap door run away?'

There was the sound of the foyer door opening.

'Quick!' Davie pressed a button and the doors closed. 'You choose, wee man,' he said.

James didn't like being stuck in the lift. It had happened once before with his sister so he said, 'Chap door run away.'

The lift went up and one of the boys said they'd start at the top and work down. Oh mammy daddy, he had heard about the boys and girls who played chap door run away. He wanted to go home. He didn't want to go home. He looked up at Davie who patted his shoulder.

'It's all right, pal. Stick with me. Best to plank your cross-bow somewhere.'

So James leaned the piece of wood against the side of the lift and waited. One of the boys took a length of wool from his pocket and wound it round his fingers.

The lift stopped at floor thirty and the boys got out. The boy with the wool tiptoed to one of the doors and tied one end of the length of wool to the door handle. All the boys began to giggle, bending over and holding their hands over their mouths, big eyes looking around, a trickle of snorts and squeaks and inhalation. Tiptoes and bent backs.

'Hurry up,' one said. His voice was a whisper.

Davie took hold of the other end of the wool and began to stretch it across the landing but footsteps sounded from behind one of the doors and the boys ran into each other, wild and feverish. A key unlocking a lock. About to get caught. They fled out of the landing door, the boy yanking the wool free from the door handle, onto the stairs, running down them fast, each boy running a few steps then putting a hand on the banisters and jumping the rest. Three floors down they stood in the stairwell with the door to the twenty-seventh floor ajar. James stood with his head down, breathing fast, and smiling.

'Okay, this one,' the boy with the wool said.

James knew his downstairs neighbours but he didn't say anything.

They were better organised this time; swifter, less gangly about their work. Doors one and four were opposite each other. The boy with the wool stood outside door one and tied the wool around the door handle. Then, with Davie standing by him, he stretched the wool across the landing to door four and tied the wool to door four's handle. He checked the wool which was taut and checked the knots which were strong. A boy stood by one door and Davie stood by the other. James watched their hand signals; one, two, three. He knew it was going to happen but he wasn't prepared for the noise of the knocking and the charge towards him as the boys ran for the door. James was first down the stairs, hooting and sucking in his lips; he even jumped the last three steps, but when he looked back, the boys weren't following. They were bunched by the door, motionless. One turned to James and scowled. Davie put his finger to his lips and beckoned for James to come back up.

'Listen,' he said.

Footsteps.

'Hold on please,' said a woman's voice. It was Mrs Cameron, his mother's friend.

Scuffling and scratching. 'Hello?'

The first tug on the wool and all the boys nearly collapsed, holding their stomachs, bunching fists into their mouths. James giggled. The wool tightened as the woman pulled her door but couldn't open it.

'My door's jammed,' she said. 'Who's out there?'

The door rattled on the other side now. Big tough tugs that made Mrs Cameron's door click shut.

A man's voice. 'What's going on here?'

The boys looked towards the door with the big voice behind it. The wool stretched across the landing. Mrs Cameron's voice again, 'Harry, is that you?' Her letterbox open and her voice coming out of it.

'I can't stop laughing.'

'Maggie, are you stuck too?'

'I'm dying with laughter.'

'I can't open my door,' she said.

'She's talking through her letter box!'

'Neither can I.'

'Something's jammed. Can you give yours a tug, Harry?'

'I'm trying.'

'Tug it harder.'

'I'm going to die laughing.'

'Some wee bastards have tied our doors together.'

'Oh my God, he's going to break the wool.'

When the boys saw the man's door lurch violently inwards and crash shut then lurch violently inwards again they ran down the stairs, floor after floor, silently, slowing up when they felt safe, until they walked nonchalantly onto a freshly cleaned landing where a pair of lift doors were opening, letting out a woman, James's mother.

The older boys put their hands in their pockets and stepped aside to let James's mother pass. Silence. Casual stances. Not a word was spoken except by James's mother. 'James, up the stair with me, please, after I give these messages to Alice.'

The boys put their heads down and stepped into the lift, Davie looking up once to wink at James, before getting in the lift himself.

'Hey, wee man, do you want your crossbow?' Davie shouted and held the crossbow between the doors.

'No he does not,' James's mother said.

In the house she ran a bath then called down from the veranda for Jennifer. She dropped a sponge into the bathwater and tested the temperature with her fingers. James climbed in.

'What were you doing with those older boys?'

James looked at her and thought before he spoke. His mother waited.

'I don't want to find out you've been terrorising our neighbours. These are good people we live among.'

'One of the boys, Davie, he caught a ferret.'

'Really? A live ferret?'

'Aye. I stroked it.'

They talked about the ferret and his mother said, 'As long as you don't bring one in the house.'

When he thought it was safe, he bent his head and splashed water on his arms and chest and changed the subject.

'Are you pleased with your wallpaper?'

'Oh aye.' She looked around the bathroom walls. 'We'll do in here next.'

James heard his sister come in.

'I found your crossbow in the lift,' she said and his mother shook her head and left the two of them in the bathroom, Jennifer sitting down to pee and laughing as James told her all about his time with the big boys.

Jennifer 1968

Jennifer watched the carpet. The wind got under it and made it billow like a sheet. She couldn't tell how the wind got there because the carpet was fitted from wall to wall. She chased the

ripple and slammed the heel of her hand onto the carpet as if
she was catching a rat. The building swayed and the tassels on
the lampshade shook. The sound of crashing pots and cutlery
came from the kitchen.

'Good God, some hurricane,' Jennifer's mother said. She
stood by the window. 'I hope they knew what they were doing
when they built up this high.'

Her father stood up and joined her at the window. Jennifer
stood up too and rested her chin and hands on the window sill.

'They were built to sway a bit,' he said.

'A bit!'

Jennifer thought they could be at sea; her eleven-year-old
hands holding onto the railing of some bulky ship, while the
turbulent air heaved them one way and then the other. She
looked down into the dark and saw shapes she thought might
be sheets of plastic or sheets of newspaper or kit from the
building sites thrown into the air or blown, twisting, onto Red
Road.

'And James is sleeping through this,' her mother said.

They were quiet. Jennifer saw a patch of condensation form
at the bottom of the window from where her breath stopped
on the cold pane. She looked up at the reflection of her parents'
faces. Gentle.

And then the building shuddered and her father nearly fell
on her and her mother screamed and the pots in the kitchen
were at it again and the books on the shelf gave up on themselves. Jennifer gripped the window ledge. Her father said sorry
hen, and her mother said right, who's coming? She took the
blanket that lay on the settee, slung it over one shoulder and
tucked a couple of cushions under her arm. 'Jennifer?'

'I'll stay and mind James,' her father said.

Jennifer and her mother caught the lift downstairs and
stepped into the foyer where other neighbours had gathered.
Mrs McCluskey, Lizzy and Harry from down the stair, Mr and

Mrs Fine; everyone from the high up floors. One old woman sat asleep on a chair.

'Terra firma,' her mother said and she sat Jennifer down and told her to put her head on the cushion and get under the blanket and sleep, which Jennifer did, but she couldn't sleep. She keeked at the men in their pyjamas and the women with their curlers and knitting, and listened to the chat. Moans, jokes, remarks – they were familiar voices and they all said they wouldn't be going back up the stair until the hurricane passed on. Each time the lift doors opened the talking stopped and the heads turned and the new refugees were greeted with catcalls and comments. Jennifer stared at the legs of everyone around her until her mother woke her in the middle of the night and heaved her up to join the others, standing and shaking themselves in their slippered feet; washed up debris on a storm-shattered beach.

Betty 1968

Betty put on her housecoat and got her man out the door with his piece and flask and straightened tie. When she closed the door she looked over her house with her ferocious eye, straightening the pictures in the hall and picking up the envelopes and papers that had slipped from the wee table. Her tea cups had shuddered on their saucers but the china on the sideboard was intact. Not so the Aynsley ladies who had toppled from their glass shelf in the display cabinet; the door had sprung open and a bouquet of flowers and tiny hand were lying on the carpet. She couldn't bear to look.

Outside, Red Road lay bruised and swollen: flattened grass on the fields, trees down, a car on its side. Wreckage everywhere. A lump of steel stuck into the side of one of the unfinished buildings. More steel lay thrust into the ground.

She would start with the landing floor, work from the outside in, and get her house straightened and correct. On the way to the mop and bucket and Zoflora she picked up her poor wee ladies and put their broken parts into a dish for Douglas to deal with when he returned from work. At least the swaying had stopped.

Opening the door to the landing, she set the bucket down on the lino.

'Douglas!'

Her husband sat on the landing, his back against the wall, knees bent, head lolling onto his right shoulder.

'Douglas, what are you doing?'

He didn't move or answer.

'Douglas?'

She rattled the mop against the bucket and was just about to rattle his arse when he started. Thank God he wasn't dead.

'Douglas, look at you!'

He held his hands out in front of him as if fighting off an attacker. 'I'm waiting for the lift.'

'No, you're not, you're asleep. Get up.'

It had been a terrible night. Douglas had sat up in bed for most of it, facing the wall above the bedstead, his hands and forehead pressed against it, moaning at every clash and clink outside. Betty had seen the night through with a few wee halfs but Douglas didn't touch anything because he said he'd be sick if he moved away from the wall.

'Oh my wee darling,' Betty said, softening, and helped him up. 'Will we get you in the lift before you get the sack and we get thrown out of our new house?'

'You can take on a few more cleaning jobs if I get the sack,' Douglas said. There was nothing wrong with him.

He stretched as he stood and picked up his briefcase and umbrella. He pressed the lift button.

'I'm cleaning away over in Knightswood today, as a matter of fact,' Betty said. 'I'll have the tea in the slow cooker.'

'Ach, that's why I fell asleep,' Douglas said. 'Look, Betty, the lifts aren't working.'

One of the lifts jerked itself down to their floor. Knocking and shouts. Young voices. Scuffling.

'Let us out,' they heard someone say.

'We've been stuck between floors. Will you get the doors open for us?'

Douglas put the point of his umbrella between the lift doors.

'Take your jacket off,' Betty said.

Douglas didn't answer and levered the doors open with his jacket on.

A gaggle of uniformed children fell out onto the landing. They milled and fretted and hopped around and spoke in high voices.

'Did you not hear us shouting?' one boy said.

'I was asleep, son.'

'My sister slept through the whole hurricane.'

Douglas yawned. Betty looked at the children and noted areas for improvement. When it was clear that the other lift was stuck too she took matters into her own hands.

'You can come through the house,' she said, 'and use the back stairs.'

It was the only way down if the lifts were broken.

'Some storm,' the boy said.

'Yes, and mind your fingers on the walls.' She led the way through the lobby and into the bedroom where she unbolted both doors and stood back to let the children pass.

'Wait!' she ordered. 'Douglas, we can't let these children out in the state they're in.'

'There's nothing wrong with them.'

'Shoes. Hair. Stains. This one's face needs washing.'

The children looked up at the adults with pale, expectant faces, brylcremed quiffs and Alice bands. Beautiful shining eyes, the lot of them. Betty felt a tug inside herself, some shift towards sadness or serenity, it was hard to tell.

Her husband laid his briefcase on the bed and knelt in front of the open wardrobe. He leaned inside and pulled out a shoebox.

Betty ran out of the room and returned with a bowl, a flannel and a brush.

'Line up!' she said.

The children did as they were told, turning their heads to peek at the bowls of potpourri, the wedding picture on the chest of drawers, the poem in a frame – *If*, it began.

'What's that, a prayer?' one wee boy said.

'It's a poem about how to live,' Douglas said. 'I'll do their shoes first.'

He told the first child to sit on the bed.

They were silent as Douglas opened a tin of black polish, dipped the bristles of a wooden brush into it and began to scrub the shoe. He asked the child to straighten his leg and put his flexed foot into his hand and he did the back and sides and toe of the shoe and then he took a yellow cloth and shined up his work. He did the other shoe and the children and Betty watched. When he was done the boy stood up and looked down at his shoes.

'Don't you go splashing in any puddles,' Douglas said. 'They need to last you a wee while.'

'I'll take over from here,' Betty said and she dipped a corner of the flannel into her bowl and wiped at a stain on the boy's jumper. 'What is that, toothpaste? Tut tut, wee man.'

'At least I cleaned my teeth.'

'Did you hear that? At least he cleaned his teeth. You're right to clean your teeth son, or you'll end up with wallies like me before you're twenty-one.'

The children turned their faces towards Betty and she gave them a righteous closed-lip smile.

When the first boy was done, Betty patted him on the back and led him towards the doors to the back stairs. 'On you go,' she said, 'and don't tell your mammy or she'll give me a row for interfering.'

Douglas and Betty worked their way through the line of

children. Betty pulled up socks and washed mouths and noses, parted hair and put a brush through ponytails.

Douglas dipped into a tobacco tin and searched for a tiny screw which he held under the light by the window and twisted into the hinge of a wee girl's glasses. He rolled the sticking plaster that he'd taken from the glasses between his thumb and forefinger and Betty held out her hand for it. 'I'll deal with that,' she said and they looked at the girl who was missing a tooth but there was nothing they could do about that.

'On you go,' Betty said and they watched her turn and wave before she clomped down the back stairs.

'You look handsome, Mr Meechan,' she said and straightened his tie again.

'Thank you, Mrs Meechan. Just imagine if we'd been allowed to...'

'Stop. Don't spoil it. You don't make the rules.'

'We could make good parents – '

'I know.'

She followed him to the back stairs and watched him go. He turned his head before he was out of sight and smiled.

'Keep working hard,' she said and went inside, bolting both doors and returning through her house to the landing where the mop stood in the bucket of water, now cold. She picked up the mats from outside her neighbours' front doors and shook them. She gathered up her special mats – the ones she stepped on when she came out of the lifts to avoid spoiling the floor – and she leaned, for a second or two, to gather herself, letting herself imagine, briefly, tidily, how life could have been.

Jean McGeogh

Once we got in we discovered that there were no stairs off the lifts and if the lift broke down the kids they would be standing in the landing saying 'shoosh, shoosh'. They had to go through your house to get onto the back stairs. And then, 'we'll miss

school' and I used to open the door and say 'no yous won't'
and they'd walk through and they'd be looking at the house
and that and the wee ones would go (to my son) 'oh I was in
your house this morning.' And maybe some of them did it
themselves, I don't know what they did but the lift would stop
and the door would open and let them out and they'd be on
the landing and I'd get up and say 'come on, out through the
house.' Always they had to go through somebody's house to get
on the back stairs.

Jennifer 1969

Jennifer's father rolled out the pastry to Elvis Presley. 'Blue
Suede Shoes'. The record player was brand new and the Elvis

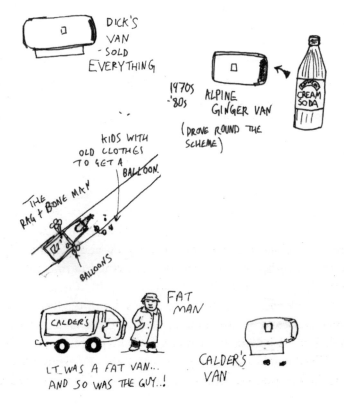

LP one of two long players he possessed. The other was The Dubliners. He turned up the volume as loud as acceptable for communal living in high flats with decent neighbours and opened the kitchen window. He liked to bake.

His wife was hanging out washing on the roof again – she'd become intrepid since moving to Red Road. With the other women, her friends now, they were like pioneers, making use of every bit of space, every facility, every aspect the flats had to offer. She was still unhappy with the lack of shops, however, and grateful for the vans that came by, parked up and sold everything. Dick's was the orange van. Calder's was the green. His wife sent the weans on errands on weekends and they came back loaded with messages for their mammy and their neighbours. His lovely wife. He'd been lucky to meet her at his age with four weans already under his belt. But she called herself a late starter and took on his children as if they were her own and asked Jim if he'd mind being a daddy all over again. Anything for you, hen. They'd worked hard in the old house, on top of each other, fighting for space. Now that they were in Red Road with the older weans moved out and moved on, he hoped life might be a bit easier for her. For them all.

He added cinnamon to the stewing apples and turned off the cooker. He took the paper from a bar of butter and ran it over a Pyrex dish. He rolled the pastry some more, palming the rolling pin to the pastry's edges, flattening and smoothing the bumps. He'd floured the worktop and the sheet of pastry lifted a treat, dangling from his fingertips. He pushed it into the base of the pie dish, his fingers creating divots where the pastry met with the wall and the base of the dish. With a quick knife he cut off the pastry that hung over the sides of the dish, leaving some to spare. More flour on the worktop and the pastry rolled into a ball again then flattened. Elvis Presley played on.

They would eat the pie after they sat down for their tea and before the weans got washed. He couldn't get over the state they returned home in. Mud in their hair, grass stains, dirt under their fingernails. He knew they were happy, but. His daughter with her Guides and Irish dancing, his son with his pals who ran about daft looking for ferrets and birds' eggs.

The apples poured nicely into the pie dish and he spread them to the sides with a wooden spoon. He took a ramekin and planted it into the apples, base up. Then he used the rolling pin once more on the other piece of pastry. It lifted well and he lowered it onto the pie, using the ramekin as a post on which to hang it. A roof on a house. Bending over the work-top, he shaped some spare bits of pastry into the letters of his wife's name and he glued them with egg to the top of the pie. Colleen. An apple pie for his wife. The edges squeezed together with flour-caked fingers. More egg to seal and glaze. Knife-slits to release the air. Four. At twelve o'clock, three o'clock, six o'clock and nine. His wife's name showing up clear. The oven hot and the pie in.

She was in the doorway with her empty washing basket at her hip.

'Jim,' she said. 'Come out here and listen.'

On the way to the veranda, she put the washing basket down. She took his hand. 'I'm covered in pastry,' he said.

'I don't mind.'

They stood together.

'What am I listening for?'

'Just listen.'

He looked and listened. His weans were down there with all the other weans and he sought them out. Noise of children playing, yes, and seagulls, but no extraordinary noise.

'I can't hear anything,' he said.

'Exactly.'

'What?'

'Exactly. There's no noise. It's finished. Red Road. It's finished.'

A VIEW TO THE WEST AND A GLIMPSE OF THE ARRAN HILLS ON THE MOST CLEAR OF CLEAR DAYS.

SPECTACULAR SUNSETS, SOMETIMES.

JIM THANKED HIS WIFE

FOR BRINGING THEM THERE

JIM

+

COLLEEN

+

THE WEANS

IN 1969.

She was right. The cranes, the huts, the scaffolding, the diggers, the men in hard hats, they were all gone. No drilling or crashing or clinking metal.

Below them the routes from building to building were busy with people passing back and forth. A few tender trees were growing up well.

'You're playing your Elvis record,' she said.

'And the pie's in the oven.'

'And the moon's out.'

The moon was there, in the fading sky, twilight settling over Glasgow.

'They've been on that moon,' Jim said.

'And they've built Red Road.'

'Progress.'

'It is, you know,' his wife said.

'Come here.'

He kissed her on the veranda, forgetting about his hands that left soft deposits of flour, a trace of white dust on her hair and face and back and arms and shoulders, his precious wife's body, her body that was strong enough to keep them all, to house them all, to love them all. Her name forging in the oven's heat. A new oven in the new Red Road.

Section Two

1970s

KERBY. TWO THIN-LEGGED boys stand on Petershill Drive, facing each other with the road between them. The first boy holds a football above his head and throws it towards the second boy. The ball arcs the road, drops in front of the second boy and bounces off the kerbstone. The first boy holds his arms above his head, palms flat. One nil. The second boy retrieves the ball, holds it above his head and throws it. They watch the ball, both boys, and see it fall and hit the kerbstone in front of the first boy. The second boy clenches his fists. One all. The first boy chases after the ball, taps it and toes it into the air, catches it and turns with quick feet. He throws again and the ball falls short of the kerb. Still one all. The second boy squints as he aims. The sun shines on his face and his hair is in his eyes. He throws.

Behind the second boy children watch a game of tennis. Some of the crowd palm the ends of tennis rackets, waiting. The game is a rough game and there are squeals when the ball is whacked out of the court and into the crowd. The net is a brick wall. The tramlines are smudged asbestos. When the game is finished, the children pick a side, run onto the court, and start a new game. Teams. Ten against ten, twelve against twelve, whatever. It's a riot of whacks and smashes and the ball can only bounce once.

The ball can bounce twice in the squash match. The squash court is the side of Two-one-three block and six boys and girls use their tennis rackets to keep the ball bouncing against the side of the building, non-stop.

Next to them, other kids play giant headers. The football is already at floor fourteen and a boy is hanging out the window with the ball in his hands, ready to let it fall. Down below another boy waits and watches the ball as it drops. He shimmies to manoeuvre his head underneath it and performs a perfect giant header. Easy. The kids clap and roar. Another boy swipes at the ball to take it up in the lift to the seventeenth floor for the next giant header. It's a slow game and while they wait they watch the squash. They turn back to the building when they hear a shout – are you ready? – and see the boy's head and arms and the football hanging out of the window. He drops the ball and the boy on the ground heads it. The crowd cheers. The boy cups his neck. A girl grabs the ball and takes the lift to floor twenty-two. The crowd waits for the girl and the ball to appear and the boy cranes his neck, looking up for the falling ball.

The Castle is hoaching with weans climbing over its turrets, making up games or just hanging about. Some of them jump from wall to wall and one of them misses and scrapes her knees on the concrete. Someone's ma shouts Alasdair, come up the stair and get your medicine and mop-haired heads turn towards the voice and then away, trying to locate Alasdair. Alasdair your ma wants you for your medicine someone says to him. What's wrong with you this week? someone else asks.

Three girls stand by the tunnel to Germiston and watch older

boys walk into the black. The girls climb the grass hill and head for the High Chaparral where they will collect feathers and bricks.

On the flattened grass behind Petershill Drive people sit on blankets and drink cider. Behind them, games of football patchwork the grass. One game, the biggest game, with the biggest boys, has barrels for goalposts.

By the railway tracks some of the older kids lob stones into the empty space on the other side. They plank good bits of brick for later. Suddenly, Gyto boys and girls come from nowhere and threaten them with weapons. The Red Road boys run back across the field, collecting footballers and weans as they run. But there's no fight yet, and the football games pick up again.

Boys and girls on bikes wheel with no hands the path between Ten Red Road and Ninety-three Petershill Drive. They're going to get bread and milk from Dick's van. Someone's mammy chucks down money wrapped in bread paper and shouts that she wants totties and good biscuits.

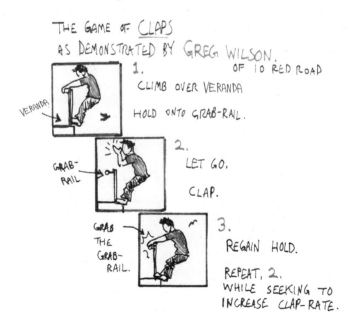

THE GAME OF CLAPS
AS DEMONSTRATED BY GREG WILSON.
OF 10 RED ROAD
1.
CLIMB OVER VERANDA
VERANDA
HOLD ONTO GRAB-RAIL.

2.
GRAB-RAIL
LET GO.
CLAP.

3.
GRAB THE GRAB-RAIL.
REGAIN HOLD.
REPEAT, 2.
WHILE SEEKING TO INCREASE CLAP-RATE.

They look up and see Greg Wilson, the quiet boy, who climbs over his veranda, holds onto the rail and leans out, twenty floors up. They see his mates on the ground looking up, holding their stomachs and their mouths. They see Greg let go of his hands and clap then grab the rail. Again he lets go his hands, claps twice, then grabs the rail. Three claps. Four claps. It goes on. And on. Spellbinding. He could fall, the children think. But he never does. And at the kitchen window next to the veranda, Greg's mother, does the washing up, waves and smiles – 'hiya lads' – at his pals down below.

In the shed next to Ten Red Road boys play Brag and watch older kids scramble onto the ledge that runs around the building just above head height and sit smoking, with their legs dangling over the edge.

Broomknowes School is empty but there's a football game going on in the playground. There's football on Little Wembley too, with its immaculately-cut grass.

Weans climb the Chippy Hill. They play in the disused railway that collects water when it rains. They fill bottles from drainpipes and soak whoever they choose to soak. They avoid the adults.

Inside, the buildings are teeming with weans; hanging about the landings, sitting in bedrooms looking at dollies, jumping in the lifts and making them jam, winching on back stairs, climbing up the narrow tunnels between floors where the electrics are kept, and throwing Action Men from windows, watching their parachutes take them softly to the ground or trap them, dangling, over window catches several floors down.

Inside and outside, there are weans who don't return home until their mothers call them from verandas or send their huffy big sisters down to get them. Hours spent with each other; the kids who leave the house at five to nine to go to Broomknowes Primary and those who march under the road through the tunnel – another tunnel – to St Martha's Primary or Albert

Academy or over to All Saints or Barmulloch Primary. What team
do you support? Fine. The kids don't care.

Dares, bother, mischief, games, fun. Stones, feathers,
tadpoles, dens, bikes. Boxing. Bird-nesting. Tournaments. Peever.
Skipping ropes. Water fights. Football.

Hunt the Cunt.

'You're the Cunt,' said Ewan.

'No way,' said Brendan.

The other boys nodded and moved towards him.

'I don't want to be the Cunt.'

'It's your turn.'

'I'm always the Cunt.'

'We won't batter you hard.'

'Yes, you will.'

Brendan looked around him but there was nowhere to
hide. The boys were blocking the entrance to his building. They
must have planned this in advance.

He tried one last time. 'Can we play something else? Can
we play football?'

'After you've had your doing.'

'Aw no.' Brendan put his hands on his head.

Ewan was his best mate. It was because he won the squash
and Ewan didn't. It was because he played good tennis too and
had the kids from Ninety-three block stopping to watch him.
Miserable bastards if they made him be the Cunt because he
was good at something.

'Twenty, nineteen...'

Brendan ran away. He didn't know where he was going to go.

'Eighteen, seventeen...'

His brother wasn't home or he could have chapped his
door and hid in there.

'Sixteen, fifteen...'

The best bet would be to lead them away from his building,

do a circuit of the flats and try to get back to his house before they caught up with him.

'Fourteen, thirteen...'

Down past Thirty-three block and out came Davie Kerr with his owl and his air gun and a line of weans following him.

'All right Brendan,' Davie shouted, the owl flapping as it sat on his gauntlet, the weans with their shoe boxes, off egg collecting, watching the bird as they walked.

'No, I'm fucking well not,' Brendan said and ran on. He could hear the boys counting, still. Soon they would charge at him like fucking Vikings and they would catch him and his doing would be brutal because he won the squash and got full of it. He had a right to, but.

Or he could just give up. Alfie did that once and the boys were so disappointed in him they let him off and found something else to do. But Brendan had a feeling that the boys wouldn't be satisfied today until they'd got him good and proper. He wondered when he and Ewan could be sending their Action Men out the window with their parachutes on, as that's what he really wanted to be doing now.

The caretaker was on his veranda. Brendan ran past him and looked up. He saw the caretaker clock him and look over his head up Petershill Drive. The boys must be coming.

'Help!' Brendan said and regretted it.

'Eh? What's that, wee man? I can't hear anything, the weans are too noisy.'

Brendan flicked him the fingers. The caretaker hated him.

He could go to Jimmy's dad's house – he was only three up – and bang on the door, but Jimmy would just let himself in the door and they'd get him. Silently.

There was the tunnel to Germiston. It was right in front of him. He ran to within a foot of it. But he just couldn't. There could be boys from Germiston hanging about the other end – he knew what happened when you got so far inside that tunnel; you couldn't see in front of you and you couldn't see behind you. Everyone was scared of the tunnel.

He heard the boys coming after him. 'Cunt!' they shouted.

So he ran up the slope onto the grass where the football matches were going on, and for a while, he felt free of the boys charging behind him as he threaded a path between the players. As long as he didn't get in the way of anyone's ball he would be okay. Past the white-walled community hut where the older boys boxed. He was puffing hard and slowing down. How long had he been running for now? Five minutes? Ten minutes? Once he ran for twenty minutes before they caught him and he was so tired and his doing was so bad he might as well have lain down and taken it after the twenty second countdown. He sneaked a look behind him to see how close they were. Oh mammy daddy, the whole fucking football pitch was after him now; a great charging throng of boys running at him, glee in their faces, with mad Mark Dougan leading the charge who his pals had banned from playing Hunt the Cunt last summer because he was such a bammy bastard when he caught anyone.

He thought through his options as he tugged his breath in and pushed sweat off his forehead. The railway tracks were a sprint away. If he was lucky he could tumble down the embankment and be across the tracks and maybe a train a mile long would come by and the boys wouldn't be able to catch him. But he would be trapped over on the Gyto's side and those bastards would give him a worse doing than his own side would. So the railway tracks were a no go.

He was too late to chase after Davie and his owl and the line of weans. He and Davie went bird-nesting together. Davie could point his air gun at them all or set his owl on them – but the wild shrieking mass of boys, and girls now too, was between him and Davie. Thirty-three Petershill Drive was the closest building. Nup. Keep out in the open where people – adults – could call a halt to the thrashing.

Brendan's only option was the Glasgow Hire and Transport Company. He ran towards it, seeing the trucks get closer and larger. He turned round once and saw the crowd spread like the wake on the Rothesay ferry. He kept running, his legs heavy and his forehead prickling. He could hear shouts still. Ewan's voice, 'Give up, Cunt,' and 'Mark, go easy on him,' and he knew that the fun was still very much in this particular game.

As he ran, Brendan heard a truck's engine start up and he scanned the cabs to see which one would move. It was his only hope now and when Brendan saw a truck snake itself out of the concrete truck park towards the exit, Brendan ran like his life depended on it. Which it did. The crowd was still behind him. Some had given up the chase – fuck, he must be a good runner. Put that on the list of talents for Brendan MacDonald along with tennis and squash why don't you Ewan Geddes. He'd done it hundreds of times before, got away with it and not got away with it, but failing was not on his mind today. Brendan sprinted for the back of the truck and leapt up for the hudgie of his life just as the truck's engine drove its slow procession through its gears, left onto Petershill Drive and away down the road. Brendan turned. Hands grabbed at his legs. Big wide open mouths with frenzied teeth. 'Fuck yous, you baw bags!' he shouted, one hand cupped around his mouth, the other gripping the back of the truck, his arm taking his whole weight as he leaned out. 'Get it right up yous!' He swung himself straight and held on to the truck as it roared down the road. He saw a woman with a message bag walking towards the flats, he saw the postman on his bike with his bag of mail. Then he pressed his forehead to the truck's metal back, held on tight and gave himself up to the jiggling and rumbling and jolting and jerking of his escape.

Davie 1970

The boys waited for a bus to pass and then crossed Red Road.

'Are you sure, Davie?'

Brendan was up for most things but Davie knew he was scared of Avonspark Street.

'I've got my air rifle.'

'They'll think we're starting a war against the Avey Toi.'

'No they won't.'

They wheeled their bikes because they agreed it looked less warrior-like, but both boys had practised jumping on them in seconds in case they had to escape.

'Which house?'

'My ma said it might be the last one on the right.'

'Right up the other end of the street. We're going to get battered.'

'No, we're not.'

With the Red Road towers behind them, they walked.

The boy's ma opened the door. She wore glasses.

'We're looking for Malcolm White.'

'Put that air gun down before you say another word.'

Davie put the gun down and laid his bike on the ground too. He took the newspaper cutting from his pocket.

'We're looking for Malcolm White, the one who was trapped up the Campsie Fells, when he went nesting, it says here.'

The woman paused.

'Malcolm, come here a wee minute.'

The three boys stood with their bikes out the front of Malcolm's house. The boy Malcolm pumped his tires and offered the pump to Davie and Brendan. They did theirs too. Malcolm tightened a screw and wiggled his handlebars.

'Have you seen *Kes*?' Davie said.

'I fucking love that film.'

'I'm going to get a kestrel. I had an owl but I let it go.'

'You got one in mind?'

'There's a nest on the Shovel gorge, where you...'

'Where I fell, aye. Are they hatched?'

'Aye. Four younks. Nearly fledged. I'm going to take the biggest one. Reckon today's the day.'

'I'll help you.'

Davie and Brendan looked at each other and smiled. They set off down Avonspark Street, back the way they came, towards the flats, riding their bikes, Davie with his air rifle tucked under one arm, all three of them with shoe boxes tied above their back wheels. Malcolm's bike had a flag on a bendy pole that came out of his seat back. Some boys came out of a house and waved at Malcolm. He waved back. His pals looked like they knew how to fight.

'What was it like, when you were trapped up the Campsies?' Brendan said.

'I made a den. I was fine. It was everyone else who was worrying.'

'Aye right.'

'Aye fucking right.' Malcolm's bike skidded to a stop and Davie remembered Malcolm's association with the Avey Toi.

'I'm going to keep it on my veranda,' Davie said and Malcolm looked away from Brendan and stared at Davie.

'You need to get a license to keep a kestrel.' He started pedalling again.

'I've got a license.'

'You need a garden and outdoor space.'

'Don't you worry, I fixed it.'

The Red Road Flats came at them blank and massive as they turned from Avonspark Street and pedalled up the hill.

'Which building do you stay in?'

'Thirty-three Petershill Drive. The one behind us.'

'It's like space, watching you at night. You look like rockets, all of yous.'

'We watch you too,' Davie said. 'The car chases and the fights.'

The chat quietened down as they cycled hard.

Past Stobhill Hospital, through Bishopbriggs, on to Milton of Campsie on their precious bikes, parts swapped or stolen then fitted tenderly. Tyres made do, bells screwed on and thumbed to test. Seats patched with parcel tape.

'What's your best egg?' Malcolm said.

Davie thought. He wanted to impress the boy from Avonspark Street but he didn't want to get found out. 'Heron,' he said. Which was true.

'I've only just started nesting,' Brendan said. 'My best one's a blue tit.'

'Mine's a buzzard,' Malcolm said.

Davie and Brendan glanced at him respectfully then hunched their shoulders over their handlebars and pedalled on.

Wheeling into the Campsie Fells. Yellow tufts of grass, piebald stones, rabbits hopping about, a bothy, trees beckoning at the edges of the grassland. Paradise. The biggest playground, all theirs, no cunt in sight. And treasure to find. Species to look up in books back at the library. A kestrel to catch. The boys hid their bikes and tumbled through the grass. Halfway up a hill they stopped to look back on Springburn and Barmulloch but other hills were in the way and they saw nothing but grass and open air.

'What was it like, really, when you fell down the cliff?' Davie asked Malcolm when Brendan was up a tree.

Malcolm picked the bark off a stick. 'I swore on my mother's life I'd never steal another egg, I'd never steal another part for my bike, I'd be good for my ma, if only somebody would rescue me.'

Davie nodded.

'Was your leg broke?'

'Aye.'

'Did you think you were going to die?'

'I don't know. I didn't know if it would ever end.'

'Were you frightened?'

The boys looked around them at the Campsie Fells.

'Aye, it was scary.'

Brendan climbed down the tree and sat on a branch just above their heads. He passed down an egg and when Davie had it softly in his palm, Brendan jumped from the branch and joined them. The egg was still warm; delicate as a bubble of air, a precious thing.

'Song thrush,' Davie said.

'Wrap it,' Malcolm said. 'You keep it. You found it.'

So Brendan found the first egg, wrapped it carefully in a leaf, and walked the slowest from that point on, his shoebox held in front of him like some gift for a king as they went on the hunt for more. They would blow the eggs later.

After a day roaming the Fells they went to the nest with the kestrel chicks.

Lights in Stobhill Hospital shone from every window. A streaky sky. Cool grey roads. The boys rode gently with hands squeezed around brakes. They stayed on the footpaths and slowed for ladies with message bags. A bus trundled ahead of them, going steady, nobody at the stops it passed. Davie saw the backs of heads on the top deck and the bottom deck.

'Will you get a doing off your ma?' Brendan said to Malcolm. 'Because it's nearly dark.'

'She's working tonight. I'm going to stop at my pal's and swap my bell for his puncture repair kit.'

Malcolm's tyre was on its way to flat again and his chain kept falling off.

They cycled in silence to the junction of Broomfield Road. The owner of Welshies was shutting up shop, a few people stood beside the chip van, the bus indicated left for the stop at the bottom of Red Road.

Davie didn't know how to end the day with Malcolm. He

wanted to go bird-nesting with him again. He wanted to meet this pal of his who collected eggs too.

'Anytime you want to see my kestrel, just come up.'

'Aye, will do.'

Malcolm nodded and the boys put their feet to their pedals.

'Oh fuck,' Malcolm said and stared down the road.

From Avonspark Street, a mass of men with swords and sticks and bottles ran onto Red Road. No noise, just the shape of them all, bent and charging, weapons held from raised arms. The men ran towards the bus and two men jumped off the bus and ran into the scheme. A couple of the Avonspark Street guys chased the fleeing men but most of the guys surrounded the bus. A window was smashed. Shouts and screams and women's voices. The bus rocked as the men got on and God, it was like a cartoon, seeing the men cracking their weapons onto the men on the top deck at the back, the cowering shapes of them through the back window, the men with the weapons doing their violence over and over. And then coming off the bus in single file, stepping off and shaking themselves, as if returning from having a piss, checking the road up and down and then crossing back to Avonspark Street, thriftily, edgily, swiftly. Job done. The bus driver started the engine, the lights in the bus flashed on and then the bus was away, turning right down Petershill Drive.

'I don't know what that was about,' Malcolm said. He seemed as if he was trying to shift the shock from his face.

'No, me neither,' Davie said.

'I'm getting my eggs home,' Brendan said.

'Yeah, you look after they eggs and that kestrel,' said Malcolm.

The boys cycled slowly. Davie wanted to ask Malcolm if he would be all right, going the same way as the men who did the beating, but he supposed Malcolm knew them; they might be his brothers or his brothers' friends and if they weren't, it didn't

matter, because they would know him because he lived there
and he was from their side.

He prayed that his kestrel – he'd named him Kes like the kestrel
in the film – would be okay on the veranda. From *Falcons and
Falconry* by Frank Illingworth he'd learned what type of perch
the hawk needed and how to build it. There was another book
he'd ordered from the posh bookshop in town but he needed
to wait a while longer before the shopkeeper gave up on him
returning for it and put it on the bookshelves. Then Davie
would go back and steal it.

Jesses round the kestrel's ankles. A leash attached and tied
to the perch. Food; bits of chopped mouse he'd shot over on
the High Chaparral. Just the right amount of food to keep it
calm but ensure it was hungry enough to man. The noise of
men returning home from the bars and clubs in town worried
him though. You wouldn't get that sort of noise in the Campsie
Fells. The bird would probably be frightened. Davie wanted
morning to come so he could get up and take care of it.

'Get to sleep,' his brother said.

'How did you know I was awake?'

'You're wriggling.'

'I can't help it.'

'Thinking about birds.' His brother laughed and turned over.

Davie lay for a few more minutes and got up when he
heard a key in the lock. He was relieved to have something else
to think about. His older brother stood in the dark kitchen,
washing his hands in the sink. Davie tripped over his hold-all.

'You scared the shite out of me,' his brother said.

'Is that a new suit?'

'Do you like it?' His brother turned on the light and the
fluorescent bulb flickered above the immaculate kitchen sur-
faces. 'I got it from Gerald's. First time I wore it tonight and
it's been a success.'

'I got my kestrel.'

'You never.'

'I'll show you.'

Davie took his brother to the veranda and they walked the few cold steps to where Davie had set up the perch.

'Fuck, it's awake,' his brother said.

The chick's eyes were open and alert and sharp and it watched Davie and his brother.

'Go to sleep, Kes,' Davie said.

'You haven't called it Kes?'

'What's wrong with that?'

'You couldn't think of your own name?'

'I didn't want to.'

'You should have called it Gringo. Or Big Baws.'

His brother touched the kestrel with the back of a finger and then took his hand back.

'You're a hard wee fucker, aren't you?'

The view from the veranda wasn't a good one. They were too low to see much other than the back of Sixty-three Petershill Drive and the tops of the swings in the kids' playground below. Davie wished they were higher up so that Kes could see hills or at least more sky or other birds.

His big brother leaned against the railing and they watched two men walk along the path below them, bottles clinking in bags, murmuring as they walked.

'There was an ambush on the bus earlier,' Davie said.

His brother turned his head and spoke sharply. 'How do you know?'

'We were coming down the road on our bikes. The Avey Toi, they charged across the street and got the bus, smashing it up. They gave someone a right doing. We saw.'

'Aye, I heard they stabbed a fella.'

'Why?'

His brother lit a cigarette and threw the match over the

veranda. 'Something to do with a score to settle. Gang members from another area. I heard it was vicious.'

'It was like a war, I'm telling you. An ambush.'

'Just don't you be in the wrong place at the wrong time, all right.'

Davie decided not to tell his brother about Malcolm from Avonspark Street.

'Come on.'

They closed the door on the kestrel and Davie watched his brother empty change and bus tickets from his trouser pockets. He often compared lives with Billy Casper from the film and wished he could meet him in the countryside one day and say to him you'll never guess what I saw or what my brother said or done, because he had a feeling he and Billy Casper would get along well.

May 1971

There were a few other cleaners standing with her at the bus stop at five-thirty. Solitary cars slipping along the grey streets, the sun nowhere, the sky a great black yawn over their heads. Barely a light in any window. Her son still sleeping. Mrs Orr, her blessed neighbour from up the stair, who let herself in to wake him every morning for school, said it was like waking the dead, the way he slept.

The morning was fresh about her face and so quiet she thought the whole bus queue would be able to hear her stomach working away at her porridge. The bus came and stopped for the ladies. She sat with Betty, who cleaned houses over in the West End but today was doing an early-morning shift at an office in the town. She started up right away.

'You're looking well, May.'

'I always try.'

The bus turned right down Petershill Drive. Betty turned in her seat and looked straight at her.

'You've done your hair different.'

'No.'

'You've put a colour in it. You've changed your perfume.'

'No, Betty.'

'If I was to guess I'd say that you were trying to impress somebody.'

'Chance would be a fine thing, hen.'

If May was honest, she would say that she was tired. She would say that her divorce and the years in the Calton had caught up with her. She would say that she didn't quite believe there wouldn't be thumping on the door or frightening phone calls. But something in her wouldn't let her be too tired or too feart. So she coloured and curled her hair and wore lipstick and told herself to come on May. And yes, there was a man at the Health and Welfare where she cleaned. The caretaker. Called Alistair McBride. Who had a gentle wave in his hair and thick sideburns. But if she ever had any godforsaken time to even speak to the man let alone attempt to impress him, could somebody please tell her where that time was and how she was to fit him in with her two shifts at the Health and Welfare and the night shift at the Shettleston Club and her son who'd been through enough already in his dear short life.

'You're blushing, May,' Betty said but May thought it was more likely to be anger in her cheeks than anything else. Romance was easy. The rest was hard.

The boy who sold the totties at the door, he told her there was a fella loitering about the foyer asking for a May Thompson. He had a tough-looking face, so the tottie boy said he didn't know anybody of that name and the man stared at him all the time he waited for the lift. The tottie boy was big enough to handle himself now but he seemed worried the day he knocked on May's door and told her all about it. And then it had been Hogmanay and she'd had a great time in her neighbours' house, and the accordion and singing and dancing and banter had taken her mind off things.

'My lovely neighbours are moving out,' Betty said. 'They've bought a house in Cumbernauld.'

The bus went past some empty stops lit by orange streetlights. Nothing was open. A man walking his dog along the road was all May could see.

'I don't want to move, do you?' May said.

Betty shook her head. 'I'd love a wee back and front door though.'

'I'd miss my view.'

'I wouldn't miss the lifts. Did I tell you this?' Betty had the best stories. 'The other day I was waiting on the lift to take me down to the ground and when the doors opened I got the fright of my life. Two undertakers standing bolt upright and a coffin leaning against one of the walls. It was Mr O'Keefe, God rest his soul. He died in his chair and they had to bring him down standing up because the lifts are too small to lay a coffin flat. There's no dignity in that.'

'He wouldn't know.'

'Oh, I wouldn't be so sure. I'd know. If I stayed long enough in Red Road to die in my chair I'd know I'd be going down in the lift standing up in my coffin. No, I shall be in Cumbernauld in a wee front and back door when I die. Easy in, easy out. This is me, hen.'

Betty stood up.

'Did you get in the lift with him?'

'Did I what? No, I gave the man some privacy and took the stair.'

'From fifteen up?'

'Aye, I know. I was nearly ready for a coffin myself when I got to the bottom.'

May watched her step off the bus and pull her good fur coat about her. Then she got off the bus too. She walked through the still-dark morning to Ingram Street and when she got to the Health and Welfare, she saw Alistair unlocking the doors.

Inside, she offered to make him a cup of tea because she always had one after she'd done the dishes in the wee staff kitchen. She told him she'd leave it on the worktop for him as she knew he went about the building turning on lights and checking the place and she wouldn't know where to find him. He rubbed his hands together and said that would be grand and then put his hands in his back pockets and May was sure she saw him looking at her hair. Unless he was skelly. They were like a pair of sparrows twitching and fussing about each other. I haven't got time for this, May thought, and turned her back on him, plunging her rubber-gloved hands into the soap suds.

Her son had asked about his father the night previously. He'd said he wanted to look at his old house in the Calton. Why would you want to do that? May said. Because a boy in his class at school stayed with his da on the weekend and they'd gone to see the football together.

'Your da doesn't live in our old house anymore,' May said. And he wouldn't take you to the football anyway. He wasn't that sort of da.

It troubled her though, that Red Road wasn't enough for him, as it was for her. Or maybe she wasn't enough for him.

She did the toilets and the toilet floor, vacuumed the corridors and the rooms, polished the desks and window ledges. She emptied the bins of the previous day's rubbish and shook out fresh bin bags, pressing them into the baskets.

When she was folding her apron and putting it into her bag Alistair came into the kitchen with his mug from earlier in the morning.

'Lovely cup of tea.' He smiled and rinsed the mug at the sink.

'I meant to make another one for myself,' May said, 'but I was behind with my work this morning, I don't know why.'

'Me too,' Alistair said. 'Must be Monday.' She knew he ran a boxing club on weekends and took some of his older boys to amateur fights. He seemed like a man used to himself. Fit. Trim. He didn't wear a wedding ring.

'Let me make you another one,' he said, and May didn't want to say no, even though she had a bus to catch and plenty to do in the house before she was back to work again.

'If it's no bother,' she said.

'Not at all.'

He took a fresh mug from the cupboard and put it on the worktop. Then he filled the kettle with water and set it to boil. He opened the cutlery drawer and found the tea strainer that May knew was there because she'd washed and dried it earlier that morning. He put a spoonful of tea into the teapot and turned to her. Then he turned back to the kettle.

'It's a slow boiler,' May said and Alistair said, 'Aye.'

When the kettle boiled he lifted it straight away and steam shot out of its spout.

'Watch yourself,' May said. She hated that phrase and didn't know why she'd said it. It reminded her of him.

A few moments later Alistair tinkled the spoon against the side of the teacup and stirred in May's milk. He turned the teacup and passed the cup to her, handle first. Fair hairs on his fingers.

'Where's yours?' she said.

'I'm not having one.'

'Oh, I wouldn't have said aye if I'd known.'

'No, no, on you go, sit down. You work bloody hard, May.'

Alistair pulled a chair from under the table. May sat.

'Thank you.'

He waited for her to take a sip. May blew on the top of her tea but couldn't sip because it was still too hot. She smiled.

'You take your time,' Alistair said, and when he was almost out of the door he added, 'Are you doing your afternoon shift?'

'Aye.'

'And your shift at the bar?'

'Aye.'

'You work too hard, May.'

'Alistair, it's either that or I lose my house.'

He nodded as if he understood.

'I've drunk in your bar before,' he said.

'I've never seen you.'

May wondered what drink he would take. She thought he might be a heavy man or he might swill a half in his glass and nurse it in warm palms. She would look out for him.

'I like the bands. And the dancing.'

May looked up.

'Do you, Alistair?'

He nodded. They smiled.

'So long.'

He tipped an imaginary hat and went away.

May waited for the tea to cool but felt anxious sitting there with nothing to do. She knew if she didn't leave now she would miss the bus, and she'd only catch it if she ran anyway. It felt pretty pointless to be sitting here with a cup of tea that wouldn't cool down, when if she really wanted a cup of tea she could have one back in her house while the washing was soaking in the sink. She tipped a glug down the sink and filled the teacup with cold water. It was still too hot to drink. She checked behind her. Alistair was gone. She tipped the tea down the sink, ran the tap and swished the lot down the plughole. A quick rinse of the cup, the teapot emptied, swilled and dried, put back in the cupboard, and then she was away out of the building towards home. If he asked, she'd tell him it was the best cup of tea she'd ever tasted.

Davie 1971

'Need any potatoes, missus?'

'Aye son, give us two pound.'

Davie ran to the sack he'd left between the lift doors and

took out a two-pound bag. He held the bag while the woman dipped into her purse.

'That's for your trouble,' she said and Davie put Fred Aston's money in his money belt and his tip in his shorts pocket. This woman was a good tipper. She wore rollers underneath her hairnet and had painted nails. Today they were pink. Davie humphed the sack back into the lift and waved as the doors closed and he went down to the floor below.

'Any potatoes missus?'

If he sold his sack of potatoes Fred Aston would give him another one from the back of the van and then he would collect him and drop him in front of more high flats. He and the other lads – there were five others – did the area: Sighthill, Red Road, Germiston. It made good money but hurt his back and his fingers from the lifting and carrying. He was so hungry he would have bitten into a potato had he not done it before and got a mouthful of starch and dirt.

At Red Road he did one of the long blocks; the posh blocks, his pals from Thirty-three Petershill Drive called them. Totties hauled from the van, through the foyer doors and into the lift, his forearms dirty from reaching into the sack, his face sweaty and speckled with mud. The lift wobbled its way to floor twenty-seven and he began his routine and his patter with the women who came to the doors. On the fifteenth floor, before he could get a foot out of the lift, Betty Meechan was at her door instructing him.

'Use the mats, son. Don't let your dirt spill onto the floor. What have you got for me?'

She always asked him what he had.

'Any totties – '

'I can't hear you from over there. Come to me, please.'

He hopped over the mats that went from the lift to her doorstep.

'Any totties missus?'

'Well, I'll be having my ham today so I'll need totties for that, my joint of beef tomorrow, my steak pie on Monday and my mince on Tuesday. The mince will do for two days so we'll have that on Wednesday as well and on Thursday and Friday we'll have links and soup. So, the only day I won't need totties is...'

Davie put his hands in his pockets while Betty worked out how many pounds of totties she needed. He thought about Kes and hoped his brothers weren't poking at her. His da would keep an eye on her. I'm proud of you for taking falconry seriously and committing yourself to looking after a hawk, his da said to him frequently. Davie always told him he would never give up on Kes.

'Better give me half a stone, son.'

Mrs Meechan gave Davie the money and told him to wait there.

'What's that?' he asked when she handed him a soap-sized parcel of white paper.

'For your kestrel.'

Davie smiled and looked properly into the woman's face. Her glasses made her eyes look huge. The curls at her forehead were like his granny's curls. Her cheeks seemed soft. Perhaps she'd given him some of her week's meat.

'How did you know?'

'I've seen you over on the field you weans call the High Chaparral.'

She stepped back from the door and Davie saw her slippers just before it closed.

'Thank you! Thank you so much, missus!'

He unwrapped the parcel. Inside was a mouse.

The door opened again.

'The caretaker's cat brought it in and I told him not to get rid of it, because I knew a bird who'd make swift work of it.'

'She will,' Davie said, and felt, perhaps, a little disappointed. He put the parcel in his pocket along with his tips.

When he walked with Kes to the High Chaparral with the line of weans following him he looked up at Mrs Meechan's house. She wasn't on her veranda and he couldn't see her at her window because the sun was shining, making all the windows flash black and gold. He told the weans to stand well back, then he set the hawk down and began his circles, Mrs Meechan's mouse attached to the leash that he whizzed around his head; a tip for a boy, a meal for a hawk.

Matt Barr

There was a steel fire escape that ran up one side of the building and at top of the fire escape there was a door onto the roof of the building. We used to spend a lot of time up there because it was somewhere that nobody else was. And the views from there were fantastic. It was very windy. There were concrete slabs made into a fence with four-inch slats that you could look through. And above that there was a wire safety net. It was supposed to stop you climbing any further but we used to get on top of that. And there were also kestrels that had nests on the top of the buildings so we used to go up and try and catch them.

Davie 1972

His ma brought two letters into the kitchen. 'One's for you, Davie,' she said and Davie's spoon fell into his bowl, splashing milk onto the table.

'Who's it from?'

'I don't know.'

Davie took the letter and turned it in his hands. He wondered if he should wait to read it with his pals because he could guess who it was from.

'Open it,' his older brother said.

So he did.

'Dear Boys,' Sir Phillip Glasier wrote. 'I don't mind you

boys writing to me so frequently, but will you please include a stamped addressed envelope from now on.' And then he answered their question on when a kestrel might be ready for free-flight.

'Tight bastard,' his brother said and he took the letter. 'Sir Phillip Glasier wants a stamped addressed envelope so he doesn't have to pay to write to the weans from the multi-storey.'

'I'm going out.'

Davie took his air gun with him. The boys from the long blocks were playing giant headers. There was a kid hanging out of one of the high floor windows and a kid on the ground waiting with his chin skywards.

Davie shot a rat and carried it by its tail back to his house. Outside his building, he saw another rat running out of the back of Sixty-three Petershill Drive. He put his dead rat on the ground, knelt down and aimed.

'I wouldn't if I was you.'

It was a man's voice with polis shoes. Davie twisted himself around and saw a big policeman standing over him and another one standing next to a panda car. The rat scampered out of sight.

'I was going to shoot that rat.'

'It looked to me like you were aiming for those windows.'

'I wasn't. I keep a kestrel. I feed it rats and sparrows.'

'We'll see what your parents say about your air gun and your kestrel. Where do you stay?'

If he expected Davie to be worried, he wasn't. The polis always got it wrong. His da was at work but his ma would tell the polis that he'd never shot a window in his puff.

'I need to get my rat.'

'Leave the rat.'

'Fuck's sake,' he said under his breath.

The weans waiting for the lift fell silent as Davie and the policeman joined them.

'What floor are you, son?'

'Six.'

The policeman pressed the button with a strong finger. And when he looked down at his watch the weans did the lift trick and the lift shot straight up, right past Davie's floor, to the top of the building.

'Help! It's not stopping!' one of the weans said before the policeman pressed number six again and said, 'If the lift doesn't stop at floor six this time, I'm lifting the whole lot of you and you can spend a night in the cells.'

'All right, Officer.'

They stepped onto Davie's landing. The policeman knocked on the door.

'I could let us in, I've got a key,' Davie said.

'No.'

His older brother answered the door with a piece of toast in his hand.

'Ah, Officer, he's not been in trouble again has he?'

'Ian, where's my ma?'

'She's not in.'

'Are you sure?'

'Aye.'

'Just tell the polis that I keep a kestrel and I shoot rats not windows.'

The policeman said, 'Is his mother or father not in?'

'Not the now, no.'

'Tell him I keep a kestrel.'

'A what?'

'Tell him Ian. I got the air gun for shooting rats and sparrows.'

'You've got an air gun?'

The policeman took a notebook from his pocket and opened it. Davie pushed past his brother and told the policeman to follow him. He found his letter from Sir Phillip Glasier on the table in the living room.

'There,' he said. 'A letter about my kestrel.'

The blue tit he'd taken as a chick and raised in the house was sitting quivering on top of the television.

'There's my blue tit,' he said. He headed for the veranda and checked that the policeman was following him. Kes was there, on her perch.

'And there's my kestrel.'

'Jings,' said the policeman.

He stared at the kestrel. 'Are you allowed to keep kestrels on your veranda?'

Oh shite. Davie felt sick. He wanted to launch himself at his brother and batter him.

'Aye, I'm allowed. I've got a license.'

'To keep a kestrel on a veranda? I really ought to see that license.'

Davie felt his cheeks flush. He should have said he was shooting out windows; the polis would have given him a dressing down and would have been away up the road by now. Davie's brother's face looked worried.

'I think our ma threw your license away didn't she?' his brother said and Davie nearly gave up there and then. He wanted to lie down and thump his fists on the veranda floor.

But he was saved. A brown shape fell from the sky. All three – and the kestrel – stared at it. It seemed to float past Davie's veranda and then it splintered and shattered when it hit the ground. A wardrobe. Smashed. Gone. Cheers from somewhere up above. Calls of what the fuck? And that was the policeman gone too. He ran through the living room and flapped his hands as the blue tit flew close to his head.

'I could do you for wasting police time,' he said, looking back at them all.

The brothers stood on the veranda.

'Who do you think threw the wardrobe?' Davie asked.

'Who knows? Who cares?'

'Do you think he'll be back?'

'I doubt it, the big diddy.'

Davie bred mice on his veranda from then on and made sure he took his air gun far away from the Red Road Flats.

Jennifer 1975

Jennifer and James called them the doorstep weans; the four children who moved into the Campbells' old house and waited on the landing for their mammy to come home. Their mammy went to work early and the children got themselves out for school and back from school on their own. They didn't play.

The doorstep weans were there again when Jennifer and James came in for their tea. The youngest boy lay on the floor and chewed the strap of his satchel, eyes fixed as a baby's. The girl leaned against the door and drew pictures on her legs with a biro. The older boys blew across the top of their ginger bottles. Two Dunns bottles each.

'Hiya,' Jennifer said.

The children stared, not rudely, but keenly. Jennifer put her key in the door then turned back to look at them. The elder two, the boys, were still staring. Their faces grey-pale. One of the boys blew across his bottle again and behind his head, their dog barked.

'Your dog wants out,' James said.

The boy slammed his hand against the door and the dog stopped barking.

'When's your mammy coming home?' Jennifer asked.

The children shrugged and the small boy, the one lying on the floor, turned himself around and pressed the soles of his feet against the wall. Tatty, holey shoes. Ripped laces.

Before Jennifer could turn her key, her mother had opened the door and stood there in her swirly dress and knee boots that Jennifer liked to try on.

'In,' Jennifer's mother said. 'All of you. Come on in.'

The weans stood up and gathered their things. Gentle heads of hair and tough shoulders. Jennifer's mother touched their backs as they walked past her through the doorway.

'She's staying out later and later because she knows I feed them,' she said to Jennifer and Jennifer looked back at their door, behind which the dog had started up again.

Jennifer's mother fed them toast and beans with an egg and they sat around the table. She stood behind them and watched them eat. She poured milk into metal tumblers. The bigger children ate quickly but the youngest savoured every mouthful, eating one baked bean at a time. They all drank quickly and put their tumblers on the table, looking up for more.

'Got any ginger bottles?' one of the boys said.

There were two empty ginger bottles by the sink. Jennifer's mother picked up one and gave it to the boy.

'What about that one?' the other boy said.

'That's for James. You two will have to share.'

James clenched his fist and put his elbows on the table.

There was a knock at the door.

'You need to get ready for Guides if you're going,' Jennifer's mother said.

The knock again and Jennifer's mother went to the door. Sounds came through to the kitchen; rapid speech and a high laugh. The four doorstep weans looked up and smiled at their mother when she came in, unbuttoning her raincoat.

'Oh, you've been fed!'

The children looked at their plates.

'I'll have that wee bit of toast if you're not eating it, Daniel.' She took it as a bird would and pushed her fingers against her lips. She seemed distracted, busy, her voice filling the room.

'Sit down,' Jennifer's mother said.

'No no, hen. I'm in a rush. I can't keep up with myself today.'

The youngest child put his arms around his mother's legs.

'Aiden, you big sook,' she said, but hugged him.

'I want you to stay home with us.'

She told her children to stand up and come with her. 'You've bothered Mrs Ryan enough already.'

'Thank you for feeding them,' she said. 'We'll have tonight's tea tomorrow then, won't we, eh?'

The older boys wrapped their arms around their ginger bottles. James stayed at the table. Jennifer got up to put her Girl Guide uniform on and saw her mother and the weans' mother talking at the door.

'Look, Colleen, you're helping me out greatly,' their neighbour said. 'I can't keep up with myself. I'm working round the clock. I don't get a penny off their dad.'

The woman's dark eyes seemed to demand a response. She stood too close to Jennifer's mother. Beyond her, the weans fidgeted and agitated on the landing. Their mother turned to look at the floor.

'It was my turn wasn't it? I'll do it tomorrow.' She raised her voice. 'Right, you lot, in, I'm not in the mood for any nonsense.'

Jennifer's mother closed the door and walked back into the house, a shade of worry on her face.

As she got changed, Jennifer heard her mother say to James, 'When you've had your peaches, take that ginger bottle over to the boys across the landing.'

If her brother said anything Jennifer didn't hear, and when she was buttoning her blue blouse she heard the click of her front door opening and then closing a few seconds later.

Jennifer called the lift and heard shouts behind the doorstep weans' door. While she waited, their door opened and one of the boys came out with the dog.

'He's already done his jobby on the veranda,' the boy said, 'but my mammy told me to take him out anyway.'

When they were in the lift he put his fingers to the burnt plastic lift buttons and said, 'Who done that?'

'I don't know.'

'Someone who likes burning things. My sister likes burning things.'

Jennifer realised she hadn't even heard his sister speak.

Davie 1975

Waving to his granny out the window, away home after her Sunday dinner, and his wee brother walking her down to the bus stop. A beautiful day. A meal and a laugh round the table.

Three guys approach two guys, casual, as if they would share a smoke. The wind picks up. Litter rolls in the road.

His wee brother recognises it just as Davie and his brothers do, standing at the window. His brother stops and holds his granny's arm. One guy runs away. Gone. The three casual guys they grab the guy who is left and push him to the ground, face down. Two of them hold him and the other guy takes a blade, like a blade from a pair of garden shears, and holds the handle and stands astride the man and stabs him in the back. The man screams and the two men keep him down while the man with the blade takes it out of his back and stabs him again. And when he stabs him the next time he jumps up first and he keeps jumping and he keeps stabbing.

Davie's granny, she shrugs off Davie's brother's arm and runs to the men and hits them with her handbag. No, Granny, no, Davie's brothers at the window say and watch their wee brother try to pull their granny away. There is blood on the pavement, blood in the daylight, and the man on the ground isn't moving. His back is bloodied. Davie's granny is pointing and shouting and her handbag is going crazy. The man has stopped stabbing and all the men, the three of them, step away and turn in circles, staring at the onlookers, holding their arms out from their sides as if to say anyone got anything to say about this? They glance at Davie's granny who is shaking her head.

'Poor Granny,' Davie says.

'Your poor Granny's seen it all before,' Davie's mother says who has come to stand by the window. 'Ian, go down and see if she's all right. Davie, go next door and phone for an ambulance.'

The caretaker comes out when the ambulance is away and cleans up the blood. Pink suds remain on the road and pavement. A patch of wet that dries in the light and breezy day.

Jennifer 1975

Half-past eight and the sky was serene, music came from some of the houses, teenagers hung about. Outside Ten Red Road two policemen ran towards a group of boys with sticks and cigarettes but they didn't stop at the teenagers. They ran inside the doors.

'What's going on?' Jennifer said to the boys.

'Go round the corner and look up.'

She walked around the building and stepped away from it. 'Oh my God.'

A boy's body was flat against the side of the building. Way up. His hands gripping the window frame, his feet on the tiny ledge. Skinny. Motionless. Jennifer was sure he was the boy from across the landing, the youngest boy, because he clung to the building three floors from the top, on floor twenty-eight, her floor. Across in the slab block people stood on their verandas watching. A woman stood on a high-up veranda and waved her arms. The boy stayed flat against the building. Tiny.

Jennifer ran into the foyer and called for the lift. When she got to the twenty-eighth floor all four front doors were open. Jennifer's mother and brother and their two other sets of neighbours were there.

'They broke open the door,' Jennifer's mother said. 'Come on, we'll see if we can do anything.'

They went into the fragile house. Nothing there. No pictures, no furniture. Three of the doorstep weans standing by the milk crates they used as chairs. The policemen had their hands on the youngest boy's shoulders and walked him into the living room. His face was grey with terror, his body shook, his wee legs buckled. And then he cried 'mammy, mammy!' and his cries ripped his face and his eyes shut tight.

Jennifer looked at the children.

'It was a dare,' the girl said. 'But he said he wasn't going to do it so we forgot about it and then we heard him shout and we saw he was already out there.'

'We thought he'd climb back in,' one of the boys said.

'But he got stuck. He kept saying he was going to fall.'

'Mammy told us never to open the windows.'

'Sit down,' Jennifer's mother said to the children, and to Jennifer, 'Get a blanket or something.'

She pushed the milk crates together and the four children sat close, their hands tight around their knees. Jennifer looked in the bedroom for a blanket and found one. The bedroom was as bare as the living room. Just a mattress on the floor, two dolls and two crossbows. Her mother put the blanket round the children's shoulders and they sat quietly. The youngest boy still shook and his brothers and sister put their heads close to his.

Jennifer watched the adults talk. One of the police asked her mother where the children's mammy was and she said she worked nights as well as days.

'The wee man was petrified,' the policeman said.

'Whatever possessed him?'

'Are there no safety catches on the windows?'

'There are, but they're easy to undo,' Jennifer's mother said.

The police took notes and their radios crackled. A pile of

mail lay on the floor by the television set next to another pile of coats. The doorstep weans made sobbing sounds; tiny squeaks and gasps. Heads together, the girl's long hair spilling over her brothers' shaven heads. Jennifer felt terrible for them and wondered if she should kneel down and say something. But they weren't crying, they were laughing. Jennifer put her hand to her mouth and the weans looked up at her, their eyelashes wet, their eyes shining. They drew their heads back together and Jennifer tried to listen to the words they whispered to each other but she couldn't make them out. The boy who asked for the ginger bottle was saying something through his laughter, his face red right up to his shorn blond hair and the other three were creased up, shaking their heads, sounds catching their throats, and finding something so funny. Eventually the girl drew the blanket up over their heads and they sat on the crates with it covering them completely. That's when the police and the adults turned to look at them.

Jennifer's mother took the children back to their house when the police said they weren't to stay on their own in the house and if nobody took them in they would call the social and have them taken away. They would need to call the social anyway. Jennifer's mother took cushions from her couch and the children lay down and slept.

Later that night, the doorstep weans' mother knocked on the door. She was subdued when Jennifer's mother told her about her youngest boy.

'I can manage,' she said and carried each sleeping child back to her house, mouth open, fingers curled, a soft bundle in her arms. Her eyes had tears in them when she came for the last child.

It took a few days to work out what she'd done because the flat was nearly empty anyway and peeking through the letterbox to see the bare floors and walls was no different to before. But when the children no longer sat on their doorstep waiting for their mother to come home and when the police and the social work knocked at Jennifer's house to enquire after the family and after that the caretaker arrived to let the man from the Corporation in, it was obvious. She'd done a moonlight and taken the kids with her.

Matt Barr

There was gang stuff that happened. I was about sixteen. A couple of boys. They came from Avonspark Street, the gang, and they got them over the railway, they caught these two boys from Blackhill. They weren't actually bad guys, they seemed like nice boys. The ringleaders started attacking them and there was a big crowd, there was maybe about forty kids, aged from ten right through to about nineteen. The boys had been punched, blood all over, their noses were bust, teeth were knocked out and the rest of the crowd were joining in, they were really going to get seriously hurt, you know. I sort of felt sorry, I could see the fear in their eyes, and I felt really sorry for them and I thought I've got to do something here otherwise these guys are going to get really badly hurt. One of the boys from a really notorious family he said we've got to do something here and I said if you're with me, let's step in, so we

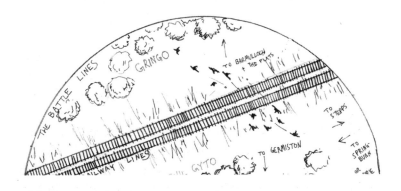

*said, ah, come on, they've had enough, they've had enough,
and because there were two of us we stopped it. And I could-
n't believe it, he took the two guys, he said you've got to get
away from here, come on follow me. He took them into his
house, he hid them in his house for the afternoon, you know,
and cleaned them up and everything and helped them get away
from the area, before they got caught in an area they weren't
supposed to be in. So there were some kind things happened
that you didn't expect.*

Davie 1976

They started slow and relaxed, a Sunday, a dewy, bright morning,
the most beautiful day of the year. Six boys. Davie was there,
Brendan, Brendan's younger brother Paul, Malcolm from
Avonspark Street and two more boys from Ten Red Road, Tam
and wee James Ryan. The boys walked south along the train
tracks, bird-nesting. It was too early for trouble from the Gyto
across the tracks and there were no trains on a Sunday – the
electricity was on overhead but there was no need to listen out
for the rattle of carriages. Peace. They climbed the cool walls
of one of the tunnels and felt for holes and nests. It was too
dark to see what kind of eggs they'd pulled out but they were
able to guess at them from their size. Outside the tunnel in the
bright morning they held out the eggs on dirt-blackened hands
and any they did not need they returned to the nests. Always,
they left ample eggs in a nest.

Malcolm from Avonspark Street had a bag of pear drops
and he shared them with the other boys. Davie scraped his
tongue on an edge of the sweet and thought there might be
blood mixed with his spit, but he didn't care, he was having a
brilliant day. Some of the boys walked along the rails, the sea-
grey tracks going on and on beyond their outstretched arms.
Davie found a stick and beat the weeds at the side of the
tracks. There were mice and rabbits for shooting but he hadn't

brought his airgun. The air was thick with pollen and his eyes watered. Because the weather was warm the boys shed jumpers and tied the arms around their waists. There was an agitation to the way they smacked their sticks against the weeds at the foot of the embankment or spun the stones they aimed at tree trunks. They stopped to light cigarettes and kick the toes of their trainers against the bolts on the sleepers. Girls. They'd all winched a girl, except for Brendan's younger brother. They'd all pressed their cocks against a girl on the back stairs and felt under her top for bare skin and nipples. They'd all been punched. They'd all been belted. They'd all dogged school. They'd all asked men outside the off-license to buy them cider or wine.

So the bird-nesting was a comfort. Nostalgia, almost. They walked in single file through a tunnel. Brendan hooted and his echo filled the black air. Coming out into the light they listened for noise of other boys or gangs but heard nothing.

Malcolm from Avonspark Street ran towards the next tunnel, the one close to Petershill Station, with electric pylons either side. He pointed at a bird's nest high up one of the pylons. If they climbed it, they could stretch for the eggs, he said. Davie wanted to climb. He thought the nest might be a kestrel's nest and he wanted to be the one to take an egg from it. Brendan climbed the other pylon, to stretch his legs, he said. The other boys watched from below.

'Oh boys, I think there's going to be eggs,' Davie said, as he reached his hand towards the nest.

'Bring them down, bring them down!' the boys shouted and one of them hurled a stick past Davie's head that clattered against the pylon.

'Fucking pack that in,' Davie said.

Brendan climbed higher up the other pylon and sat casually on the metal. 'How many's in there, Davie?' he said. Then he spat at the boys on the ground below and got Malcolm from Avonspark Street on the head. Malcolm told him he had better stay up that pylon because he would knock him out when he came down.

Davie stretched as far as he could stretch. He walked his fingers along an egg and rolled it into his grip.

'Got one.'

Brendan spat again at the boys. Spit hit a wire, making it hiss.

'What eggs are they?' wee James Ryan asked.

'Kestrel.' He'd been right.

'Oh ya beauty,' Brendan said.

'Come on Davie, man, bring it down,' the boys said.

'I will.' His hand that held the pylon was sweaty.

'How many's in there?' Brendan asked again. 'I want one.'

Davie transferred the egg to his other hand, managing to keep the egg cushioned in his palm while gripping the pylon with his fingertips. He stretched again and counted the eggs.

'Four,' he said. 'I'll just take the one.'

'Bring it down,' the boys said again.

Tam and Malcolm from Avonspark Street began to argue about who should keep the kestrel egg. Brendan spat again and the wire hissed.

'Listen to that, boys,' he said.

Davie manoeuvred himself away from the nest and took the egg out of his precarious grip. He breathed out. And as he rested, holding his body close to the pylon with the egg clutched in his fist close to his heart, he heard the explosion and saw Brendan fall from the pylon onto the tunnel and slip to the track and dirt below. Brendan lay as if he was still falling, as if the rude ground had stopped him when he wasn't ready to be stopped. When he didn't move his friends came to him and Davie climbed down the pylon.

'Is he breathing?'

'Brendan,' his brother said.

'Take his pulse.'

'Brendan,' his brother said.

'Don't move him.'

'Why not?'

'Because you're not supposed to.'

'Brendan.'

'Can you feel his pulse?'

'I don't know.'

'Let me try.'

'I saw him move.'

'No he didn't.'

'Brendan.'

'Come on Brendan, wake up.'

'Brendan.'

'Is he dead?'

They were crying. All of them. The big tough boys were breathless and crying. They ran to the people at the bus stop by Petershill Station, who stood with their papers and hand-bags like figures in a painting, and they shouted and pointed the way they'd come and said with their red desperate faces that their friend's been burnt and please, please help them. But the people at the bus stop, perhaps scared of the big tough crying boys who charged up the embankment, didn't help them. So the boys ran to the hospital on Petershill Road and Davie felt the egg knocking about his pocket as he ran and he took it and threw it and didn't look to see where it landed and he and the boys ran screaming to the front gate where they saw the security guard who they knew because he was a man from the Red Road Flats.

'It's all right boys,' the man said. 'I'll get it sorted.'

'Brendan,' said Brendan's brother.

'That's his brother,' Davie said as the security man used his radio.

'Stay here, I'll get it sorted.'

The boys hung on to the man's actions, staring and weeping. When they heard the sirens Davie wanted to run away and so did the other boys but the security man said, 'You need to stay and show them where your friend is.' They stayed.

When the police and the ambulance men returned, they carried a stretcher with a red blanket over it and they took Brendan away.

At his funeral, the boys wore their darkest, smartest clothes and didn't like to look at each other. Afterwards Davie sat with Kes on his veranda and stayed there till it was dark, looking down at his trousered legs, tracing his finger over the nylon, or slumping his head against the wall and staying as still as he could, watching Kes peck and preen and peer sharply at her world.

On his own, he rode his bike to the Campsie Fells and freed Kes. He left her jesses on and turned his back. She would survive, he thought. That night he returned to the railway tracks and hurled hard stones at the Germiston gang.

John McNally

There's a wee story. I was in the local. There was a power cut. Mind the power cuts? No light or anything. No lifts. The lights went out at certain times. And well, I walked up twenty-seven storeys. I was up the wrong flat. I had to walk down again. And this is the God's truth. I walked up and I was stone cold sober. Twenty-seven storeys. Well I couldn't believe it when I saw the door. Good job I never tried to open it.

Jennifer 1977

A bag of sugar, butter, condensed milk. Heated in a pan. Not boiled or else the mixture would turn to treacle. Spread flat to cool in a tin. Then cut and bagged and sold at chapel. Jennifer's fingers still tasted of the tablet she'd made at Guides. Almost too old to be going now and preferring the lure of the town and the boys from school, she went, still, out of habit, because of her pals and because of nights like the one she'd just had where they made more tablet than she'd ever seen. The Guide leader had given all the girls a couple of pieces to take away with them and Jennifer ate a chunk while she waited for the lift.

Two boys, younger than Jennifer and new to the building but already running riot in it, were in the lift when it arrived. They didn't get out, and as Jennifer stepped in, they pressed all the buttons to all the floors using a stick because the plastic buttons had long been burned off. The boys leaned against the walls and stared at Jennifer.

'What are you eating?' one said.

'Tablet.'

'Any left?'

'Nup.' She smiled.

The lift made its slow climb up the building. The boys had quick eyes and nervous legs, yet they stared too, as if they were interested in Jennifer.

At floor fourteen they ran between the closing doors and shouted back, 'We seen you winching on the back stair!'

Jennifer laughed but was glad her father or anyone she knew wasn't with her. She wondered if her brother knew who the boys were. They were his age.

The boys ran like rats in the building. They took turns to climb through the fireman's hatch in the lift's ceiling and sit on the top in the dark, not moving and holding on tight as the lift went up and down. It was the berries. They returned, legs first, jumping to the floor of the lift, their faces worn out from adrenaline. Oh man, try it from the very top to the bottom. We'll put it on the fireman's switch so it won't stop at any floors. Outside they found a jobby and wrapped it in newspaper. It stank. One of the boys held it in front of him, away from his nose. The other felt for the matches in his pocket. They took it in the lift to the floor where the miserable git lived, put it outside his door and bent down to set fire to a corner of the paper. It took off beautifully. Three loud thumps on his door and then they raced through the fire door to the stairs and watched through the glass. Five, four, three, two, one. He opened his door in his dressing gown and slippers and black-rimmed spectacles, and his eyes and mouth were holes of surprise when he saw his burning doorstep. Three huge steps with his slip-pered foot onto the flames. A pause, surprise again and that sweet look of disgust at the shite on his slipper. The boys took off and howled and whooped down the stair and didn't care that they were giving themselves away because that old cunt wouldn't have the legs to chase them. What a laugh.

When Jennifer was in the bathroom she heard the lifts going up and down and shouts and thuds and supposed the boys were still playing. She took off the make-up that her mother had shown her how to apply and splashed her face with water. When she pressed a towel to her cheeks and eyes she could smell the roof; she could always tell when her mother had dried clothes at the top. There'd been a good wind today. She cleaned her teeth. Murmurings from her parents as they tidied up. Her mother's boots back in her wardrobe. A glass of milk and a glance at the news and then bed.

From out of black sleep, her father woke her. Her eyes stung in the bright room.

'Get up now! Move!' he said.

She didn't have time to speak. He pulled at her arm, drag-ging her up.

'Shoes, coat, out now!' he said and he left her room and she heard him waking up her brother who cried a distressed, sleep-filled moan.

'Wake up James, this is serious,' he said.

Her mother came into her room. She said, 'Jennifer, are you ready?'

Her mother wore her coat and slippers and carried her handbag. 'There's a fire,' she said.

'Where?'

'A few floors below.'

'Oh my God.'

'Yes. Hurry up now.'

The faint smell of burning, she recognised it now. It took her seconds to put on her coat and shoes. Her father was pushing her brother out of his bedroom.

'My football cards!' Her brother reached into his room but Jennifer's father turned James's shoulders back towards the door.

'I should take the photos in case it all goes up,' her mother said.

'No, no, out, all of you!'

Jennifer smelled the fierce smoke when she stepped onto the back stairs. Clanging footsteps above and below them. She held onto the rail as she walked and listened to one of their neighbours.

'It's on twenty-three floor,' he said. 'One of the empty flats.'

Lights were on in other buildings. No stars. Smoke low in the sky. Streetlights showing empty streets, except for fire engines. Jennifer was out of breath. She thought she might fall. Her mother coughed and sounded like she would never stop.

'Mind your backs folks!' A man's voice shouted from above them. And then again, violently, 'Mind your backs!' and Jennifer looked up and saw firemen. She stood close to the wall and let them pass. They carried a colleague who lay flat in their arms, black streaks on his face, his eyes closed, the toes of his boots pointing to the ceiling. The firemen travelled fast down the metal stairs.

'Is he dead?' she heard James ask.

'Shoosh, son,' her father said. Then, 'I don't know. Perhaps he's injured. The heat.'

An elderly couple, Jennifer knew them, they lived on the sixteenth floor, struggled down the stairs ahead of them and Jennifer slowed as people in front of her slowed.

'Go by us,' the elderly man said.

'Don't be daft,' somebody said.

The elderly woman began to cry. 'I can't go any faster,' she said. 'I can't go any faster.'

'You're all right, hen,' somebody else said and they all slowed on the stairs.

The sprinklers came on above their heads and wet their hair and shoulders and made the stairs slippery.

'I didn't know they had sprinklers,' said Jennifer's mother.

Jennifer saw more fire engines coming from all the main roads that led to Red Road. Gusts of smoke-smelling air came at them on the stairs. More firemen charged up, their heavy boots ringing on the metal, quick in their heavy gear, tanks on their backs and masks on their faces.

Jennifer and her family reached the ground and stood in Red Road looking up at the fire which was full and blazing. A fat cloud of fire, cloying and smothering and swallowing the windows and verandas and sides of the building. Residents gathered in the street, looking at the fire. People shouted from their verandas in the long block opposite, and all around them there were voices and screams and sirens.

Jennifer's father gathered his family to him and said, 'Are we all right? Is everyone okay?' and Jennifer and her mother and James nodded and turned their heads back to the fire.

'My wedding dress is up there,' a girl shouted and stretched her white arms out. 'Oh God, my wedding dress is hanging up in my burning house.'

She cried and a woman put her arms around her and the

girl put her hands over her face. Jennifer knew she was getting married to Christopher McGeady who she'd met at the Sky Lounge and they were going on their honeymoon to the Isle of Mull and she'd had her dress made by her aunty who was a seamstress.

'My poor wedding dress!' the girl howled.

Somebody opened the doors to the school and somebody else shouted to the people in the street that they could take the weans in there to sleep for the night. Men and women carrying sleeping children walked through the crowd towards the school. Most of the adults stood and watched and Jennifer watched too because it was horrifying and wondrous. She thought of her house with all their things in it.

'I took my budgie and my policies,' she heard Simon Forbes say and he laughed because he joked about everything. He'd been on his own for years but he always joked. His budgie cage swung as he talked.

'Did you bring your policies, Ma?' Jennifer asked.

'We don't have policies,' her mother said and because there was nowhere else to go they walked towards the school with the other tenants who wandered about dazed and upset in their nightgowns and pyjamas. They stepped onto the pavement as another screaming fire engine came down the road. The fire was still huge and billowing, the wind pushing it round the sides of the building. They left the people in the street and watched the fire from the doorway of the school, unable to take their eyes off it.

Morning. Smoky, burnt air. Ten Red Road standing spent, chastised, with blackened sides and gaping windows, the top floors skewed and aslant. Officials stood outside its doors while residents of other buildings went about, going into the shops or walking to the bus stop. A man from the Corporation taped a sign to the door.

'You can't come in.'

'My house is in there.'

'That makes no difference.' His face was tired, as if he'd been up all night, which he probably had. Jim didn't try to argue.

'Have you any idea when we'll be allowed back in?'

'A day or so, maybe. They might let you in to get essentials, I don't know.' The man from the Corporation nodded towards the primary school. 'There's a meeting in there at twelve.'

Jim put his hands in the pockets of his coat.

'Was anybody hurt? It was some fire.'

The man used his teeth to tear a piece of sellotape and smoothed it softly over his sign.

'Aye, it was some fire. A wee boy lost his life,' he said and Jim let his breath out in a sigh.

Red Road was quiet, the news about the boy silencing any laughter or chat. Just the seagulls, louder than ever, cried out. Jim spoke to a neighbour who'd also slept in the primary school overnight and now couldn't stop staring at the building, he said. He wore his slippers and dressing gown, and his pyjama trousers hung over the backs of his slippers, touching the ground. The men stood on the corner and Jim's neighbour rolled a cigarette.

'The firemen couldn't get in to twenty-three/two for ages.'

'Is that where it started, aye?'

'Aye, twenty-three/two.'

'That house was empty.'

'They'd left their furnishings though. It must have seemed like a playground for a couple of wee boys.'

'Do you know the family?'

'No. One boy got out alive, I don't know how. A miracle if you ask me. The other boy, he didn't survive.'

'His parents, the poor souls.'

'Devastated, I bet.'

Jim's neighbour put his tobacco in the pocket of his robe.

'I gave my lighter to a fella in the school this morning,' he said, 'and he never gave it back.'

'I don't smoke, pal,' Jim said and his neighbour walked away to the paper shop to see if anybody there would light his smoke for him or let him have some matches for free.

The meeting in the school was crowded with people standing up at the back and at the sides of the rows of chairs. The people from the Corporation held out placatory palms when somebody mentioned asbestos. The injured fireman, it turned out, had inhaled the asbestos and smoke and collapsed. It lined the ceilings and walls, they knew that.

'We're going to make it safe,' an official said.

'The whole building's at a tilt,' someone else said. Which it was. The fire's heat had buckled the building's steel insides.

'Yes, that's why we'll move some of you out for a wee while. Everyone from floor nineteen and above.'

'Where?'

'We're working on it.'

'When can we go in and get our belongings? We've got nothing here.'

Some of the men and women got angry and many of the folk were desperate to get out of Red Road anyway, so they used the fire as an excuse to insist on never coming back.

'We like Red Road, don't we?' Jennifer heard her father say to her mother. 'It's handy for our work, I know, but we like it anyway, despite its problems.'

'Aye, I don't want to move,' Jennifer's mother said and they listened as the men and women at the meeting got angrier and angrier.

Finlay McKay

We had two bedrooms and a box room. You could put a bed in the box room and a wee bit of furniture and it had no windows so you were in complete darkness. Any time of the day, it could be any season, and it would be complete darkness and you'd wake up and couldn't see your arm or your hand in front of your face. It was great for hangovers. My mum put a drying rail up and that's where she'd hang the washing, in this tiny wee box room. It must only have been about seven feet long and three feet wide.

I suppose it would have been cold because it was right at the end of the building. When I was really young I'd go in there if it was windy. If it was really windy it would rattle the windows and the building would be swaying and if I was scared I'd go in the box room. I always remember shouting for a fur coat. My mum would come in with her fur coat and I'd get under that so it must have been cold.

I think some folk used to just put junk in there. But we put a bed and a wee cabinet and a wee record player or a tape player in there. We drilled a hole in the wall, which was a no-no because of the asbestos, but we drilled a hole in the wall and plugged into Mum and Dad's electrical supply. It was great, it was a great wee room.

Ricky 1977

Ricky loved the lumber room so much. It was definitely better than sharing a bedroom. His mattress fitted brilliantly on the floor and he got peace all night. His ma and da had let him clean the place out so there wasn't any junk, just his Action Men and mattress and he could sleep in there whenever he wanted. No windows either so morning light didn't bother him. It was the best room in the whole house. Yes, he had to take turns with his brothers but let it be remembered that he cleared it out and made it into a bedroom in the first place so he should get first choice.

'I missed the fire? Why didn't you wake me?'

'Never wake a sleeping baby,' his ma said.

'I'm not a baby, I'm nine.' Ricky put his elbows on the table and cupped his cheeks.

His ma raised her eyebrows and he took his elbows off the table.

'How many fire engines were there?'

'Oh, about twenty.'

'Twenty!'

'It was on the radio, they came from all over. Dumbarton, Helensburgh, Falkirk. It was some fire.'

Ricky couldn't believe it. He'd never seen firemen putting out a real fire. It was his dream to see that.

'How many firemen?'

'I couldn't say, son. Hundreds?'

'Oh God.' Ricky put his head in his hands again and wished he hadn't slept the night in the lumber room. His ma told him about the people in their pyjamas and the dogs and weans, the cameras and journalists with microphones, the bright white TV lights. Polis. The place buzzing when they finally went to bed and still buzzing when they woke.

'Some fire,' Ricky said and ate up his breakfast, eager to get out and see Ten Red Road for himself.

His pal Tommy lived in Ninety-three Petershill Drive. They met every morning and made the short walk to school. The first thing Tommy said was, 'Did you see the fire?'

Ricky paused. But not for long.

'Aye, it was mental! Twenty fire engines, a hundred firemen, TV cameras.'

'Flames a mile high!'

The boys added detail after detail to their story, passing Ten Red Road and gasping at the burnt structure, smoke up their nostrils and in their throats. They stood outside their school and saw grown-ups where schoolchildren would have been, standing in twos and threes and fours in the playground, treading all over the games and patterns marked out on the concrete.

'No school!' a kid from their class shouted as he ran past them and away.

The boys didn't wait for anyone else to tell them different. They walked back the way they came, then went off to the grass behind the Little House on the Prairie, the community hut that stood alone on the field, and played long shots with the football Ricky took with him wherever he went.

Jennifer 1977

While the Corporation worked out what to do, they let the residents of Ten Red Road who lived on floors nineteen and beyond back into their ruined houses.

'I don't want to go,' Jennifer's mother said because she'd talked to a neighbour who'd said she'd broken down when she went through her door and saw her house of ten years wrecked and all her possessions useless.

'Jim, just take what you think we can salvage,' she said and waited at her mother's on Dykemuir Street where the family were staying.

Jennifer went with her father and James and a couple of suitcases. They caught the lift to the eighteenth floor then walked the rest. They stepped onto their wet landing and her father put the key into their door. There was a terrible smell of smoke, the air in the lobby was damp, the carpets sodden and there was fungus on the walls. Their panicked beds were wet through. Books, carpet, curtains drenched. Jennifer and James filled their suitcases with clothes and items they thought could be salvaged. Their father took photographs that weren't ruined, for Colleen, and his bottle of malt, and documents from a drawer, even though they were wet.

'Say goodbye to our house,' he said and Jennifer and James did that. Jennifer stepped once more on to the veranda because she liked the view.

In the living room she found her father shaking his head and looking as sad as she'd ever seen him.

'See this,' he said and put his fingers to the red wallpaper with the swirls.

It slid to the floor with only the lightest of touches.

'Your mammy's wallpaper,' he said and they shut the door behind them and walked down the stairs in silence until Jennifer said, 'We'll get another house for you to decorate, Da.'

And they did. Sixty-three Petershill Drive. Twenty-four/four. Fair play to the folk who wanted out; out of Barmulloch altogether, out to a new house in a different part of Glasgow, but not for the Ryans, with the easy walk to Provanmill and their kids settled in their schools and Colleen with her friends in other houses and her own ma just up the road. No. A new house. A new view. Red Road changed and changing but the Ryans sticking with it.

Section Three

Ricky 1978

SCOTLAND! NINETEEN SEVENTY-EIGHT! The World Cup Finals! Scotland's year. Scotland's decade. Scotland's finest hour! Ally MacLeod's words in his head. Everybody's da and even their ma was going to be watching the first match. Scotland v Peru. Scotland! Ally's Army! Scotland!

Ricky booted the football up the pitch for his pal Tommy to run on to and take goalwards. His was a kick worthy of the 1978 World Cup squad. He'd be fourteen for the next world cup and eighteen for the one after that. A Scottish footballing legend, that's what he was going to be. Oh Scotland.

He was out playing as long as he could contain his excitement. His mammy had already kicked him out the house because he couldn't sit still and wait. From the numbers of boys out playing, Ricky guessed their mammies had done the same thing. Red Road was hoaching with weans and footballs and flags. The Saltire flapped from windows and verandas. A badge. A statement of allegiance. The most exciting summer of Ricky's life. Boof, the ball came to his feet and he saw a quick, sneaky pass down the wing to Tommy. Boof.

Suddenly, boys began to run. Hundreds of them. They took off. Some carried footballs, others just ran in their sannies or football boots and they ran as if the world was ending or beginning. Weans shouted down from verandas and waved up their brothers and sisters.

A slow, guttural chant started up; *We're on the march with Ally's Army!* dragged from the boozy bellies of a group of men who staggered past Ninety-three Petershill Drive.

Ricky ran with his pals to One-five-three. He would watch

the match in his house. Tommy was coming with him. His brother would be there and his ma and da and anyone else they'd invited in. Oh mammy daddy it was too exciting.

It felt like hundreds of weans were waiting for the lifts and it was a scrum of elbows and shuffling feet and wee pointy shoulder blades. Scotland! Scotland! Their shouts cracked against the painted walls. May McBride came in with her husband Alistair and she put her hands over her ears.

'Oh you boys are making an awful racket,' she said but she laughed and looked around the mass of twitching, twittering boys.

'He's up the stair already,' Ricky said to her. 'He wanted to watch the build-up.' Ricky was pals with May's son. They went to school together.

'That's my boy,' she said.

A lift arrived and the boys surged in. Five, ten, fifteen, twenty, thirty boys squeezed themselves into the silver-walled lift that was meant to carry eight adult bodies at the most.

'You should let May into the lift, boys,' Alistair called out, his hands on his wife's shoulders and her hands on his.

'It's all right, we'll wait for the other one.'

'Okay, just this once.'

They stepped aside and Alistair pulled on the lapels of May's raincoat and drew her lips towards his.

'I'm not letting that lift get away,' Ricky said and he and Tommy pushed past some hesitant boys who'd only just moved to Red Road and squeezed themselves in. The lift was hot and smelled of mud and sweat. A tiny boy sat on the shoulders of a big boy. Hands reached to the number panel until a boy took control and, because he knew where all the boys lived – they all did – he pressed the buttons himself. The doors shut and thirty boys' toothy faces looked up at the ascending numbers that lit up above the doors. The lift stopped at the second floor and several boys berated the boy who squeezed himself out.

'You should have taken the back stair you lazy cunt,' one said.

'You can't get in the back stair, you can only get out.'

Ricky couldn't speak now. He closed his eyes and felt his stomach flip and squirm. Jordan. Dalglish. Gemmell. Burns. Masson.

'Are you all right?' Tommy said.

'Aye. I just want to be in front of my TV,' Ricky said through clenched teeth and a barely-open mouth.

The lift set off again and a cheer went up. Scotland, Scotland! The boys began to sing and bang the lift walls with their fists. More boys jumped up and down and the lift went on up. Then it stopped. Just shook and stopped. Sudden silence. Ricky breathed in and opened his eyes. All the boys looked at the doors. The tiny square window showed no light; they weren't even nearly at a floor. Still in silence, the boy who was good at working the lifts, the one who put it on the fireman's switch or got it to miss floors or stay still when new people were in for the first time, squeezed a path through the boys and got to work. He tapped a few buttons, got a bunk up from another lad and fiddled around with the lift panel. Nothing. The lift didn't move.

'Try jumping,' a boy said.

So they all jumped, hoping that it would kick-start the lift in the way some of them had seen their fathers jump-start their motors. The lift didn't move.

'Try shouting,' another boy said and they screamed and bawled and shouted for help.

'Where's the caretaker?' somebody said.

'In front of his telly with his baffies on,' Tommy said.

'Oh God,' said Ricky and he thought he might greet.

The boys went quiet again. Tommy began to laugh. 'I can't believe this is happening.'

'It's not funny,' Ricky wailed and said nothing more.

Ricky couldn't believe it. He just couldn't believe it. Even if the caretaker found them he knew they'd never get a lift engineer out while the game was going on. They were stuck and he was missing Scotland's finest footballing hour. He told himself that the lifts in Red Road were cursed and doomed and he would never take one ever again.

At eight forty-five a boy looked at his watch and said, 'That's kick-off,' and the boy with the tiny boy on his shoulders said, 'Matty, I can't hold you up anymore. You have to get down.'

The boy with the watch began to count down the first-half minutes and somebody made up a commentary that had Jordan scoring a hat-trick and Rough performing a dynamic and stunning save.

'And Graeme Souness with his thunderous left foot floats the ball to Rioch's feet. What a joy to watch.'

Ricky closed his eyes again. The boy with the watch counted down a full forty-five minutes then fifteen for half time then another forty-five and when they were well into twenty-six minutes of injury time they heard the caretaker shouting to them and telling them that help was on its way.

'What was the score?' Ricky shouted.

'You don't want to know, son,' the caretaker shouted back.

'We do!'

'Three-one. To Peru.'

'Oh pishing, shiteing, typical Scotland.'

'There's always Iran.'

'Ach well, it can't get any worse.'

June Aird

The bus stop used to have a lane all the way through and it was a pathway, a busy, cheery pathway. You used to walk all the way along and you'd come to my Aunt Molly's. And she would have a brae, you went up a brae to my Aunt Molly's, and there'd be chutes and swings kind of built in. And we used to play on that. Because Aunty Molly was a wee bit better off than her other sisters you knew you were going to get some chocolate biscuits. You just loved going to Aunty Molly's.

She was a character. Everybody knew her. Her pastime was the bingo. Bingo was a social place. She won vast amounts. She won lots of different things. They'd have a play-off – you shout 'house' in one game then you'd get a special ticket to play in another game and they linked up the bingo halls – and Aunty Molly got the star prize of going to London to see Miss World. She took one of her sisters with her.

Ricky 1980

A weird-looking man came into the flats and a few minutes later they heard a thump and a bang. Ricky and the boys played kick-ups outside the shed as people came home from their work. There were two footballs between them and although there were no rules as such, it worked out that two boys played against each other, keeping up their footballs until one of them missed. When Murdo Johnson had a shot they mostly just watched him because the boy was brilliant and it was like watching a keepie-uppie exhibition with the football bouncing off his neck and head and toes and knees and even his arse at times. He would probably go on to be a professional player if he kept on being so good, and fair play to him. The guy never even smoked or anything.

The weird-looking man had walked quickly past them. He wore denims and a khaki jacket and carried a rucksack. He could have been a teenager or he could have been older, it was hard to tell. His hair was cropped close to his skull and his face was weird; a bit mad-looking. He didn't seem to want to look at the boys even though they looked at him; they said hiya to everyone who came in or out because they knew everyone. But Ricky had never seen this guy.

Tommy chucked the football to Ricky and he started his turn at keepie-uppie. Murdo Johnson had the other ball and started really showing off. Ricky stopped after a bit and held his ball against his side and watched. Murdo flicked it behind him and then kicked it up over his head and nudged it back into the air with his thigh. Then there was a thump and a bang. Murdo looked up at the boys but carried on with his kick-ups, not show-off ones now, just simple keepie-uppie ones.

'I'm going to see what that noise was,' Paul said. He was a wee boy, only about eight.

Murdo carried on and Ricky started again, knocking the ball into the air with just his head. He could be as good as Murdo if he put his mind to it. And then he mishit the ball and it flew towards the wee boy Paul who was coming back from round the back of the building. Paul didn't pick up the ball. He let it roll past.

He said, 'There's a dead guy round the back.'

'Shut up,' the boys said and Paul said, 'I'm telling you, there is. There's a dead guy.'

They were used to seeing men lying in funny places. And women too.

'He's not moving.'

Ricky went with him and as soon as he saw the guy he knew that he was dead. It was the guy in the denims and the khaki and his head was underneath his shoulders because of the way he'd landed. His arms were snapped and lay at strange angles. There was no blood at all, just this frightening-looking body.

'He's dead isn't he?' the wee boy Paul said.

Ricky looked up and saw an open window way up high.

'Aye. I think he's a suicide. He's jumped.'

'He only went in the building two minutes ago,' the wee boy said.

'I remember.'

They told the other boys who came to look too and some

put their hands to their mouths and peered and they all stood at some distance from the poor body on the ground.

'He's not from the flats is he?' Tommy said.

'He came here to get killed,' the wee boy Paul said.

All the boys went together to tell the caretaker about the dead body and they stayed together while the caretaker waited for the police to come and take statements. They each told the police more or less the same thing. A weird-looking man came into the flats and a few minutes later they heard a thump and a bang.

Jean McGeogh

We liked Perry Como, and his shows, we liked that. I hardly watched the telly I was always working, Christ. Well, I worked in the Shettleston Club and I knew all the songs they were playing and the bands and the music. No, I never had time to listen to wirelesses. I hardly watched the television by the time I washed myself, maybe took a bath and got into my bed.

I mind one time the boys came in. I think they were nineteen, eighteen and they all came in and that, and I was in my bed and ah, I smelt this lovely smell of ham coming through to me and I got out of my bed and they were all in the kitchenette, we had a wee table with benches and that all done, and I went do you think this is a bloody Reo Stakis hotel, come on! And they would go, Get into your bed, Jean, you're tired.

I just loved them. I knew they weren't any trouble. If they weren't in my house they were in another neighbour's house. They were good boys. They were no trouble. You still worried about them.

Ricky 1981

In the pitch-black lumber room Ricky's alarm sounded. He darted a hand from under the covers and turned it off before anyone heard. He pushed his way through the washing that

hung from the drying rail and grabbed a pair of his mum's
tights, put on his black clothes and opened the door. The
house was asleep. As he tiptoed through the lobby he nudged
a picture with his shoulder and grabbed it with blind hands
but it didn't fall. He felt in his pocket for his door key and then
opened and closed the front door. On the landing it could have
been daylight the way the lights buzzed and lit up the floor.
Except that he sensed everyone was sleeping. Even the spiders
and the flies. He called for the lift and when the doors opened
he saw a man lying on the lift floor and nearly shat himself. It
wasn't a junkie. It was Mr Murray from floor nineteen, asleep
and stinking of booze.

Outside in the dark, Tommy whistled for him with such
subterfuge that it made Ricky laugh out loud. Tommy had the
paint and was dressed in black too with boot polish on his face.

'Can you see through they tights?' Tommy said.

'Aye, no problem.' Ricky tucked the legs down the back of
his coat. 'Right, we know what we're doing don't we?'

'Aye. You hold the paint pot. I'll paint. Go.'

They ran. Tommy dipped the brush into the paint pot and shuffled backwards like they'd seen the men on the streets do when they painted the yellow lines. They started the line from one end of the low wall, took it down and then across and then up the way to the other end of the wall. They did the tramlines and the T to make the serving boxes. One side of the wall and then the other. Quick work. When they were finished, the boys sat on the wall and swigged the Irn-Bru that Tommy took from his pocket. The white lines glistened. Ricky saw a rat. It nosed the kerbstone on the other side of Petershill Drive, then crossed the road and stopped by the painted lines but didn't tread on them.

'Good rat,' Tommy said.

'It must know there's wet paint.'

'That rat smells a rat.'

An engine sounded and the boys looked up to see a police car going slow down Petershill Drive. They were off the wall and running around the side of the building so fast that when they peeked round the corner of One-five-three and looked back up the road, it seemed as if the patrol car had hardly moved.

'We got away with it,' Ricky said.

When the police car was away, its headlights nosing the dark road and its engine soft, the boys said goodnight.

Mr Murray was still in the lift. He woke and yelled out and bashed his head against the side of the lift as he tried to sit.

'Don't hurt me,' he said. 'I'll give you my money. It's in my pocket. Take it. Take it all.'

He pulled coins and a crumpled pound note from his pocket and the coins spun on the lift floor. When Ricky bent to pick them up he remembered he still had his ma's tights on his head.

'It's all right, pal,' he said and put the money into the man's boozy hands.

Ricky pulled off his ma's tights before he went back into the house. He folded his black clothes and put his pyjamas on and slept. He woke up in the pitch-black lumber room, wondering if it was morning yet.

Wimbledon! Björn Borg headbands! McEnroe tantrums! Towels and sheets and mops and buckets flung out of cupboards as kids search for tennis rackets. Strawberries and Pimms! What? Ma, chuck us down some money wrapped in newspaper so we can get some ginger from the van!

Oh my God, somebody's painted the tennis courts. Was it the caretaker? Was it fuck? There's tramlines and everything. We can play doubles. That wall there's the net. Who was it? Who cares? Can you serve? Doesn't matter if you can't. Just skelp it over the wall – the net! – and try not to aim for anybody's coupon. Allan Scott, he's the best player in One-five-three. He'll take on the long streak of piss Robert Hawley from One-two-three. Oh my God, all the kids want to play tennis and they're standing with their rackets around the court and the best bit is when they play five-a-side or ten-a-side and everyone just keeps hitting the ball over the net and it goes on and on and on all day until the mammies call from the verandas and tell the weans to come on home for their tea.

Ricky and Tommy act casual. No, we don't know who painted the courts, they say. Must be legends, whoever it was. Wink wink. Tommy's whistle again, just for Ricky to hear.

Iris 1982

They came from their flooded house in Avonspark Street. Vandals got to it and wrecked her roof and the Corporation moved them high up in Sixty-three Petershill Drive.

Iris, her daughter, Pamela, and her son, Scott. Iris was unused to the height of the place. Despite watching the towers for years from her low-down house she'd never been inside Red Road. And here she was now, twenty-four up and able to see her old roof and the roofs of her old neighbours' houses, roofs of cars and buses, and warehouses. String-like roads, patches of grass, pylons, trees, hills. Some view, if only she wasn't so feart to stand at the window and look.

Ricky 1982

They met in the same place as last time at three a.m. on Sunday morning, wearing their black clothes. Hardly anyone was around and anyone who was was buzzing on something or other. A few lights in a few windows and a dog barking. That was all.

'We could fill our pockets like in *The Great Escape*,' Ricky said.

'Aye we could, but these are better.'

Tommy handed Ricky a shovel and some bin bags and they walked in the dark to the far fields. The two boys bent over their shovels and filled their bin bags with dirt. Ricky pushed the ends of his ma's tights over his shoulders but they fell down and got in his way again.

'Tommy, do me a favour and tie these ends for me or tuck them down the back of my coat,' he said.

'Just take them off.'

'Good idea.'

Ricky took them off and wiped his face.

The boys dug in silence. A train rattled past and they stopped to watch and stretch their backs and when they bent to dig again their movements were economical and slight as if they belonged to another time when the fields were farmland and men and women bent to knife cabbages from their stalks.

It took them hours to fill the bin bags and drag them to the football fields and then to pour dirt into the holes and divots made by the boots and falls of endless games of football. They stamped on the earth and pressed it into the holes and walked on, scanning the ground for more holes to fill. Ricky couldn't stop. He said so to Tommy and Tommy agreed, saying just imagine the boys tomorrow when the pitch isn't fucked up anymore. They went on until the trains came more regularly and the sky lightened and they could see the shapes of singing birds in the trees and on top of the buildings; a kestrel taking off from the top of Thirty-three block, some crows pecking at the grass under the trees by the tracks.

'I was born in those flats,' Tommy said when they stopped.

'I know you were. So was I.'

'No, actually born there. In my ma and da's bedroom.'

Ricky looked at his friend. 'I never knew that.'

'Aye. Born in Red Road. Bred in Red Road. Died in Red Road.'

Ricky looked at his friend again. 'Really?'

'We'll see how life pans out.'

They walked back towards the flats side by side, knees muddied, shovels trailing, bin bags hanging at their sides like upturned cabbages, the clouds overhead grey and half-lit, the fields around them green-grey and ready.

Pamela 1983

Pamela and her pal ran towards the ice cream van. Its music drew them up from the swing park and they joined the line of weans in ankle socks and shorts. They licked their oysters and got vanilla on their noses and chins. Nicola trailed her skipping rope as they walked, the wooden handle bouncing off the ground.

'It's him!' Pamela saw her da walking away up Red Road, jeans and a T-shirt, a paper in his hand, and ran to catch up with him. Ran straight into the ice cream van – bam – on its way out of Red Road. Up in the air she went and when she came back down she hit off the ice cream van again and ended up on the road. But she got up, no bother. Her da didn't see. He was out of sight.

'Are you all right, hen?' the ice cream man said.

'I saw my da. I was wanting to talk to him. I've missed him now.' Pamela's knees were grazed.

'Where do you live? I'll take you home.'

'My ma's at bingo,' Pamela said and she held the man's hand in the lift as her body began to hurt. Nicola chewed her fingernails.

'I'll be back tomorrow with a present,' the man said when she was sitting on the couch and he was trying to leave. 'I'm glad you're not hurt bad.'

'What will he bring you?' Nicola said.

They switched on the television, even though the day was a scorcher and if Pamela hadn't been hit by the ice cream van they would have been running about daft outside.

'I don't know. I'm so excited.'

'Maybe he'll bring you ice creams.'

'Aye, hunners of ice creams. Or sweeties.'

Pamela's ma found the bruises in the bath and she was livid. She said she'd have words with the man when he came back but he never did. No present for Pamela.

Donna McCrudden

I had friends in other blocks and I had friends up the same flat as me. I had a really good neighbour. She moved out before me. She'd been there a long, long time, I think since the flats opened. She moved to one of the houses on the Red Road. We would babysit for each other and things like that and have nights out together if there were any nights going. And then when the kids went to nursery I got to meet a lot of other people from a lot of different areas, but I kept good friends with my neighbours for years until they all moved away. My kids they went to nursery in the flats and they got to meet a lot of friends there as well, but I never really let them out too often on their own. They couldn't reach the buttons on the lift for a start to get up or down because they were way up high. And if

they did go out to play, one of my daughters was more street-
wise so she used a stick to press the buttons. Either that or they
had to wait till an adult came or somebody older and they
would press the buttons for them.

Ricky 1985

Ricky and Julie went to different schools. He went to Albert
School, she went to All Saints. So they met around four o'clock
down by the tennis court and talked about music. Julie with
the flick and pink lipstick and Ricky with his boxing fists and
football. He made her a tape of David Bowie songs. She told
him about Bob Dylan and said she would record one of her
da's tapes on the tape-to-tape and give it to him.

'What was the first record you ever bought?' Julie asked
and when Ricky told her it was Jimmy Osmond's 'Long Haired
Lover from Liverpool' she leaned into him and put her fluffy
head on to his chest and laughed and laughed.

They hid up her back stair and winched. She told him if
her da caught them he'd cut his balls off.

'You wouldn't let him do that to me.'

'I'm only saying. It's not up to me.'

Julie lived on floor twenty-seven of Two-one-three Petershill
Drive. She once took Ricky and Tommy and some of their
other pals up to her house to look at the view. Her da watched
them from behind his newspaper and asked questions. When
she offered to show them the roof, he said, 'Five minutes or
I'm coming up after you.'

Afterwards, Julie told Ricky that her da thought the other
boys dressed smart, but not Ricky.

'That's because I'm not into that kind of music.'

'I know what music you're into, my long haired lover.'

Ricky believed Julie's da would hurt him, no bother. No fat
on him which was impressive for an old guy. He had fingers that
looked like they would crush flies, his forearms were covered

with black hairs and his movements were quick and surprising. He once took Ricky's football from him and threw it off the veranda – just hurled it.

Another time, he stood right close to Ricky when Julie was out of the room.

'Julie tells me you're a boxer.'

'Aye, well, I train with Alistair McBride in the community hall.'

'Do you compete?'

'Not yet.'

Julie's da laughed. 'Not competing? I see. I bet you haven't even sparred.'

Ricky wanted to tell him that Alistair had started introducing a spar at the end of each training session.

'I used to box.'

That's all Julie's da said before he left the room. Alone in Julie's living room, Ricky stared at the picture on the wall of the boy with the tears. Everyone's house has that picture, he thought.

That evening, in the lift on the way down, Julie and Ricky held hands. She wore perfume. She must have just put it on because her neck was wet. He touched her silver name which hung on a chain and sat just below her throat. Julie put a hand in the back pocket of his jeans and Ricky leaned his head against the lift wall and had conflicting thoughts about his stauner; his bloody cock was out of control – she might think him disgusting if she saw – but then again it was such a right rare feeling and God she was gorgeous.

'My sister's got an empty tonight,' Julie said.

Ricky opened his eyes.

'She's away in Dundee. I've got the key. Do you want to stay there with me?'

'Just me and you?'

'Aye. I'm not inviting all your mad pals too.'

'Oh, Julie.'

He put an arm round her shoulders. At the next stop a woman in her Sally Army uniform stepped into the lift. Ricky took his arm from Julie's shoulders and waited for the questions to start. Dutifully, they stated how they were doing at school, what their mammies and daddies were doing the night and their opinions on the various huge dogs in the flats.

'You youngsters have a good evening,' she said when they got out.

'We will.'

A Friday night.

'So shall we?' Julie said when it was just the two of them.

'Oh, aye,' Ricky said and they went to find Tommy so he could cover for them.

Tommy was helping some of the weans with their hatchets. He was finishing them off for them – stamping with his stronger feet to flatten the soup can and shaping it so it looked more like an axe blade.

'Find me a tack or a nail and I'll fix it to your handle,' he told the weans who went off searching.

When Julie and Ricky asked if he'd cover for them that night, Tommy said, 'Aye, no bother,' and the three of them worked out their story.

'So this is how it goes,' Tommy said. 'Ricky, you're staying with me the night, Julie, you're staying with Karen Brown. And I'm staying in my house on my Jack Jones because no lassie will have me.'

'Taking one for the team, Tommy, cheers pal.' Ricky was so excited he could hardly stand still. He kept looking at Julie to check she hadn't changed her mind. Her hair, her peachy cheeks, her gorgeous rack, oh God, he couldn't believe she wanted to be alone with him in an empty house.

The wee boys came back with nails and half a brick and Tommy squatted to bash the nails through their hatchet blades and onto their wooden handles. He slashed one through the air when it was done and then shook it in front of Ricky's face. 'If I find out you've been messing with my daughter, I'll chop your prick off, you dirty wee... prick.'

Ricky looked at Julie and Julie just said, 'We won't get caught.'

Tommy gave the hatchet back to the boy and the weans ran off, waving their weapons in the air, roaring and cussing.

'On you go then, go tell your lies to your mammies and daddies.'

Ricky left Julie to make the arrangements and walked back to his house. He passed some of the boys he spent evenings with. They were dressed alike, in skin-tight trousers, big boots and jackets with ribbed elastic trim at the waist. They swung sticks or kicked stones and Ricky guessed they were heading out to the railway tracks to have a go at the Gyto.

'Ricky boy, you coming?' one boy said.

'Not tonight fellas, I've got an empty with my bird.'

The boys shouted out appreciatively, 'Getting your hole, wee man!'

Ricky played it down but thought, would he? Would she? Is that why she arranged to get the empty? Did she want to sleep with him? Should he get johnny bags from his big brother's room? Yes, he should. Oh, it was fucking amazing. Julie was a soft-skinned, gentle girl. He might be getting his hole with a girl he actually liked.

Their lies told, they winched in the lift they took to her sister's house in Birnie Court, even in front of people, they didn't care. The house was on the fifth floor and Julie shut the door behind them and turned on the lights. Her sister had painted the walls purple and lime. She had a framed poster of New Order on her living room wall and heart-shaped cushions.

'Did she say you could use her flat?' Ricky said.

'No,' Julie said. 'But she wouldn't have given me a spare set of keys if she didn't want me to use it.'

He wasn't going to argue. They kissed in the kitchen and Julie put her hands down the back of his jeans. His belt was quite tight and he wanted to loosen it. He felt her tits and got a hand beneath her bra. Oh God. Then they made coffees and moved the heart-shaped cushions to one side in order to sit on the couch.

'We've got the whole night,' Julie said and smiled at him and he felt sick and sweet.

She put her feet in his lap, like he'd seen women do on the television, and he put his coffee cup on the floor and took off her socks. She had pink toenails and the softest feet he'd ever felt. He'd only felt his own. He tried to massage her feet the way he thought she might like; stroked them and played with her toes – not too tickly yet not too rough. She told him his hands were warm and lovely and as he massaged, more confidently now, she talked about her da losing his job and how he shouted at the television and said Maggie Thatcher was a vile, evil cow. She said she'd heard him crying in the bathroom one night.

'I'm going to stay on at school and get a decent job,' she said. 'I want to be like your ma and my ma. And my da, if he could. I want to work. I might be a nurse like your ma.'

When he'd finished massaging her feet he lifted them to his face and kissed her soles. She giggled, and when he let go, she pressed them against his groin and Ricky thought the sudden silence between them would kill him.

There was a knock at the door. Julie took her feet out of Ricky's lap and they sat still on the sofa. The knock again. And then a scuffle at the letter box.

'Hello.'

It wasn't a voice Ricky recognised.

'Catherine, are you home, honey?'

A man's lazy, drawling voice.

'What do we do?'

'I'll tell him we're house-sitting.'

Ricky stood up and when he opened the door he saw a man in his twenties with thin shoulders and a moustache. He carried a hold-all.

'Catherine's away,' Ricky said. 'I'm house-sitting with her sister.'

'Okay, pal, it's just that Catherine said –'

The man knelt on the doorstep and took things out of his bag; an iron, a radio alarm clock, a watch.

'She said she wanted a couple of Sony Walkmans. I can do her the two plus batteries for twenty-five quid.'

He stood up and piled the batteries on top of the two Walkmans and held them out to Ricky. 'I've got another man wanting them so you'll have to take them now as I can't guarantee when I'll get any more.'

Ricky started to close the door. 'You're all right, pal,' he said.

'Catherine ordered them.'

'She might have ordered them but she's away and I'm no giving you twenty-five quid because I haven't got twenty-five quid.'

'Take them anyway and she can pay me when she gets back.'

'I don't think so.'

'Catherine won't be pleased with you. Or me.'

'You're a tryer.'

The man smiled and scratched his cheek.

'Beat it,' Ricky said and closed the door before any trouble could start.

Julie was in her sister's dressing gown and coming out of the bathroom.

'Oh, hello,' he said and Julie said, 'I thought we could have a bath. My sister's got bath pearls. I put one in. It makes the water all silky.'

He thought it was the most erotic thing ever. He lifted his arms and she took off his T-shirt and touched her finger to a bruise he'd got from sparring with one of the boys. She undid his jeans and he helped her pull them down, over his feet. He took off his socks and then as she undid her dressing gown and slipped it over her shoulders, he lowered his pants and was suddenly shy of his body. They hopped into the bath and sat opposite each other, bent-backed, cupping water in their palms and letting it fall on each other's shoulders. She put her wet hands on his face and neck and chest. He wanted to say do you like my chest hair? Do you like my muscles? I can do one-armed press-ups, I can pull my chin over a bar. He smoothed her hair from her forehead and watched drops of water fall from her earlobes. 'Look at you,' is what he said and he couldn't take his eyes off her tits.

'The bath's quite a squash and a squeeze isn't it?' she said.

'Sit between my legs, turn round,' he said and just as he was anticipating the feel of her wet back against his chest and her beautiful knees cupped in his palms there was another knock at the door.

'Ignore it,' Ricky said, 'it'll be our friendly door-to-door salesman.'

But the knocking continued. Julie swished the pearly water with her hands and cocked her head as she listened.

'Isn't that Tommy?'

'Julie! Ricky! Julie! Ricky!'

It was indeed Tommy. And his shouts were urgent and loud.

'Julie! Your da's on the warpath!'

'Oh God.' Ricky and Julie crashed out of the bath and while Julie dried herself, Ricky put a towel round his waist and opened up for Tommy.

'Oh Ricky, please,' Tommy said and put his hand over his eyes.

'What's happened?'

'I'm sorry, mate, Julie's da rang my house and asked if you were there. I said you were, but then he said he wanted to speak to you and I couldn't say you were on the shitter or anything because he would have just waited till you were off so I had to come clean and say that you weren't with me. He's rung Julie's pal and knows she's not there. You better get out sharpish.'

Julie came out of the bathroom, dressed. 'Get yourself home, Julie,' Tommy said.

They left the flat in a few minutes and Ricky and Tommy snuck away to Ricky's house while Julie walked to her own house, running her fingers through her damp hair, combing and shaking out the knots. Ricky silently wished her luck.

The boys with the hatchets ran past them, shrieking and cavorting, and Ricky put a hand to his balls and his cock and thought he'd better appreciate them while they were still there.

Helen McDermott

I've been stuck in the lift with the dog. We weren't allowed dogs on the flats. But I had a dog when I stayed on Avonspark Street so I got authorisation for me to take the dog into the flat. One day I was coming down with my Staff, and my Staff sensed there was a dog on the landing further down. The man who owned the Alsatian was going into his house and he took the Alsatian dog's leash off so when my lift came down, the lift door opened, the big Alsatian seen the Staff and the Alsatian breenged into the lift and the two dogs were fighting and I was in the lift with the two of them. But the man, right enough, the man who owned the Alsatian came running out and he grabbed his dog because my dog would have done the Alsatian in. So what I had to do was, I'd watch for the Alsatian going out and coming in then I'd go down with my dog. I used to stand at my window and see him coming out the foyer. I seen him going on the field with his dog, right, and he'd walk his dog, right, and then he would come up to the flats to come in the flat so I used to time him to go in the lift. I'd wait maybe ten minutes for him to go into his house and then I'd come down with my dog. That was about four or five times a day.

Ricky 1985

He was on his way back from the biggest telling of his life, so far. Oh, Julie's da, he didn't stop for about half an hour, just pointing his finger in his face and roaring at him. Ricky saw his grey fillings and wet spitting tongue, his black nose hair and his shiny red forehead. Julie's da wouldn't let him move. He just had to stand and take it while Julie's ma came in and out the room, tidying up and putting knives and forks on the table. Then Julie's da called Julie in and the two of them stood side by side while Julie's da read the riot act.

'This girl is not a plaything for dirty wee scheme boys. Especially not proddy wee scheme boys. If you touch her ever again I will kill you with these bare hands. Don't think I haven't done it before. You think you're some ticket with your boxing and your football, but listen to me, son, I could have you for breakfast, I could do you without even breaking a sweat.'

Ricky doubted that as Julie's da was in fact sweating quite heavily.

'This is your first and only warning.' He turned to aside to cough, his fist bunched against his mouth and his hand gripping his thigh. He coughed and coughed. Julie and Ricky looked at each other and rolled their eyes and Julie touched her fingers to Ricky's and squeezed his hand. That's when he felt aroused. Oh Christ, please don't let me get a stauner in front of Julie's da, Ricky thought. He took his hand from hers and looked at the wall where he saw a picture of a sultry Latin woman with slicked-back hair. No, not that one, where's the greeting boy? There he is. That's more like it. The poor greeting boy.

'That's all I'm saying on the matter,' Julie's da said and he looked like he needed a sit down or a Viennese Whirl or something.

'I'm sorry, Mr Doyle,' Ricky started to say.

'Son, spare me. Fuck off.' He waved his hand and dismissed him.

'Catch you later, Julie,' Ricky said.

Julie smiled at him.

'Julie, you're in for six months,' said Julie's da and Ricky shut the door behind him.

In the lift on his way back he met his pal Innes and told him about his telling, the spit that flew from Mr Doyle's mouth and him feart to move to wipe it off his face.

'Oh you have my sympathies,' Innes said.

'She's to stay in for six months. I can't as much look at her any more.'

'You'll never guess what happened to me,' Innes said.

'What?'

'I'd been out with Mhairi one night. We'd been up the town and she had to be back by half-past ten so we were in the lift in her building and I was coming up to her door with her to see her safely in. And it was just us in the lift. But then it stopped. Broke down. There was nothing we could do to get it going again. We tried calling out but nobody heard us. Caretaker's watching *Sportscene* or out sparko with his vodka so he never came. Nothing to do but stay the night there. Do you get me? I made a nice wee rug of my coat for us to sit on and a pillow of my jumper and kept her nice and warm. Do you get me? We were happy as Larry. Her ma was having a hairy canary right enough, but we were fine.'

'You jammy bastard,' Ricky said.

'We were in there till seven in the morning. Had to smash out the wee window to get some air in. And that was the first night we'd spent together. In the lift. Do you get me?'

'You jammy bastard,' was all Ricky could say and feared his days with Julie were long gone.

With his ma's fur coat over him for warmth, he spent the night in the lumber room, and slept on till well into the day. The darkness suited him. The lack of sound was good too. Red

Road would be full of weans and junkies and bingo women
and he wasn't in the mood. Julie, Julie, Julie; her knees on
which he almost put his naked hands.

'Come on, Ricky, up,' his ma said when she opened the
door and set down her washing basket.

'Can you not wait till I'm out of my bed?'

She didn't hear him or she ignored him because she
unhooked the drying rail rope and let it slip through the pulley. The rail dropped an arm's reach from his head. She shook
a pair of pyjama trousers from the washing basket and hung
them over one of the rails.

'Mind my eye,' Ricky said.

'Mind my way,' his ma said.

But he didn't get out. He leaned on his elbow and watched
her.

She hung up his Sta-Prest trousers and his waffle trousers
and a couple of his dad's shirts.

'They've come up well, your new strides,' she said.

'Aye.'

Wet clothes dangled above him. He pushed a trouser leg
out of his face.

'I'm having a shower.'

'Good. It's midday. Go and box or something.'

He took the pulley rope off his ma and hoisted it for her. The
pulley squeaked. When he'd hooked the rope over the cleat his
ma patted his arm and said, 'Thanks, son.' She asked about Julie.

'Did you have a row?' she said.

'Not as such.'

'Did she dump you? If she did that's the biggest mistake
that lassie's ever made.'

'No, Ma, no, leave it.'

Ricky's ma said all right then and pulled the creases out of
a T-shirt that hung from the rail.

He helped Alistair lay out the mats in the community centre, hauling each one from the pile of blue and it felt good to do something physical. It felt good too, to put on the sparring gloves and hit the speedball. He got a good rhythm going and only stopped when he saw Russell out the corner of his eye, staring at him. Russell annoyed Ricky. He always had. Perhaps it was because he had the hots for Julie. Perhaps it was because he was a better boxer than Ricky. Whatever, Ricky thought he was a wee dick.

'What?' Ricky said.

'Nothing.'

'You're putting me off.'

'Let me know when you're done on that speedball.'

Rude. Full of himself.

Sick of Russell staring, Ricky moved on to smack the punchbag. Alistair took him to one side and told him to drink some water and calm down.

'Skip,' he said and handed him a rope. Ricky drank and skipped and watched Russell be a cock at the speedball where some of the younger boys had stood to watch.

'Ricky, shall we try you and Russell out with a wee practice spar?' Alistair asked.

'Aye, fine.'

Six two-minute rounds. The boys put their kit on – gum shield, groin guard, head guard, sparring gloves – and checked their boots were tied. Alistair held their gloves together and then stepped aside.

Jab. Jab. Jab. Ricky probed with his left hand, keeping watch for Russell's right hook which Alistair said was the best in north Glasgow. He kept moving, tried to mix it up with a range of punches. But Russell ducked away from each one and got him with a body shot then came in straight away with an uppercut. Didn't hurt.

After three rounds the boys were fighting well. In fact it

was a fucking brilliant fight. Two welterweights really giving
it some. Ricky could see the wee boys watching at the edge of
the mats. He could hear the squeak of his shoes and feel his
breath coming in and out hard. He sniffed blood back up his
nose and looked over the top of his gloves. Jab, jab, uppercut.
Missed. Keep moving, keep fluent. A couple of body punches
and in with a hook. Got him. It was a proper ding-dong fight.
Ricky felt nothing, no pain, no fear, just adrenalin. They
fought on. One round to go. Ricky was determined to outfight
Russell. Fight your own fight, he told himself. Don't let his
punches rattle you. Mix it up. Keep moving. When Russell got
him in the ribs and knocked the breath out of him he couldn't
help but lean into the pain. But then he got caught by Russell's
right hook, followed by an uppercut and then another right
hook. Floored. It felt as if he'd been pushed down the stairs.
Oh fuck.

Alistair called time, stretched his arms and brought the
boys together, held the back of their wet necks and said, 'That
was one spirited fight, boys. I watched Marvin Hagler and
Tommy Hearns last night and you were better. Keep it up.'

The boys nodded.

'But lads,' he said, 'keep your fighting in the gym, eh?
You've both got promise so don't get sidetracked by anything
going on out there.' He flicked his head towards the door.

Ricky and Russell said yes Alistair, they would keep their
fighting to the gym, and avoided each other's eyes.

Despite being knocked down, Ricky felt better. He zipped
his tracksuit top and slipped on his tracky trousers and, outside, poured water over his head even though the day was a
cold, damp one, the sky like a grey dish towel.

Red Road was mental. Looking up at Thirty-three Petershill
Drive he saw the glue sniffers from Avonspark Street doing
their high wire act again. A crowd of people watched from the
ground as the glue sniffers balanced on the girders that stuck

out of the very top of the building. Arms out for balance. Black silhouettes tiptoeing against the dirty sky. One guy walked to the end of one girder and onto the beam that circumvented the building. Round he walked. Fearless. A gust of wind or a wrong step could send him falling to his death. Pumped, Ricky walked to the Broomfield Tavern to see if they would serve him.

Matt Barr

I remember getting caught by the police when I was running in the Germiston flats on the other side and my shoe fell off and an old grandpa with his shopping caught me and held me till the police came. I was the only one of my side to get caught but thirteen of the Germiston lot got caught so I was arrested with them. We got locked in the caretaker's office at the back of the building and I was shaking – oh my God they're going to batter me – but then we started talking and I think they realised I was just a normal kid and they were normal as well, they weren't really bad people when you talked to them. I got caught and done for that.

Pamela 1985

He must have jumped after his breakfast. Her ma had gone to her work at eight-thirty and she hadn't returned to tell her not to go downstairs, protecting Pamela from another death, as Pamela knew her ma would. So he must have jumped after he woke. Or perhaps he'd been up all night staring at the window from which he'd finally flung himself. Pamela knew it was a man because she saw his black boots sticking out from the white sheet. Police and the concierges stood near him. An ambulance with its open doors was parked close by.

Pamela kept clear. She boked on the path to her friend's building and wiped her mouth with the back of her hand. Looking up at the building she tried to imagine how anyone could let themselves fall down its sheer sides. Unless he was a junkie and out of it or thought he was flying or something, as had happened before, she'd been told.

Her pal was waiting for her outside One-eight-three Petershill Drive. She didn't wear her school uniform either.

'My ma's given me two pound,' Nicola said.

'Someone's jumped,' Pamela said and suddenly she cried.

An arm around her shoulders, a cigarette. A sharp tug of wind and litter scuttled in circles. Something metal clanked against something else.

'Let's do the mats,' Nicola said. 'It's too cold to stand around.'

'Birnie Court. Away from the polis,' Pamela said. And so they walked.

They passed a man who had a dog on a lead. He was confident, the man, and when his shorn dog stopped to piss on the concrete, he scratched his face and said, 'All right lassies.'

'All right, Trevor,' Nicola said.

Pamela looked at the stripes on his trainers.

'Jellies, lassies?' he said.

His hands went into his pockets.

'Nah, you're all right,' Nicola said.

The girls smiled and Trevor smiled back.

'Tell your sister I was asking after her,' he called as he walked away.

'My sister's pal,' Nicola said. 'He knows everyone. Can get you anything.'

They did the mats and it was a buzz, a blast from the past, a reminder of how they used to be three or four years ago. They caught the lift to the top of Birnie Court and gathered up the four mats from the four doors. Nicola held open the landing window and Pamela pushed the mats out one by one. Then they ran down the stairs to the floor below, throwing all those doormats out too. On one floor they stopped to watch them crash to the ground, leaning far out of the window.

'You must be mad to jump,' Pamela said but Nicola can't have heard her, pulling her arm and dragging her down the stairs before they got caught. They did the whole building, pissing themselves and running away. What to do next?

Ricky 1986

There was a problem in the flats with joyriders. If you had a motor you better expect it to get nicked or wrecked. Or else guard it. Ricky walked back from his football game, his studs clicking on the concrete and Tommy's too, which reminded him of a time when he was just a boy and all the boys would walk back to their houses with mud-streaked legs and elbows, their studs click-clacking on the ground and Ricky in his trainers would wish for a pair of boots with studs so his footsteps would make the same beautiful noise. They were nearly men now, with bigger thighs and more sweat. One of the older guys, in his twenties, had started to recede and another had let the drink spread out along his belly but Ricky was the fittest and strongest he'd ever been. He still wanted to be a fireman.

Ricky was worried about his car because the paintwork was scratched on the driver's side and when he'd gone to drive it one night he was sure he disturbed a couple of dark-clothed sneakit-looking boys. It made him more angry than he'd ever felt to think of some little shites messing about with his motor.

He and Tommy went to the Broomfield Tavern. Ricky drank his cider and wiped his mouth. The football had rid him of some of his energy but he still felt sharp and anxious about his motor. Another gulp of cider. Bob Marley sang out from the jukebox.

'I think I need to give those wee shites a warning. Make sure they don't come anywhere near my motor again.'

'All the kids carry knives now,' Tommy said.

'I'm aware of that.'

He leaned towards Tommy and told him what his elder brother had brought him back from Russia. Tommy shook his head and laughed and said, 'Are you serious?'

'Oh aye.' He pressed his lips together then ran his tongue over them and sniffed. Took another swig of cider.

'Don't get yourself in trouble over a motor.'

'But you see, Tommy, it's more than a motor. It's the work and the saving and the waiting. And it's mine. I'm not having anyone tear into my car just because they feel like it. No, I'm not.'

'My ma likes watching the polis chase the joyriders.'

'I know. All the old dears do. Telly's crap these days.'

They stayed for more pints and leaned back in their chairs as the jukebox played Marley and Madonna and the warm air made them yawn into their fists and wipe water from the corners of their eyes. The landlord asked them if they wanted someone to stretcher them out they were lying so far back in their seats.

Outside, daylight was gone and cold wintry air was in its place. They walked briskly through Red Road. Ricky checked for shapes at the doors of cars and vans but there was nobody about. Too early. His legs were stiff. He kicked a Lucozade bottle out of his way and told Tommy he was going home to see if his ma had boiled up the soup she'd promised to make. A couple of figures crossed in front of him. They stopped by some parked cars and Ricky wondered if they were going to have a go at one of the cars but he heard the tinkle of a dog's chain and saw them move off with a fat Staff. A trickle of dog's piss shone in the light from a streetlamp as he passed.

'Come on and I'll show you what my brother brought back.'

Tommy held the sword with two hands above his head and lowered its point to the floor. Then he swung it from left to right and right to left as if charming a snake. He let go a hand

and made wide zigzags. Then he stroked the side of the blade and put a finger to its edge.

'Ricky, pal, that is some sword. Is it a genuine Russian Samurai sword?'

Ricky paused. 'Aye, I think so. I'm going to hang it on the wall above my bed.'

'What if it falls off in the night and kills you?'

'Okay, I'll hang it away from my bed.'

Tommy held the sword in his flat palms. 'I don't like it. You need to be careful, Ricky. Don't get into trouble with this.'

They were all saying things like that; Tommy, Julie, his ma. Tommy was even making threats to leave Red Road altogether. He said he could feel himself going wrong; he'd been in too many scrapes, had too many warnings from the police, and finally realised that hankering after the easy days with the footballs and tennis and water fights was a waste of time. Ricky said he didn't believe he'd ever go and Tommy said he would have said the same until now – watch this space.

'Go back to the boxing,' his ma said to Ricky and he always said no, he preferred football. Russell was heavy into smack now so there was no one he wanted to batter. But he felt like battering the bastards who broke into the cars and crashed them for laughs.

'I'm away for my tea,' Tommy said.

'See you after. Keep an eye out the window for the joyriders. Don't do anything stupid. Like leave.'

He sat up well into the night with his sword at his side. His ma asked him what he was doing and he told her he was looking at the lights and the view. And when she'd gone to bed he saw three figures creeping towards the parked cars on Petershill Drive. Black-clad. Young and troublesome-looking. Not a second to spare. Into the lift, his sword in his hand, ready to give them the biggest shock of their car-thieving, joyriding lives.

The roar started as he pushed himself through the foyer doors and rounded the corner to the cars. A scrawny wee shite of a boy ran away and Ricky followed him, holding aloft his sword which curved down his back like a pelmet or a mane. The kid was a fast runner and he cried out oh mammy mammy mammy as he ran and he sounded like a goat or a horse or a baby. Ricky heard his own throat making noises he didn't mean to make. High, violent noises. The kid was right to be crying out for his mammy. Ricky chased him along Petershill Drive, past One-two-three and Ninety-three and when the kid turned right to run past Sixty-three block Ricky dropped the sword and lunged at him. He caught him and he pushed him against a brick wall. His head stoated off the wall and the kid began to greet.

'You weren't greeting when you were trying to steal my motor.'

'I wasn't stealing anyone's motor.'

'Yes, you were.'

Ricky hit him hard. The kid's head stoated off the wall again and Ricky's knuckles hurt. He went for him again and the kid ducked his head and Ricky hit the wall. He kneed the kid instead and kicked at his legs.

'I wasn't stealing your motor.'

'Yes you were.'

'I wasn't. I wasn't.'

'Yes you were.'

Ricky didn't want to stop and he didn't think he could stop. He kept hitting the kid and kicking the kid and there was blood now and the smell of piss.

'You don't know what that motor means to me,' he said and he was nearly greeting too now, his head so angry, so fucking on fire with the nerve of this stupid boy.

The boy said, 'I promise you, it wasn't me, I wasn't trying to nick it. I was going home. I promise you, I promise you,' and when Ricky left him lying on the ground and turned to pick up his sword the boy said 'Oh mammy mammy no, please don't kill me' and he shouted for help.

Ricky put the point of the sword to his soft neck and thought about pushing it down hard. He could, he could. The kid deserved it. He could fucking murder him. He could teach him a lesson. He had a Samurai sword. So angry. So much fucking fury.

'Ricky, no! Ricky!'

It was his ma's voice and he saw her running towards him, her house coat open and flapping at the sides. She held out her arms and ran awkwardly. The sight of her, her voice, her house coat, her slippers that she was struggling to keep on her feet, stopped Ricky. He took the sword away from the kid's neck and stepped back.

'You put that sword down and leave the poor boy alone,' his ma said and Ricky was afraid of what she would say to him and what she would think of him.

His ma knelt alongside the greeting boy and smoothed his fringe from his forehead.

'You're all right, William,' she said. 'You're all right.'

The boy whimpered. He was bruised badly. He turned his head this way and that and called for his mammy.

'We'll get you to your mammy,' Ricky's ma said. 'You're all right. It's over.' She pointed at Ricky. 'Do you know who this boy is? He's the butcher's boy. He's Andrew Cullen's wee lad. What were you playing at Ricky?'

Ricky gripped his right hand with his left, the sword still in his hand. 'He tried to steal my motor.'

'No he didn't.' His ma's voice cracked as she shouted at him.

'No, I didn't. I promise you, I didn't.'

'He's the butcher's boy. Look at him. He's got a van. What does he want with your car?'

'I saw him.'

'No you didn't. You must have seen someone else.'

She looked at the kid and put her hands inside his clothes, on his waist and then felt his ribs. The kid cried out. She inspected his face. He was cut badly on his cheekbones and his mouth. There was blood in streaks on his neck. His hair was wet with blood.

'And you,' she said to Ricky and her voice was grave. 'I told you to put that sword down.'

Ricky looked down at his hand and his sword. It made an awful grating sound on the concrete as he put it down. Then there was quiet as Ricky's ma helped the boy to his feet. The boy whimpered but he no longer gret.

'It's okay. It's over,' Ricky's ma said again to the boy but she looked at Ricky.

Ricky couldn't meet her eyes.

'You'd better get out of here,' William said. 'If the polis catch you with that, you'll get done. Look.'

The kid nodded at the buildings next to them. Sixty-three and Ninety-three. Lit up windows, rows of them, and heads at the windows. More lights flicked on in more windows. Yellow squares lighting up the dark.

'Go away,' his ma said and Ricky picked up his sword and ran home, past his car, which was still there, and into his building.

He put the sword under his bed and waited for the police.

He waited to get caught for weeks. When his ma took him to the butchers to apologise, the butcher's boy, said, 'I guess you thought I was someone else. I saw three lads running away just before you came out and chased me. I guess it was them you should have got.'

Ricky nodded and noted the bruises still on the boy's face and couldn't look at the boy's da who stood at the back and hacked a cleaver into a cow's leg.

Ricky's ma told him that it was time to get his act together. If you get a criminal record the Fire Brigade won't touch you, she told him. These antics of yours, they're over, she said, or you're out.

The police never came to his door. Ricky kept the Fire Brigade in the back of his mind while he worked his first job for the social. Tommy moved out of Red Road for a new start.

The police came to someone's door, however. The family who lost their son in the fire, they lost another son to a car crash. He was a joyrider, ten years old, and chased by the police one night he drove his stolen car into a lamppost. It killed him instantly.

Ricky bought the father a drink whenever he saw him in the Brig or the Broomfield. It was the least he could do. And when he felt like doing something stupid or revengeful, he thought of the sword and those lights going on one by one in the windows all around him.

Section Four

Concierges 1986

JOHN THOUGHT HE MIGHT have put too much milk in George Mallion's mug of tea because he didn't touch it. They stood in the main office and John pointed out the televisions with the black and white CCTV pictures, the key cabinet, and the paperwork on the students who came and went, some only in the building for a term, some a year, and some for longer.

'You'll see when I show you around, the first thirteen floors are ordinary council tenants, floors fourteen to twenty-seven are the student flats and each student has a bedroom to themselves and they share a kitchen and a bathroom. The three top floors, twenty-eight, twenty-nine and thirty, they're the executive flats.'

George wanted to ask what was special about the executive flats but John answered the buzzer and let in a girl whose eye-linered eyes looked wide into the camera.

'I'm here to see my friend Kat,' the girl said.

'On you go,' John said and the men watched her get into the lift.

'Heavy into politics, Kat is. She's a good lassie, but.'

John picked up his radio. 'The only difference with the executive flats is that they've got a better quality curtain and the baths are green, not white. Pistachio, actually. Are you going to take your tea with you?'

'I'll just drink it.'

George swigged it as if it was ginger, drank the whole mug in one, and wiped his mouth. Then he put the cup down on the desk and picked it up again.

'Do you want another one? Are you thirsty?'

'No, I just can't drink it when it's too burny.'

John stood in the main office and watched George go into the kitchen and rinse his cup. George was a tall skelf-like man. He seemed to have hollow trouser legs and too-long arms. Apparently he was a long-distance runner. John hoped he wouldn't be too jumpy for him. He liked to ponder, not charge.

'Have you always worked in the high flats?' George asked when he came from the back. He clasped his knuckles and pushed his palms outwards.

'I was on the Manpower before here,' John said. 'My year was nearly up. I jumped at the chance of working here.'

'So it's not true what they say about Red Road?'

'Oh don't get me wrong, it's not paradise. You'll get to know the community police and there's a reason for that. But I like it. Are you ready to go up the stair?'

Today they had the flat inspections. When their colleague Allan was back to man the office John took George to floor twenty-seven and told him they'd work downwards and when George got the hang of it, they'd split up and take a flat each to make things go more quickly. As the lift passed floor twenty-three John told George about the community flat, the pool room, TV room and the library and study room and said they held meetings in one of the rooms from time to time. George thought the place wasn't as bad as people had suggested it was. His colleagues were all right too; laid-back, friendly, and they seemed to like their work and their tenants.

'We're not ready John, can you come back?' a girl said in twenty-seven/one. She held a broom when she opened the door. The flat smelled of toast. George looked beyond her down the corridor and saw the Hoover cord on the floor.

'We'll do flat two first,' John said.

A boy in pyjamas opened the door.

'Did we get you up?' John asked.

The boy said no and led them into the living room where

two more boys sat on the couches. George wanted to rush to the window to look out at the view. But he didn't. A Scottish Saltire and the flags of Canada and Nigeria were pinned on one side of the room. There were bowls on the floor with the cocked ends of spoons and forks sticking over their sides. A duvet was slung over the back of one of the couches. There were beer cans with cigarette ash on their tops, books, newspapers, crisp packets and two-litre bottles of Irn-Bru. George looked at the carpet and saw pieces of food and dirt and paper. The other boys wore pyjamas too. *Number 73* was on the television. George couldn't see a Hoover or a broom or a duster. There was a black bag, however.

John leaned his hand against one of the walls. 'Did you forget about your flat inspection?' he said.

The boy who answered the door shook his head earnestly and gestured towards the black bag. 'We were just about to start on the living room.'

The other boys shifted their shoulders and turned their heads to nod affirmation.

'So you've done the kitchen and the bathroom?'

'Oh aye.'

George had never heard anyone say oh aye who didn't have a Scottish accent. They left the boys in the living room and went to the kitchen. The worktop had been given a smeary wipe, the floor was swept to a certain extent and the dishes done. The washed dishes were piled high on one side of the sink, plates stacked on pots, cups at angles, and a shoal of silver cutlery next to them.

'You'd think they'd never seen a dish towel,' John said.

He moved to the cooker and said, 'No way. Right, that cooker's not been touched so we'll tell them to get it cleaned and we'll come back in two hours.'

He looked briefly in the bathroom and came out saying, 'They're living in a midden.'

When the concierges returned to the living room the boys were off the couches, their bare feet treading amongst the debris on the floor and their bare legs bending to throw rubbish into the sack.

'Can we keep our beer pyramid?' one of the boys said and popped the end of a Marathon bar out of its packaging and into his mouth.

'You can keep your beer tower but everything else has got to be ship-shape when we come back in two hours.'

'Okay, John, sorry John,' they said and John softened.

'Why don't yous boys take it in turns to do a clear-up once a week and then all do the clear-up the week of the inspection?'

The boys seemed taken with this idea and said they would do that starting from next week. George and John left them as they sat back on the couches and began a conversation about which one would go first on the clear-up rota.

'They'll never do it,' John said and as they waited outside the first flat again he told George that one time he'd gone up to sort out a broken Hoover in one of the flats only to find it wasn't broke, the bag just needed changed.

The same girl opened the door and led them into a thoroughly cleaned flat which now smelled of furniture polish and perfume. The windows were pushed wide open in the kitchen and the living room, and cool air shook the curtains.

George did walk to the window in this flat and looked out on South East Glasgow. He could see the water towers of Easterhouse and the motorway and the houses and rooftops that just went on and on. And in front of all this, tearing up the view, the other high rises with all the windows and the first slab block yellow and brazen in front of him too.

'You can do the next one on your own,' John said.

Flat three had three girls in it. One was from Aberdeen, the other from Lewis and the third from Malaysia.

'What are you studying, girls?' George asked, leaning on the chest of drawers that was in the middle of the living room floor. He thought it was an odd place for a chest of drawers but was too interested in the girls' studies to give it more thought. Nursing, biomedical sciences and sociology, they told him and offered him a cup of tea.

'No, no, thanks girls. Your flat's looking great,' he said and joined John on the landing. In the lift John asked George how he'd got on.

'Aye, it was a cracking flat,' George said. 'I wouldn't have my chest of drawers in the middle of the room, but.'

'Am I hearing right?' John said and looked up at George.

Out of the lift on floor twenty-six and up through the fire door to the stairs.

John took a couple of steps towards the door and gave it a couple of thumps.

When one of the girls opened the door he said, 'Let me see what's under your chest of drawers, Marie,' and she said, 'Oh John, sorry, we had a wee party and I think somebody dropped a cigarette.'

'You think.'

'So we put the chest of drawers over it.'

George gave John a hand to move the chest of drawers. On the carpet was a triangular-shaped burn mark.

'Some cigarette,' John said and the girls got a warning and a ticking off about ironing on the carpet and when George and John were in the lift to floor twenty-six John admitted that he didn't like this aspect of the job because one, he didn't want to be checking up on how people looked after their houses and two, he didn't want to be faced with their filth either.

George went into the next flat ready for anything and on the lookout for strategically placed items of furniture.

Iris 1987

'You never know the minute,' Iris's neighbour said because her husband had died and then her son within six months of each other, and now someone had knocked off all the brass on her door, just lifted it while she was still in the house; her bell and her wee ornaments, everything. Life was cruel, she said, and now it seemed bizarre.

'You're up to high doh, Margaret,' Iris said, whose own husband had died too, a few years previously, and just recently she'd fallen in the rain on the wet path below the Chippy Hill and snapped her ankle.

'They wouldn't care I'd collected them over twenty year.'

'No, they wouldn't. They wouldn't care.'

There was a noise from one of the lifts, chat and coughing, and the women paused while it passed. Margaret shook her head and fiddled with the clasp on her bag.

'Will you come in for a cup of tea?' Iris said.

'No, doll, I'm going to speak to the concierges and see if they'll give me a lend of their phone. I want to ring Frank and ask him to get me a new nameplate. Just my surname, no initial.' Frank was her remaining son.

'That's it, Margaret.'

Iris's dog came from the kitchen and Iris put out a hand and held its collar.

'Are you just in from your work? Go on in. Don't wait on me,' Margaret said so Iris shut the door and rubbed her hands together because it was cold and shooed her dog into the living room.

The budgie was fussing in its cage so Iris opened the door and put her hand in, guiding the bird into the room. At the window she watched the weather over Royston and saw a fitful sky. She remembered the time when she was too scared to go near the windows because of the height, too afraid to stand even to look at the view, let alone clean the glass. She got used to it, but in bad weather, when the house shook, the fear and the vertigo came back. On the field below Shug Skinner walked his Alsatian. It humped its back and shat and Iris thought it made a change to see it shitting on the field rather than the veranda, the dirty pig. She didn't expect Shug would clear his dog's shite off the field.

Her daughter wasn't home and neither was her nephew or son and although it rattled her, not knowing where they were – none of them would be where they ought to be – an hour or two's peace was appealing. She put her uniform over the back of her chair in her bedroom and changed into her comfortable clothes. Her tubigrip had left ridges of red skin on her bad ankle and Iris scratched before she stood up to get her paper and sort out a cup of tea.

Someone chapped her door. The dog barked.

'Zeus, baby, stay!' Iris said and the dog sat and panted at the entrance to the living room.

It was another neighbour, Colleen from across the hall, sad and worried-looking, her husband standing behind her in their doorway.

'Is your nephew still staying with you?' Colleen asked.

'Aye. How?'

'Because my house has been broken into and I may as well tell you I think it was him that done it.'

Iris held up her hand. 'Now wait a wee minute,' she said.

Her neighbour glanced at her husband and said, 'Iris, I'm sorry, but we know it was him.'

'Have you got any proof?'

'Aye, he was on the landing, wasn't he Jim?'

Jim nodded. 'Aye.'

'That doesn't mean he did it.'

Colleen explained how he was hanging about the landing as they left to go out in the morning – told them he was waiting on

Iris's son to finish getting ready. When they returned, their front door was open and their television and video gone.

The couple were no bother. His pipe-smoke and her mince wafted onto the landing whenever they opened their door. Iris loved the way they dressed up for each day, Colleen with the elegant waves in her hair and Jim with his tidy shirts and jumpers. Iris remembered how Jim had hated retiring from his work as he said his body and brain were still firing and he ought to be using them. This is how we can improve life for the working classes, he told her often. He read and sang and redecorated. And Colleen knitted. A pair of good souls who asked her occasionally to get their paper and rolls when Iris got hers and Iris obliged, noting the trembling of Jim's hands and Colleen's cough as they took their messages from her. She was in no mood for accusations today, however.

'Right, leave it with me,' she growled and left them on the doorstep.

Nothing in the house. No telly or video stashed behind the couch. Zeus was frisky and followed Iris about the house. 'Stay! Baby!' Iris roared. The dog collapsed in obedience.

'Right, well, I can assure you there's nothing in my house.' Her hand gripped the edge of the door, ready to push it shut then slam it. But she noticed Colleen's watery eyes – another one crying on her doorstep – and she slowed herself down.

'You're welcome to come in and see for yourselves,' she said. 'This time, I can assure you, it's not him.'

'No. Come on Colleen,' Jim said, his hand around her shoulders as they folded themselves back into their doorway.

'What will you do for your telly?' Iris asked, remembering that she had her shows she wanted to watch.

'I expect we'll go to Rediffusion on Springburn Road – it's where we got the other one,' Jim said.

'Right then.' Iris paused. 'You can come in my house and watch my telly if you want.'

'Oh no, hen, the radio will do for now.'

Jim and Colleen waved and Iris shut the door on the polished landing floor.

The dog followed her into the living room and curled himself next to her as she sat on the couch, stretching her bad leg out in front of her, reaching for the remote control and switching on her own television that her reformed, on-his-last-chance nephew would know better than to go near.

When the windows became black and Iris had pulled the curtains on the wind and the rain, her daughter came home smelling of mud. She crashed into the living room, her skin sweaty and her fingers dirty.

'Ma, I'm starving,' she said and Iris watched her eat the piece she'd made and covered in clingfilm.

'Where's your brother?'

'At the new girlfriend's.'

'I don't like you dogging school,' Iris said and Pamela ignored her, tearing at the bread with her teeth, kicking off her DM boots while she chewed. Pamela no longer pretended to go to school, wearing her uniform to leave the house and changing at a friend's house. Normally she came home for her tea and left again to hang about with her pals.

Iris always said it, 'I'll send you to Balloch if you go off the rails,' and Pamela always replied, 'Aunty Jessica can't even raise her own weans.'

It reminded Iris. 'Colleen and Jim across the hall are accusing your cousin of nicking their telly and video.'

Pamela laughed and pulled her legs underneath her, reaching across the table for one of her ma's cigarettes.

'If he has, he's an eejit,' she said.

Iris loved her daughter. 'I telt them in no uncertain terms that he hadn't done it,' she said and she lit up too, and blew fierce smoke into the room.

Her daughter's hair was long and curly. A pal had helped her perm it in the bathroom and it had taken them all day. She had lively eyes and a recklessness about her – as if her body couldn't cope with the speed of itself.

'He told me he's staying off the drugs.'

'Is he what?' Pamela said and picked at a nail. She left the room and Iris heard her opening the fridge in the kitchen.

'I like him,' Pamela said when she came back. 'He's all right.'

'Well, I told Jessica I'd look after him.'

The wind shook the walls of the house and the milk swayed in Pamela's glass. The budgie flew from surface to surface making a racket.

'Bastarding wind, pack it in!' Iris shouted and her daughter laughed and Iris patted Zeus who was whining on the couch next to her.

Pamela joined her mother and the dog on the couch. 'Ma, you hung my clothes up in the drying room didn't you?' she said.

Iris said she did.

'Because my tops were still there but my tracksuit wasn't and it's not in my room.'

'I washed your tracksuit with your tops and other stuff and I hung them all up.'

'Well some bastard's pinched it.'

'Some bastard's taking the piss out of us.' Iris told Pamela about their neighbour's brass and wondered if the same person was going round taking everyone's stuff.

Pamela stubbed her cigarette out and swore at the walls. Iris turned the volume of the television up.

She heard her daughter crying in her room when they'd both gone to bed. At first she'd thought it was the wind at the windows because the foul weather was raging on but as Iris lay there, her arm still stretched and touching the switch of her bedside lamp she recognised her daughter's sobs. 'Hen,' she called and tapped the wall gently. A thump came back, then more sobs. So Iris swung her good leg and then her bad leg onto the floor and tiptoed past her sleeping dog, into her daughter's room. It was the same. 'I miss my da,' Pamela said and there was pain in every sob, her eyes clenched shut, her fingers at her cheeks. Iris patted her daughter's hot back and shoulders, smoothed the nightie over her skin and shook her head in the dark. It wasn't going away, her daughter's grief. It had trapped her, invaded her, led her one way and then another. The house swayed and Iris gasped. Pamela laughed. 'Bastarding wind,' she said and pulled the duvet over her shoulders.

Iris was just about to switch off her bedside light when she noticed the bolt undone on the door to her back stairs. Opening the door and checking the adjoining door's bolt, which was undone too, she thought of her nephew. The master criminal. It was a perfect way of getting in and out of her house, unseen. Knowing she was bound to find something, she checked the bed and her bottom drawer and flung open the wardrobe. Inside the wardrobe, on top of her shoe rack, wrapped in towels were wall clocks. Four of them. The thieving wee shite.

Sleep was not necessary for Iris that night. She sat in her robe, as her budgie's cage swung and great showers of rain crashed onto her windows, and waited for her nephew. She would wait all night if she had to but knew it might not be too long before he showed himself, not liking the rain, not wanting to be humping stolen goods about in inclement weather. As soon as she heard the key in the lock she was up, finger pointing, roaring.

'Right, you!' she said and skelped his baseball-capped head. 'Out. You're not staying here. Take your clothes and your wall clocks and fuck off.'

'Aunty Iris, I don't know what you're going on about,' he said and Iris jabbed her finger into his face.

'I'm not a fool. You're the wee fool,' she said. 'I told your ma

I'd help you start again here, but no, you've been stealing other people's stuff and storing it in my wardrobe. I had poor Colleen and Jim at my door this afternoon. No telly and video. At least you didn't have the cheek to plank that in my house too.'

'Aunty Iris, let me stay. I'll give you one of the wall clocks.'

'I've got a fucking wall clock. Out. Clock off.'

She slammed her door and put on the chain.

'Aunty Iris,' he tried the letter box.

'Zeus, bite!' Iris said and her letter box crashed shut.

Iris watched the television for a while to calm herself. Her budgie's cage swayed with the wind outside but the budgie slept. It was quiet in her daughter's room so, finally, as if up in the boughs of some great creaking tree, Iris slept too.

Pamela 1987

The lift opened at floor fourteen and Shug Skinner got in with his Alsatian. The dog sniffed her Farah trousers and Pamela showed it the sole of her trainer when Shug Skinner wasn't looking.

'Can you smell Zeus?' she asked it, to wind Shug Skinner up.

Shug Skinner tugged on his dog's lead. 'How's your ma?'

'Aye, she's fine.'

Two men with suitcases got on at floor seven. Margaret Anderson got on at floor six and spoke to Shug Skinner, telling him about her lost brass ornaments. More people got in, including two prams and a priest and Pamela stood as close as she could to the side of the lift to give them room. Shug Skinner's dog stretched its head in her direction and Pamela bared her teeth at it, checking first that Shug Skinner wasn't watching.

'Shall we do the mats again?' said Nicola when they'd met by the slab block nearest the shops. The concrete underfoot was patchy with rain, the buildings themselves dull and cold-looking. They lit up cigarettes first and walked round the entrance to the bingo to the shops.

'Nah,' Pamela said.

'Shall we go to your house then?'

'Nah. My ma's off work.'

'Shall we get wasted?'

'That's my tracksuit,' Pamela said.

Pamela pushed her hair out of her face and stared at a boy, about her age, standing at the burger van. He put his hand in his pocket and paid the vendor for a roll. He let go the paper napkin and it fluttered to the floor. Taking a step towards the boy, Pamela saw the man from the burger van come out of the side of his van and stoop to pick up the napkin. He said something to the boy which Pamela didn't hear and neither must the boy because he walked on and didn't turn round, biting the roll as he walked. Pamela walked faster. Nicola followed behind and when Pamela reached the boy the first thing she did was snatch his roll from his hands and hold it in her outstretched arm.

'What?' the boy said and made an attempt to grab his roll back and when that failed he angled his shoulder and elbow into Pamela, perhaps to barge her, but Pamela wasn't fazed because she liked to fight and if he'd ever been to where the gangs fought at night above the blind tunnel he'd have seen her there wailing and ducking and lashing and hurling whatever weapons she could find.

'I'm not giving you your roll back till you give me my tracksuit.'

The boy looked surprised, as if that was the last thing he expected to hear.

'What? It's my tracksuit,' he said.

'No it isn't. And I can tell you why. See on your arm, your left one, there's a wee burn mark. I done that by accident when I was looking for my door key and couldn't get in the house.'

The boy scowled and checked his sleeve, casually, as if checking for dog hairs.

Pamela grabbed the material between thumb and forefinger and pointed to the burn mark.

'There. Thieving wee shite.'

'I didn't steal it. My ma bought it for me.'

The boy's disgruntled face and his open mouth threw Pamela. The kid was riled and looked ready to sprint away. There was something about him that was earnest.

'Who did your ma buy it from?'

'Her pal from the pub.'

'Right. Her pal from the pub,' Pamela said. 'Well, her pal from the pub has lifted it from my drying room and flogged it to her. Off.'

The boy didn't hesitate. He looked down at his chest and unzipped the tracksuit top. He shrugged his arms from the top's sleeves. Pamela took the top from him and tied it round her waist. The three of them stood for an instant staring at the boy's tracky bottoms. A seagull cawed above their heads. A woman wheeled a tartan trolley out of Kwik Save. The smell of sweet onions wafted on the breeze. A rusting car painted gold, with suitcases on its roof rack drove slowly in and out of the concrete area where the shops were. Pamela didn't know what to say. Her friend did.

'Off,' Nicola said.

'No way.' The boy hitched the tracky trousers high up his waist.

'Off. Now,' her friend said and the boy looked about him, up at the sky where the seagull still flew and behind him towards the slab block.

'Can I take them off over there?' he asked and Pamela said, 'Aye all right.'

They walked round to the entrance to Thirty Petershill Court and the boy mumbled, 'I only live on floor two. It's too cold to take them off here.'

They stood in the lift in silence. Outside his door, the boy knocked, shouted for his ma, pulled down the tracky bottoms and handed them to Pamela. The girls rattled down the stairs just before his mother opened the door and shouted after them.

'All right lassies!' Trevor shouted. His dog was on its side, scratching itself.

The girls waved. Pamela felt like kicking the air. She rolled up her sleeves and they left the towers behind them, walking on the wet grass towards the trees and the tracks and the tunnel and the boys from the Gyto.

Concierges 1988

John read the incident book.

'Here, read this, George,' he said. He and George had relaxed into a happy partnership that was two years long now. George could be a bit of a doughball at times but he clocked on to John's humour and he had a sense of humour of his own too. They'd not been able to stop laughing about the new student – the boy from France – who'd come into the office in his swimming trunks with a towel under his arm asking for the pool room. And the thought of him taking the pool cues from George and saying no I want the swimming pool, still made them laugh. Or the girls who complained about their flatmate who kept dead mice in her freezer and it turned out she'd a snake in her room. John had a phobia of snakes so George had gone in and told the girl that he would put the snake down the chute if she didn't get rid of it.

'Why did you say you'd put it down the chute?'

'I don't know. That's the worst place to put it isn't it? We'd all be feart to go near the bins.'

'No shit, Sherlock. As long as she gets rid of it I don't care where it goes.'

They liked the students. The executive flats were gone and after their first year many of the students stayed on in the block, taking rooms in flats on the top three floors or the first thirteen.

'This here. "Anthony from flat thirty/one complained again that somebody had taken his breakfast cereal from his room. Concierge went up and found no break-in. No explanation. Student questioned as to whether he was remembering correctly."'

John flicked back through the incident book and found a similar entry. '"Anthony from flat thirty/one accused concierges of breaking into his room and stealing cornflakes. Assured tenant that concierges did not break in and steal cornflakes."'

John and George were on the back shift after a couple of days off.

'Anthony's the one who couldn't work the washing machine,' John said, as if that explained everything.

George took the buffer and went off to do the landings.

Later, Anthony came into their office, his eyebrows at anxious angles.

'My breakfast disappeared again,' he said. He wrung his hands.

'What did you have, son?' John said.

'Cornflakes.'

'Did you have sugar with your cornflakes?'

'Yes.'

'A little milk?' said George.

'Yes but...'

'Now, was the milk cold or did you warm it up first?'

'I don't think you're taking me seriously.'

The young man's eyes were disappointed. They made John stop laughing. He looked again at the young man, and saw something honest about him, saw the man who left for university at eight-fifteen and returned from his labs at six-thirty, who put his messages in a rucksack to save on carrier bags – John had seen him once with the contents of his rucksack on the landing floor: he was looking for his door key – saw this honest young man and realised he was completely and profoundly spooked.

'Start again, son,' John said.

'I put my bowl and a packet of cornflakes on the table in the living room. I went back to the kitchen to get milk. I read an article from yesterday's paper. It was about greenhouse gases. I forgot about my breakfast. I went to the toilet. And when I came back my cornflakes were gone.'

'Are you sure you put the cornflakes on the table?' John was determined to sort this out for the poor wee lad. 'Maybe you only thought you got them out of the cupboard.'

'No, I took them out of the cupboard. There's a space on the shelf where they were.'

'Are you sure?' John asked.

'Yes. It's happened before.'

'How many times?'

'Five.'

'Five?'

'I told you after the first and second times. And then the third and fourth times I didn't tell you because I didn't think you'd believe me.'

'And is it always your cornflakes?'

'Aye. One time it was a bottle of Pepsi as well. This is my fifth box of cornflakes. They're not cheap.'

John watched Anthony put his key in the lock and push on the door.

'They were here,' Anthony said and he pointed to his table. It was a small square table with one chair. There was a spoon, a bowl, a cornflake, and nothing else. John looked around him. He paced to one wall and the other, as he imagined a detective would.

'Shall we retrace your steps?' he said to Anthony and Anthony took him to the kitchen. He showed him the cupboard from which he took his packet of cornflakes. 'And you see, I have no other cereals,' he said. 'And I have no bread. So I haven't had breakfast.'

'Get yourself a roll and bacon from the van on your way to university,' John said and his words seemed to cheer the young man.

The young man took him from the kitchen to the table in the living room then back to the kitchen where Anthony showed him the paper with the article on global warming.

'And then I went...' The student made to go to the bathroom.

'We can skip that,' John said.

John checked all the doors – the back and the front – and saw no sign that they'd been forced open.

'Look, son, I don't know what to say to you. Are you sure?'

The boy's eyes were angry. He held out two empty cassette cases. 'They've taken my tapes now. They're missing.'

John tapped open the tape deck on his tape player but it was empty.

'I want the polis up here,' Anthony said and John stopped suddenly.

Up the stair again with the community policeman who checked the doors and windows like John had done.

'It's an unsolved crime, right enough,' the community policeman said. 'Are you sure he's the full ticket?'

'He seems to be, but you never can tell.'

Back in the office George showed the polis CCTV footage of a couple of lads trying to put a crowbar down the side of a car door.

'I can tell you who they are and where they stay,' George said.

'An easy one at last,' the policeman said and took the boys' names and addresses and went off to chap their doors.

The cornflakes mystery unsolved, the concierges left at the end of their shift. John never liked leaving for the day with an issue unsolved or unattended, but there was nothing he could do with this mystery.

Two days later, Martin, the concierge from Petershill Court, flagged him down on his way to the paper shop.

'See up there,' Martin said. He pointed to the top of Ten Red Road.

'Aye.'

'I saw someone up there and I had to do a double take. He was right at the top. How many floors up do you go? Thirty isn't it?'

'Aye, thirty.'

'He was hanging onto the outside of his veranda and then he scaled the side of the building and climbed over the next veranda along. I wanted to shout up to him to be careful but I was afraid to break his concentration in case he fell.' Martin's face was red and animated.

'When?'

'Five minutes ago.'

'He climbed out of his flat and into someone else's?'

'Aye, Spiderman. Right across the side of the building.'

'I know who that is. Thanks pal, you've just solved a crime.'

Back in the office John identified the man; an HPU, Homeless Persons Unit, who had been moved into Red Road while the flat he usually stayed in was repaired after a fire. He hadn't been in the building long. Was obviously hungry and not afraid of heights. Another call to the community police. After the dressing down, John wrote in the incident book: *Cornflakes mystery solved. Man climbed from veranda of thirty/two to veranda of thirty/one and broke into Anthony Docherty's flat. Case closed.*

Pamela 1988

They stood in front of her mirror, Pamela and Nicola, and behind their reflections was the open window and beyond that, all of Glasgow, it seemed.

'Don't say I look like a boy.' Pamela turned her head to see her profile.

'I feel like battering you. I should have stopped you,' her friend said. 'Your curls were gorgeous.'

'Suits me, for fighting.' Pamela's hands were sticky with the mousse she'd used to spike her hair. Her neck felt bare so she zipped her ski jacket to her chin and wiped her hands on her jeans.

'I bet your ma had a hairy canary.'

'I like it. Richard likes it.'

They stood a little longer in the mirror, the two friends. Nicola passed her lipstick to Pamela. Pamela checked her pockets for everything she would need.

'I'm going to do hairdressing,' Nicola said and Pamela looked at her. It surprised her in a way she couldn't understand.

'When?'

'August.'

'Where?'

'Central College.'

'I would have thought you'd do something with numbers,' Pamela said eventually.

'Nah. Shall we go?'

Pamela checked her hair again in the mirror and replaced her sleeper earrings with studs. Then she looked around her bedroom for her boots.

'What are you going to do?' her pal asked.

'I don't know,' Pamela said. 'I don't really care. Now where's my boots?'

The girls were used to searching for Pamela's lost clothes or shoes. When they'd checked the wardrobe and the piles of clothes on the floor they lay on their bellies on Pamela's bed and took a side each, pulling up the valance and sticking their heads underneath.

'Here they are,' she said, pulling them out by their laces.

A bottle rattled out of one boot. Pamela picked it up. It had a chemist's label and her brother's name on it.

'Come and look at this,' she said.

Nicola turned herself around and crawled to Pamela's side

of the bed. They lay there, the girls, on their bellies, looking at the bottle.

'I reckon my brother planked these,' Pamela said.

'In your boot?'

'Aye.'

'What are they?'

'Temazepam. Jellies. He called the doctor out the other night. Said he was freaking out, because of my dad.'

'Give us one then,' Nicola said and Pamela looked up at her pal. She'd never taken one before. Glue and fighting had been enough.

The lid was difficult to undo – it just clicked round and round – so Nicola took the bottle from Pamela, pressed hard on the plastic cap with her palm and twisted it off.

'How many?' she said.

'Look at the size of them. They're not going to do nothing to me. Two?'

They took two.

The walk across the field was exciting as they waited to feel something. Their boots swished on the damp grass. Gulls cawed overhead. And when Pamela's ma shouted from the veranda 'Don't you be out late,' they only turned and waved, her warning cry ineffectual, her body and waving arms tiny against the vast wall of concrete around her.

Back in Pamela's bedroom the girls lay on their backs. Afternoon. Still wearing the previous night's clothes.

'That wee guy from Blackhill took four off me. I just took the two and I can't remember the rest of the night,' Pamela said.

'You were out of your face, buzzing glue an all.'

Nicola drank from a can. 'Check in all your shoes,' she said and the girls upended all the shoes and boots they could find but there were no more planked jellies.

'We'll buy some. Or I'll get a script,' Nicola said.

Pamela spiked up her hair and looked at the ceiling. Her head was sore. The night's events were patchy but she knew that Nicola went off with some of the guys from Avonspark Street and she and Richard sat against the wall of the community centre and listened to the shouts over at the railway.

Nicola laughed. 'I ended up down at a house in Sighthill, chapping the door and demanding to get in. I was like that, I stay here, and the person inside was like that, no you fucking don't, this is my house. My uncle found me and got me up the road. He'd been to a pal's.'

'I thought those wee things wouldn't do nothing for me.

Sure did,' Pamela said and then her ma put her head round the door and said, 'Can you get me twenty Mayfair and bring them up the stair before you go out.'

'All right, Ma,' Pamela said and followed her mother into the living room where the table was set up for her card game with her pals from the bingo.

Nicola stood in the doorway and said, 'I start my course in three weeks.'

Running through the town to take a script to Boots as the workers clog the bus stops and pour down the hills to Central Station. Running through the sizzling lights, the black sky leaking its rain, the script in Nicola's hand and Pamela running behind, dodging the people with bags and brollies. Running through the town to catch Boots.

'I can't sleep is what I told my doctor. It was easy. My nerves are jangling, can you give me something for my jitters?'

In Boots they take the paper bag with the pills rattling inside. As carefully as the pharmacist taps out the tablets from the big bottle they cup their hands and tap out with a forefinger two, three, four jellies. Swallow them.

The fighting was funny that night. She got lamped with a brick and the skin above her right eyebrow cut and bled. Her tracksuit was filthy from where she fell. The boy who threw the brick jumped about. I got that guy a cracker, he said and Richard said That guy's my girlfriend and the two of them fought, clamping arms and heads and punching ribs in the dark. Pamela watched them lunging at each other on the top of the embankment on the other side of the lines.

Stones and bricks and bottles. Pamela and Richard kept each other in sight, Gringo girl, Gyto boy, meeting up after the police sirens and the flashing blue lights signalled the end of that night's fighting. The useless police, seen from miles away, giving all the fighters time to scramble through the under-growth and Pamela and Richard a chance to winch.

She used to meet him when it was quiet and the girls from their side went to meet the boys from his. His mouth tasted of lager and mints. He liked to fuck standing up. Pamela thought she loved him. She pure fancied him. He said he liked her hair either way; curls or spikes. He took her to see Scheme and they both joined in the fighting that went on while the band played. He said he felt fierce about her, got done for breach several times then disappeared to live in Greenock with his uncle.

Kat 1989

Kat Fisher was indignant for the tenants of Red Road, for the tenants of Glasgow, for the tenants of Britain and the whole capitalist world. It made her so angry. Shame on electricity companies that charged their highest prices for metered elec-tricity in rented flats that were generally the domiciles of the poor and the struggling. Shame on Glasgow City Council for installing the meters. Shame on everyone for not stamping their feet and refusing to take this crap from the multinationals. It annoyed her even more because she always paid her electricity bills on time and now she and her two flatmates were being penalised. And one of her flatmates was tight enough. They'd never have the lights on any more and the television would be censored. At least the heating was included in the rent.

   The wind shot leaves and dust around the tarmac when she left the building. It lifted the skirt her sister made her high up her thighs and she had to hold it flat against her legs with her hand. Her black woollen tights kept the chill off and the wind didn't matter to her hair which was tousled and bowl-cut any-way. Hardly anyone about. She walked on to the bus stop. John, one of the concierges, waved at her.

'I'm not talking to you, John,' she said.

'Oh. What have I done today?'

'You could have stopped them putting the meters in.'

John used a hard-bristled brush to sweep up bits of wet cardboard box. He made a pile of the cardboard, and the bristles made a sharp noise on the concrete. He leaned on the broom and said, 'I knew I'd get a telling from you. It was coming, but. The electricity board were up here every five minutes cutting off someone's supply.'

'That's not the point. They're charging their most expensive electricity to those that can least afford it. We're all in thrall to big companies and we all let it happen.'

'Aye, you start the revolution, and I'll join in,' John said.

'I will.'

Kat tucked the billowing ends of her scarf into her jacket and put her hands in her pockets.

'John,' she said. 'My da's coming to visit this weekend. Can I borrow the Hoover?'

'Aye, sure you can. Tell him to park in front of the cameras and we'll keep an eye on his motor.'

'Thanks.'

John began to sweep again and Kat walked to the bus stop, her notebooks and textbooks heavy in her bag.

Pamela 1989

Nicola stopped coming up the stair. Pamela saw her from time to time with a snakeskin handbag. She changed her hair colour then kept it blonde.

New friends took tablets out of their pockets and chased them down with Irn-Bru or Buckfast. It was easy not to leave Red Road. Sofas in high houses were comfortable.

'I've never done a Ouija board,' Pamela said.

The new friend, Sarah, cleared stuff off the wee table and Pamela watched her take things out of a shoebox.

'We done it ourselves,' Sarah said and the other new friend sat on a cushion and crossed her legs.

'Close the curtains.'

Pamela went to pull the curtains across the shitty day and kicked the leg of a man lying in the corner, his body half in shadow.

'Oh my God!' she said. 'Who's he?'

'My ex, Liam,' Sarah said. 'He comes here to sleep.'

'I thought he was dead.'

The man rolled onto his side and pulled a blanket over his shoulder. 'I'm still alive, honey,' he said. 'Five minutes more.'

Pamela saw his sleeping feet sticking out of the blanket, a toenail showing through a hole in his sock.

'We're ready,' Sarah said.

The Ouija board was well used. Sarah put a glass in the middle and the girls held hands.

'Will we try and get the wee boy again?' the other new friend said. 'Close your eyes.'

The room was quiet. Pamela heard a slow breath from the man in the corner and then nothing. The fridge buzzed.

'Darren, are you there today?'

Pamela opened her eyes and saw the girls with their eyes shut tight. The other new friend, Kirsty, swayed. Her shut eyes twitched hard.

'Darren, are you with us?'

Nothing.

'Right, well you're obviously playing with your wee pals today,' Sarah said. 'Who else shall we do?'

They looked at Pamela. Pamela shrugged.

'My granny,' Kirsty said.

'We always do your granny and she always says your granda's a cunt.'

Sarah tapped the glass against the board. Pamela kept quiet but she thought loads. She thought about her da up there.

'Right, will we do my uncle Tam then?' Sarah said and the girls were quiet again. The man in the corner rolled over and yawned.

'Shoosh,' said Sarah.

Pamela closed her eyes and thought of her da. She could no longer see him in her head but she heard his voice and followed the sound of his voice. It was taking her somewhere.

'Fucking Christ!' Sarah shouted. 'She's took a fit.'

Kirsty was shaking, her eyes rolled back into her head, spit coming from her mouth. Great shudders in her body, her knees coming up and knocking the table, Pamela not knowing which way she was going to fall.

'Lie her down,' the man in the corner said. He was up, in his socks and boxers and T-shirt, pulling her, sliding her legs along the floor from under the wee table.

'She's got a spirit in her,' Sarah said. 'Oh my fucking God, she's taken on a spirit.'

And Pamela thought of her dad.

'Get a spoon!'

Someone was shouting. It was the man. To her.

'You, get a spoon from the kitchen.'

Pamela ran and her legs were sick with fear. Her dad. Her dad. Her dad.

The man lay the shaking girl on her back and put the spoon in her mouth.

'Get back,' he said and knelt at her head, putting his palms on her forehead and cheeks as she thrashed about.

'Get the spirit out,' Sarah said and she was crying and screaming and shaking herself.

'It's not a spirit,' the man said. 'Somebody get an ambulance.'

Sarah phoned downstairs and the concierge said he'd send for an ambulance and the three of them waited while Kirsty fitted and sweated on the floor.

'Vodka, Ponstan, Temgesics and hash,' Sarah told the ambulance woman when asked what Kirsty had taken.

They'd done something else as well, Sarah wasn't telling. Pamela didn't even know what it was but had put it in her mouth and swallowed it with her vodka. She pressed her back against the wall and watched the procession out of the house; Sarah first, to open the doors, the ambulance woman at the head of the stretcher, Kirsty flat out with the drip in her, the other ambulance man at the back and the man in the corner last, carrying her bag and cardigan.

She stayed pressed against the wall as they closed the door, imagining her da, as crazy as ever, wondering about the spirit world.

Kat 1989

Kat filled the Belfast sink with water. She put a compilation tape into the cassette player in the kitchen and turned the volume up loud. She loved the Bunnymen. While she waited for the sink to fill she put away some clean dishes and stored an empty Irn-Bru bottle with the others under the sink. It was just a few bits of underwear and a couple of T-shirts she had to wash. She tipped a scoop of washing powder into the sink and stirred the water with a wooden spoon. Then she heaved the clothes around the sink with the wooden spoon, prodding at them as they puffed up out of the top of the water. She put the spoon down and rubbed two socks against each other then rinsed and squeezed them and put them on the draining board. They dried their clothes on the drying rail they kept on the veranda. Sometimes, in winter, the clothes froze as they hung, but it wasn't cold enough yet for that.

There was a knocking at the door. Her hands were wet and she grabbed a dish towel. A man stood at the door. His nose was long and his cheeks thin and he wore a heavy blue wool coat.

'There is somebody home!' the man said, all smiles. 'I was knocking and knocking. I could hear your music so I thought there must have been someone in.'

'Sorry pal, I didn't hear you.'

'You students and your loud music. You're all the same. What are you listening to?'

'It was Echo and the Bunnymen. Now it's The Smiths.'

'Oh aye, The Smiths. Morrissey. To die by your side, what a heavenly place to die.'

He looked into her eyes and flirted with his own. 'I like Billy Bragg.'

'Do you?'

'Aye.'

He took a hold-all from his shoulder and knelt down to open it, his hands tugging at the zip and pulling out some of his gear and resting it on the top of the bag.

'See this, I can offer you any of this – clock radios, Walkmans, Tippex – very, very cheap, or, if you tell me what you need, I'll get it for you, darling.'

He looked up at her and his chin jutted out as he smiled.

'No thanks pal,' Kat said.

'Are you sure? I can get you clothes from Next. Next is good quality gear. What do you want? Jeans? Tops?'

'Do I look like I dress in Next? Look at me.' Kat laughed and looked down at the long, holey jumper that she wore over her leggings.

'You look lovely. Stationery, then?'

'I'm all right for stationery, ta.'

The man sniffed and put his things back into his hold-all. 'Is there anyone else at home who would be interested?'

'Nobody's at home and nobody's interested, sorry pal.'

She wanted to close the door now, in case he got nasty. She didn't think he would, because he seemed like a harmless chancer, but things could turn easily. She shut the door on him as he went across the landing to the Kenyan and the Indian students' door. The boys wouldn't be taken in but there were a few new arrivals who needed telling.

'I'm only saying this for your information, to put you in the picture. You can do what you like. We can all make our own decisions. But this is what I would advise you not to do while you're staying here.'

The new students watched Kat, some took notes, some screwed their faces up as if they couldn't quite hear or quite understand. Perhaps she was speaking too fast. A Malaysian couple sat at the back and their boy played on the floor with the pool-table triangle and balls.

'Don't use the ice cream van. The one parked out by the bus stop. It doesn't sell ice creams. I don't think I've ever seen it move. Just leave it be. That's none of our business. Don't buy drugs from anyone in the area, don't borrow money from anyone in the area, stay out of the pubs and stay out of the bookies. Now, shoplifters will come round the doors selling stuff that they've nicked. Or they'll ask you what you want and steal to order. If you get involved with them and they get a fine they will come back asking for a contribution to their fine and if you don't give them a contribution you will start getting problems. I'm not saying don't do it but if you do get involved with a shoplifter this is what's going to happen. Okay?'

The students nodded their heads. The wee Malaysian boy put his face through the pool triangle. They seemed raw, these new students; girls from the Islands, boys from the Highlands, postgrads from India, Kenya, Nigeria, Spain. More families like the Malaysian family, come to Red Road from miles away to study hard.

'Lastly, for food, there's Frank's the Chippy or the Five-in-One,' Kat said. She pushed her fringe out of her eyes and counted on her fingers. 'The Five-in-One does pizza, chips, jacket potatoes, burgers and...'

She stopped and looked at John.

'Kebabs,' John said.

'Aye, kebabs. And Frank's the Chippy does pizzas too.'

Kat told the students that if anyone wanted to join the Labour Party club at Strathclyde University or Glasgow Tech they could come to her or her flatmate and she would sort them out. And the meeting was over unless anyone had any questions.

'Is there a telephone in the building?' somebody asked.

'No,' said John, 'and there's no swimming pool neither.' The students were silent as they stared at John. 'Just a wee joke,' he said and he tapped the wall with his knuckles and left.

Pamela 1989

'Pamela?'

The voice came from the blue sky.

'Pamela?'

Some fucker pulling at her leg and the voice coming at her again from the blue sky.

'Pamela?'

And then she smiled with her eyes closed.

'I'm not leaving her here. She can hear me,' the voice said.

'But is she straight?' Some cow's voice who Pamela didn't recognise.

'I very much doubt it.'

'Do I look full of it? Because I am full of it.' Pamela tried to sit up but branches got at her face. 'Ah, fucking sticks, sticks in my face.'

Nicola put her hand on Pamela's face. 'Come here, pal,' she said. 'Come this way and we'll sit you up.'

Pamela let herself be rolled out of the hedge. She put her arms around her friend and hugged her shoulder.

'Hello Nicola.'

'Hello Pamela.'

Pamela smelled her friend and kept her nose in her neck. She felt her friend's hands untucking hair from her collar. It was long again.

'What are you playing at, sleeping in the hedge?'

'What time is it?'

'Ten in the morning.'

Pamela laughed. 'Oh no, I've overslept.' She felt her wet face.

'Blood.' It upset her. She wiped at it.

'It's not blood,' Nicola said.

Pamela looked at her fingertips, wet but not bloodied. 'What is it then?'

'Rain,' the other girl said.

'Aye right, rain.'

'It's been raining, Pamela.'

Pamela laughed again and shook her head. She looked up at the blue sky with fat clouds at its edges.

'Do I look full of it?'

'Yes, you do.'

'Your pal doesn't like me.'

The girl walked away and took something out of her rucksack. Nicola moved from her knees to the pads of her feet and put her hands under Pamela's shoulders. She helped Pamela stand and when she was standing steady she flicked a hand over her clothes, removing dirt and leaves.

'Will we get you home for a wash?'

They walked towards Sixty-three block. The other girl had put headphones in her ears and was putting a cassette into a Walkman. Pamela needed a shite but she didn't want to say. She walked a bit faster.

'That's it,' Nicola said and held onto her hand.

A fire engine screamed around the corner. The girls were close enough to see the firemen in the cab.

'Noisy fucker,' Pamela said.

They followed in the wake of the fire engine and watched it stop.

'That's your block,' Nicola said.

They didn't go into the entrance because the fire engine was parked outside and the concierges were holding their hands out to stop people. There was smoke in the sky so the girls walked around the building to have a look. Smoke like a snort of breath came from one of the verandas. A bubble of smoke, ineffectual against the building's grey bulk. It turned into wisps the farther it got from the veranda and slipped into the clear blue air. A small fire. But still a fire. People watched from the ground, their faces tilted up towards the grey. Pamela looked at the men standing at the foot of Thirty-three block, smoking their cigarettes, talking through their own smoke. She saw one man. He was leaning, his face in the sun's shadow.

'Isn't that your ma's house?' Nicola said.

'Eh?'

'Is that your ma's veranda, or the one below, I can't tell.'

'It's not my ma's veranda,' Pamela said.

She looked again at the man she recognised with his dark hair and the sun's shadow on his face, leaning against the wall of the building, a flat foot against the wall. He was looking at her. Straight at her. His hands were in his pockets. She wondered what he had in his pockets for her.

'Are you sure?' Nicola said.

'Aye, I'm sure, it's not my ma's house. See you after.' She walked towards the man and shook her leg as she walked because it was stiff from where she'd lain in the hedge. The man didn't stop looking at her and when she got into the shadow with him she saw that he was smiling at her and he was waiting for her. She would go with him to wherever he suggested, have a shite, and do what he wanted to do.

Her neighbour, Keith Smith, ran past her. 'Pamela, your ma's house is on fire,' he said as he ran, his hands clenched into fists, his eyes brave.

'All right, Mr Smith,' Pamela said under her breath, as the man, Liam, Sarah's ex, held out his hand for her and she leaned forward to kiss his lips and give him her tongue.

Kat 1989

Six fifty-five a.m. Fern was waiting outside the shop and nearly finished her cigarette. Kat helped her pull up the shutter, drag in the newspapers and rolls and pull the shutter down again. They sorted *The Suns* and *The Heralds* and *The Daily Records* and the one *Guardian* and started putting piles of magazine inserts into the newspapers. It was like John Menzies. Fern's gold bracelet tapped against the inserts as she worked. Kat yawned.

'What did you do yesterday?' Fern asked her.

Kat said, 'I went to the student union.'

'After your vigil?'

Kat looked up and checked Fern wasn't being snide.

'I saw you,' Fern said. 'I was walking by and I saw a bunch of student types who looked exactly like you. And then I saw you with your wee boyfriend.'

'You should have stopped.'

'I didn't have the time.'

Kat didn't say this but she thought that apartheid in South Africa would never be abolished if everybody said they didn't have the time.

The newspapers were full of the poll tax and Kat wanted to read more than just the headlines as she sorted out the papers. Dissent was gathering. People were angry, especially in Scotland where Thatcher had pissed on the poorest and made so many – so many – people jobless.

Fern pointed a finger at a picture of Maggie Thatcher. 'I'm not paying her community charge,' she said and tapped her finger.

Kat raised her eyebrows.

'Me and Tommy Sheridan, we're not paying,' she said.

'And the rest.'

'I suppose you'll be at the demonstration at Birnie Court.'

'Yes I will. Will you?'

'I live there, so I suppose I will be. Shall we open up? You get the shutters, hen.'

Kat pulled on the door and bent to heave up the shutters. Her arms were stretched above her head and she was just about to turn to push the shutters right to the top with the bar that they kept inside the door when a man jumped out at her. He held a flick-knife at his waist, and told her to get inside the shop. Fuck. She did as she was told.

'Open up the till and give me all the money,' he said. The man was in his fifties and he wore a denim jacket and looked as if he was too old and tired for robbing but had no choice in the matter.

Fern was already behind the counter and she opened the till and took out the ten pound note and the five one pound notes and held them out to the man.

'Any change? I want all the money in the till.'

'There's a fiver's worth of change.'

'Give it to me. And forty Mayfairs. All the Mayfairs.'

Kat watched Fern gather the change into her fists and put it in the man's hands. He put some of the change into his pockets and a couple of coins dropped to the floor, which he didn't pick up.

'Now the fags.' He stabbed his flick-knife into the air and Kat stepped backwards, knocking a Pot Noodle off the shelf.

Fern gave the cigarettes to him and he backed out of the shop and when the door was closed Fern said, 'Our usual start to the day. Couldn't wait for his giro.'

Good God. When they were robbed they were to call the owner who would come to the shop, unlock the safe and give them twenty more pounds of change, as that is all he would allow in the till at any one time. And he didn't allow too many packets of fags on the shelves or jars of coffee on display either. Just in case. And it always was the case that one day or the next, they'd get robbed, Fern told her. You'll get used to it, she said and Kat felt embarrassed to be breathing so heavily and unable to stand still.

The police came but said to Kat, 'You didn't see anything did you? You wouldn't recognise the man, would you? You're a student. You live round here. You have to live in this community and you didn't see anything.'

'No, I didn't,' Kat said, but she saw the man later that day. He'd set up a card table, outside the shop and he was selling the cigarettes he'd stolen, asking folk before they went in if they wanted to get them from him as he was cheaper than the shop.

Donna McCrudden

It was quite frightening because I remember one day my daughter went down in the lift and there was someone drunk and smelling of drink. I think she was about seven, and the shop was just down at the bottom of my flat, and at that time the basement was down where the shops were and the lift went right down to the basement, out the basement into the shops and she was to get a loaf, and because we didn't have stairs on our landing the lift was the only way to get out, or through your back entrance and down the back stairs. So she was in the lift and the lift door only opened so much and it got jammed and there was a drunk man in the lift with her and she started screaming and the next thing, she pushed the bread through the floor and the plain loaf was broken and all the slices of bread were on the floor and the lift went away. It went up to the top floor and you could hear her screaming all the way up. The lift went up to twenty-four. The drunk man must have got off at another floor. And the good thing was that the girl on the twenty-fourth floor was a friend of mine and she knew exactly who she was and got her back down to mine, in some state.

Pamela 1990

Sounds of breathing. Everyone breathing. She lay in the hall with her head pushed against the skirting board. Her jeans unzipped and the waistband tight around her thighs. Her knickers pulled down too. They must have come out into the hallway and fucked there.

He was in the kitchen holding a cigarette over a saucer, looking out the window. She watched the end of his cigarette as she zipped up her jeans and pulled her hair away from her face.

'I've got something to do today,' she said. 'Something important. I can't mind what it is.'

She turned on the tap and put her mouth to the water. Then she coughed into the sink and spat. Gravel in her chest. No milk in this house. A kettle and spoons. A used tea bag in the bin. She leaned across Liam for the kettle and filled it with water. Then she set it to boil and rinsed some mugs.

'Help me, Liam,' she said. 'I have to do something today. What day is it today?'

'Saturday.' He tapped his cigarette and a tower of ash fell onto the saucer.

The tea was weak.

'We have to put Kirsty outside,' he said. 'I can't do it myself.'

His arms were the skinniest they'd ever been; scabbed, sore, translucent skin. His fingers shook.

'Why?'

'Are you a fucking eejit?'

It pissed her off, the way he spoke to her, but she didn't rise to it because she relied on him to find them more smack. That's how it worked.

'We'll have to put her outside and then fuck off.'

'What time is it?'

'Are you not listening?'

'I've got something to do today, Liam, and I can't remember what it is. I'm thinking!' And then she realised.

'Who did you say?'

'Kirsty.'

A squeak from her throat. A flutter of the muscles in her face. She couldn't control them.

'God rest her.'

Liam turned on the tap and held his cigarette under the running water. He rinsed ash from the saucer.

'Are you sure?'

'She's grey and stiff with a mouthful of vomit.'

They walked into the lounge and Pamela heard the breathing again.

'Is anyone else dead?'

They lay, the rest of them, like children; soft arms, gentle knees, parted lips, a whistling nose, a flickering under the eyelid.

Flips started up in Pamela's belly. Metal in her mouth.

'They're all breathing.'

'Why Kirsty?' It hurt to cry. The pain knocking about her head, something swollen in her throat.

'Come on and we'll get her outside and then we'll go.'

They took a thin arm each. Pamela gripped Kirsty's wrist and felt the chain she wore against her palm. She wasn't heavy but Liam was weak and worse than he'd ever been. Kirsty's hair spread behind her. Her head bumped along the floor. They put her out on the back stair and Liam put his hands in her pockets and took out a cigarette lighter and a tissue. He kept the lighter and threw the tissue on the stairs. Pamela didn't have time to say goodbye because Liam took her arm and pulled her back into the house and out the front door.

They stood in the lift, stinking and silent with their thoughts. Pamela was thinking about what she would say to Kirsty's ma. She thought she would visit her own ma.

Liam walked away. His tiny jeans hung scrunched around his arse. He held an arm behind him and said to Pamela, 'efter.'

It was easier to cry on her own. On the corner of her ma's

building, children hung about. They were restless and excited, some jumping, skipping, clapping, twitching their legs. Noise. From further down Petershill Drive came the sound of horses' hooves. The children surged towards the noise. Above her, on the verandas, her ma's neighbours clapped and shouted out. She thought she heard her ma's voice shouting Go on yourself Nicola, but she couldn't see her when she raised her head to look. She would be on Colleen's veranda. Nicola came in her horse and carriage with her husband at her side. The horse flicked its tail and shook its head as it walked. Nicola waved. Her husband wore a kilt. Her dress was white and she wore a tiara and a veil.

Maybe she caught Pamela's eye as she scanned the crowd on the street and all the way up the building, well-wishers hanging out the windows and leaning on the verandas, but she didn't wave. She was a bride.

The best man got out of his car, put his hands in his pockets and threw a shower of coins into the crowd of weans. The weans screamed. They bashed heads and threw themselves onto the rolling and spinning coins. The best man lifted his arms again and threw more coins. A coin for every child. They chased them before they rolled into the drain, distracted by another shower.

The horse and cart and Nicola and her husband were away down the road. The best man held his palms above his head and said no more. A couple of coins rolled Pamela's way. She bent to pick them up and went after two more before she heard the heckles and reprimands from the people on the verandas and then she went up the stair to sleep in her ma's lounge, if her ma would let her.

Section Five

Kamil 1990

KAMIL'S TAXI DRIVER dropped him in front of Kwik Save and told him to walk around the slab block to find the concierge in number Twenty Petershill Court.

'This building here, this is my one?' Kamil asked. He could see neither the top nor the sides as he looked through the taxi window. It was vast, and the people outside seemed blasted with cold and wind and bad temper.

The taxi driver told him as he took his money, 'I'll give you one piece of advice son: act like you're up for a square go at all times, even if you're keeking your breeks. That's my advice. Take it or leave it.' He picked something out of his tooth, tooted his horn, turned on the tarmac, and drove back onto Red Road.

Kamil picked up his cat box and suitcase and walked the giant width of Petershill Court and around the thin gable end to the other side. There, he saw the three red columns stuck onto the beige that he would later learn were the stairs, built not long previously so that tenants didn't have to walk through other peoples' houses to the back stairs when the lifts broke down.

'You'll have viewed the flat already?' the concierge said as he took the keys from the hook.

'No. I just took it. I didn't care where I went, I just wanted a house.'

'Fine,' the concierge said. He slid his swivel chair away from his desk and joined Kamil out the front by the visitors' hatch.

'Just you and the cat?' the concierge said and looked down.

'Aye. We can't live without each other.'

They walked back into the cold and on to number Ten as the clouds began to spit rain. There were silver buttons on a panel by the door which the concierge showed him how to use.

Then he pressed a plastic fob to the security panel and the lock released. The concierge pulled on the door and a coin hit the ground and rolled away on the concrete. He looked up. So did Kamil. He saw the ghost of a closing window.

'On you go, son, call the lift. I think I know who that little bastard was.'

Kamil went through to the foyer of his new block and looked back to see the concierge standing legs wide with his arm pointing vigorously somewhere high up the building.

Kamil put the cat box down and read some of the notices pinned to the wall: Credit Union in Twenty Petershill Court, Red Road Football Team, Samaritans. He saw a sign with a card saying *Two* slotted into it. Then he saw the silver lifts and pressed the buttons to call them.

'You only need to press the one,' a man said as he walked into the foyer. He had a moustache and sideburns and rain-ruffled hair. 'You press the one and it calls the both of them.'

He whistled briefly then said, 'What's your cat's name?'

'Fluffs.'

The man smiled. 'New to Red Road?'

Kamil nodded.

Three girls with ponytails of plaited hair skated through the lift's opening doors. As they clattered their way through the foyer, pulling the hoods of their anoraks over their plaits, the concierge held the door open and called in, 'You go on up, son. I've just seen one of the community polis and I need to have a wee word. Your flat's fine. I checked it this morning.' He threw the keys and Kamil caught them. 'I'll come up and chap your door in a wee while. All right?'

'Aye.'

The foyer was suddenly quiet. The man with the moustache got in the lift and put his arm out to stop the doors from closing.

Kamil dragged in his suitcase and went back for his cat.

The walls were metal. No mirrors. There was a metal panel

of numbers that stretched up the wall, higher than his head. He could touch each side of the lift if he held his arms out.

'Small, isn't it?' Kamil said.

'You'll get used to it. If you tell me which floor you want we can get going.'

'Oh, aye, nineteen.'

The doors slid shut and the lift took off.

'I'll make a prediction that you're in flat nineteen/two.' The man didn't look at Kamil. He looked up at the red numbers above the doors. Kamil noticed his thick nasal hair.

'How did you know?'

'It's the one that's always empty.'

'Is that so?'

Kamil looked up at the numbers too.

'Do you want to know why?' Sly eyes keeked sidewards towards Kamil's.

Kamil knew there would be local types ready to tease him so he said nothing. But as the lift approached floor nineteen he said, 'Go on then.'

'It's haunted,' the man said and nodded his head. 'Aye, that and you've two house-breakers either side of you.'

The lift wobbled as it stopped. 'On you go.'

Kamil took his case and his cat and stood on the landing. 'Why is it...?'

'Haunted? You'll find out. You might want to call your cat something else by the way.'

The lift doors shut and Kamil stood alone with his cat and four doors.

As he opened his own door and walked into the muffled quietness of his flat Kamil prepared for ghosts but unless a ghost had shat all over his living room, there was only pigeon shit to contend with. It covered everything; floor, table, sofa, chair, heater, veranda. Even the light that hung from the ceiling was splattered with white shite. The place looked like a midden and Kamil was only eighteen. He wasn't keen on cleaning. His ma had cleaned his last place: of course she had; it was her house.

Two fat grey feathers lay on the carpet and Kamil threw them over his veranda. He looked out at his view. It was strange, like the view a child would have holding onto the legs of his mother and looking up; him halfway and her going up beyond him. Concrete, glass, smoke-grey cladding, red cladding, beige cladding, the tops of shops, the rain invisible and the air damp and thick.

When he let Fluffs out of her cage she stalked his flat and he followed her into the pale kitchen and the bedroom with the built-in cupboard, and the chilly bathroom. As if hunting down pigeons the cat dabbed her paws under the bed and around the back of doors then leapt onto the arm of the sofa and stayed there, her back humped and her tail erect, her eyes wide and freaked. She was either sensing pigeons or phantoms. When she bolted for the front door and leapt at the door handle as she'd done in his ma's house he let her out and stood in his doorway watching her walk edgy circles around the floor tiles.

The lift doors opened. A man and a woman got out. They carried message bags and the guy carried a wee boy.

'Cat,' the boy said.

'Want to stroke it?' said the man. He was cheerful, amiable, skinny.

'She's a bit unsettled,' Kamil said. 'She might scratch your wee boy.'

The guy put his bags down and hoisted his kid higher on his hip. 'No touching,' he told the boy. 'The cat's a bit spooked. Just moved in?'

'What's it called?' the boy said.

'Fluffs. Aye, first day.'

'What do you think of your house?'

'It's all right. Apart from the pigeons.'

'You have to keep your veranda door closed, mate.'

'Aye, it seems that way.'

'No you really do. And your windows too.'

The guy seemed serious. He picked a cigarette from behind his ear and twirled it in his fingers. Then he said, 'I hope you settle in okay. If you need anything, just chap the door. I'm Adam.'

'I will, I will. Thanks, pal.'

Adam put his boy on the floor and let him stroke the cat and the cat seemed to like the boy. Kamil relaxed.

'Say ta-ta,' Adam said.

'Ta-ta,' the boy said.

The cat danced about the doorway, seemingly fine.

'I've met you now,' Kamil said. 'So it's just the two house-breakers to go.'

The guy held his hand out for his son to hold but he said nothing. So Kamil continued. 'Old boy in the lift. Told me my house was haunted and I had two house-breakers either side of me.'

'Ta-ta,' the boy said again to the cat.

'He's right on both counts. I don't steal from my neighbours though, you're all right.' The young guy tapped his cigarette and said, 'Call down to the concierges, they'll help you clear up that doo shite.'

When he was back in his flat, Kamil made sure his veranda door was shut and checked the windows too. He put his tea bags and milk in the kitchen and then called down to the concierges.

'And do you want me to stick a broom up my arse on my way up, son?' the concierge said.

It wasn't the concierge he'd met before. Kamil didn't know what to say or what to think or where to start. He sat with his cat for a quarter of an hour and then began to clean up the pigeon shit. He took a pair of pants from his suitcase, ran them under the hot tap, squeezed some washing up liquid onto them that his ma had put in his suitcase and began scrubbing.

An hour later, Adam's girlfriend knocked on the door with a mug of milk. Adam and the wee boy followed her in.

'Let's have a look at your house,' Adam said.

'I've nothing in here yet.'

'Don't worry pal, I won't take anything from you. Nor will Jack. That's a promise.'

'Jack?'

'Number three.'

'Thanks but I've got milk already,' Kamil said to Adam's girlfriend.

She opened his fridge.

'So you have,' she said. 'You didn't look that organised. I thought you were a student.'

'I'm not a student. I work in a restaurant.'

The woman said 'oh right' and stared at him. She seemed on the verge of asking him something and Kamil felt nervous, standing in the kitchen with the wee woman with the back-combed fringe studying him so blatantly. He was glad when Adam came to get her and said, 'Yer man's flat's the same as ours, except our bathroom's here and our living room's here.'

They filled the house. The cat sprang about with them.

'You've got one of they big wardrobes too,' the girlfriend said. 'Adam uses ours. I can't get a look in.'

Kamil didn't doubt it.

'And here's where they jumped,' Adam said. He turned to see where his son was playing, out of earshot, lowered his voice and said, 'Two guys. High on drugs. Tripping. First one thought he was being chased and leapt out of the window. Second one thought he could fly. One after the other. Splat. Look down.'

Kamil unlocked the window and pushed the glass. Leaning out, he saw the long drop.

'See that dark patch on the Kwik Save roof? That's where they landed. They had to rebuild it. The ghosts came back to haunt the flat they jumped from. Well, I don't know if both of them did, but one did definitely. Nobody stays in this house. Nobody lasts.'

He turned to look at Kamil, as if daring him to dispute what he'd said.

'I'll be staying,' Kamil said and the man shrugged his shoulders and glanced at his girlfriend.

'Suit yourself.'

They left.

The ghosts tested Kamil that same day. He ran a hot bath and soaked in the suds from his shaving foam. The bath was all right. His cat was all right. She lay curled on the bathroom floor, enjoying the heat and steam. Kamil closed his eyes and let his head sink under the water. When his ears were submerged he heard a couple of loud thumps and sat up to work out where the noise was coming from. Water clogged his ears and as he tipped his head to one side to clear the blockage he heard his door rattling, as if someone was shoving a hand in and out of the letter box.

'I'm in the bath,' Kamil called.

The letter box rattled again and there were tough raps on the door.

'Come back in a minute,' he shouted but whoever it was either didn't hear him or didn't want to come back in a minute.

The chapping was loud, bossy, aggressive. Kamil pulled himself out of the bath, wrapped a towel around his waist and strode to the door as the thumps and rattles became ridiculous. But when he opened the door, nobody was there, not a soul. And not a sound. No footsteps tapping up or down the stairs, no lift whirring up or down the shaft. Kamil walked slowly around the landing, checking for evidence of a person just away. Then he knocked on Adam's door.

Adam held a screwdriver in his hand.

'Was that you chapping my door just a second ago?'

'No, mate.'

'Did you hear anybody chapping my door?' Kamil was aware of his voice coming out panicked.

Adam paused. 'I might have heard a knock or two. Look, pal,' Adam changed the subject. 'The polis are probably going to show up later and I've got to be somewhere else. If you hear them giving my missus any hassle will you come out?'

Kamil said he would and made to go back into his flat.

'You reckon it was your ghost then?' Adam said.

'I'm not suffering it if it was,' Kamil said.

He shut his door and tried to calm himself.

'Stay if you're staying,' he said to the ghost, 'but don't give me any hassle. You're the one that jumped out of the window. I live in this flat now.' He stood in the bathroom trying to decide whether to get back in the bath for another soak or give up and get dressed. He put one foot in the water and was astride the bath when the door thumped and rattled again.

'I'm not having this. Give me peace! Stay and behave or fuck off,' he roared into the steamed-up bathroom air.

He threw open his front door and came face to face with the concierge who stood with a mop and bucket and bottle of bleach.

Silence. Kamil hid his naked body behind the door. The concierge held out the mop and bucket and bleach and when Kamil didn't move, put them on the floor.

'My partner told me you were having a bit of bother with the pigeons,' he said.

'I was, aye.'

'Everything all right? Nothing upsetting you?'

'Not now, no.'

The concierge stepped backwards and raised a hand. Kamil closed his door and whispered to the walls, 'Don't give me a showing up again, ghost. Bob. That's your name. That's what I'm calling you. You're just an ex-tenant who likes your old flat. I'm onto you. This is your last warning, Bob. Give me some peace.'

He dressed, apologised to the cat for leaving her alone and went to his work in the restaurant, baffled.

Helen and Sharon McDermott

Helen: It was roughly about eight pound. You just had to take your luck. I used to sit in a foursome, there were four of us and then when the interval came, you had a fifteen-minute interval, and you'd bring the cards out and sit and play ordinary bingo with the cards till the session started up again.

Sharon: When I was pregnant I started going with my ma.

Helen: I used to say to her just get three books. She didn't know how to use the books. So I had six books and she had three and she didn't know how to play for a single line so I'm trying to watch my book and watch hers at the same time. That was actually nine books I was playing between the two of us. I said never again are you coming back to bingo.

Iris 1991

'You come to the bingo with me,' her ma said when Pamela was seventeen weeks pregnant. 'Come on hen, it'll give you a boost.'

So Pamela sat with her ma and the ladies and her ma kept an eye on her books even though Pamela could play fine by herself now. In the interval she went to the toilets and had a look at the clothes the women were selling. Some of the tops were nice but Pamela didn't have enough money and she knew she'd get too fat to wear them soon so there was no point buying them. The pregnancy was a distraction. Once it started moving she thought she'd cope better because the kicks would remind her to hold her course and her nerve. The midwife told her to imagine standing on a boat and pulling on a rope to get her through a stormy sea. Pamela found listening to the Talking Heads helped. She couldn't say why.

'I'll put the chest of drawers from my room into yours,' Iris said. 'Will you move back just before or just after the wean's born?'

'I don't know, Ma, we haven't decided.'

Her ma's knuckled fist rested on the table. The interval ended and the next game began and the women looked at their books. Pamela did well. She was concentrating better now, despite being pregnant, and her numbers flew in.

'And Liam, how is he doing?' Iris asked.

'I just leave him to it now,' Pamela said.

The caller called another number on Pamela's book and Iris leaned over and squeezed Pamela's hand and said, 'Go on hen.'

Neither of them had the next number.

'What does his ma say about the wean?'

'She doesn't want to know. He borrowed some money off her and never gave it back and she said she's had enough and wants rid of him.'

'That's a shame. It's not the wean's fault.'

Pamela had the next number. And the next and the next. A forty-four, an eighteen and a fourteen.

'Ma, look.'

'You've got a line, Pamela, well done, you've won something.'

The game continued. Nobody shouted 'house'. Pamela only had a thirteen to go. As each number was called and nobody shouted, Pamela looked up at the board to see which number was going to be called next. It was never a thirteen.

'You know you'd be better getting shot of him if he's not clean,' Iris said.

'Ma, give me peace, I only need a thirteen.'

Her number still didn't come but neither did anybody else's winning number and Pamela was restless as she waited. Come on, come on, come on, come on.

It killed her. A woman shouted and if the woman didn't shout, Pamela would have won. The next number came up on the board after the woman shouted and the next number was thirteen.

'I would have won. Look, I would have won.'

Pamela stood up. She pointed at the board and grabbed her ma's arm.

'I see it,' her ma said.

The board had a huge figure on it. Twelve thousand pounds.

'What we could have done with all that money,' Pamela said. But she didn't win the money.

'No, you didn't win,' her ma said.

'Fucking bingo,' Pamela said.

'Don't upset yourself,' her ma said. 'Really, you mustn't. If mummy gets upset, baby gets upset.'

Pamela sat down and did a double take at her ma, spouting the baby books at her, but stopped herself from retorting because she saw only concern in her ma's face and her ma reached out and stroked Pamela's cheek and jaw. They walked arm in arm as other women bustled to get on the bingo buses.

'Some amount of money I could have won,' Pamela said.

'I know, hen, I know. But you won a line. Do you want to give me your thirty-nine pounds and I'll keep it aside for the wean?'

Pamela gave her mother thirty pounds and kept back nine. She told her ma she would get chip suppers for her and Liam. Iris put the notes in her purse and said she would keep them with the rest she'd saved back in the house. There was a lot to invest in the new baby.

Kamil 1991

The footsteps and floor-creaks became normal. Kamil would lie on his bed in the mornings or the evenings and hear sounds of someone walking in his living room, and this happened so frequently that he came to see the ghost as a kind of flatmate; one who didn't bother him and never used the last of the milk. The cat took to arching her back and rubbing herself against nothing. Kamil could only assume that she was pressing herself up against the ghost's legs. The thing that concerned Kamil was other people. A friend house-sat for a night and phoned after fifteen minutes saying he couldn't stay because the chest in the bedroom had spewed out one of its drawers, tipping its contents onto the floor. Kamil doubted a girlfriend would put up with anything like that.

One night the cat jumped in front of him as he walked from the living room to the hall. Spitting and shaking, it made as if to protect Kamil from something. On that occasion, it wasn't fine to imagine some benign housemate padding around in his slippers and sharing the couch with him; whatever it was had made his cat evil and angry and petrified. Kamil picked up his keys, coins and coat and fled.

He wanted a drink. His options were the Brig or the Broomfield Tavern. Until then he'd avoided both but that night he took his chances on the Brig which was dug into the concrete, down a flight of stairs and at the end of fifteen yards of unlit alleyway. Windowless. Exclusive. Noisy. Kamil approached it without getting jumped. He opened the door and the noise stopped. He suddenly felt as if he was the only Asian in Red Road. Perhaps he was; the only non-student Asian anyway, the only one who put his head through the doors of the locals' pubs. But to turn back now would be worse than walking through the silent tables to the bar. So he strode on and ordered his pint, and after a while people began to talk again.

Kamil stood at the bar and drank and noticed the pool tables with red cloth, the darts board, and watched a man he thought must be the landlord walk from table to table collecting glasses, saying a word or two. The barmaid wiped up spills with a cloth. She took more money from Kamil and then removed a comb from the back of her up-do, smoothed her palm over her hair and put the comb back in.

People approached him and asked where he was from.

'Govan, originally,' he said and watched while they took him in, questions forming on their furrowed foreheads.

'Before that?'

'Nowhere else. The Southern General? I was born here.'

'Oh right, pal. Do you stay in Red Road?'

'Aye.'

No bother. Just nosiness.

'You looked a wee bit nervous walking in here, son,' a man said.

'Do you believe in ghosts?'

'No.'

Kamil told him the story and the man said, 'I don't feel sorry for you. I feel sorry for your cat. You left it in there while you shat yourself.'

Oh God, the poor cat. Poor undeserving Fluffs. He'd put hell into her life and left her. But he couldn't go back until he'd got a few inside him. He couldn't go back.

'My cat can handle herself,' he told the man, remembering the words of the taxi driver.

'I've heard that some of these houses are haunted, right enough,' the man said, and that seemed to close the conversation.

A woman came into the bar and people turned their heads but didn't hush their conversations. As she walked down the centre of the bar with the tables and chairs either side she put the strap of her handbag over her shoulder. She stood beside a man who'd nursed the same pint for as long as Kamil had drunk two. The man looked up and pulled a stool from the table. The woman sat. She didn't remove her coat. The man seemed to be defending himself while the woman shook her head.

'Is it an Indian restaurant you work in?' a man who drank Guinness asked Kamil.

'No, it's not, pal.'

'Are you a chef?'

'No, a waiter.'

The woman stood up and the table wobbled as she gathered her bags. The man steadied his pint glass.

'Do what you fucking like,' the woman said and walked back through the pub and pushed both hands against the door. The man breathed in and as he breathed he made as if to move but then he must have decided otherwise because he turned his head away from the door, tipped his glass and drank the remains of his lager, and brought the glass to the bar.

'Same again please, May,' he said.

'Haven't you got a home to go to?' the barmaid said.

'There's too many people in it,' the man said. He took his pint back to his table and placed it next to his paper. Kamil ordered another drink and a crowd gathered; acquaintances of the man he was talking to, all keen to know who he was and what he did and where he lived. The Brig was all right. A few of the men had ghost stories of their own. They all felt sorry for Kamil's cat.

Michael 1991

Michael was glad he was alone. The peace was so rare and delicate it made him want to sleep. When it was just him and Kay he liked his peace and quiet, but now, with Kay's best pal and Michael's brother taking turns on the sofa or the lounge floor, there was never a moment's peace. Kay was out shopping. His brother was at work. Trish, Kay's friend, was at her ma's. Michael pressed play on his Waterboys tape, rolled his sleeves to his elbows and washed his hands. He put onions, carrots, lentils, barley and a couple of stock cubes onto the work surface. Sharp knife and chopping board. Big metal pot. Salt and pepper. The kettle was already boiled from the coffee he'd made. He took the grater from the drawer and gave it a rinse because there were smears of cheese left on it. Then he laid his hands on the chopping board and looked out of the window. He sang the words of one of the songs in his head.

He picked up an onion and a key turned in the lock. Fuck.

Trish came into the kitchen, looking as if she'd smoked her giro. Michael cut the bum off the onion. She put a paper bag onto the side.

'Pie. My pie. Don't touch.' She opened the window. 'Where's Kay?'

'Gone shopping with her ma.'

'She could have waited for me.'

'Go and follow her in. She'll be at the bus stop. She's not away long.'

Trish opened the fridge.

'Where's my ginger?'

'In there somewhere.'

'Oops,' she said. 'I thought you'd scooped it. What you making?'

'Soup.'

'I love soup.'

'So do I.'

She watched him as he peeled the skin off the onion and chopped it in half.

'I can make really good soup.'

'I've never seen you make soup.' Michael had only seen Trish make a joint.

'Shall I can give you a hand?' She put her ginger back into the fridge.

'No, you're all right. I like the chopping.'

She lit a cigarette and took a saucer off the draining board.

'Me and Kay want to have a party,' she said.

'Listen, Trish, we need to talk to you about something.'

'Who needs to?'

'We do. Me and Kay.'

'Kay's not here.'

'Aye, but we've talked about it. She knows I'm going to bring it up with you.'

'Bring what up?'

He scraped the chopped onion to the corner of the chopping board and started on another one. 'We've been thinking.' He peeled the onion's paper skin and it crackled. 'If you're staying here with us for any length of time...'

'Kay said I could.'

'I know, we're not saying you can't. But if you're staying here and using the electricity and eating the food...'

'I go to my ma's for my tea. I don't eat here.'

'You do sometimes.'

'And I buy my own food. Don't I?' She pushed the pie out of the bag and took a bite. 'See. My own food,' she said. Flecks of pastry stayed on her lips. Some fell on to her jumper.

'You do eat the food sometimes.'

'No I don't.' She was getting agitated. He didn't want her to get agitated.

'Whatever,' he said. 'We were just thinking that seeing as you're staying here now, you could put a bit towards the food and the electricity.'

She stopped chewing. He pushed more chopped onion to the side of the board and got the next one.

'That's some amount of soup you're making,' Trish said.

'Aye. It's for Kay to take into work.'

She ate her pie then went into the living room. He finished the onion and topped and tailed the carrots. Quickly now, Michael grated the carrot, made up stock, sweated the onions and poured the whole lot with the lentils into the big pot. He shook salt and pepper and wished he'd bought a hough. A final stir, the lid on the pot and the heat turned down.

'Trish!' he called. 'Are you in for a wee while?'

'I might go to my ma's for my tea.'

'Okay, but are you in for the next hour?'

'Aye.'

'Do me a favour, turn the soup off after an hour.'

'Do I do add anything to it?'

'No, but if you get up for any reason, give it a stir.'

She'd tidied the lounge and had stacked his uni books and papers and pushed them to the edge of the table. A wash bag was on the table now, with cotton wool, nail varnish and nail files taken out.

'Michael.'

'What?'

'Tap us a fag.'

He threw one to her and opened the front door. A man stood outside. He wore a khaki anorak and trainers. In his hand was a six-pack of Tennent's. Michael was surprised.

'What do you want?' he said. He thought the guy was one of her next door's punters.

'Is this Trish's house?'

'This is my house,' Michael said. 'She sleeps on the couch.'

'My turn on the sofa bed tonight,' Trish said. Michael looked round to see her wearing lipstick and smelling of Kay's perfume.

'Hiya Stephen,' she said. 'Come on in.'

Michael left them to it.

Incident Book 1991

On routine inspection of back stairs of Ten Red Road Court, concierge found body believed to be friend of tenant in flat eighteen/three. D.O.A. Ambulance and police called. Body taken away. Not suspicious. Drug overdose. John.

Michael 1991

The Broomfield Tavern wasn't a place to study and Michael knew he was kidding himself on that he'd get his reading done. But after he'd chosen a seat where he could keep the whole pub and the exit doors in his sights he took his book from his bag anyway. The pub was busy with Saturday afternoon drinkers. One of the televisions showed horseracing. The other one showed football. Men rested pints on the barrels that stood between the tables and the bar. The smell of onions came from Michael's fingers as he flicked through the pages of his book. He looked up when the pub fell silent and saw the Asian guy from the Brig walk in. The football commentary carried on, like the hesitant music in some saloon bar, but everything and everyone else was quiet. Horses jumped silently. Punters held glasses and stared. Michael thought the Asian guy was brave. He didn't seem bothered by the sudden silence and he went straight to the bar as if he had some business to take care of. Michael heard him order, 'Give us a pint of Tennent's please pal,' and the pub was still silent. A couple of known BNP supporters were in. They stood along the bar from him and stared. The Asian guy paid his money, picked up his pint, turned from the bar, and that's when Michael waved at him. He couldn't have him pick his way through the silence and find a seat.

'There's a space here,' Michael said.

'You were in the Brig the other night,' the Asian guy said and sat down with his back to the bar.

Talk rumbled through the pub again and Michael patted the seat next to him and said quietly, 'Mate, come round here so you can see who's round about you. Always best to in here.'

The Asian guy moved seats, Michael closed his book and they exchanged names. Some guys with kit bags and sweatshirts came into the pub. Nobody bothered looking at them; Michael recognised them as locals who played in the Red Road football team. Most of the guys had been born and bred here.

'You recently moved in?'

'Aye. You?'

'Nah, moved in a year ago,' Michael said.

A man with a gentle face walked slowly to their table. His name was Terence and he collected the glasses. The landlord didn't pay him, Michael said to Kamil, when he'd moved on.

Instead, he allowed him to drink the leftovers in the glasses he collected. So Terence was always in and he always had a drink.

Suddenly Kamil sat up in his seat, stuck his arm in the air and waved. 'Hiya!' he shouted. A girl was waving at him, in the same boisterous way. Michael recognised the girl. She always came in with a crowd of crazy-looking people at her table. Men who looked like they'd stick the head on you for sneezing near them. Girls who could drink six of everything in the bar and still stand to dance on the tables. Kamil stood up and set off towards her with his pint, turning back to Michael to say, 'I work with this lassie.' The pub fell quiet again and heads turned to watch Kamil's big footsteps over to the girl and her crowd. When the girl put her arm around him and told him to sit down, the talk started up again. Michael watched Kamil and the girl and thought if they hadn't shagged yet, they would do soon. They were so into each other, her, touching him all the time, him big-eyed and beaming, all of them knocking back their drinks. He seemed to have a way of making people laugh. Even the tough-headed guys that sat with them were creasing up.

Michael wanted Kay. The girl that Kamil knew reminded him of Kay. The same sensibility; sweet and young and gorgeous, but feisty and most likely utterly demanding. Good luck to Kamil. It would be eventful. Michael picked up his book again, drank the last of his pint and was wondering if he'd head home to see if Kay was in when Kamil came past looking for the gents. I'll introduce you to Michelle in a moment, Kamil told Michael and walked on to the toilets. One of the guys who stood at the bar near the BNP men put down his pint and followed Kamil in. Nobody else seemed to notice or to care. Michael was horrified. He watched the door and listened for violence. He argued with himself; should he go in or should he stay out of it. Or was he being paranoid. He checked the BNP men at the bar and thought they seemed slow and casual. Kamil's lassie was clapping her hands and screeching at something. Her pals were laughing too.

Perhaps he was being paranoid. But nobody came from the toilets. It was long enough for Kamil to have had a pish now.

Michael nearly physically jumped when the pub doors burst open and a man walked in. 'Da!' Kamil's lassie shouted and the man unzipped his jacket and shook the rain off it as he walked towards his daughter. Michael clocked the BNP men clocking Kamil's lassie's da. Nothing from the toilets. This was a fucking mental pub. Nobody would see anything if the polis asked but sure as hell they'd all bundle into a fight wielding chair legs and ash trays if provoked. He stood up. He'd go in. And then the toilet door snapped open and the guy who followed Kamil in came out first. He turned around as Kamil came out and the two men stared at each other. Kamil stepped forwards. He looked ferocious and strong. The guy walked away and shook his head at the bar. Kamil stepped close to Michael.

'Are you all right, pal?' Michael said.

'Fucking guy came in and wanted a square go. Said what was I doing chatting up his ex-girlfriend. I said aye, all right, I'll give you a square go, come on outside. And then he backed off. Fucking shitebag.'

Kamil's eyes were black and shining with adrenalin. He licked his lips.

'Are you all right, pal?' Michael said again.

'Aye. I'll give him a square go if he wants,' Kamil said and he breathed deeply and looked over his shoulder.

The lassie, Michelle, waved again, and shouted 'Kamil, come and meet my daddy.'

The BNP men put their glasses on the bar and walked past Michael and Kamil, out of the pub.

'Are you coming?' Kamil said.

'Nah, I'll go back and check on my soup. See you after.'

'See you after.'

Michael stepped out to the cool air, saw the BNP men walking away on the other side of the road, and went home for his soup.

Trish and her pal were crashed out on the couch when he
returned to the house. The television showed pictures of those
silent horses again. Trish stretched a naked arm and waved at
Michael. She yawned. The house smelt of soup and hash. His
brother's boots were under the table by the window.

'He home?' Michael said.

'Gone for a sleep on your bed.'

'Kay?'

'No.'

He went into the kitchen. Trish had switched the cooker
off like he'd asked but she'd also eaten some soup. A lot of it.
The pot had orange rings on the inside, where the soup had
once been. Three blatant bowls sat unwashed in the sink.

They were putting their clothes on when he came into the
living room. The guy was struggling into his combats and
Trish grabbed onto the back of them and jumped, pulling them
up over his arse. The pair of them laughed and fell back onto
the sofa and Trish reached for the remote control. There was
nowhere to go. Nowhere even to beat his fists against the wall.
They all had to fuck off out of his flat. Once before, after a
row with Kay, he'd sat out where the chute was and now he
did it again, taking a black coffee and a couple of ginger nuts
and his book. He closed his eyes and leaned his head against
the cold wall and stayed there until Kay found him and said,
'Michael, get a grip.'

She took him into the lounge for a smoke and a drink, put
a Bob Marley tape into the player, and the night turned into a
session where all the soup got eaten and they sent Stephen, Trish's
man, down the stair for more drink, because nobody had
work or uni the next day and nobody seemed to want to stop.

Kat 1991

As well as the job in the paper shop, Kat took a job going round houses collecting forms and conducting interviews. It's for the census, she would say to people with sudden fear on their faces, believing she was from the social or the police or the housing. They would let her in and sit her down while she asked the questions and wrote their answers if they needed help with their forms. Birnie Court was one of her blocks and she was back again to get the houses she'd missed the last time. The same houses were deserted. A peek through the letter boxes showed piles of letters on the hall floor, bare boards and little else. Giro drops. But one such house had a woman and a boy in it. The boy rode a tricycle in the hall and the woman took Kat past him and into the living room.

'Oh sorry, apologies, I've not got my carpets yet,' the woman said. 'Or my couch.'

She made Kat sit in the only chair which was an armchair and Kat didn't want to but the woman leaned against the wall and told her on you go. Kat asked her questions and recorded the woman's answers. Age: twenty-three. Dependents: one, aged two. Job: unemployed.

'I was an auxiliary at Stobhill,' she said, 'but I can't work it round my son.' Her boy pedalled himself into the living room. 'Does that count?'

'Well, yes, but I need to put what you're doing now,' Kat said. 'It's to record this moment in time.'

The woman leaned against the wall and stared at her boy.

'That's you done,' Kat said and the woman, when she closed the door said, 'Thanks for coming.'

Kat saw too many women like her and too many households with no men in them. Too many families with no income because their jobs had gone or they couldn't afford childcare. Does anybody see this? Kat thought, does anybody know we're here?

Helen McDermott

You had a good view from the flats, you know, looking out the window and that, pass your time of day. I used to sit at the window for hours, watching people coming up and down. And night-time, the young ones used to steal the cars, knocked-off cars, motors, and drive round with police getting after them. You had some view watching the motors going out and in, you know, getting chased.

Michael 1992

It was an early start. Out of doors while the sun was buried under the sky. The walk down Petershill Drive in the smirr, through the blind tunnel, into Germiston, right on to Royston Road then left at the lights and down the road to the Blochairn fruit market. Barely a car on the road and a day's grafting ahead of him. Then the walk back at the end of the day, arms aching from lifting the crates and cartons of fruit. That's why he borrowed the work van after his workmates told him he'd be daft not to, especially because the gaffer was away for a couple of days. That's why he drove it home from the fruit market the night before and parked it outside his building. That's what he told himself as he stood by the van at six in the morning surveying the damage. The wee triangular window was smashed in and the radio gone. Turning desperately, as if he would be in time to catch whoever did it, all he saw were the still, knowing forms of the buildings around him. Not a soul. So he drove down the roads he used to walk down and instead of driving with the heating and the radio on, pushing back against the driver's seat and stretching his hands to meet the steering wheel, he sat hunched and agitated, ruminating on how he could fix the window without his boss knowing. It wasn't even a nice van. The radio was shite. They'd steal anything, but.

Iris 1992

Iris had promised her neighbours she'd get the papers and rolls for them so after a cup of tea she took Zeus with her. In the foyer there was a gorgeous wee bedside table that one of the rich folk had chucked out. A couple of other items were there too, including a mirror – but Iris already had a mirror she was happy with – and a wall clock, but having no desire to see another wall clock she didn't want that one. She told herself to remember to call in on the concierges when she was back with the messages. After walking Zeus on the empty field she popped into the paper shop. Zeus waited outside and she bought her cigarettes off the student lassie who didn't mind that she asked to pay for each set of papers and rolls separately so as not to get confused with the money.

She walked into the concierge office and the concierge stood up.

'Graeme, that wee bedside table down there, it's been thrown away, hasn't it? Because it would do for Pamela and Liam's bedroom with the baby.'

The concierge held out his arms. 'I've been buzzing you for the past half an hour. I was on my way up.'

'Did you guess I'd be after it? Second Hand Rose will have that.'

'No. It's Pamela.'

'What's happened? Has she phoned?'

'The hospital did. They've a message for you.'

'Oh good God.' Iris felt as if her legs had snapped. She held onto the concierge's arm.

'It's good news,' he said. 'She's had a baby girl.'

Iris cried. She put her hands over her face and they shook as she cried. Graeme kissed her cheek and told her that visiting hours were from eleven until twelve-thirty and the midwife said that Pamela was fine and the baby was pink and healthy.

'That baby wasn't meant to come out for another three weeks.

I don't know if Pamela even had her bag packed. Oh Christ, I need to clean my house. They'll be bringing the baby back.'

The concierge said he'd run the messages up the stair to the elderly folk and if Iris left her key with him on her way out, he'd drop the bedside table up for her. Iris dabbed at her eyes with her knuckles and went upstairs with Zeus to prepare for the hospital and the baby.

Michael 1992

His workmates called him a jammy bastard because he'd got away with it. A guy at the fruit market had a pal who worked at a scrappies so the two of them drove the van to the scrappies and they got a window and fitted it there and then. When the gaffer came back he never noticed.

The long walks home weren't too bad that week. Each afternoon the Glasgow sun was out, throwing itself against the windows of the Red Road Flats. One afternoon he came down Petershill Drive and saw a woman taking a baby out of a car. The woman was tall with a graceful bobbed haircut. A younger man and woman stood next to her, holding hands. They all watched the baby and as Michael passed, he saw a pink new-born face amid the blankets and the wool.

Kamil 1992

He began by taking her home from the restaurant and seeing her in to her building safe as he sat in the car. Then she invited him up and showed him the damp on her walls and opened the doors to her freezing rooms. She asked to see his flat and soon after they were sharing a bed and not long after that she moved in with him. Unlikely love, to others perhaps, but proper heartfelt, spirited love to Kamil.

'I've got this ghost,' he said. 'Bob. He doesn't bother me. Are you all right with ghosts?'

'Aye, fine. The more the merrier.'

Like Kamil, the pigeons bothered Michelle more. And anyway, the flat was hardly ever quiet enough to hear footsteps or goings on because Michelle liked her indie pop and talking on the telephone and the house was always full with her crazy pals. Her da came up from time to time and talked to Kamil about golf. One time he showed him his golf clubs.

'I got the message,' Kamil said to Michelle, later.

The pigeons kept coming. He spent a morning throwing two and one pence pieces at the window to scare them away.

'Want to pack that in? I'm trying to read my magazine,' his missus had said.

Kamil pinned a bed sheet from the veranda railing to the concrete ceiling. It kept the pigeons away but it blocked the sky out too. They read the Saturday papers for a while until a pigeon saw its way behind the sheet and careered about the veranda, flying into the soft puff of the sheet and the hard glass, fluttering and squawking.

'I can't stand this,' Kamil said and he was scared, more so than of Bob the ghost or the tough guys in the pubs.

They fed the cat and shut the door behind them.

Kamil paced about on the landing while they waited for the lift. His neighbour's door opened a crack and Adam poked his head out.

'Oh, hiya pal, it's you,' he said and raised his arm and his eyebrows and shut the door.

'We could ask him to get us a telly,' Michelle said.

Kamil furrowed his brow and looked at her.

'No,' they both said as the lift arrived.

'Where are we going?'

The doors slid shut. Kamil looked at the lift buttons.

'I've pressed the ground floor, son,' a woman in a beige coat said. Michelle smiled at her.

'Will we get some hash in for the weekend?' Kamil said and pressed a button on the lift.

The woman shifted her handbag on her shoulder and tightened her mouth.

'I'm all out of marijuana,' their dealer said when they sat on his couch. 'My supplier taxed me a bit too heavily and I didn't get as much as I usually do. But I've got these.' He opened the neck of a scrunched paper bag and took out a bottle. 'Co-codamols 500 milligrams.'

'Nah, you're all right,' Michelle said and they stood up.

They tried the next block. Sometimes they got their hash from Trevor with the hat and the mad dog. He usually invited them in and made a ceremony of presenting his stash before they bought it. But this time he shook his head and put a foot between his dog and the door and said he was all out.

'We know Kyle,' Kamil said. Kyle was their pal who knew everyone and got everyone anything. He was a helpful pal to have. Use my name any time you need it. It'll get you far, he used to say to them.

'I know you know Kyle.' That was all Trevor said, then before he closed the door he said, 'How are you keeping, Michelle?'

'Aye, all right,' Michelle said and when they were back in the lift Kamil said, 'You know some crackpots.'

'I can't help that,' Michelle said.

Finally they tried a dealer they'd never been to before in a block they knew barely anyone in. One-eight-three Petershill Drive.

'Will we try Kyle's name?' Michelle said and Kamil said yes but shat it. He didn't know whether to make himself look full of it or inconspicuous but eventually opted for the swagger.

Floor fourteen had a fluorescent light that flickered. Three of the doors had doormats, plants, wee brass ornaments and one had an umbrella leaning against the wall, point down. The last door was plain. No name. Kamil knocked. Nothing. They waited, listening for footsteps. Kamil knocked again. Still nothing.

'You sure this is the house?' Kamil said.

'Aye,' Michelle said. 'Kyle told me about it.'

She knocked this time. Nothing. Knocked again and suddenly a hand pushed the letter box open. Michelle shrieked and stepped back.

'What are you wanting?' a voice said. The voice was young and wary, its tone hard.

Kamil bent towards the letter box.

'We know Kyle,' he said.

'That wee prick.'

'We don't know him that well.' Kamil turned to Michelle and shrugged but Michelle said, 'That's my pal he's talking about.' She had a way of speaking out that landed him in it. Kamil put a finger to his lips.

'Eh?' the voice said from the letter box.

'Listen, mate, we were told you could sort us out with some hash. Kyle sent us your way.'

'You can tell Kyle that if he comes near this house again with his fucking fake tenners, I'll toe his balls.'

The voice sounded too young to be toeing anyone's balls.

'Is your da in, son?' Kamil said.

'Aye.' The boy stopped. 'How much are you wanting?'

'A half Q.' Kamil's back was aching. 'Why am I bending down talking to a letter box?' he said to Michelle, who shook her head.

'Listen, wee man, open the door will you and go get your da.'

'Wait there,' the voice said.

Footsteps sounded and Kamil looked around. 'Bit mental this,' he said and Michelle tapped her heel on the floor.

The footsteps returned and a grubby hand came out of the letter box again.

'Fifteen quid,' the voice said. It was the same boy. 'Give us the money and I'll pass out your gear.'

'Aye, right you are,' Kamil said. 'Open the door.'

'No,' the voice said and then it went quiet. Kamil could hear himself breathing. Michelle had stopped tapping her heel. He had fifteen quid in his pocket.

'Are you gonna give me the money or what?' the voice said.

Kamil stuffed the notes into the boy's hand and watched as the letter box closed. He stood in front of Michelle and waited and when nothing happened he shook his head and cursed Kyle. As he was clenching his fist, ready to thump the door and walk away, the letter box opened again and the hand held out a tiny clingfilmed package.

'Now fuck off and mind and tell Kyle he's getting toed,' the voice said.

'Wee prick,' Kamil said quietly and took the package just as the door with the umbrella outside opened. An old gent in a cap and smart shoes came out and picked up his brolly. He glanced at Kamil and Michelle and Kamil thrust his fist into his pocket.

'The polis raided them last week. I don't know how long they'll keep up this cloak and dagger shite. It's getting right on my tits, I can hardly hear my telly.'

He called the lift and stood silently with his back to them. Kamil and Michelle got in the lift with him when it arrived and they all stood silently as it took them down to the ground.

Concierges 1993

Mrs Donoghue called up for a wee bit of help on the same day that Mr O'Brien threw himself off the thirtieth floor. She wanted help to move her couch out from the wall because she said she'd taken a notion to clean behind it. They did it on Saturdays, the suicides, or when the weans were coming home from school. That's how it felt anyway, but if he added them all up, and he didn't want to, maybe he'd find no pattern whatsoever, just a bunch of tortured human beings. John went up at the end of his shift, just before the back shift started. Mrs Donoghue kept her house awfully neat.

'Poor Mr O'Brien,' she said. 'What a terrible shame.'

She was right. He'd only moved into the flats a few months ago, without a home because his wife had kicked him out, but most of the residents knew who he was because he looked so bad. He didn't shave and rarely washed his hair. He looked at his shoes when he walked. He struggled to get words out and John used to have to lean close to him to hear and it irritated him, which he didn't feel proud about but there it was. And he'd made an awful mess throwing his body onto the concrete. Nobody should come to that. It was a terrible waste and a terrible shock.

'So this is the couch to be humphed, is it?'

Mrs Donoghue took the cushions off it and moved her Hoover and its cord out of John's way.

'I've had this settee twenty-three years,' she said. 'And there's not a mark on it despite all those grandweans of mine clambering all over it.'

'Aye, you keep your house nice,' John said and moved one side of the couch at a time, lifting it out from the wall. There was very little dust behind it.

'You sit for a bit,' Mrs Donoghue said and pulled the Hoover behind the sofa and switched it on. John looked at the telly. The horseracing was on and John wondered if Mrs Donoghue had had a wee flutter. She did from time to time and made it known to practically the whole block that she was seventy pounds to the rich or thirty-five or fifty or whatever it was. That reminded John.

'Mrs Donoghue,' he said when she'd finished her hoovering. He stood up and pushed the couch back against the wall. 'You know if someone comes to your door selling stuff just say you're not interested, right?'

'Sit yourself down again, son.'

John sat and leaned forwards.

'Or if you get someone asking to borrow stuff over and

over, you just say no, or you tell me or one of the concierges about it.'

'I'm an old woman, son, but I'm not an eejit.'

'Okay.' She was right. He needn't have worried. There was no shocking and no telling Mrs Donoghue.

'So who's been robbed or conned or led up the garden path then?' she asked.

'Well,' John said. 'There's a lady in Twenty Petershill Court. She got some new neighbours in and thought they were very nice and friendly but they kept knocking on her door and asking to borrow tin foil. And she just thought they must be doing an awful lot of baking. But they borrowed all this tin foil and never brought her in any baking at all; no cakes, no biscuits, nothing. So they keep on borrowing the foil and she's too polite to suggest they buy their own tin foil so one day she says to the concierge, Martin, "Would you mind, son, just saying to that young couple could they buy their own tin foil for their baking in the future." Martin hits the roof and tells her it's not baking they're doing. And he tells her what it was for. You know what they were using it for, don't you?'

'Aye,' Mrs Donoghue said and took off her housecoat. 'Heroin. Or yon crack's the up and coming thingmy nowadays isn't it?'

'Just you watch who comes to your door.'

She put the cushions back onto the couch and plumped them into the corners. Then she pulled in the Hoover cord and wheeled it into the hallway.

'Is that you done for the day?' she said.

'Aye, I'm on my way home now.'

John made to stand up but Mrs Donoghue said, 'Will you have a wee orange before you go?'

'Oh, no thank you.'

'Go on, how about a wee half?'

A wee half might be just the ticket. It had been a bastard

of a day with Mr O'Brien throwing himself off. It made John think about his Uncle Charlie who was under the doctor for this, that and the other and was making all sorts of threats. People seemed to struggle through this life.

'Aye, I'll take a wee half,' John said and looked about Mrs Donoghue's immaculate living room with the Mills and Boon books on the shelf and the lampshade with the cream tassels and the cross-stitch pictures in frames on the wall and sewn onto the front of cushions. He pulled a circular cushion from behind his back and studied it. Freedom Come All Ye, it said in stitching on one side and it made John smile.

He looked up just as Mrs Donoghue came back into the living room with two plates. She handed one to John and kept the other. No glass. And on his plate was half an actual orange. There was his wee half. He ate it, but, and listened to Mrs Donoghue tell him about the bingo she was going to that night, as a treat for spring-cleaning her house. The orange was sweet. He had such a thirst on his way down the stair that he was tempted to take George into the Brig for an actual wee half but knew he oughtn't socialise with the people he worked for. I'll just knock this up as another one of my Red Road stories, he thought and went on home.

Kamil 1993

'Come on and we'll go to Leigh and Gary's house,' Michelle said one Friday night in the Broomfield Tavern. A nutty white boy had threatened Kamil in the toilets again.

'Who do you think you are?' His chin jutted towards Kamil.
'I'm not interested, mate.'
'You will be fucking interested when I take you outside.'
'Come on right now then.'
Kamil prayed the guy would back down like they always did.
'I'll get you later then.'
Michelle stroked the back of his neck and looked defiantly

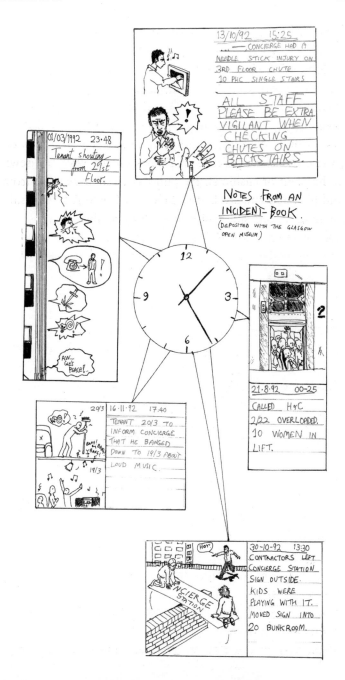

NOTES FROM AN
INCIDENT-BOOK.
(DEPOSITED WITH THE GLASGOW
OPEN MUSEUM)

round the pub. Her best mate had taken up with Kyle and the four of them drank up and went to Leigh and Gary's.

Hash. Bliss. Cushions, couch, soft carpet. Lights from other flats making the buildings seem closer than they really were. Table with Rizlas, lighters, pots and packets of dope, teapot. Happy faces. Leigh and Gary with their haircuts and no nonsense. Kids at the granny's so bunk beds for anyone who wanted to stay the night. Michael and Kay already there. Warmth and chat and smoke-filled air. Take That.

'Get that crap off the stereo,' someone said.

The girl who liked Take That tutted. Michael chose a Bob Dylan tape and put that on. It was a good, happy crowd at Leigh and Gary's. Michelle's best mate stood at the window and said, 'Look, that's my living room.' Kamil stood with her and looked where she pointed at a yellow window directly across from the window at which they stood.

'What's going on in all those rooms?' Michelle's pal said.

They talked about what to do later on. Michael's pal's band played in the Furlong in town and it was decided they'd head over there. Leigh and Gary would stay and smoke some more because that's all they wanted to do.

'You'll never guess what happened to me,' Michael said and told them he'd nearly been hit by a falling nappy, thrown from a window in One-five-three block.

Kamil said once he'd nearly been hit by a falling pan loaf. Michelle said the wind blew her off her feet one day and she fell on the path outside her building. Michael said he'd just missed being hit by a roller skate. Kay said she saw a kitchen worktop sticking out of the grass, with the concierges pulling on it, trying to lever it out of the earth.

'You know, pennies don't speed up if you throw them out the window,' Gary said, 'so you wouldn't get killed from a penny hitting you on the head.'

'You would from a kitchen worktop,' Leigh said.

Gary's voice changed. 'Whoa whoa whoa, what the fuck do you think you're doing?'

Michelle's pal's boyfriend was in the corner of the room, holding a lighter underneath some silver foil. He looked up.

'What?' The lighter went out and he flicked it on again.

'Pal, we're not into that here. You can't do that in this house.'

'I'm not bothering anyone.'

'Yes you are, me.'

The guy seemed confused. Gary stopped the tape and turned on the big light. People rubbed their foreheads. Kamil got up for a pish but before he went he watched Kyle fold the foil over his smack and put his gear into a small tin. He stood up slowly, scowling, knocked over a can of coke and kicked it with his foot.

'Are you coming?' he said to Michelle's pal and she got up too and put on her coat.

They walked past the people sprawled around the living room and didn't say goodbye. Gary turned off the big light, Kamil went to the bathroom and he heard the Take That fan saying 'Can we put 'Could it be Magic' on?'

'No!' Lots of voices shouted at her.

'Hippy cunts,' she said and Bob Dylan carried on with 'Sad Eyed Lady of the Lowlands'.

Incident Book 1994

7.47 p.m. Saturday. Jumper. Police and ambulance called. D.O.A. Suicide not tenant of Ten Red Road or any of the Red Road Flats. Concierge cleaned up and washed concrete. Window on thirtieth floor landing secured.

Michael 1994

Today would be the day he finally got some money off Trish. No longer a student, he didn't qualify for help with anything anymore and he hadn't got a job yet. He wanted something he'd studied for, some kind of job in the community, working with people he understood. Kay still worked.

'No, Kamil,' he said as he passed him on the way out of the pub. 'I can't have another one, I'm going food shopping and I'm getting a tenner off Trish because it's giro day.'

'Good luck,' Kamil said.

Fate or something produced Trish. She was walking towards the entrance to Two-one-three, their building.

'Hey,' Michael shouted. 'Tenner.'

Trish stopped and turned.

'All right, Michael?' she said and smiled.

He wondered if she'd heard him.

'Hand it over,' he said and held out his hand. 'We're going shopping.'

'Michael,' Trish said, 'look what I've got. Put your hand in my pocket.'

'If it's a tenner, I'll put my hand in.'

'It's better than a tenner. Go on.'

Trish's cheeks were flushed and the wind stuck strands of hair to her pink lips. She held open her pocket and Michael saw the edges of a crumpled paper bag.

'Go on, Michael, put your hand in.' She was teasing him. He knew it instantly.

'You don't want to go shopping now, do you?'

'No. Where'd you get them from?'

'Donald.'

He didn't know who the fuck Donald was but he said oh aye and they caught the lift to the flat.

'Will we wait for Kay?' he said.

'If you like.'

They didn't wait for Kay or his brother. But they did leave them some and when Kay came through the door not long after, they stood up and said, 'Hmm, what's for tea? Shall we have mushrooms perhaps?' and Kay ate what was left for her and

said, 'Who left my cornflakes out, was it you?' and Trish said no
it definitely was not her, she didn't eat anything in this house
except mushrooms, and Kay said, 'You ate our soup, you eat our
crisps and now you've eaten my fucking cornflakes.'

'You're always eating our food,' Michael joined in.

'I am not.'

'You are so.'

'And you shag in our bed,' Kay said.

'No!'

She did. Michael and Kay had worked it out from the rum-
pled sheets and condom wrappers.

'You eat our food and you shag in our bed!'

Kay was laughing and Trish picked up the box of cornflakes
and said, 'I bought these cornflakes, you lying bastards. Look,
that's the shop next to where my ma stays.' She pointed to the
price label.

'Well that's the only thing you've bought this year.' Kay
grabbed the box but Trish held onto it. They fought with the
box and Trish won and tipped the packet over Kay's head and
Kay swatted her hand through her hair and grabbed the box
off Trish and shook it as if she was shaking confetti and
Michael grabbed a handful of cornflakes and put them down
Trish's back and Kay's front and the two girls pulled at the
back of his jeans and shoved their hands full of cornflakes into
his pants.

'Come on,' he said. 'We'll get a carry out and a fish supper
and sit on the grass.'

And that's what they did, the three of them smirking as
they walked until they flopped onto the grass by Birnie Court.

They ate their fish supper and lay on the grass, Kay curling
herself into Michael's body, his arms around her, one hand clasp-
ing the side of her head, Trish with her arms wide at her sides.

'Fuck, they're huge, aren't they?' Michael said.

They looked at the blocks, so close and so high Michael

felt they might fall over and flatten them. The way the clouds moved made the blocks seem as if they were moving too.

'Wow,' Kay said.

'Gravestones.'

'Eh?'

'Gravestones.' Trish said again. 'This place is a cemetery.'

Kay shifted her position. Michael cupped a hand over his eyes and stared.

'Fucking great gravestones. That's what they are.'

She was right; they stood with their lower floors in shadow and the tips of them in soft sun, reaching from the ground, tilting towards the sky or God or whatever else was up there.

Kamil 1994

One Friday night Kamil went with Michelle and her pal and Kyle to Leigh and Gary's house but Leigh and Gary turned them away at the door.

'We're not having anyone round tonight,' they said.

'You're joking.'

'No we're not.'

The four of them stared at each other and then back at Leigh and Gary. 'We just want some quality time together. We never get any time on our own.'

'Kyle, fuck off for a second,' Kamil said and when Kyle had gone through the door to the stairs, Kamil asked them, 'Is it because he's with us? We've told him he's not allowed to smoke any of his drugs.'

But Leigh and Gary assured him that it wasn't because of Kyle, they just wanted a night in to themselves. That was that.

Kamil and Michelle and the other two went back to Kamil's house and threw Kyle out at the door. They told him to go and do his thing and come back when he'd finished because they weren't having anyone smoking heroin in their house. He came back half cut and the other three were half cut and he said to them, 'Do you want to do something dead funny?' Of course they did.

He led them outside to the phone box and called the police. Putting on a conspiratorial voice, as if he and the police had an understanding, he said, 'There's a guy jumping about with a gun. Aye, he's acting like a lunatic. One-two three Petershill Drive, nineteen floor, flat three.' He gave the police Leigh and Gary's address.

'Now we take our seats and watch the show,' Kyle said and they went to Michelle's pal's house because she had a view of Leigh and Gary's house from her living room window. They laughed in the dark at the thought of the polis arriving with their battering ram and raiding Leigh and Gary's, their place loaded with hash because it was a weekend and they usually got an ounce in on a weekend. When the police turned up with their vans, the four at the window laughed and laughed and wished they could be closer to see the look on Leigh and Gary's faces. They saw enough to nearly make them die laughing. In the yellow room across from them they saw police coming in heavy handed, lifting cushions, pointing and gesturing at Leigh and Gary who stood flailing and shaking their heads as the police did over their place.

'Oh my God, they're tearing up the couch,' Michelle whispered and they stopped laughing after a while because the police pulled the stuffing out of the couches and stayed in the flat for nearly an hour, searching.

Kamil and Michelle walked casually out of Michelle's building and went to the Broomfield for a quiet drink, vowing never to let on that they knew who'd called the polis on Leigh and Gary, as they knew they'd inevitably be asked. Any number of men promised access to guns in the Broomfield. It was a currency. Everybody talked about them. The police knew they were about.

'He's a crackpot,' Kamil said about Kyle.

'Aye, he's getting worse,' Michelle said. 'It's my pal I worry about.'

'It was funny, but.'

Incident Book 1995

Fire in supermarket. Fire brigade attended and broke into main doors with force. Fire subsequently put out. Bingo hall below damaged.

Iris 1995

Iris was furious. She'd planned to go to the bingo on Saturday and take Pamela, and Pamela had agreed to go with her and be in her company which would have been a relief and a pleasure. Now the bingo was closed indefinitely and there were rumours that it would never reopen. The water from the firemen's hoses had leaked to the bingo hall below and the whole place was saturated, apparently. All the electrics and upholstery ruined. She stood outside the supermarket with Zeus waiting for the owners to come by and survey the damage. She planned to put her finger in their faces and tell them she knew it was an inside job, that she'd seen the stock run down for the past few weeks and that they'd ruined the lives of hundreds of women. She stood with her dog and watched the youngsters walk by in their groups or cycle by, standing on their pedals. Nobody from the supermarket came. A couple of rats shot past the entrance to the Women's Centre in the slab block. A man about twelve floors up tipped bread from a bread bag.

Nicola, Pamela's old friend, stopped to say hello. Iris hardly ever saw her. Her hair was long. It suited her.

'How's your man?' Iris said.

'He's working the day. He's all right.'

'One that's still got a job, hang on to him.'

'I know,' Nicola said. 'Tell Pamela I was asking after her.' She paused and smiled. 'Tell her I'm expecting. Due next June.'

'Oh that's lovely,' Iris said. 'Pamela's got a wean. She's three now. They live with us.'

She called Zeus, who didn't need a leash, and went to the paper shop for her fags.

She told the young student lassie that she couldn't believe there would be no more bingo buses, that there would be no more chance of her winning any money, of having something to spend above and beyond what little she knew was coming in every week.

Kat 1995

Kat watched the woman with the dog leave. She would miss the bingo buses too, because the women were always popping in for mints and magazines and it made the day go quickly.

Two Saturday girls worked with her and Fern. They spoke in whispers as they stacked the shelves, and Kat never understood why they didn't like her to join in. Sex. They talked as if they were wee wifeys. Men. Condoms. Catholic roulette. Perhaps they didn't think Kat had ever had sex. She did some catching up when she got to university, yes, but she knew about condoms, she knew about the pill, and she didn't intend to have a baby before taking on academia. You know you can insist on a condom, she wanted to say to the girls who said their men, their older men, well into their twenties and them still in their teens, didn't like the feel of them.

A woman came in the shop and the girls stopped whispering. Fern put down the Saturday supplement she was reading and said, 'Can I help you?'

'Twenty Marlboro Lights please.'

The girls and Kat turned their heads to stare at the woman.

'Will you be wanting anything else?'

Kat thought she was going to say 'Ma'm' as she'd done once before but she didn't, she just tilted her head deferentially.

'Give me one of your lighters too,' the woman said and picked coins out of her purse.

They all stared at her back as she pulled on the door and stepped outside.

'Marlboro Lights,' one of the girls said.

'Who does she think she is?'

'I've never had a Marlboro Light.'

'What's wrong with a plain old Embassy No.1?'

'Some people have more money than sense. They should take away her benefits.'

Kat laughed with the others. They never sold Marlboros. She used the price gun to put tickets on some cans of soup and one of the girls took them from the counter where Kat stood and put them on the shelves. Fern pulled the other packet of Marlboro Lights to the front of the shelf and stacked the boxes of matches.

'Will I put the kettle on?' one of the girls said.

'Her man hits her,' Fern said and the girls held onto the things they were pricing or putting away and stopped to listen. But Fern didn't say any more. She just pressed her lips together.

One of the girls started up. 'I'd hit her if I was her man. Torn-faced cow.'

'It hurts to be hit, you know,' the other girl said and she coughed into her sleeve.

Fern picked up her glass of water from behind the counter and said, 'No one's saying it doesn't hurt.'

Kat remembered, perhaps they all remembered, the time she'd come into the shop with yellow smudges on her jaw and cheekbone and none of them said anything. Not then, not ever. No one said anything to anyone ever.

The door burst open. Two men, unsteady on their feet, came to the counter and waved their arms. One carried a penknife, the other a broken bottle. With their drug-ravaged faces they weren't frightening, but their voices were loud and because they demanded money and because they were carrying weapons, the women didn't refuse them. Kat and the two girls moved to stand next to Fern. They watched her open the till and they all stood still and firm while the men crashed out of the shop.

Afterwards, shrugs, half-smiles, a few words, then, 'Right, if nobody's going to put the kettle on, I will.' Fern clasped her hands together and went out to the back shop.

Azam Khan

I remember one time I went to the chippy for a pint of milk because we ran out of milk so I only had thirty pence, forty pence, whatever milk was, and I had to go up the hill – there was a wee hill there, I think they called it Chippy Hill. So I was going up Chippy Hill, went up there, got my milk and I was coming back down and there was two drug addicts standing there and they were like that, got any money? Giz your money. And I was like that, no, I haven't got any money on me, I only had enough for a pint of milk. And they were like that, giz your milk then. I said, that's not gonna happen here and they're like that, giz your milk or we'll stab you. Again, like I says, Barmulloch was one of those places where if you were pushed about by one, everybody was going to push you about so you had to turn round and go like that, fucking stab us then. I'm not giving you my milk. You had to stand up. And because they were drug takers and all that there wasn't much to them so I pushed one of them and he fell down Chippy Hill. The other one just ran off. And when I walked down Chippy Hill he was at the bottom and was like that, you didn't have to do that, you could have just said no. And you're like that, don't do that again. But aye, in that way, it kind of prepared you for life because you had to be a tough guy and you had to toughen up because there was a lot of nutters walking about.

Iris 1995

She should have been excited about the party she was throwing
for her son, but Pamela was off the rails again. The wean wasn't
enough to keep her clean.

She opened her door and the girls were there again saying
they had money for Pamela that they owed her. Iris let them in
and watched them talk to Pamela as Lauren played on the
floor. The girls needled at Pamela, Iris could tell. They were no
good and they didn't care.

'Ma, will you watch the wean for an hour?' Pamela asked.

'I'll put her to bed then,' Iris said.

'Would you?'

Liam was long gone out of the house. Iris kicked him out
because she found needles in the bedside drawer when she was
looking for nappies. And Pamela would be next, God help her,
if she didn't draw back from whatever road those girls were
tempting her down.

The wean didn't sleep well. The wean gret a lot and suf-
fered from constant colds. But the wean was a wean. She was
the most precious thing Pamela had and Pamela was messing
it up.

'I need to talk with you, my lassie,' Iris said as Pamela was
leaving.

'I know, Ma,' Pamela said. Iris knew she knew. But she
couldn't stop.

As the family and the neighbours arrived for the party, Iris told
them to tiptoe past Pamela's room where Lauren slept. She put
Queen on the stereo and then somebody found a tape of seventies
hits and that got the dancing started. Her son had a look of
shock on his face when the lights came on in the living room
and people jumped out at him, bursting party poppers and
chucking balloons in the air. Carol from up the stair did the

stripogram, as she'd promised, and had them screeching and shrieking as she sat on the table and burst out of her bra.

Lauren woke up with all the noise and asked where her mammy was. Iris held her close and told Carol to make herself decent, gave her the twenty quid she'd offered for the strip, and the adults put their happy, boozy faces close to Lauren's and kissed her smooth cheeks and said she was the dead spit of her mammy.

Pamela didn't come back till the morning. That was it. She had to go.

Kamil 1996

The cat hadn't bothered with anything until the day Michelle's best mate turned up knocking on the door. She was with her boyfriend, the same one, who'd done some time in prison. Kyle had his hands in his pockets and his hair combed down onto his forehead. He didn't look at Kamil; only at the cat that sprang into the hall and hissed and arched its back. The two of them barged in, Michelle's best mate zipping and unzipping her jacket, playing with her fingers, jerking her head and speaking quickly and tearfully.

'They're going to hurt the weans,' she said.

'What?'

'They're going to hurt the weans.'

Over and over, the energy of the pair. 'They're going to hurt the weans.'

'Who?'

She didn't stop for breath, her voice climbing higher and higher. They moved into the living room.

'Sit down,' Kamil said. She didn't sit down and kept on talking. Her man followed her in and began to talk over her and Kamil watched Michelle, caught between the two of them, turning her head, her face frightened. She looked at Kamil. He told Kyle to shut up.

'What is it? Who's getting the weans? Whose weans?'

'My niece and nephew. I'm looking after them for the weekend.'

'If we don't give them fifty quid,' Kyle said.

'Who?'

'The dealers. They're coming back in half an hour,' Michelle said. She was back on the zipping and unzipping.

'Basically,' her man said and he sniffed, 'we owe them money and they came back for it. When we didn't have it they said they'd come back and kick the shit out of everyone in the house. Including the weans.'

'Get the weans over here then,' Kamil said and Michelle nodded.

'So we need fifty quid.'

'Aye, but get the weans over here first.'

'Can you give us fifty quid, but?'

It was Kyle again. His voice took on something else, a nip, a brittle note. Michelle looked at her friend.

'What's going on?' she said and her friend cried. She slowed her speech down. She put her head on Michelle's shoulder and then she said, 'I'm really sorry Michelle, I wouldn't ask but I'm feart for the weans, for what they'll do. I don't care what they do to me but I need to pay them off.'

Kamil went to his wallet and felt for notes.

'I've got twenty quid.'

They almost reached out for it. He saw their mouths open. Michelle's best friend touched her zip and looked at her man.

'You haven't got any more?' Kyle said.

'Go get the weans.'

'Aye, we'll bring them over. Can I have the twenty quid?'

They were desperate; heads genuflecting, eyes keen and shameless. Kamil went to put the notes back in his wallet but looked at Michelle. She shrugged and said, 'She's my pal, Kamil, better give her the money.'

When she took the money Michelle's friend folded it carefully and put it in her pocket. She bent down and said, 'Hiya Fluffs.' The cat purred and nuzzled.

'See you after,' Michelle's friend said and Michelle nodded. She walked to the window and picked up a photo in its frame, then put it down again.

'Mind you bring the weans over,' Kamil said.

'Oh yes, oh yes,' Kyle and Michelle's friend said and they looked high, elated, delighted, as they walked out of the house.

Kamil and Michelle waited in for the weans but they never showed.

'We'll check on them in the morning,' Kamil said.

'Aye, I expect they're not even with her.'

She was right. The next day Michelle's best friend told her that Kyle had made her make up the story about the dealers and the weans as it was the only way they could get some money for a hit. They were desperate, she said. They'd have died without a hit. Michelle shouted down the telephone. 'You're my best friend and you did that to me? We went to school together, nursery together, we grew up together, we were dead tight me and you and this is what you do? You wanted your hit and you used those weans and our money to get it. Fuck the money, I don't even want the money, it isn't about the money.'

She pressed her knuckles to her cheeks and cried, standing by the window. A pigeon landed on the veranda and Kamil picked up a one pence piece and threw it. The pigeon flew away and Michelle turned into the room.

'Leave the pigeon alone,' she said and she was red in the face and Kamil took his fingers away from the pot of coins. The cat hopped onto the back of the couch and meowed.

Sharon McDermott

My pal asked me to keep a hold of her wee lassie while she went to the hospital. I said aye but I have to take my son to a Christmas party this afternoon so you'll need to be back for that. And I needed to go to the Rottenrow so I took the wee lassie with me. I went to the Rottenrow and then I think I went into town and then I came back, and there used to be a wee van that used to sit at the bottom of the flats and I went in and said have you seen my pal? and she said have you not heard and I said no what is it? – and her wee lassie was standing outside the van – and she said she's took an overdose and she's lying dead. And I was like, oh no, and I still had her wee lassie with me. So I went up the flat and everybody was outside this lassie's house, so I went up and shouted through the letter box and these two big polis just came out and said who are you? and I gave my name to them and they said who's the wee lassie? and I said that's my pal's wee lassie and they said do you know what's happened? and I said I've heard something but I don't know. And they said can I have a word with you outside on the landing? and I went out and the window was wide open and the lassie was sat outside waiting and they said she's dead. And I said what am I going to do with this wee lassie, will I take her to her granny's? The polis said we'll deal with that, but this lassie, she was only about four, and she came out and she's seen the window and she was like that, where's my mummy, where's my mummy, is my mummy okay? and it was instinct I think.

Kamil 1996

Two weeks later Kamil saw Kyle at a party. The sound of his voice caught him as he walked down the hall. He'd taken to mugging folk, Michelle told him, and there he was, telling his war stories with all these rapt faces listening to him say how he'd threatened this person and harmed that person and how the young guys now called him the Godfather of Springburn.

'You wee dick,' Kamil said.

'You what?'

Kyle scowled at Kamil who stood with his shoulders big and his hands out of his pockets.

'You want to watch who you're talking to,' the wee Godfather said.

'See you, you're nothing but a dick,' Kamil said and Kyle stood up and put his hand into his jacket as if he was going to pull something out so Kamil hooked him, hard. The room was covered in patterned carpet and Kamil saw the wee prick's face clear against the pattern before he walked coolly but quickly out of the door and up the road to the Broomfield.

Michael 1997

Three weeks later, in an empty house at last, Michael cooked lamb chops and totties and peas for Kay's birthday. He expected her in at six. He ate his plate of tea at eight and when she came in steaming at eleven and said she wasn't hungry, he smashed her plate onto the landing floor. Peas rolled everywhere. The lamb sat cold in a pile of gravy. Kay didn't even take off her coat, but got back in the lift and went out again. Michael sat in the hall and only stood up when his neighbour, the blue nose with the King Billy poster, opened his door and said, 'I thought someone was out here.'

'Not happy with your cookery?' he said and Michael got his mop and brush and cleared up. When Trish got in she told him she would have eaten Kay's dinner.

Kay came back at midnight and got into bed beside him.

'Happy Birthday,' Michael said.

'I'm pregnant,' she said.

'No.'

'Yes.'

'Did you do a test?'

'Two. I'm pregnant.'

He turned to hold her body because he thought she might be afraid. He saw her blinking in the dark. He was afraid too.

'It'll be all right,' he said.

'Aye.'

He wanted it. He was pleased. Delighted. Dear God. They'd be parents. It'd be beautiful. And Trish, she would surely have to fuck off now.

Concierges 1997

Wee Theo Orr was moving out of his flat on the thirteenth floor. He was moving down the stair to a house on the fourth floor because he couldn't move about much and it was closer to the ground if the lifts broke down and he had to walk. He came into the concierges' office with his paper and rolls. John and George were on days.

'Boys, would you mind giving me a wee hand shifting a bit of furniture?' He was full of business, waving his paper in one hand with his bag of rolls in the other.

'Aye, no bother, Theo,' John said.

'What time do you want us?'

'I'll get my breakfast into me and then I'll buzz down to you.'

'Right you are.'

John said that some of the tenants trod a fine line between respect and taking the piss but he liked wee Mr Orr. He sometimes gave him a cheeky racing tip and although John wasn't a betting man, he would put a couple of pound on Mr Orr's tip and it paid out near enough every time.

'So, we'll help Theo with his flit and then we'll see what's what,' George said. 'Who are they flowers for?'

'Sandy. You know Barbara, she went into labour a few nights ago and he says she raced in here saying Sandy, it's time,

it's time, the baby's coming, I'm in labour. So he phoned an
ambulance but fifteen minutes later it still hadn't arrived so he
says Barbara, hop in the car and I'll run you down to
Rottenrow. He got her there in time and her ma came in this
morning before you got here and said to give these flowers to
Sandy. Barbara got overloaded with them in the hospital and
she was sharing them out, like, to say thanks.'

'So where's the baby now? Where's Barbara?'

'Home.'

George gasped. His eyes went to the CCTV monitors. 'There's
a tiny wee baby in this block.'

'Aye. I never saw it. She'll bring him down when she's ready.'

'Welcome to Red Road.'

George gulped his tea and walked with his mug to the
kitchen.

'I tell you what,' John said, 'I'm surprised there's not been
more near misses in these flats with all these people over the
years. We should be trained in midwifery.'

'Careful what you wish for,' George said.

They left Allan in charge of the office and went up the stair to
Theo Orr's house. His door was open and his twin brother and
twin brother's wife were there too.

'We'll take the small things, the black bags and boxes and
the like. If you chaps could take the big items that would be
grand,' Theo said.

There were quite a few big items.

'All this?' George said.

'There's a wardrobe in the bedroom that needs to go down
too. Thank you boys, you're a great help.' Theo Orr was pan-
icking a bit, John could tell. He kept pushing his specs further
up his nose and changing direction in the living room, not
quite getting anywhere.

George and John took off their jumpers and made a start. They shifted a table first and left it in the landing outside the lift. They moved a sideboard next and a drawer fell out so they put it down and took out all the drawers and left them on the couch. When they were in the lift a couple of kids with a bike tried to get in too and George said, 'Boys, it's not going to work now is it?' and when they were gone he said, 'Is it me, or are the young team getting more and more dense?'

The flit went on for an hour and a half. A bed, a wardrobe, a telly and its stand, a nest of tables, a framed photograph of the Rangers 1972 European Cup Winners Cup team. Wee Theo Orr began to visibly relax. He'd got his sister-in-law working in the new house, unpacking boxes and putting crockery on shelves. He shook his head and looked about him, his old house bare with rectangles of bright clean carpet on which furniture had stood.

After the last piece of furniture he said, 'Lastly, I'd be so grateful if you'd take a picture of me,' and he stood by his window and his view and John snapped him portrait and landscape with the window wide open behind him. 'I won't see a view quite like this again.' Theo put the camera cord around his wrist and walked with the concierges to the door.

'Oh wait a wee second,' he said. 'Something for your trouble.' He came back with a carrier bag with cans of lager inside and George and John said, 'Oh Theo, you needn't have,' but when they were alone in the lift they said that they were looking forward to a cold lager at the end of their shift.

'See, you don't mind helping somebody out if you know you're appreciated,' John said. And then he laughed. 'Sandy and his flowers and us and our beer. I know what I'd rather have. He hasn't even got a missus to give his flowers to.'

Allan was desperate for a piss when they got back to the office and he got up from his chair in what seemed like a huff but when he came back from the toilet he laughed and showed the boys the incident he'd written in the incident book. *Maureen made another complaint about her neighbour's noise.* John looked at his watch.

'I'm not getting into that today. She can suffer Angus scraping butter on his toast for one more day. The woman's off her nut.'

'Scraping is scraping,' Allan said. 'It made it to the incident book.'

'It can stay there. George, gonna put these beers into the fridge so they'll be nice and cool for when we get home.'

George took the beers from the carrier bag and said, 'Oh look, there's the lager lovelies on these cans!' He held one out. 'Hello Susannah and your apple basket.' He put the bag on the table and took the cans out one by one. 'Mary, June, hello again Susannah and two Normas.'

'Let me see,' John said and George passed him a can. 'I thought they stopped these years ago.'

'Which lovelies do you want to take home with you?' George said.

'Can I have one?'

'Did you shift any furniture, Allan? No, you did not. So you can share Sandy's flowers.'

'Get yourself to fuck.'

John said, 'Wait a wee minute' and shook his head. With a finger pointing to the can's expiry date he walked over to George. 'Read that.'

'07/88.'

'07/88. That's eight years ago.'

Allan let out a laugh at the same time as answering the phone. 'Hello Ten Red Road Court concierge,' he said as George and John looked at the expiry dates on all the cans and put them back into the carrier bag.

John put the bag into the bin.

'Not taking your Tennent's home, boys?' Allan said when he was off the phone.

'I don't want to poison myself tonight,' George said. 'I've got a half marathon on the weekend.'

'If the students were here we could give them to them for their collection.'

'If the students were here we would be able to drink them because they would be in date.'

'I'm just saying they would look good on their beer towers.'

Allan picked up the incident book and wrote in it.

'Boys,' he said. 'That was the community police. They've had a call from Maureen, saying she's got a nuisance neighbour and can they come up and sort it out.'

The two fellas on the back shift came into the office and George and John put on their coats.

'Welcome to the mad house,' John said and George said 'Don't drink the beer.'

'The beer in the bin with the models on,' Allan explained. 'I used to collect them.'

'You're welcome to them. If wee Theo Orr comes in the office, ask him how long he's had they beers in his fridge for and if there's anything else he finds in there, we're not hungry or thirsty.'

Kamil 1997

Kamil worked hard in his new job. His shifts on the street with the teenagers in Possil ended at ten and he finished his evening in the office, writing up notes and leaving messages for the next day.

Michelle phoned. He almost didn't answer because he was headed for the door. 'Hiya, gonna do me a favour?' she said.

'I'm leaving now.'

'Good. I'm starving. Can you jump into a kebab shop and get us a kebab or a Chinese or something?'

He'd eaten a burger at eight when he was on the street.

'Can you not make yourself a piece and we'll go to the supermarket tomorrow. I'm so tired.'

'Please, oh please babe. Jump into a kebab shop or a Chinese or something.'

He'd do anything for her. So he jumped into a Chinese and read a newspaper while he waited. It was hard to read anything because he was exhausted. The kids he worked with were hard core. They had a pinch of respect for him based on where he lived but they were hard going all the same.

The man in the Chinese gave him free prawn crackers and he tore a hole in the bag, put them on the front passenger seat and ate them as he waited at the lights and drove on home. He was hungry after all.

When he got to Petershill Court he saw two police cars parked outside and blue and white tape strung across the entrance to his building. The police let him through and up to his house.

Concierges 1997

The concierge stationed in Twenty Petershill Court watched the man on the CCTV monitor. The only person in the foyer, he carried on as if he was out of his face on drink or drugs, pacing, head down, his hands jerking in his pockets. He was a sight, but not an unusual sight because the flats were full of junkies and drunkards and odd bods. He kept an eye, however. A tenant rang down and asked if a parcel had arrived for him. The concierge checked the shelf in the office and said no, nothing had come.

Another tenant, Jack McGann, let himself through the doors of building Ten and joined the man in the foyer. The two men, he could tell, were wary of each other; Jack stood still, his hands clasped behind his back, his rucksack between his feet, and his eyes flicking towards the other man and back to the lift. The concierge saw all this on the CCTV monitor. The other man sidestepped along the far wall, his back pressed against it, back and forth, from one side of the wall to the other.

When Jack McGann moved to press the lift button again –

perhaps it was never pressed in the first place – the strange man went for him. He pulled a knife from his pocket and stabbed Jack McGann's side and plunged the knife in and out of his body. Jack McGann, he opened his mouth and tried to turn his body away from the man but the man stabbed his back and kept stabbing him. Oh sweet Jesus, the concierge said and called the police and ran to the man's aid. The attacker was gone and blood spread out on the floor. Jack McGann was conscious but he was dying.

'Don't leave me,' he said and the concierge knelt in the blood and put his jumper under Jack McGann's head.

His breathing was shallow. He lay on his side, his cheek buried into the wool of the concierge's jumper, eyes blinking.

Does it hurt? the concierge wanted to ask and prayed that it didn't, that his body had gone beyond pain. He checked the wounds, tried to stop the bleeding, took off his shirt and tried to plug the gashes in the poor man's body.

'Don't leave me,' Jack McGann said again and the concierge knew that he knew he was dying and there was no time for running for relatives. His dying wouldn't wait.

'You're all right,' the concierge said and Jack McGann said again, 'Please don't leave me.'

'I won't leave you. I won't leave you.'

It was too bright a place to die. Too cold and bright. 'I won't leave you,' the concierge said.

He tried to resuscitate him and when the ambulance arrived the paramedics tried too but the concierge knew Jack McGann was gone and he knew the point at which he'd gone. The man had let his head sink heavily into the pillow of his jumper, he'd stopped struggling and seemed to turn in on himself; eyes, breath, chest, turned in and stopped. He didn't breathe again.

Kamil 1997

Kamil and Michelle stood in their flat and counted. They knew it took him five or six minutes to drive home at ten o'clock at night. The man was stabbed at eight minutes past ten. The attacker had been hanging about the foyer since ten o'clock and the man, the dead guy, he was the only person through the door. Kamil knew it could have been him.

'This place is going to ruin our lives,' his missus said.

'I was lucky, I was lucky,' Kamil said and he found it hard to concentrate. 'You can't protect yourself against that, can you? Sudden acts of violence. You can't avoid that, no matter how tough people think you are.'

They made up their minds quickly.

'We're moving out,' he said to Michelle and Michelle sorted them out a house miles away.

Three weeks later they were gone.

Iris 1997

It was a blousy morning, the clouds light, the wind docile; mild for December. Iris went to the paper shop. She got the papers even though Colleen sometimes did them on a weekend, but Jim had phoned saying Colleen wasn't up to going out that morning; she was unwell and he'd never seen her like that before. Iris delivered the papers and rolls to her elderly neighbours and when she was back on her own floor, she chapped Colleen's door to check on her.

Jim was anxious.

'She's out of sorts,' he said.

'That's not like her.'

'I'm after giving her a cup of tea and she's not drunk it. Will you come in and see her?'

'Aye, no bother.'

Iris went into his house and opened the door to the bedroom. Colleen lay across the bottom of the bed.

'Come on Colleen, stop your carry on,' Iris said. 'Get up doll, get up.'

Colleen didn't move. She lay as if in a stubborn sleep.

'She's not well,' Iris said and she called down to the concierge and told him he'd better get up quick because there was something wrong with Mrs Ryan.

'No, come up the now,' she said, when the concierge said he would be along in a minute.

Jim told her that Colleen had been under the weather of late, with her usual cough and aches and pains, but she'd been fine the night before, wrapping presents and trying on her Christmas outfit.

'She's maybe worn out with the stress of Christmas,' Iris said.

When the concierge arrived, Iris left Jim in the living room and took the concierge in to see Colleen. He knelt at the foot of the bed and gently touched her shoulder and forehead and neck.

'Iris, she's dead,' he said.

Jim didn't believe her but when the concierge told him too that his wife was gone, he sobbed in his chair. Iris waited with him while the ambulance came. He was so upset, so sorry that she would have to go down in the lift, dead. They'd always said they wouldn't let that happen to each other, he told Iris, that they would get each other out before they had to be tipped up and leaned against the lift wall.

'Don't worry yourself, Jim, please,' Iris said. 'You weren't to know. You did your best.'

She couldn't console him.

Michael 1997

Michael and Kay slept in the lounge with their baby in her Moses basket alongside them. It was warmer in the lounge. The bedroom was on the gable end and the mould wasn't good for her, they decided. The baby was a girl. She moved as if underwater still, her fingers painstakingly curling and uncurling, her tongue poking through her tiny red lips. When they caught a glimpse of her full, open, indigo eyes, they agreed she took their breath away.

Michael knew Kamil was scared to return to Red Road but he came with Michelle to see baby Lisa and when they were inside, and the baby was bundled asleep in his arms, he had to give her back to Kay and turn away from them all. Michelle put a hand on his shoulder but he left the room. She told Michael he was acting strange since the stabbing and wasn't coping great.

They left, all together, to see the lights in George Square. The baby slept and woke for milk twice. It was exciting, being in town with the Christmas shoppers and the actual day almost upon them. Trish met them on Buchanan Street and tried to persuade them to have a drink but when they'd said goodbye to Kamil and Michelle, they told her to jump in the taxi with them and they'd have one back at the house for old time's sake.

Concierges 1997

Christmas Eve. The concierge office dripping with decorations. Tinsel, paper chains, shiny silver snowflakes that popped open like light shades and twirled gracefully on thin string. The office warm and bright. Moira, the latest addition to the concierge team, in flashing snowman earrings. George and John in Santa hats and fluffy beards. Tins of biscuits on the desk and shelves, the lid off the Quality Streets and most of the strawberry ones gone already. Mince pies in the fridge. The Christmas songs

tape on a loop. The postie dropping off sacks of parcels and
George and John and Moira taking turns to ho-ho-ho the
parcels to their recipients.

Mrs Donoghue calling out as she came down the corridor
and George jumping up to take her arm and escort her in.

'There's a wee present for you in my handbag, son. Take it
out.'

So George clicks open the clasp and pulls out her purse.
'Thank you very much, how much is in there?' he jokes and she
laughs her old, deep laugh and says, 'No you daftie, the bottle.'

There's a bottle of Bells inside and George says, 'Oh no, that's
too much,' and Mrs Donoghue says, 'I didn't come down here
to argue with you. Take it or I'll wrap it round your head.'

George kisses her and so do John and Moira and Moira
takes her back up the stair. John writes his shopping list for his
whiz round the town when his shift finishes at seven. They
leave as mammies and daddies arrive, carrying shopping bags
with wrapping-paper rolls sticking out, beads of rain on their
hair and arms, like snow. John just misses his bus and George
offers a lift, even though it would mean going into town in the
opposite direction, but John says no, he's happy to stand, on
Christmas Eve, and watch the world go by. A black cab pulls
up and lets out a young man and two young women. The young
man lifts a pram from the taxi and inside the pram's rain cover
a baby sleeps. One of the women hangs carrier bags over the
pram's handles and the man begins to push. The woman puts
her hand in the young man's back pocket and the young man
stretches his arm over her shoulders and pushes the pram with
one hand. The other woman walks alongside them, turning in
to talk. They take a right off Red Road and walk into the flats,
and on into Christmas.

Iris 1997

Iris stood at the window and spoke to her daughter.

'I have to give the weans their bikes,' she said.

'Is there anyone in the house?'

'Aye. He's there.'

'Have you knocked?'

'No, not yet. His daughter's just left.' She paused to inhale and the house was so quiet, the gentle pop of her lips leaving the cigarette end could be heard. Iris saw her reflection in the window and twisted the telephone cord in her fingers.

'No, there's been comings and goings all day,' she said.

'Could you get them tomorrow?'

'I could. But he might go to mass.'

'Aye.'

Her daughter was smoking too. Both their voices were soft and low. The night did it to them. Or perhaps the occasion.

'I'll give you money for your taxi tomorrow. Have you got it up front?'

'Thanks, Ma.'

She saw cars on the Broomfield Road.

'So what will you do?'

'I'll chap his door now.'

Iris finished her cigarette while they talked about the next day. Her daughter was having a good, clean run since her boy was born. The wee man had turned her round again. Liam was back and worse than ever. He was well into his life now, as was Pamela, and Iris didn't like to think in last chances, but she felt if there was any time Pamela needed to stay clean it was now.

'Get to sleep now, else Santa won't come.'

'Night, Ma.'

She propped open her front door and went in her slippers to Jim and Colleen's. Lights were on and she could feel the warmth from his house as the door opened.

'Christmas Eve,' Jim said as he opened the door.

'Aye. Have you had your family up?'

'Jennifer and my granddaughter. They're away now. James is picking me up tomorrow morning. The weans asleep?'

'That's why I'm here. I'm awfully sorry, Jim, the bikes, we need them for Christmas tomorrow.'

'Oh good God, the bikes. Come on in.'

'I didn't like to ask you.'

'I've been staring and staring at them all day. I should have remembered.'

'Not at all. You've had enough to worry about.'

He wouldn't let her wheel them out herself. He took them from his living room into hers and asked her where he should lean them; a girl's bike and a tricycle. She showed him a space by the wall underneath a hanging print and he placed them there.

'Do you think you'll sleep?' she asked.

'The doctor gave me pills. I don't know if I'll take them.'

'Will you stay for a wee half?' she asked.

'No, dear, I'll be by myself.'

She stood at the door as he crossed the landing. He passed the lift and turned back to Iris, his fingers touching the wall.

'I'm not having her back up here for the wake,' he said. 'The lift's too small for a coffin. I won't do it to her again.'

'She'd understand.'

Concierges 1997

Christmas Day. Carols on the radio. Prayers. 'I Wish it Could be Christmas Every Day'. 'I Saw Mummy Kissing Santa Claus'. Pre-recorded Wogan. Ho ho ho. The shops closed except for the paper shop. Rain not snow. The incident book with a list of drunken events at twelve, one, two, three and four in the morning. Now, the block was quiet.

'We'll start on the mince pies,' George said.

'And a cup of tea.'

Church and chapel goers stood in the lifts with their good coats and umbrellas. The children clutched one toy each to their chests, the lifts crowded and no space to zoom toy aeroplanes or jiggle baby dolls. 'Me-he-he-heeeeerrrrry Christmas,' George warbled on the lift intercom and the church and chapel goers looked up at the camera and waved. A man, clean-shaven for the first time in weeks, gave the vicky and winked. A baby on another man's shoulders widened its eyes in surprise and almost cried but a wee girl looked up, gabbled some baby talk and put her hands out to touch his legs.

The lifts went up and down all morning and George and John endeavoured to cry 'Merry Christmas' to each and every lift load. Cars pulled in and parked outside the building and in the car park at the back.

At lunchtime George and John unwrapped their pieces. George had thick-cut ham that his missus had bought for Boxing Day. John had beef as his missus had roasted a joint for the Christmas Eve tea and they would have it again with cold roast potatoes and coleslaw and horseradish sauce that evening.

'All we're missing is a cracker,' George said and John said 'Oh, Mrs Donoghue's not so bad.'

Theo Orr's grandweans charged into the office with a four-pack of beers.

'Thank you very much,' John said and checked the expiry date.

'Tell your granda thank you very much. We'll drink them in eight years time.'

'He wants a favour off you.'

'Does he now?'

'My mammy's cooking the Christmas dinner and we've got too many people and not enough chairs. My granda says can you shift six chairs and one of your tables from the community flat so we can eat our Christmas dinner in one sitting. My two uncles will help you.'

'That's what he told you to say, was it?'

One of the boys wore a Celtic jersey and the other a Rangers top.

'What does your granda say about your Celtic jersey?'

'My ma says he's not allowed to say nothing.'

'Quite right.'

John put his piece down on the desk and said to George, 'Will I go, or will you?'

'I'll go,' said George and John said he'd do the next one as they were bound to get more requests for furniture before the day was out. He turned up the radio which was playing The Pogues and Kirsty MacColl and ate his delicious beef piece.

When George came back he told John he'd caught Theo Orr's next-door neighbour trying to shove three cardboard boxes down the rubbish chute.

'The landing is piled high with boxes,' he said. 'Every door, there's about six boxes outside.'

'It's started,' John said.

So, when George had eaten his piece and they'd finished another cup of tea they set about clearing the landings, holding the lift at the top floor and putting in all the cardboard boxes and black bags of wrapping paper, and dropping down the floors until they'd piled the lift so high and full of boxes they couldn't see each other when they squeezed themselves in.

'Merry Christmas, partner,' said George as the lift shot to the ground floor.

'Merry Christmas, partner,' said John and put his arms wide around the towers of cardboard boxes to stop them falling down.

Section Six

Concierges 1999

A PLANE-LOAD OF MEN, women and children would arrive at Glasgow Airport. They would come on a bus to Red Road. The media would be there.

George and John prepared the flats for their arrival and laid out keys on the desk in the office. They unstacked chairs and put them in rows in the community flat and placed a table at the end of the room for the press conference. It was busy on the phones with Glasgow Housing Association people calling. Moira and Allan were on too.

George and John watched the news, they read the papers, they knew what was going on in the former Yugoslavia, where a tenant once went on his summer holiday.

Mrs Donoghue buzzed down and asked if perhaps somebody could pick her up some tablets for her headache if they were going out themselves, because she was feeling awful bad and her daughter wasn't due until teatime tomorrow. Ah, Mrs Donoghue, her timing was impeccable. Allan held the phone away from his mouth with his hand covering the mouthpiece and whispered, 'What do I tell her?'

The bus was expected. They'd had the call from the airport.

The concierges looked at each other and looked at Allan. Mrs Donoghue was nearly ninety now with no sight in her right eye. She hadn't left her house for going on two years and the concierges never saw her unless they took up mail or messages.

'I'll go,' John said. He picked up his coat and his radio. 'If they arrive, just radio me and I'll come straight back.'

There was no bus pulling in as he left Ten Red Road and turned right to go up the steps to the shops. In the chemist, a girl was causing a row over a suspect prescription and John waited as the pharmacist and the shop assistant convinced her that her script wouldn't be dispensed. The girl slammed into the door as she left. 'I'll be back to batter you,' she said.

'No you won't,' the shop assistant called after her. Her voice was suddenly energetic and loud.

'Cow,' the girl shouted as the door closed.

The shop assistant raised her eyebrows, tilted her chin, turned away from the door and looked directly at John.

'What can I get you, honey?'

'Forty-eight Nurofen please, hen.'

'That all?'

'Aye.'

She took the pills from the shelf and tapped the price into the till. The pharmacist stamped a prescription.

'Three times now, Ali, someone's been in with that same script,' she said to the pharmacist without looking up.

She put the Nurofen in a paper bag and handed it to John. 'Take care, honey.'

John folded the receipt and put it in the bag.

'See you after.'

The girl was outside the door and she approached John, holding her script out, the cuffs of her sweatshirt frayed.

'Gonna take this script in for me and get it dispensed? Please, my ma's really desperate for these pills.'

'You were just in with it. I heard you and I heard the chemist.'

'Gonna try again for me?'

'No, pal.'

'It's her arthritis, she can't relax because of it.'

John looked towards Ten Red Road and saw a bus pulling in. 'I said no.'

'Okay, no bother, calm yourself.' The girl walked away, pushing the script into the back pocket of her jeans.

John watched the bus's careful arrival. It drove past the

entrance to the block and parked in front of the lock-ups where the bingo buses used to sit. He saw grainy faces through the windows, upturned eyes and unmoving mouths. John looked around him, trying to see Red Road for the first time, taking it in as if it was new to him. On a sunny day light glinted off the windows and the mustards and greys and reds of the flats were grand-looking. But today the place was stark. The buildings' rendering was dirty and so was the ground on which he stood. Other people had stopped now, like him, and he didn't like to stare but he couldn't help it. The people who stepped from the bus were in a terrible state. Some were bandaged and others had sticks or crutches. Some were elderly. Some carried children in their arms. They filed off the coach and followed the woman from the GHA. None of them carried luggage. Nothing. His radio crackled. It was George.

'The coach is here.'

'Oh I see them.'

In the office George and John and all the other people there helped allocate flats. Some of the children spoke English but very few of the adults did. When John took people to their flats he showed them the storage cupboards, the view from the windows – if it was a good view – and the white meter heaters. Their faces were so tired-looking. The empty rooms echoed with their footsteps and their coughs. They had nothing to put down, nothing to lay out on the table or place in a drawer. John left them.

Hanging about on the first floor landing was a loose-tied, suited photographer hack who didn't want to impose but wondered if any of the Kosovans would be interested in speaking to him for his newspaper article.

'They're just off the plane. No,' John said. 'You're not supposed to be in here.'

'Yeah, yeah, I know that, I just thought I might get to speak to someone before the press conference.'

'Out.'

John walked behind the journalist as he left the building and told him to stay away. Then he found a police officer. 'You polis are going to have to do better at guarding the entrance. I've just evicted a journalist who knew fine well he shouldn't have been where he was. Do your jobs.'

Back in the office, two young boys came in. Brothers who'd translated for their parents when John was settling them in.

'Are we allowed to go outside?'

That floored John. He didn't know what to say. 'Aye, on you go.'

The boys turned to walk away.

'Hey,' John said, 'you don't have to talk to anyone who shoves a microphone in your face. Just you stick together. Be careful.'

The boys nodded and gave John the thumbs up sign. John wondered where they would go; if they would walk as far as Petershill Drive and the grass beyond or whether they would stay close to the building, circling the base of the block, within the thickening ring of police and press and residents.

The residents of the Red Road Flats and the houses across the road whose front doors or bathroom windows or gardens were overlooked by the high steel flats responded vigorously to Tron St Mary's campaign to collect clothes and furniture for the Kosovans. Some had seen them arrive off the bus and had returned to their houses shaken and horrified, others had been told about the poor souls and the terrible state they were in; fleeing a war-torn country and arriving with nothing. The concierges received black bag after black bag of donations and when the press conference was over they opened up the community flat and spread everything out on some tables they'd put together. There were some quality items; clothes and shoes, bedding, rugs, crockery. Then they suggested to the Kosovan men and women that they come up, or down, and choose things that they would like to have. The asylum seekers were grateful and enthused and this enthused the local people more and they raked through their own belongings again and returned with more black bags. Eventually, the concierges said enough was enough. 'Take your stuff to the church,' they said. 'We're full to bursting.' There was a feeling among the local people that they had done good, that they couldn't stand by and see so many poor souls suffer. They're on our turf, Glasgow, and we'll look after them.

Ermira 1999

Ramiz clapped his hands and silenced the young people in the community flat. He looked at the concierge who stood in the corner with his keys.

'Okay, some of you know me,' he said. 'I'm Ramiz. My job is an interpreter. I'm Kosovan Albanian but I came to London first, last year. I didn't have to flee like some of you.'

Ramiz looked at Ermira and paused. She touched her hands to her knees and avoided his eyes. Ramiz was Ermira's brother-in-law. His English was fluent. He told jokes to the concierges and they laughed. Always he was on at her to do something with her days because she was too old to go to the school in Hillhead with the other teenagers. But she wished he'd leave her alone to watch television.

Ramiz started speaking again, in English this time because, he said, it was essential that they improved quickly.

'You need to learn Scottish words. Glaswegians speak quickly. There's a whole new vocabulary here. Wean. What's that?'

Nobody spoke.

'It means child. Next one: messages? What are they?'

'Like a note or a letter,' said a guy Ermira knew from the plane.

'Ahah, no! It means shopping. You go to the shops for your messages. Isn't that right John?'

The concierge nodded his head and pushed out his lips as if to say, why not?

'Who wants to have English classes? Tell me?'

Hands went up and Ramiz said he would take names at the end of the meeting.

He then said he wanted everyone to enroll on courses at the colleges on Cathedral Street. A vocational course that will give you a job. Hairdressing. Food technology. Computing. I'll help you, he told them, and Ermira knew he would. And her sister would too, because they were like that. Driven. Passionate. Caring. But they hadn't fled to Macedonia and lost their mother in the mess at the border like she had.

Lastly, Ramiz brought out his recent acquisition, one that he'd told Ermira about already. In fact he'd saved one for her and it was in her house, in a handbag she'd taken from the table-loads of donated clothes.

'Here. For all of you. This is a free bus pass from First Glasgow. Use it to explore your new city. Be careful and have fun. Remember, come to me and tell me what you want to study.'

While Ramiz and the concierge gave out the bus passes Ermira left the room. She heard Ramiz call her name but she didn't turn back to see his hopeful, energetic face. She would see it later, back in the house. There would be no avoiding it there.

Beki

Everywhere you go you would see same furniture. If I went to my friends you would see same furniture but different colours. They had furnished flats. Okay, my mum had red furnitures. My mum's flat went for red. Red carpet, red sofas, there was one three-seat sofa, two chairs, three tables, small ones, one kitchen table like dining table with four chairs. Bedrooms were mattress and all that, they were like pink, wardrobe was light brown, light pine. I went to my friend she had same but in green. Most of them were green, red and like yellow with green. It was so funny. Wherever I go I see same size of house and same furniture. That's why people didn't get jealous of each other, the neighbours, because nobody had better than anyone else.

Pamela 1999

It came out aggressively because Pamela was tired and wrung out and not doing well.

'Ma,' she said, 'You know my favourite tracksuit, the one that got nicked that I got back, did you give it away?'

'It's been in the bottom of my wardrobe for about ten year and you've never mentioned it in about ten year so I took it to Ten Red Road for the Kosovans. And don't give me a row about it, I'm not in the mood.'

Pamela tapped her cigarette onto an ashtray. Her bones were tired and her back hurt.

'No, no, I don't mind. I saw it.'

'Where?'

'On a boy. A Kosovan boy.'

'I hope you didn't rip it off him like you did the last lad.'

'No, no, I just saw it.' Pamela smiled.

Iris was making tea for Pamela's two children.

'Do you want some?' she said.

'No, I can't eat nothing, my stomach's all tight,' Pamela said and she sat on the couch and chewed her fingernails before she went home to the house she lived in by herself. She came to see her ma and the kids on good days. Her kids were growing up well. Lauren had the most beautiful long hair. Callum could count to ten.

Concierges 1999

The first time they caught the boys on camera playing about in the lifts they let it go because they were good boys from a good family. All the Kosovan families were good families. The boys didn't smash windows or kick in cars, they weren't aggressive and they didn't answer back. But the time they opened the fire hatch on the ceiling of the lift and climbed through was different. Serious, dangerous and foolish; it was everything that angered John and George after everything they'd seen over the years.

'Get down, now!' George said through the intercom which shocked the boys and George and John left Moira in the office and went to find them. It took them a wee while because thirty floors of evading capture gave them good odds. They got them though, with the help of Moira on the radio and a short spell of running up the stairs which wore them out but was enough to surprise the boys on their way down.

'You're coming with us,' John said and put them in the lift with him and George. No back-chat, no refusing to go, no threatening to call the police if they touched them, which the young ones did now.

At floor fourteen they took the boys to their front door and knocked on it. The boys' parents motioned for George and John to come in, like they always did, proffering them juice and fruit and making them sit for a while.

'No, no, thank you,' John said. 'Boys, will you tell your parents you're in trouble with us.'

The boys nodded and spoke in Albanian.

Their parents looked from one concierge to the other and laughed.

'Did you tell them?' George said.

'Aye,' one of the boys said and spoke again in Albanian.

The parents talked briefly, as if conferring, and pointed to George.

This wasn't going the way George and John had thought it would.

'Tell them we're sick of you playing about in the lifts. It's dangerous,' John said.

Again, one of the boys spoke to his parents in Albanian.

Their parents widened their eyes and smiled and ruffled the boys' hair.

'If we catch you doing it again you'll be in trouble.'

More talking and gesturing and innocent-looking eyes and again, smiles from the parents. The mother said 'Thank you'.

One of the boys volunteered something else although neither George nor John had asked him to translate anything and the parents laughed and motioned again for George and John to come into their house.

'Thank you but we'd better get on. Another time.' George turned to the boys. 'You tell them we'll be watching you. You've been very bad boys.'

A burst of Albanian and the parents ruffled their children's hair again.

When they'd shut the door John said to George, 'Keep an eye. It's all we can do.'

Ermira 1999

Ermira stood at the window with her brother. He was taller than her. Thin and tall with awkward teenage arms. He'd started at the school in Hillhead and took two buses each morning and afternoon with the other kids.

'You should see the West End,' he told her. 'It's like a different country.'

A fat seagull glided past the window. The day was grey.

'See if it will take this,' her brother said and took a slice of bread from the bread bag. He pushed hard on the window and tipped it up so that it turned in on itself. The cold wind hit them. They held their bare arms out. Wind rushed over Ermira's wrists. Her brother threw his bread up into the air. They looked down, following the bread and watching the seagull, seeing if it would swoop to catch it as it fell. It didn't. Ermira looked up to see the bellies of more gulls gliding on the air currents. Some pigeons flew about too, but with less grace.

'Ramiz was looking for you,' Ermira's brother said and Ermira flopped onto the window frame and let her hands dangle out of the window. Her brother grabbed her T-shirt and pulled her upright.

'Stop that. How old are you?'

'I wasn't going to fall.'

'I know, but.' He paused. 'He said have you made a decision.'

Ermira's brother shut the window and she leaned her forehead against it.

Ermira had made a decision but she couldn't see how she would be able to sit and learn in a college with her head jumping the way it did. Her brother leaned his forehead on the window pane too. Wind sprayed rain onto the glass and whistled through the gaps in the frame.

'Ramiz is a bully.'

'No, he's not.'

'He should concentrate on looking after his own wife and kids. Weans.'

'Tell me what you're going to study?'

Maybe it came from the woman in Macedonia who had taken her in when she'd lost everyone.

'Tell me what you're going to study, Ermira.'

'Did you look for me at the border?'

Her brother shot her a look. 'You know we did.'

'How hard did you look?'

'Very hard.' He kicked a foot against the wall.

Ermira knew her brother and her parents didn't like to talk about what happened at the border. So they didn't. When she asked them they acted guilty and told her they'd found each other in the end so the trick was to look forwards now.

But no one but Ermira had seen the man the Macedonian family had taken in as well. He apologised for crying but cried all the same. Like Ermira he had no luggage – that was left behind and lost in the crush – but he'd crossed the border on his own and said his whole family was gone. The Macedonian man sat up with him on hard-backed chairs by the window and the woman put water and cotton wool on his injuries. She made up beds and Ermira cried in hers for much of the night.

'You're going to do childcare, aren't you?'

'No.'

'Catering.'

'No.'

'Hairdressing?'

Ermira paused. 'The Macedonian woman, she couldn't have children and she loved children, so she asked if she could sit with me and brush my hair because she'd always wanted to brush her little girl's hair. I let her brush my hair and all the time I was thinking that she wasn't my mother, that only my mother should brush my hair. And then I felt bad because she'd taken me in so when she said have you had enough, I always said, no, you can keep going, and she kept brushing. I thought I might have to stay there in that house with those people forever. I didn't even know that she'd let me or want me to. I thought I might have to go to Britain with the man who'd lost everything. He was like a madman. I didn't know how long I should stay there at the border waiting for you and looking for you. I thought you might have gone on without me.'

'But then we found you.'

'Yes, you found me.'

'From the message on the wall in the community centre.'

'Yes.'

'So look forwards, Ermira.'

'All right, little brother.'

A plane flew low and loud across the sky. Ermira left the window and sat on the couch. Her brother threw her the remote control for the television.

'So it's hairdressing isn't it?' he said.

'Yes.'

'In memory of the woman who brushed your hair.'

'Yes, because I thought bad things about her and I feel guilty. Poor woman. She couldn't have any kids.'

'That's no reason to do something.'

'I need to have some reason.'

She could have said more. They could have talked on. But the Saturday football programme was on and her brother liked to follow the football in the Scottish leagues and the English leagues, so they sat together on the couch and watched the men with microphones standing in the empty grounds giving their thoughts on the matches to come.

Hairdressing. Her brother would let her practise on him. Probably.

Khadra 2002

Six months after the attacks in the United States, Khadra came to Glasgow via a camp in Kenya and God knows where else. She spent a week in a hotel in Argyle Street. Then they sent her to Glasgow Airport. A special centre in which people like her could be processed, the planes landing and taking off while she sat in the room waiting. A passenger could get across an ocean in the time she sat in that room. The tension was tough on her body. It made her sick.

When it was her turn they took her into a room and told her to stand against a white wall and before she was aware of what was happening they took her photograph. Click. Flash. They didn't ask to hold her fingers but they took them and rolled each one on an ink pad and then on a piece of paper, their own latexed fingers manipulating her fingers, pressing them firmly. She thought they were finished with the ink but they held on to one of her hands and pressed it, palm down, to the ink pad and took its print. They took the other hand and did the same. As she wiped her hands with the cloth they gave her she watched a woman take a cotton bud and plastic bag and indicate that

Khadra should open her mouth. The woman rolled the cotton bud on the inside of her cheek and put it in the plastic bag.

Then they spoke.

Tell me how you came to Glasgow, they said. Name? Date of birth? Where are you from? Khadra spoke no English. They got her an interpreter and the interpreter told the officials what Khadra said. I am from Somalia, an island called Koyama. I'm twenty-four. I'm here alone. I don't know how I got here. Really? Yes. I was drugged. I escaped to a refugee camp in Kenya and then I got here, somehow, and they left me outside the doors of the Scottish Refugee Council. Do I have to tell them everything? It's best to.

My parents aren't alive anymore. My dad was shot. My mum was raped. I was raped. My mum died. I escaped. The political and religious situation in Somalia is such that you are persecuted if you hold different beliefs to the people who take control of your area. If your ethnicity is different, you are persecuted too. I am mixed race, a minority; my dad Indian, my mother Bantu. We were persecuted. As I said.

The officials didn't look at her. They studied their computer screens and paper documents. Khadra still felt sick with the telling and the tension. She was hot. It was horrific.

'You understand you would do better to be married,' the interpreter told her when the officials had paused in their questioning. 'A Scottish man. Then it will be harder for them to kick you out. You'll get your status in three years.'

It confused her, what the interpreter said. It made her faint with the shock of the sentiment and she didn't have words to say that she wasn't here because she simply wanted a better life but she was here because she had to be here, because she had to escape before she died too. It made her weak to think that one of her own people, a Somali woman, could make her feel so utterly and desperately alone. She sat quietly in the chair while they finished processing her.

They sent her back to the hotel in Argyle Street where along with the other asylum seekers she stuffed her pockets at breakfast with rolls and cheese to eat in her room later in the day. She wasn't lonely. We're all asylum seekers, we're all fucked together, they said and she agreed. With the thirty pounds they gave her each week she went with another woman to Boots and studied the labels on bottles, trying to find one that contained shampoo. She learned the words for currency first: pound, pence, one, two, three, four, five. When a woman asked for eight *pun* she stared confused, cloth covering all but her eyes, until the cashier turned the plastic screen to face her and said *that*.

She knew the world was jittery about Muslims and terrorists. Someone spat at her on Argyle Street.

Onwards. On the advice of other women she saved her cash because once they processed her she would be on vouchers that had to be spent at specific shops.

At five in the morning they knocked on her door and told her to get in a van. Other women came out of their rooms carrying bags and children and when the doors shut and the van drove off the women thought they were going to a detention centre. The officials didn't explain anything. They didn't speak.

The van pulled up at a warehouse and the officials opened the doors. They gestured for the women and children to climb out of the van and go into the warehouse. No kindness, no civility, just strong arms and thick coats. Still early in the morning, some-where in Glasgow. If they were to be lined up and shot, this is how it would be, Khadra thought.

Inside the warehouse, the officials called them one by one and Khadra realised they weren't shooting or detaining or taking them away, they were giving them homes. Homes in Birmingham, homes in Manchester, homes in London and homes in Glasgow. Khadra had picked Glasgow. They'd asked her at the airport and she'd chosen to stay in the city her fate had brought her to.

'Here's your flat number,' the official said. 'Twenty-three/two. Twenty Petershill Court, Red Road Flats.'

They opened the doors of the van and told Khadra and the women and children to get in. The van stopped at other high rises in Glasgow and let people out. She said goodbye to some of the women she knew. She and another Somali woman were let out at Red Road. Two men met them at the doors of the van. One man took her to number Twenty Petershill Court and they got in the tiny lift. On floor twenty-three he opened her blue door and said here is your flat.

The first thing she noticed was the light slamming through the windows. She went straight to the living room window and stood up against all that light and saw in front of her the most amazing view. Hills called the Campsie Fells, the man told her, and stood behind her while she looked out in silence. Then he left her to her asylum process. Welcome, I hope you're happy here, he said as he closed the door.

Jim 2002

Jim couldn't stop thinking about Colleen. He missed her. Nearly five years gone and it didn't make a difference. She could be sitting up in bed next to him, telling him she'd had enough reading and could he turn the light out now, she was so present in his head. Right there. For her, as he did occasionally, to wind her down to sleep, or coax her into loving, he sang his song.

> *The moon was rising above the green mountains*
> *The sun was climbing beneath the blue sea*
> *As I stray with my love to the pure crystal fountain*
> *That stands in the beautiful vale of Tralee.*

In the concert party at Alive and Kicking, the centre he went to every day, he was to step forward after May and Donald and Erica's second sketch, and sing this song. The first verse unaccompanied. Then the pianist would join in. And finally the whole concert party would come in with their harmonies. He would put his hand on his chest and sing for Colleen.

Oh go to sleep, you daft old fool, lie down and put the radio on. He did so, pulling the pillow from Colleen's side and holding it tight to his chest and belly and groin.

Khadra 2002

A letter informed Khadra that her application for asylum had been turned down. The trip to Leeds and the interview with the Home Office had come to nothing. She would have to leave or appeal.

'Appeal then,' her Somali friend said.

'How long will that take? Months?'

'But they won't send you back yet.'

'I'm going to choir,' Khadra said.

On the bus to Partick some boys asked her what she was wearing underneath her abaya. Her English was slow and hesitant but she told them a Spiderman costume. The boys blew pieces of bus ticket through straws and asked where her cousin Osama Bin Laden was hiding. When they kept up their taunting she moved seats and sat next to a woman who turned her face to the window.

It was a nothing world she lived in. Living in a flat halfway to the sky, thinking up sentences in Somali, Katchi, French, Swahili, Gujarati, yet fighting to find words in English, travelling like a stranger on buses – even with her face uncovered people still avoided her eyes – and having the fate of her body – her physical body – where it would stay and sleep and eat and piss – crossing the land on printed paper in self-seal envelopes.

'Don't you miss Somalia?' her Somali friend said to her when they broke their fast together later that night.

'No, I do not,' Khadra said.

'But Somalia is still in me,' her friend insisted. 'It's us.'

'Somalia isn't me. It nearly killed me.'

'You'll regret it if you turn your back on your homeland.'

'I'll regret it more if I get deported.'

Khadra ate a piece of lamb and wiped sauce from her lips, finding comfort in food and quiet and the company of her friend, even though her friend and she were finding less and less to agree on.

Farah 2003

And there's that girl again, calling for her brother. She shrieks his name. Jalal. Jalaaaaaaaaaal. It's a performance and so annoying I can't study. I wonder if it's the girl who gets in the lift and presses number twenty-one. She wears a scarf bunched around her neck. It could be her. She looks as if she has the voice of a banshee.

She shrieks again. I guess her veranda must look out to the football pitch. Ours looks out to the other blocks. They say the views are good up here. Our view's shite.

Jalaaaaaaal! She sounds tough. She also sounds funny. I don't know a single girl here.

Jalal and Mariam 2003

Jalal sees his sister wave her arms above her head from her spot on the veranda. She's wearing her school uniform. She looks tiny, not tall. Hers is the loudest voice he's ever heard. She puts it on. She practises it. She yells over his bed in the mornings to waken him. He knows she'll be laughing at herself and the way her voice sounds. She's two years older than him.

Blacks v Scottish again tomorrow. The guy from Side Kicks blows his whistle and Jalal leaves the boys on the football pitch and the girls on the basketball court and runs home.

Sixty-seven, sixty-eight, sixty-nine, seventy! Yes! Seventy seconds from ground to front door. No stops. Twenty-one floors.

'Mariaaaaaaam!'

She's on the veranda and she jumps when he shouts.

'Pack it in, eejit.'

'You're wearing lipstick.'

'No I'm not.'

They stand on the veranda and Jalal shakes the pigeon net. If he tries, he can look through the wire squares and see the town laid out below him and not notice the pigeon net. If he squints he can make the net come into focus and become all he can see or concentrate on.

His sister's phone bleeps.

'They want to come after school tomorrow. They fancy the asylum boys.'

His sister goes to school in town. She doesn't go to the Big Roch like he does. She has a pal from Sighthill who used to live at Red Road and the girls at their school like them because they take them to meet the asylum seeker boys.

'Me?'

'Not you. The older ones.'

'Like Mustapha?'

'Aye.'

'It's Blacks v Scottish tomorrow.'

His sister says they don't want to stand around in the cold watching the boys. Maybe they'll come another day or talk to them after the match.

'I bet the Scottish girls will want to watch.'

After their tea Jalal and Mariam stand on the veranda and watch their mother. She likes them to observe her walking around the football pitches and the fields beside the far trees. Keep watch over me, she asks, and her children poke their faces through the pigeon net and watch her walk.

'Why doesn't she go in the day?' Jalal asks.

'There's Mustapha down there.'

A teenager shoots at goal. It's not a big game. There's just a boy in goals and four others. The shot goes wide and Mustapha throws his head back and turns on the spot.

'Too busy.'

The boys on the pitch play on. Mustapha is the best player. The other boys are younger and less coordinated.

'Where's mum?' Jalal says.

'There she is.'

They look through the green and the dusk to the trees alongside the railway line and see her, small and silent.

'Why does she go off walking like that?' Jalal says.

Mariam doesn't answer.

The game below goes on. Mustapha sidesteps around a small boy and the boy topples. Mustapha goes out wide to avoid another boy and weaves the ball around him. In front of goal he looks up. But a man is next to him and the man chops Mustapha's legs and takes the ball off him and boots it hard. Jalal and Mariam hear the thud of the man's kick from their veranda. It's a goal. The wee boy between the sweatshirts has his arms by his sides and stares at the big man. When the big man runs back towards Petershill Drive with his arms wide and chin jutting, the wee boy walks to retrieve the ball. Mustapha stands up and limps a couple of steps.

'Who was that?' Mariam asks.

'It's a man called Ebi. He does it all the time. If you're on his side in Blacks v Scottish and you skin the ball, he hits you. He forgets all about the game and starts chasing you around the pitch. He gets angry.'

'Why does he bother?'

'He caught me doing chap door run away and knocked me down. We don't chap his door any more. I don't know why he bothers. Actually I do. He likes to frighten us. Says we don't know nothing, we haven't seen what he's seen.'

Their mother is walking alongside Broomfield Road. They see her turn her head when a dog barks. The dog is in the middle of the field, jumping and pouncing. Its owner throws a stick.

'Why do grown men play in the Blacks v Scottish matches? I thought it was just for boys.'

'It's not. They're big matches. People take it seriously.'

The teenagers are quiet for a while. Mariam stares at Mustapha and thinks of the girl at school who fancies him.

'Hey Mustapha!' Jalal calls but Mustapha doesn't look up.

He calls again. Mustapha bounces the ball on the pitch and throws it for one of the younger boys to head.

Mariam takes a huge breath and calls 'Musssstaphaaaa!' She puts extra emphasis on the last syllable of his name and her voice falls from high to low until she runs out of breath. It's an excellent call and they both laugh. She loves it when she makes her brother laugh.

Mustapha looks up and waves, puts his fingers in his mouth and whistles.

'That same time I got knocked down we went to Sixty-three building and played chap door run away. The boys, they tricked me, they said I had to stand in front of the door, count for ten seconds after I chapped it and run into the lift. They said they'd hold the doors open for me. They didn't hold the doors and I was stuck on the landing. The door opened and this really old man answered it. He said hello and I had to make something up. I asked if he wanted his floor cleaned and he told me he didn't need me to clean it because the concierge did it with a buffer because they didn't let him do it himself anymore. He was too old. What's a buffer? I thought he was going to shout at me but he was friendly. He said this ground here, before the flats, used to be cabbage fields. He said he saw these flats being built. He said he worked over there, at the top of that hill.'

'A buffer's a thing that makes the floor shine. There's mum.'

'She's going quite fast.'

'She's going fast now because she knows we're watching. Call her.'

'Muuuum!' Mariam roars. She makes her voice crazy.

'She didn't hear you.'

'Mum!'

Jalal shouts too. They've forgotten Mustapha who stands and looks at them then goes back to his football.

'Muuuum!'

'Mum!'

They compete with each other. Mariam is still the best but Jalal is good too. He can't do it without laughing though.

Their mum is on Petershill Drive now. She looks in their direction.

'Mum!'

A twitch, an almost imperceptible switch from casual to urgent. Their mum glances up at them and Jalal waves and shouts again.

'Don't. She'll think – '

It's too late. His mother begins to run and she looks up as she runs and they can see worry in her face. She's not a good runner and her arms pump the air.

'Oh no, she'll think it's something bad. She'll think it's dad.'

'Or a knock at the door.'

'She'll think it's news from the solicitor.'

Mariam makes a cutting motion with her arms in front of her but that seems to make things worse.

'Oh, look at her face.'

She runs out of view and Mariam and Jalal go in from the veranda and stand at the door, waiting for their mother to burst out of the lift.

Farah 2003

Stupid kids who do not stop shouting from their balconies. It is not funny. This is not funny. I can't study. Shouting from your balcony doesn't help you or change your situation. You're still an asylum seeker. Shouting makes you dumb and stupid, hanging out of your cage. My dad is tired. My mum is tired. They're tired from sitting and doing nothing because they're not allowed to do anything except hand in their vouchers and get their food and travel to solicitors and appointments and wait. How can I study when I don't know if I can stay? Who will accept me for Medicine if I can't promise I will stay on the course? You shout up there and your neighbour jumps out of her window because she thinks they're knocking on her door. You shout and my mum takes her antidepressants and my dad gets fat because he has nothing to get up for. I want to be a fucking doctor and I can't afford the exams to even try to be a doctor. My guidance teacher says I'm cynical because I'm in the system. You're in the system too so why are you laughing? Why are you yelling from your balcony? Is four years not long enough to wait here? Do you want to wait another four? Don't you care that if your application fails and you go back your parents could be beaten or go to prison? Or your parents will leave you – leave you – or try to have you adopted or hide you, but leave you – so that you don't have to go back. Shout your stupid shouts from your veranda. Make your friends and play your games. Pretend it's not happening in this building. Pretend the man next door to you isn't gay and won't be executed if he returns. Pretend the woman up the stair didn't get raped and raped and raped. Pretend your friends didn't witness their brothers or fathers or uncles being killed. Pretend they didn't see their mother pick up their baby sister and run as they ran too. Pretend they, out there, the Scottish, don't hate you, pretend their newspapers aren't full of you and how they hate you. Pretend it doesn't kill you to get in the van and leave your house full of possessions and go to the airport and then for them to say, oh no, it's okay, your appeal has been granted, or oh yes, you're going, and if you don't go quietly, we'll tie your hands together with plastic and sit on you. Pretend the world isn't in chaos and nobody gives a damn as long as they've got money and someone to blame. Pretend it's all about the number twelve bus or the number fifty-six bus or mucking about in the lifts or cheeking the old people. Or about religion. Or about God. Pretend people don't jump. I want to be a doctor. I really want to be a doctor. I want to be a doctor.

Her fingers touch her bedroom window. Red Road is outside. Nothing else. Her father coughs. Her mother's onions fry.

Iris 2003

The concierges couldn't believe it and they didn't know what to say. They shook their heads and finally said, no, we're not letting you go.

The old folk in her building gasped and held both her hands in theirs, gold rings clinking on soft liver-spotted skin. Who'll get our messages for us, they joked. Oh Iris, what will we do without you?

It felt right though. A house with a door near to the ground. No more bastarding lifts. She could get another dog – Zeus was long gone and dreadfully missed.

The grandweans would move with her. And Pamela, who turned up one night with streaming hair and a methadone script, would come too. I'm doing it this time, Ma, she said and Iris believed her.

All packed. Lord, it was a big move, away from her pals and her memories.

Jim opened his door and looked as smart as he always did in a jumper that Iris presumed Colleen had knitted.

'It's not today is it? Oh, no, I can't cope with this,' he said.

He seemed too distressed to speak, his brown eyes desperate-looking. Iris sat in his house and drank a couple of halfs with him. He talked about socialism, he talked about Ireland, he talked about children and what a torment they were when they lost themselves before your own eyes.

'I'm never leaving Red Road,' he said when Iris asked. 'What reason would I have?'

'You're quite happy here,' Iris said.

She stood at the door and kissed him. She pressed her face to his neck and felt his chin and nose and breath on her head.

'So long, Jim.'

She wouldn't forget Jim and she wouldn't forget Red Road. She'd see it often enough when she was out and about, in Springburn or the town or anywhere with a view across the rooftops to Barmulloch. Over twenty years in the same house. Good times, on the whole.

She would keep slithers of memories in her head, of her Red Road days, and sometimes the memories would come back all at once; a shower, a sieving of remembering, like the way the asbestos covered the house once, when the wind blew and shook the walls.

Khadra 2004

'You should write it all down,' Khadra's Scottish friend said to her. He was more than a friend. He let her lie quietly against him when she was tired of being an asylum seeker.

'I can't bear to write it all down,' she said.

'It makes a good story.'

'Not when you're in it.'

The first appeal had gone well. Leave to remain. Leave to remain! They stood on the veranda that night and counted stars.

Nine days later – there were ten days in which to do it – she received a letter saying the Home Office were going to appeal.

Back to court.

Thandie 2004

At their door, Thandie, Mhambi, and daughters one, two and three. Just moved in. The man who knocked asked for baby milk. Thandie, a primary school teacher, Mhambi an electrical engineer, the girls aged nine, six and not yet one. The baby in her mother's arms, the girls' heads at hip height and waist height, next to their parents' young legs. The man at the door, their neighbour, leaned towards them with his hands in his pockets as if to apologise for himself and asked again for baby milk.

'Of course you can have some baby milk. How old is she?' Thandie said.

'Sixteen weeks.'

'Oh! Come in, come in.'

The girls stepped back and stood against the wall as their parents took the young man into the kitchen.

'We didn't expect to run out but she's just really hungry, you know, and my girlfriend's thingmy, she's a bit down in the dumps so I don't want to leave her, you know.'

Thandie spooned some milk powder into a glass and Mhambi said, 'Any time, just knock.'

The young man took the milk and said, 'Which part of Africa are you from?'

'South Africa.'

'Are you refugees?'

Mhambi shook his head. 'We came here because South Africa is in the Commonwealth.'

'Are you working?'

'Yes.'

Thandie didn't want to say that she was struggling to find work because primary school jobs were scarce and she needed to register with the GTCS and do a couple of courses.

'Oh right.'

It was a visit to Thandie's aunt that made them want to live in Glasgow. The friendliness, the shops, the kilts, the music. They stayed, even when the aunt moved to London. And Red Road, it was different to anything they'd known. In Johannesburg the houses were spread out, low to the ground with space around them. To live high up in One-two-three Petershill Drive, with the view and the neighbours above and below was extraordinary. It was fun. Mhambi filled the bath whenever the wind was strong because he loved to think of the steel structure allowing itself to submit to the wind and sway to stay up, and he loved seeing the water move in the bath as proof of the building's design.

The next night the young man came back and asked for more milk. Three nights passed and the young man was back again and because he was so young Thandie and Mhambi worried that perhaps he and his girlfriend were finding it hard to cope with their tiny new baby. They understood. Life with children was challenging. They gave out cupfuls and tubfuls of milk but afterwards they would stand in the kitchen and tap the sides of the milk carton to level out the remaining powder and say to each other that they couldn't continue to give away their baby milk because milk was expensive.

'Is it because we're new?' Thandie said and Mhambi said, 'I think that's got something to do with it.'

The young man knocked on the door a few days later and offered to sell them a radio for their kitchen. It had a cassette and CD player too.

'I should ask for sixty quid,' he said, 'as it's top of the range, but I'll sell it to you for fifty because you're my neighbours.'

He held out the radio but Mhambi wouldn't take it.

The young man told them that they wouldn't get it cheaper in any of the shops and he said, 'Go on, have a closer look at it.'

'We've got all the radios we need, thank you.'

The young man shrugged and told them to suit themselves and then he asked for more baby milk.

They wanted to say no but they didn't.

'I hope you don't think we're taking the piss, asking for the milk,' he said.

'Oh no, no, no.'

A few weeks later Mhambi went back to bed, in the middle of the day, a luxury reserved for childless weekends or annual leave. It was day one of his holiday and Thandie would be off work too the following day and doubtless would want to take him in search of the hills she could see from the window and was so desperate to walk on. So this was his one and only chance for stillness and sleep. Silence, warmth, a cool pillow against his cheek. He slept easily and when he woke he didn't know why he was in bed or why he'd woken. He remembered quickly that he was on his holidays and was about to turn over and put his other cheek to the pillow when he heard footsteps behind his bedroom door. He propped himself up on an elbow and stared as he listened hard. His own door began to open – was it opening? – and the hinges creaked. Mhambi watched as fingers curled around the door and an arm and shoulder and then a face peeked around but as soon as the face was there it was gone, because the eyes in the face had locked on to his own eyes and the two men – the other face was definitely a man's face – stared at each other for a violent second and then the face whipped itself away behind the door and Mhambi heard footsteps and the clicking shut of his own front door. At that point Mhambi jumped out of bed. He strode through his house, once to check that it was empty of intruders and once again to see if anything had been taken. There appeared to be nothing missing. The DVDs were still in the lounge, the television was still on its stand. In the girls' room, which was the first room an intruder would come to as he walked into the flat, all appeared to be okay. Mhambi locked the front door and went to the kitchen to boil the kettle and stood with his hands on the sink, breathing hard, adrenalin and anger fighting it out inside him, nowhere to go, nothing to do but work itself out.

When his daughters returned from school the eldest said her mobile phone was lost but Mhambi didn't tell them about the intruder. His wife confirmed that the mobile phone was left on the bed in the girls' room and the couple resolved to always lock the door and to peek through the spy hole when there was a knock on the door in case it was the young man from across the landing. No milk. No favours. Thandie hated being suspicious of people but there it was. Enough was enough.

Khadra 2004

Khadra crossed in front of the CCTV cameras. Still some slush and patches of ice on the ground. She sang the song they practised in choir. Out loud; she didn't care. A head popped up from behind a hedge. Pop. Then another. More heads. Pop. Pop. Pop. Oh God, she thought, they were like teenage hoodlums with hoodies pulled tight around their faces and silent staring faces. Yet if anything, they seemed like amateur hoodlums. One had a sweetie stick in his mouth.

'All of you behind a hedge,' Khadra said. Her English was good now. Plenty good enough to give conversation a go; to banter with the best of the Glaswegians.

The boys stared at her.

'You stopped singing,' one of the boys said.

'Did you like it?'

'Aye.'

The hedge moved as the boys shifted their positions. Some stood up.

'Sing it again,' the first boy said.

'Only if you sing it with me.'

'No way.'

'You're not singing, I'm not singing.'

She made to go and the first boy pushed a tiny boy into her path.

'He'll sing it with you. He's got a lovely voice.'

'Shut up,' the tiny boy said but looked up at Khadra.

So Khadra sang and was amused when the tiny boy joined in and more amused when the other boys behind the hedge joined in too and began to sway and clap their hands. If they were taking the piss out of her they were doing it in a good-natured way. When she stopped they looked at her with open mouths and tilted chins and there was a pause before anyone spoke.

The first boy did. 'What's that you're singing anyway?'

'It's not English. It's a South African hymn. 'Jesus is the Highest'.'

'You a Muslim?'

'Kind of.'

One of the boys began to sing the song again and laughed at himself. The tiny boy bent his knees and wiggled his bum. Khadra smiled and wished she could sit down with them and share their evening. It was making her weary, the months of her asylum; the insecurity, the boredom, the fear of what people might say, suddenly.

And there it came.

'My granny wants out of Red Road because she says she's the only Scottish person left.' The tiny boy spoke innocently, looking at Khadra as if she was a teacher, as if she could help him work things out.

She didn't know where to start.

One of the other boys helped her. 'They're just people,' he said.

Khadra nodded.

'But why can't my granny get what the asylum seekers get?' the tiny boy said. 'She hasn't had her house decorated in twenty years.'

'And the asylum seekers get brand-new kitchens and furniture,' another boy said.

Khadra attempted to say that the people she knew from the choir and the photography workshops in the YMCA, were people who had fled with nothing, who were exiled out of necessity, not because they wanted a new kitchen.

'They're building new houses,' she said.

'For asylum seekers.'

'And for us,' one boy said. 'We're moving to a new build.'

'My uncle moved out of Red Road to a house on Broomton Road and it's not a new build, it's old. And he had to get the roof fixed because it was leaking.'

It went on and on. Khadra listened, and spoke when she felt she should, and came to her old conclusions; that housing mattered, that jobs mattered, that integration mattered. That people should not be left in isolation.

They said goodbye and the boys asked her if she'd come back and sing with them.

'Aye, if you like,' she said.

The next day she went back to court, as instructed in her letter from the Home Office. In the building on Bothwell Street the woman on the bench took away her leave to remain. Why? Inaccuracies with your story. Your accent isn't from the part of Somalia you claim to be fleeing. But I... You have one more appeal.

Last chance.

Jim 2005

Jim suspected the boys were playing at their chap door run away but he got up anyway. Even to see the legs or hear the feet of living boys would be a thing, a fact of that day. And boys should play chap door run away. His own did.

His children invited him to move closer to them – Rutherglen, Stirling, London or Leeds – take your pick, they said – and he said, I pick Barmulloch. I pick Red Road. I pick living within sight of Provanmill where me and your mammy tramped each day of our working lives. I pick the view from my window. I pick my pals at Alive and Kicking. And now I'm going to pick up my glass and carry on with my wee half. Did you have anything else to say? How are the wee yins?

Yes the boys who played chap door run away were at it again. Not a soul on his landing. Not a sound.

Teenage Asylum Seekers

At night.

If you go by yourself at night you'll see it.

You need night vision goggles and you need to go at midnight.

You have to stay. The moment you hear even a click you have to start running.

Down the stairs.

You touch the lock.

You have to touch the lock and then you hear like a rattle and you start running.

No you don't, you have to kick the door.

I've seen it. Black hair.

Invisible.

It's a woman crying.

There was this woman getting raped, yeah, and she died and the next day the man died.

So there are two ghosts.

Do you remember the time we all came up here and we started screaming?

Yeah, ages ago, it was night, yeah, it was winter, it was dark, we went up to twenty-three floor yeah, and he knocked the door and you see the door open.

The rest of us just ran out.

Last time we came here we were playing football in the landing. And there used to be this metal door and somebody kicked the ball on it and we just heard somebody walking up. Everybody start running.

Thandie 2006

Music filled the flat. Brenda Fassie: God rest her soul. Oh, the songs were brilliant. Up went the volume. Thandie danced when she should have been preparing for the party. The 'Scotland's Towns' table cloth, like the dish towel pinned to the wall, was folded and ready to go on the table, the paper plates and napkins and uncut bread put out. Beers were cooling in the fridge, thanks to Mhambi. Mhambi was on the veranda organising the spot for the braai.

She turned to see her daughters watching her dance from the lounge doorway. Tall, taller, tallest. Their eyes in triplicate. Beautiful girls. All washed and dressed and hungry, probably. She swung her hips more emphatically to wind them up and the girls turned and went in the direction of their room. Thandie heard the sounds of the Black Eyed Peas starting up. So up went the volume on Brenda Fassie again. Oh Brenda, with your talent and gifts and weakness for drugs; some voice, some woman.

The volume didn't matter. Hardly a neighbour anywhere near. The nice woman across the landing, gone, the family who borrowed the milk powder, gone, and the door boarded up with a steel sheet, the other house on the landing long empty. The block sterile and silent and cold and mouldy. Sing out, Brenda.

Her husband came in from the veranda and turned the volume down to nothing. Thandie stopped dancing and was about to protest.

'Listen,' he said.

Nothing.

'I thought I heard...' He went out to the veranda and Thandie followed.

'Listen,' he said again.

'It's cold out here.'

'Shoosh. It doesn't matter.'

Then Thandie heard the noise. There were shouts from the ground and she recognised the voices. The pigeon net prevented her from leaning over and waving but she knew her friends had arrived. When they came into the flat they said they had been waiting downstairs and buzzing and calling on the mobile and nobody had come in or out of the building to let them through the door. Only a couple of teenage boys on bikes, circling. All the friends were there at once and Thandie took them into the house.

One friend gave her a bag from Solly's, the African food shop on Great Western Road. Thandie put her nose in the bag and sniffed. Maize meal and star fruit. All the African women she knew had come to the party. From as far as Yoker. Two women had Scottish husbands.

The women stayed in the lounge and the men stood squashed on the veranda. The braai – a discounted barbecue from Tesco's – was lit by Mhambi and Thandie asked him if he was ready for the beef but he said no, it had a while to heat up.

The young people in the girls' bedroom, playing R&B, the men on the veranda drinking beer, and the women, hyper and pleased and dashing around the flat helping to get the party ready. One woman went looking for the toilet and opened the door to the big cupboard. It was full of furniture. It made Thandie angry to think of the money they spent on the furniture that stayed piled in the cupboard. A hundred pounds extra a month which brought the rent to five hundred pounds instead of four. Thandie had asked the council if they would take away the couch with the holes in and the tatty chairs but the council said the flat was only furnished three years ago and the furniture had to stay. So the furniture was shoved in the cupboard and they were locked into paying the extra hundred pounds a month.

'I can't wait to move,' Thandie said.

'Do you have somewhere to go?'

'Not yet.'

The women talked about houses. Some had previously lived in Red Road and moved on to other parts of the city. Some started out in Sighthill.

'We were so looking forward to having our house up high because in South Africa, in Johannesburg, you just don't have high houses.'

The women nodded, some of them from South Africa like herself, some from Zimbabwe and recently hauled through the asylum system.

'I don't miss it,' one woman said.

'I do,' said another. 'I don't feel integrated where I am now. I did at Red Road.'

'I'm fed up of it now,' Thandie said. 'The mould is terrible. See this, come with me.'

She took the women into her bedroom and showed them the mould that dirtied the wall.

'We have the girls in with us when it's really cold,' she said. 'Wheezing with their asthma, it's no good. It gets really, really cold.'

The women sat on the edges of the bed and talked about children, about work, about holidays.

'You'll miss the view,' one woman said and Thandie agreed that she would.

'There's lots of sky,' she said. 'And I like to look at where I've been and where I want to go to. I can see so much from here. I can see where you ladies live.'

'Make the most of it,' the woman said. 'It's not the same down on the ground.'

'She had a bad experience yesterday,' one of the women said.

'I don't want to talk about it.'

It was so unexpected, the abuse, if that is what the woman was talking about. Thandie worried most about teenagers, but some were so unexpectedly charming and decent that it restored her, completely. The children her daughters introduced her to were polite and honest and clever and her daughters sounded like them now, with their Glasgow vowels and different names for everything. They forgot their Zulu now, especially the youngest, and Thandie reminded herself to speak in Zulu as often as she could so the children could have their Scottish language and the language of their birth too. So much to think about.

'Come on,' she said and the women went into the living room and she poured them wine and gave the men meat for the braai – strips of beef and lamb and some cut tomatoes – and then she put Brenda Fassie on the stereo once more. It was as if a charge went into the room. Wine gulped and glasses put down and the women started dancing to the party songs. They danced in pairs and took turns to hip dance, weaving and shaking their hips and their bums, bending their legs and lowering themselves closer and closer to the ground. The teenagers were at the doorway again. Thandie's girls and other daughters too, one in spectacles, one with a hair band tied around her curls. The girls in the doorway smiled and looked embarrassed and the women danced harder, kicking off their shoes and stepping barefoot on the carpet, showing their daughters how it is done, swaying and shaking and letting the turned-up music bring them back to something of their life in Africa, something that their African-born, Glasgow-bred children might never truly understand.

Smoke came into the room all of a sudden. The men flapped tongs and dish towels at the billowing grey. It rushed to the top of the veranda and spread out across its ceiling. The men stumbled into the house and Thandie yelled out of the door, 'What do you want, water?'

'It's all right,' Mhambi said. 'It's the fat on the coals.'

But the smoke didn't stop and it began to smell of plastic and chemicals and burning wood.

One of the women came out of the kitchen with a vase of water. Thandie took it from her and hurled it on to the veranda in the direction of the braai.

The hot coals sizzled and her husband roared as the water hit him too.

'Calm down!' he shouted but he wasn't calm himself. 'It's just the hot fat on the hot coals!'

Brenda Fassie sang out about a wedding day and Mhambi yelled, 'Turn that off!'

When the music stopped the scene on the veranda seemed less frantic. Mhambi remained out there behind the pigeon net and the sound and the smoke decreased to a puff and a sizzle. But someone was knocking at the door.

The women looked at Thandie.

'Shall I go?' she said and squeezed past the watching teenagers and opened the front door. It was the concierge.

'Are you on fire?' he asked.

'No.'

'There's smoke coming from your veranda.'

'I know, it's over now.'

'It doesn't smell as if it is.'

'Do you want to come in?'

'No, Thandie, but if you'd answered when I buzzed up and had opened the door without me knocking for five minutes I'd have been less inclined to call the fire brigade.'

'Sorry, Craig, we were having a braai.'

'What's a braai?'

'It's like a barbeque.'

'On your veranda? Just do me a favour and calm the smoke down, will you?'

They did calm the smoke down. Mhambi cooked enough to eat and when the coals were cold he folded the foil barbeques and put them down the chute. They never had another braai until they left the steel-covered doors on their landing and moved to the four apartment in Roystonhill with the garden and the beautiful kitchen and the water that didn't slosh around the bath when the wind was up. Thandie played Brenda Fassie and Miriam Makeba and her daughters didn't object. The older two went out on a Saturday night to the bars on Sauchiehall Street. Tesco's sold maize meal and some of the vegetables she liked, but she still went to Solly's when she passed.

Khadra 2007

When the French artist started his walk across the high wire
the crowd on the grass turned silent and respectful. He walked
on wire Khadra could barely see, step after fluid step, and carried
a balancing pole at his waist. A black-clad figure crossing the
air between One-two-three and Ninety-three Petershill Drive.
And he looked so confident up there, so confident that the
people around Khadra began to talk again and comment as he
walked, as if he could never fall, as if he couldn't possibly drop
off the wire.

Police stood among the crowd. Kids, dogs, families, concierges. Men and women stood on verandas. Everyone looked
up. A plane flew overhead, oblivious.

The wind was kicking about, down on the ground, and
when Khadra noticed the French artist walking backwards she
realised it was too windy for him up there on the wire. A high-
wire walker with a film crew and journalists taking pictures
wouldn't go back unless it was too dangerous to go on. He
took graceful steps backwards. Thin and high and balanced.

Then she worried for him. She imagined his foot feeling for
the wire and missing, his leg dropping below the wire and his
body tipping after it.

'Why is he going backwards?' a girl asked a woman.

'I don't know pet,' she said and sounded disappointed.
'Perhaps it's too windy. Perhaps he lost his nerve.'

When he was back on the platform at the top of the building Khadra and others in the crowd didn't move, expecting
him, perhaps, to step out again. But he disappeared and never
came back.

The crowd dispersed, carrying the mugs and key rings and
balloons that the housing gave out. Khadra looked for anyone
she might recognise. A group of teenagers stood close by and
Khadra wondered if they were the older selves of the boys who'd

popped their heads above the hedge. One of the boys glanced at her as they passed but Khadra didn't attract their attention.

On another part of the grass, children pointed shoe boxes and tin cans at the buildings and stood very still. Pinhole cameras. A woman watched them and although Khadra couldn't hear her words, she knew she would be encouraging them gently and helping them with exposure times and angles. Khadra remembered standing with the same woman in the dark room on the twenty-seventh floor of the YMCA and developing her own pinhole photographs, seeing the skewed, silent images her camera had created. She remembered, too, watching Red Road appear on the silent walls and ceiling of another dark room and gasping at the fine magic of the Camera Obscura; tiny buses and cars, wind-blown clouds, the Campsie Fells. It was a delicate art and one that had given her solace in the dark years of her asylum. Khadra was happy to see the woman still there.

Then she saw her old friend, the Somali woman she'd stepped off the bus with when she first arrived at Red Road. Two children played near her. They could have been twins. For a second Khadra thought the woman was going to turn away from her, but instead she stood still while Khadra approached.

'You look tired,' her friend said.

Khadra pushed hair out of her eyes and shrugged. 'I got my leave to remain,' she said. 'When you left Red Road I was still waiting.'

It was much more difficult to speak to her than Khadra thought. 'Video link to London. Three years of hell, eh?'

'Are you married?' Khadra's friend said.

'No.'

'Not to the Scottish man?'

'No.'

'That's a shame for you.'

Khadra shrugged again and smiled at the children.

'I don't know what I'd have done without him during those

asylum years, so I'm grateful to him, in a way. But he ended up not being very nice to me.'

'We have to go home now,' her friend said and held out her hands for her children.

Khadra looked at the creases on her old friend's face. The woman turned away. And then Khadra couldn't stop herself.

'Have you got a problem with me?'

Her friend turned to look at her and the twins stared.

'Have you? Is there a problem?'

Families walked past them towards the roundabout at the bottom of Red Road. Groups of boys kicked footballs. People with cameras and microphones approached groups of asylum seekers.

'We have nothing in common,' Khadra's friend said.

'What?'

'We have nothing in common any more,' is all her friend would say and she walked away.

Khadra stood for a while with her hands in her pockets and the wind blowing her hair and wished she was the kind of person who could hold onto things like faith and origin as if they rooted her to something, but she couldn't. Red Road. She took one last look at the place where she'd endured the process that finally gave her leave to remain and went on home.

Concierges 2007

It was a strange feeling, doing their job and knowing one day where they sat would be rubble or grass or somebody's new living room. They were told new jobs would be found if they could be found, but demolition was a way off yet. Some of the boys had moved on to other multi-storeys but John said to George that the more high rises they knocked down, the fewer jobs there would be. Some of the Sighthill buildings were on their way out. One of the Gorbals high rises was ready to go. All over Glasgow cranes with claws – munchers – were sticking their nails into walls and windows and picking off floors. And all over Glasgow they were moving tenants into new builds with front and back doors and only one set of neighbours either side.

George and John were there to wave cheerio to Mrs Donoghue. Her daughters wanted her closer to where they stayed in Bishopbriggs. They wheeled her along the corridor to the concierge office, her legs covered with a tartan blanket.

'Where have you been hiding?' John said.

'Oh, I've been up in my wee house, having fun,' she said. 'I can't get about much now.' By the nick of her, with her frail face and sloping shoulders, she wasn't wrong. George and John saw one or other of her children almost daily, on the CCTV cameras, waiting for the lift with a bag of messages. Devoted. Or loyal. Or just being good children for their mammy. One of the daughters whispered to George and John that Mrs Donoghue was petrified of being alone at night. They were considering taking it in turns to stay over until she got used to the new place. They hoped it was the right thing, moving her closer to where they lived, but away from the house she'd known for years and years.

'She liked having you concierges there,' one of the daughters said and John said, 'Aye, a lot of the older folk liked the security.'

So they went down the stair to wave Agnes Donoghue goodbye and the old woman had tears in her eyes as her daughters wheeled her out of the foyer and she kept looking back over her shoulder, straining her neck. In the end she put her pale, thin fingers over her face and the cuffs of her blouse rode up to show her white and bony forearms and her daughters wheeled her, like that, to the car and she didn't look back.

Teenage Asylum Seekers

There's Scottish people, Somalian, Pakistan, Iraqi, Iran, Afghanistan.

Congo.

Congo.
Nigeria.
Nigeria, Somalian, Scottish, American.
Iraq.
Everyone. People from around the world. Side Kicks is the
organisation. We play Blacks versus Scottish. They beat us.
Sometimes we beat them.
(Laughter)

Concierges 2008

The concierges sat in their office. Nothing showed up on the monitor. Nobody in or out. The phone rang and it was a mainstream on twenty-five floor. She said she could hear glass breaking and crashing about. John went up with his radio and torch. He didn't wait long for the lift and it was just him who got in it. On the twenty-fifth floor the mainstream tenant stood in her doorway. She pointed at the window on the fire door. Kicked in with glass everywhere.

'I think they've done it all the way down,' the woman said and John radioed George, telling him to catch the boys before they got out.

'That's them away,' George said because he saw them on the monitor, running out of the building, their mouths open like warriors. Young, some of them. Really young. Local boys.

'This will take a while to clear up,' John said and George stood up to get the dustpan and brush.

Andrea 2008

The elderly man wouldn't sit. He came through the door with a woman who worked at the centre and it was laughs and jokes at first but he didn't want to sit and he wouldn't sit. So he stood next to one of the walls that were covered with photographs of elderly people. The stage had three chairs on it and looked out on to rows of more chairs. The room was full. At the back of the hall women in housecoats stood at a hatch. And behind the women and the hatch was a stainless-steel kitchen. Alive and Kicking was the name of the building, and the hall in which Andrea sat and the elderly man stood was shiny with laminate and polish, a thousand smiles on the walls, the wood floor and wall panels in comforting tones and the air warm. Andrea had never been inside before but she knew about the Women's Centre next door where she worked once, albeit in a different building, at its old address in Petershill Court where the rats used to run past at night when she locked up.

Babies crawled along the floor at the end of the aisles in the hall. Some folk chatted. Others sat still in their seats and stared at the empty chairs on the stage. After the elderly man came folk from the GHA. And then the woman who worked at the centre returned with a tumbler of drink – a liquid coin of whisky at the bottom of the glass – and a plastic cup of water. The elderly man took the tumbler and held it while the woman poured in water. She pointed to a chair, apart from the rows of chairs, by the wall, and the man sat. He sipped his whisky and pulled at the collar of his jumper. Cable-knitted. Cream coloured and thick. The man had strong-looking eyes and when he caught Andrea staring, he raised his glass and winked. Andrea smiled. The people from the GHA asked for attention.

The meeting was brief. The flats were coming down over a period of eight years. The blocks would be emptied as new houses became ready or vacant. The needs of tenants would be taken into account as to who got the new builds, the other high rises in the city or the older housing stock in Springburn, Barmulloch and Balornock. Disturbance money would be paid.

Questions? Can we choose where we go? To a certain extent. When will we go? The tenants of the slab block at the back – Two-one-three to One-five-three Petershill Drive – will go first. How will it be demolished? Explosives. Probably. Safedem is the company. You will hear more from them. They will talk to the children in the primary schools and have an office on site for enquiries. Rent? Comparable. Although expect to pay a wee bit more for the new builds. What about the asylum seekers? They will continue to come to the YMCA. Can we watch the demolition? There'll be an exclusion zone. Best to watch it from a very safe distance. I heard there's tons of asbestos lining the walls and the ceilings. There is. We need to make the building safe.

'What if you don't want to leave?'

The voice came from the back of the room. It was a man's voice. Andrea saw the elderly man with the whisky and the warm jumper turn his head, as Andrea did, to see who had spoken. While the speaker's question was answered, the elderly man sipped the last of his whisky. The woman who worked at the centre stood over him and poured more whisky and more water in his glass.

'I thought I was the only one refusing to move,' the elderly man said and the woman said 'Shoosh Jim' and touched him on the shoulder.

When the meeting was over Andrea stood up. She walked past the elderly man and heard him say, 'They can blow me up in my house. I'm not leaving.' The woman touched his shoulder again.

'Your hair's looking lovely today, Janet,' he said.

'I knew you were coming in, Jim,' she said.

'I come in every day.'

'So it must look lovely every day.'

'No. Some days it's a wee bit flyaway. Today it's looking lovely.'

'Thanks Jim. I'll take that as a compliment.'

'Take it any way you like.'

The women in housecoats and younger men arranged the vacated chairs around long tables and elderly folk stood about and sat at the tables when they were ready. The women in housecoats were full of business in the stainless-steel kitchen.

'You don't want to go?' Andrea said. She didn't know why she spoke. She hardly spoke to anyone she didn't know.

'No, I don't,' the man said.

'Why not?'

'Because I like my house. I've lived in it since 1977 and Red Road since 1966. What on God's earth is the point of me moving somewhere else now?'

'Do you not want a nice back and front door?' she asked the elderly man.

'No. I want my peace and quiet and my view and the house my wife died in.'

Someone struck some chords on the piano and the elderly man widened his eyes. 'Now, that's a beautiful Irish song,' he said.

'He's sharp as a button,' the woman, Janet, said in Andrea's ear. She spoke softly and kindly. 'But he's upset today. He doesn't see why he should have to move at his age.'

Andrea couldn't wait to move. She'd been married and divorced and married again at Red Road, she'd raised her weans and brought in a wage and sat on sunny days with friends on the grass by the wall near the shops, but she longed to leave. It was enough now. Twenty-five years. The four boys who lived next door didn't respect anyone; they played on the landing floor as she was out there on her hands and knees trying to clean it. When the concierges buffed the floor when it was her old neighbour's turn, the boys trod mud onto the shiny floor and spilt ginger on it without wiping it up. They chapped the door and ran, scraped her door and burnt her door, put sandwiches through her letter box. Countless arguments with the boys' mother came to nothing. Andrea didn't like to argue but she felt she had to. And don't get her started on the drug dealer across the landing; the girl whose house was busy with comings and goings all day and all night.

One of the last to leave the hall, she turned to look at the elderly man who walked tall and slow to one of the tables, to eat his lunch, and then return later, presumably, to his house in the high rise. Andrea wondered which was his house and wanted, on a wee whim, to see the world from his flat, to feel his peace and quiet, to maybe understand why it was he wanted to stay.

Donna McCrudden

Fond memories? Oh aye, some good times. In summer we'd all go down and bring sandwiches and juice and what have you for the kids. We'd either just sit on the grass down beside our flat or the wall round the back at the shops, there's a wee wall that's there. We'd all sit there outside the shops and watch everybody going by with the sun shining right on us and we'd sit on the grass behind the shops, a big patch of grass behind the shops, and the kids would run about and everything. I went with one of my neighbours, she had girls as well. We'd have a radio and the girls would play with their dollies and skipping ropes.

Incident Book 2008

Schools Liaison officer looking for Evan Harrison given paracetamol for headache. Sat in office for fifteen minutes and felt better. Evan Harrison evades detection.

Andrea 2009

She met with the officer from the Glasgow Housing Association and told them her stipulations, seeing as they'd asked. Firstly, don't put that drug dealer girl anywhere near me, she said, and the housing officer understood and made a note on her paper. Secondly, I would like a new build please because I'm disabled now and I can't manage stairs and I don't want to be anywhere with lifts because they always break down.

She requested a three apartment, one bedroom fewer than the house she already had, because two of her three girls had moved out and it would just be herself and her new husband and her youngest.

'We'll see what we can do,' the housing officer said.

Jim 2009

The pills didn't help anymore. It was harder to get up in the mornings and when he was up, at half-past seven, he needed to return to bed soon after. This was something new. He tried hard to stay optimistic. He liked to hear the Chinese weans on the landing waiting for the lift. They waved when they saw him and he thought their mammy and daddy were bringing them up beautifully. The pain was a nuisance. It was a heavy pain and he told himself that he should expect pain at eighty-seven. They stopped his radio programme on a Sunday night and he was devastated. Jennifer and James bought him a television set with a CD player included and a DVD player too. It did everything but make the tea he told Janet and said he didn't know if he'd live long enough to read the manual. Janet told him to stop that talk. He showed her a letter from the GHA inviting him to a meeting with a housing officer to discuss his housing needs. I don't have any housing needs, he told Janet. I have what I need and I live in it. Janet said that she would come with him to meet the housing officer if he wanted and Jim said, aye, that might be a good idea, you'll keep me out of the jail.

Andrea 2009

Twenty-five years of staying in Red Road. Thirteen years in one house, twelve years in the other and now a moving out date – June 2009 – and a new house with a front and back door, a garden and three toilets. Three toilets. A downstairs, an upstairs and an en suite. Andrea daren't tell her mother, up the road and using a chanti po at night because she couldn't manage the walk to the bathroom. Nobody would have far to go for a pee in her house, that was plain. It was a beautiful house. She'd been taken for a look round by a man from the GHA and stood in the garden in the shadow of Birnie Court admiring the cut grass and clean windows and inside she'd been pleased about the spacious kitchen and the laminate flooring. It was a good house.

Andrea's clear-out was meticulous and time consuming. First she added their savings to their disturbance money and worked out which of the big items they would need to keep and which they could afford to replace. She wanted everything new because the house was new and the start was new. If they were careful, it would work out that they could buy a television and DVD player, settee, table, chairs, washing machine and beds, totally brand new. So they ditched the big items. Everything else they sorted into bags for the charity shops or gave away to her daughters or their daughters' friends. Andrea put bubble wrap around the paintings she'd done in Fab Pad on the twenty-third floor of Ten Red Road. She'd made a mirror too and she wrapped that and put it in the room with the boxes and stuff to take. Her daughters came up with fish and chip suppers on one of her last nights in the house and they watched the telly as if it was just another normal night, but their memories

bounced about in their chat. Andrea saw them to the lift and her eldest daughter said, look, I can reach the buttons without a stick. See you in the new house, they said, and told her off for not getting one with more bedrooms in case they needed to stay over.

On one of her last mornings she saw an elderly man coming out of the chemist as she was going in. He held a sellotaped-down paper bag in one hand and pushed his other hand against the closing door, attempting to open it.

'Too late,' he said and she said 'no bother' and realised it was the man she'd met who didn't want to leave. He wore a knitted hat and a knitted scarf and his hand shook as he tried to put his paper bag in the pocket of his coat.

'Have you had your meeting with the housing officer?' Andrea asked and the man's brown eyes were confused.

'I met you at the meeting about the demolition. You didn't want to leave.'

'I don't want to leave,' he said.

Andrea commiserated, and having done her packing and sorting, she understood what an upheaval it would be for the man.

'I'll be gone by the weekend,' Andrea said and the man nodded as if it was no surprise that another person was going.

'It's only me left on my landing,' he said.

She wished him well and he told her he was going next door to the paper shop to put on his lotto ticket for the next month. Twenty pound a month, he said. Is it worth it, because I've only won a few tenners and had four numbers once. Andrea went inside the chemist for her tablets then crossed the concrete to the burger van to say farewell to Barry.

John McNally

My wife went away about nineteen eighty-three to the hospital and I was on my own then, so this project opened and that was handy. I never left it. They offered me a house near to the ground, only five, ten minutes away but I never took it. That's why I stayed there, you know. It's hard to explain but it kind of knocks the heart out of you. I couldn't imagine living anywhere else now. I'm hoping that if I go to flats, I'm high up.

Concierges 2009

John didn't know. Perhaps he was jaded. It could have been the bag of bread that landed on his head when he stood outside the building and he'd never know where it came from because when he looked up, all the windows were shut. Not as bad as the fire extinguisher that the students smashed onto the roof of the BMW next to where he stood and could have killed him. At least they'd caught the guys that did that, though. Or perhaps it was because his job was about to go. Because they'd moved some of the concierges on already – concierges who'd spent as long as he had, or longer, at Red Road. He was told he'd be given another concierge job or an alternative job and God knows what that would be.

So the mainstreams were moving out to the new builds at the foot of the Red Road Flats but still the asylums came. Perhaps that was getting to him. This constant flow of persecuted people from all over the globe. Some globe. And locally the BNP were stirring things up snake-like, taking advantage of people's poverty and the media's misrepresentation. He saw it every day in his paper. He'd heard too many times the mainstreams say that they wanted out of Red Road because they hardly saw a white face anymore. The asylums were no bother. If anything, they were less bother than the mainstreams because they kept themselves to themselves; they didn't pester or badger or, let's face it, harass the concierges. It wasn't the same in that Christmas was quiet and a non-event and they hardly got a single tin of biscuits or a card for their work during the year and a family could be living in the block for months and he would never see them or he wouldn't recognise them when he did. But crime was down. Joyriding was finished. Drugs weren't the problem they used to be. John didn't know. Maybe it was the weather. Maybe it was the starless and moonless night that was doing it for him.

Each floor of the slab block nearest to Ten Red Road – Ten, Twenty and Thirty Petershill Court – needed to be checked. Most of the floors were uninhabited, with steel bolted onto the door-ways of each house. They had to check, though, in case there was somebody sleeping on the landing or dead on the landing, snuck in through the main doors. Although the updated door entry system in this block meant that a message was sent to the computer in the Ten Red Road office with the name of each person whose key fob accessed the doors, it wasn't impossible that somebody could get in.

Nothing. Nothing. Nothing. On his own in the lift to the top of the block, watching the red numbers go up and up and up and the tiny lift shake in its shaft. The remaining tenants were spread around the three joined-up blocks. Thirty-three lights in thirty-three living rooms. He didn't expect to see anyone until he walked all the way down to the twentieth floor. So why did it sound like there were doors closing and footsteps above? He told himself it was because the doors he'd opened to check each land-ing took a wee while to close. Simple. He couldn't explain the footsteps so he would forget about it.

'Jesus Mary and Joseph!' A man was just inside the door that went from the stairs to the landing. He was coming out of his front door and seemed as frightened as John.

'I don't expect to see a soul up here,' the man said. He was an HPU. The majority of tenants were from the Homeless Person

Unit or were mainstreams, not wanting to move to one of the
local houses but waiting until a house came up in another part
of Glasgow – perhaps one where family or friends lived. Everybody was waiting to leave.

The tenant called for the lift and John went on his way
down the stair. He still didn't know. There wasn't much chance
of him and George working together on a new job. It was a
shame. You didn't get better partnerships.

The other floors were quiet. On floor seven it was a relief to
hear a television behind one of the doors. He thought it must
be strange for the tenants left behind to live on deserted landings.
Or maybe it was peaceful. Maybe that's what people wanted
now; to be undisturbed in their houses, not to know their
neighbours, not to be living cheek by jowl.

Three in the morning. One block left to check and then he
and George would make a cup of tea and sit in the office and
keep an eye on the CCTV monitors. In the last block the
shutters to the old concierge office were pulled down and
undisturbed.

A tenant came out of the lift and lunged at John.

'It's coming,' she said.

The tenant was pregnant. It was Susie Ho. She lived with
her husband on floor nineteen and they were waiting for a
house in Knightswood.

'Oh hen, are you all right?'

'It's coming,' Susie said again and she put her hands flat
against the wall and bent over.

'Is it a contraction?'

Susie nodded and said yes with an intake of breath so that
it came out as a gasp. This was serious.

'Have you phoned an ambulance?'

Susie nodded again and cried out. When her contraction
had finished she stood up and began to walk to the door.

'Where are you going?'

'To wait for the ambulance.'

'Hen, wait here,' John said. 'We'll sit you down in the office and you can be comfortable.'

'Nothing is comfortable,' Susie said but she waited with John while he opened the door to the old concierge office, flicked on the lights and pulled out a chair for Susie to sit on. The office was like the bloody Marie Celeste, everything as if the concierges had stood up and walked out one day. Which is what they did, really. She put her legs astride the chair and leaned her body towards the chair-back but began to struggle and didn't seem comfortable. John helped her up. 'My bump's too big,' she said and then she leaned against John and roared.

'It's coming. It's another contraction. Oh God.' Her legs shook and began to buckle. John helped her to the floor and leaned her back against the wall.

'Right,' he said. 'I'll phone the ambulance to see where it is. Where's your husband, Susie? Tell me he's not up the stair.'

'He's away at a conference. He didn't want to go but I'm only thirty-six weeks. I said I'd be okay.'

Susie leaned back against the wall and put a hand on her forehead and a hand on her belly.

'You just rest there,' John said and he went to radio George to tell him what had happened but thought he'd better check on the ambulance first.

Susie began to breathe heavily, in and out through her nose.

'It's another one,' she said and she continued to breathe, her chest rising and her head turning from side to side. Her face was pale and sweaty. He made to get a towel from the back room but the operator answered.

'I'm checking on an ambulance. I've got a lady here and she's about to give birth.'

Susie moaned through her contraction and put her hands on the floor next to her and said, 'I want to push. I need to push.'

'Did you hear that?' John said to the operator. 'She wants to push.'

'Right. How regular are her contractions? Can you tell me if you can see anything? Can you see a head?'

'Okay.' John put the phone on speaker and said to Susie, 'Your contractions, how far apart are they?'

'I don't know.'

'Well that's about a minute since the last one. Or maybe less. A minute at most!' he shouted into the phone.

'Okay, can you tell me if you can see a head?'

'Susie, I need to see if the baby's coming.'

'I can feel something heavy.'

Susie lifted her hips, pulled down her tracksuit and kicked off her trainers.

'I can feel something heavy,' Susie said again. 'I want to push.'

'Yes, there's something there,' John shouted into the phone.

'Do you think it's the head?'

'I think it's the head.'

'It's coming,' Susie said.

'Okay, on the next contraction, you need to put your hand on the baby's head and hold it gently. You've got to stop it from shooting out or she'll tear, do you understand?'

'Aye.'

'Have you got clean towels?'

'No.'

'Run and get clean towels if you can.'

John leapt to his feet and Susie screamed, 'Don't leave me,' but he ran to the back office. There was a dish towel on the side next to the sink but it seemed used. He pulled open drawers, praying he'd see a pile of clean, folded towels. He didn't know this office. When he found a drawer with some dish towels he grabbed the lot. No hand towels. Nothing else of use. Susie was crying out again.

'She's having another one,' John said and he spread out a dish towel.

'Remember,' the operator said. 'Apply firm but gentle pressure to the baby's head.'

'Until the ambulance gets here?'

'No, the baby wants to be born, but you must hold its head there so she doesn't tear. How's mum?'

'She's doing really well.'

'I'm in agony!'

'I know, I know, but you're doing really well,' the operator said on the phone's loudspeaker.

'Can you see the head?'

'A little. I think it's the head.'

'Well, remember to apply firm and gentle pressure when she has her next contraction. And when the head does come through you have to support it, yes? And support the baby's shoulders. They'll be slippery. Don't drop it.'

Susie leaned her head back and roared through her contraction. 'It's coming. I need to push.' She squeezed her eyes tight shut and scrabbled at the floor. John had a sudden thought that she shouldn't be giving birth in this dirty disused office, but there was nothing he could do about that now.

He applied gentle pressure to the baby's head and felt the baby pushing against his hand. It was coming. Then the pressure eased.

'Oh my God, oh my God,' Susie said and John wished he could mop her brow or hold her hand but God, he was delivering a baby.

The next contraction came within seconds and he could feel the head wanting to burst out so he applied pressure as the head kept coming.

'How are you doing?' said the operator. 'Can you see the head?'

John was silent.

'Can you see the head?' the operator said again.

'The head's out! The head's out!' John shouted.

'The head's out?' Susie cried. 'Oh my God, oh my God, oh help me.'

'Are you supporting the head? Hold onto the head and remember to support the shoulders when they come and then the hips and legs. The baby will be slippery.'

'Come on wee baby,' John said. The baby's eyes were closed. Its face was blue and wrinkled.

Susie's cry tore into the room. John told her she was doing well. His hands were bloodied and he held onto the baby's head. Liquid surged over the baby's head and on to John's forearms and he shouted, 'There's water coming out!'

'That'll be her waters breaking. It's okay. How's mum?'

'She's doing great.'

Then the shoulders came.

'The shoulders are here,' he said and Susie cried out again.

'Well done,' said the operator. 'Remember to hold tight. Baby will be slippery.'

The operator was right. The baby was slippery. So slippery he prayed he wouldn't drop it. It was coming now, nearly all of it, body, hips, bum and legs. Susie panted and said 'oh oh oh,' over and over. John saw the cord still attached to the baby he held in his outstretched hands.

'How are you doing?' the operator said.

'The baby's out. The baby's born. The cord –'

'Clean its nose and mouth. Wipe it with a clean cloth. Then wrap it in a different clean cloth. Keep it warm. Don't pull the cord.'

So many instructions. Susie was whimpering in high-pitched out-breaths. It was hard to hold the baby and reach for a dish towel. God, he didn't want to drop it and it was so slippery. He held the baby against his chest, keeping his arms tight around it. He wiped a clean dish towel over the baby's face and waited for it to cry. He knew it had to cry. He wrapped the tiny wrinkled baby in a dish towel and then wrapped it again in another one. The cord was still attached.

'The ambulance is thirty seconds away,' the operator said. 'Is it crying yet?'

Not yet.

'Shall I give the baby to mum?'

'Is it crying? Make sure its mouth and nose are clear.' John had no more dish towels left. He wiped its nose and mouth again with the corner of a used one and then the baby opened its mouth and cried. It bleated and opened its eyes once, twice, then closed them again and cried some more.

'That's the baby crying,' John said and he felt relief in his face and shoulders and arms and he began to shake. Don't drop the baby.

Susie was quiet, shaking, her head tipped back against the wall and her eyes half open, watching her baby. Her hair was jet black compared with her pale face.

'I'll give the baby to mum, will I?'

'Yes,' the operator said. 'The placenta will be delivered soon. Don't pull the cord. The ambulance men will help you. Give the baby to mum. Do you know what you have?'

John didn't know. He must have seen because he'd had the bare baby in his hands, but he didn't know or he couldn't remember. He moved closer to Susie and as she held out her arms, he put the swaddled baby against her chest. She cradled it in her arms and her baby's face was close to her own face. The baby breathed.

John took off his coat, and encouraged Susie to lean forwards and let it slip over her shoulders and down her back. Susie was quiet. She kissed her baby's wet head.

'The ambulance is pulling up outside now,' the operator said and her voice was more relaxed now, a strange sound coming from the phone on the floor beside John. 'I'll wait till they get inside then I'll leave you with them. Is it a boy or a girl?'

Susie smiled. 'Shall we see?' she said, and John helped her pull open the cloth around the baby and peek. 'It's a boy,' she said.

'A boy,' said John.

'A boy. Congratulations. You've done really well. Both of you.'

'Thank you,' said Susie and she put her fingers to John's bloodied hand and then her fingers returned to touch lightly on the cloth that swaddled her baby.

Blue lights flashed a pattern in the foyer and John got up to let the paramedics in. The operator said goodbye. The paramedics attended to Susie and the baby boy and John stood in the doorway looking at the way they swiftly organised the scene and cleaned up Susie. He turned away and looked at the wall and then asked them if he could do anything.

'No,' they said and they had Susie in a wheelchair and the baby in her arms very quickly. And because her husband was away and there was nobody Susie could call, they took her away to the Royal.

God. A baby.

He found a mop and bucket and some disinfectant and cleaned the floor. Then he bundled the dish towels and put them in a bin bag. That was all he needed to do. The office was as they'd found it. Papers scattered on the desk, shelves of files and A4 notebooks. He would write up the incident book when he returned to Ten Red Road.

Outside, the concrete crunched under his shoes. The wet breeze cooled his damp neck and back and arms. He remembered he'd left his coat in the old office, but he didn't want to go back. It was a short walk to where George would be waiting for him in the office but one that took him some time for stopping and raising his face to the black sky and starting again and stopping to flick his wet eyes to the lights he could see in the windows of the dark towers. Oh God have mercy on us he said out loud and crossed his arms to hug his shoulders as he walked, waiting a while, out of sight of the CCTV camera, to shake and sob and get it out of his system.

Jim 2010

Jim had his meeting and told them he didn't want to leave and a week later his daughter phoned for the doctor. They took him to hospital all of a sudden because his chest was weak and infected and the pain in his arthritic hip was masking some complications. He sat in a wheelchair with a blanket over his knees as they pushed him out of his house, his pictures and trinkets and piles of books flashing by him. Down in the lift to leave Red Road for the last time.

They left his body in the chapel for a night. The same chapel as his wife. Janet came to see him and lit a candle. They said his name from the stage at Alive and Kicking when the elderly folk were at the tables eating, and told them that he'd passed away. Despite the smiling walls, the hall was sad that day and nobody felt like singing, especially the old Irish songs.

Mariam 2010

Mariam lit a candle and put it with the others in the spot outside the YMCA. She didn't know them but her brother played football with the boy. Rumours were rife and varied; they were about to be deported, they were wanted by the Russian mafia, the Canadian Intelligence were after them too. But they did jump. Tied together. And they died where they landed. Those were facts. Mariam was aware of tension and panic and fright and anger. Many people milled around. She watched a photographer take a picture of a young woman her age who lived in the YMCA too. The woman glared at the photographer and turned away, then she turned back and spoke and used her hands a lot when she spoke and her face was angry. The photographer took his pad from his pocket, listened, and wrote.

John McNally

I still live in the flats. Twenty-seven/four, One-two-three Petershill
Drive. G21 4QU. Same flat since when I first moved in. 1969.
Any people that I know have left, they say they kind of miss it
because they were well laid out. There were no stairs or that.
It's the view that actually kept me there. My living room looks to
the west with the whole of Glasgow spread out in front of me
and believe it or not I can see the Arran hills. And Thursday and
Friday there the sunsets were absolutely beautiful. Thursday and
Friday were beautiful. For a daft old man like me, an old gas
worker talking about sunsets, is there a name for it, aesthetic?

Concierges 2010

George came back one night with a tiny black and white cat.
It stayed in his arms contentedly when he sat on the desk and
stroked its head, rubbing his fingers between its tiny black ears.

'I found it by the fire escape door,' George said and put the
cat against his chest like a baby and stroked its back. The cat
wriggled then curled itself into George's lap.

'Whose is it? Is it hungry?'

'I don't know. It kept following me. It wouldn't leave me.
Go put some milk in a bowl, John.'

John got up from his chair and went out the back to the
fridge. He splashed some milk into a bowl and put it on the
floor in the office. 'It's the bowl Moira uses for her cereal but
she won't mind,' he said.

The cat lapped the milk until there was none left in the
bowl and sat neatly next to it.

'Put a bit more in,' George said.

John did so, for the cat, although he wasn't sure why George
couldn't get up and do it himself.

The cat drank the rest of the milk.

'We'd better leave some for Allan and Moira's tea the morra,'
John said and put the milk back into the fridge.

'How about that tin of tuna of Moira's? We'll get her another one tomorrow.'

'How about it?' John said.

He took the tin and a can opener and put the bowl on his desk. The cat leapt onto the desk and watched him open the can and fork out some chunks of tuna and brine. When he put the bowl on the floor the cat jumped down and ate.

'I don't think that cat's eaten for days,' George said. 'So, what will we call him?'

John looked at the cat and said, 'Toots. He's only a wee baby cat. Toots.'

George said, 'Not Red as in Red Road Court?'

'No. Toots. Allan won't let us keep it.'

'We'll keep it quiet for a bit.'

The cat cleaned its whiskers with its paws and curled up under the desk on top of a hold-all that contained George's running kit, just in case he ever felt like running home.

John noticed the funeral cortege first. On the CCTV monitor a slow procession of black cars and ordinary cars came down Red Road. Slow and dignified. The first hearse stopped beyond Ten Red Road opposite the YMCA building and the other cars stopped behind it. John and George went through to the office at the back and stood on the veranda in their shirt sleeves. Instinctively John thought about lighting up but he kept his cigarettes in his pocket and watched the line of cars. Barely a noise on Red Road except the hum of engines. The air respectful. No wind. A bitterly cold white day.

'Who is it?' George said.

'I don't know. An old mainstream? Look at the Glasgow families in the car.'

Faces turned towards them, tipped to look at the high towers.

'Not Agnes?'

'Her family would have let us know, surely. We'd have gone.'

'Look.'

In front of them, elderly folk came from the doors of Alive and Kicking and stood in coats and hats in the forecourt. They looked down at the funeral procession.

'One of the old folk.'

'Funny we don't know who it was and we've been here so long.'

'We'll ask the concierges on Petershill Drive.'

People on the street stayed still. Mothers held pram handles, men stood with arms by their sides, phones clutched in their hands. A boy tugged his dog to sit by his legs. Mainstreams. Asylums. Passersby. Still.

The cortege began to move and the first hearse drove around the roundabout and came back up Red Road. Full of flowers. A honey-coloured coffin. The drivers in black coats looking straight up the road. The other cars looped around the roundabout. Some cars peeled off down Petershill Drive and drove fast away. But most of the cars were there for the procession and came back up Red Road behind the cortege, the passengers' faces turned again towards the flats, while the coffin lay straight and flat in the hearse, the passengers turning for one last look at Red Road.

George and John came out of the cold and worked the rest of their shift. Seven days on, four days off. Seven days on, four days off. Switch to nights. Seven days on, four days off. Seven days on, four days off. And so on. And so on. And so on. Till the tenants were gone and the buildings only steel and girders and ghosts stories.

Epilogue

RICKY'S BACK. He's read about the demolition in the *Evening Times* and wants to see his old house. A woman with a pram pushes a toddler on a swing in the swing park on Petershill Drive. A man, bent as if he would fall but for his legs continuing to move, passes by with message bags. And there's nobody else. A few parked cars. Perhaps the sound of children playing in the nursery, or perhaps the sound of faraway seagulls. In the Safedem office, Ricky waits for the manager to come off the telephone and sees on the wall a diagram of his slab block; Two-one-three, One-eight-three and One-five-three Petershill Drive. Every house is marked as a square and some of the squares have crosses in them.

'The crosses show that we've safely removed the asbestos,' the manager says. He gives Ricky a hard hat.

When they walk outside the manager points out the tents that the workmen go into when they leave the building.

'We don't cut any corners with asbestos,' he says. 'We have a three-stage airlock. One metre by one metre squared; three of them. In the first one, they hoover themselves down, in the second one they strip off and give themselves a wash with their masks still on, in the third one they put on a clean pair of overalls and make their way to the shower unit. And then they go through the whole process again. Overalls off, paper underwear and masks still on, soap, shampoo, and then everything gets stripped off.'

'We used to break chunks of asbestos off the veranda and use them as chalk,' Ricky says and the manager shakes his head and seems as if he is about to speak, but doesn't.

There is metal fencing around the slab block. The building looks sickly with its pale cladding and hollow windows. It's derelict and huge; a useless hulk of a building that's too dangerous to topple.

'So, you're One-five-three? We haven't started on that one yet.'

'Aye. That's mine,' Ricky says and points up the building to the top and counts down the windows to the twenty-fifth floor. He finds Julie's house in Two-one-three. 'And that one', he turns away from his own block and looks up Petershill Drive, 'that's Tommy's.' He makes sure he finds their windows. It's important to see the actual windows on the actual buildings.

'Have you been back since?' the man asks.

'Not to my old house. I was back on a job once, a kitchen fire, but it was in Sixty-three.'

'So you're a fireman?'

'Aye.'

'Shall we go in?'

They go in, and the man takes charge, opening the doors, pressing the buttons on the lift and holding the keys as if it's Ricky's first time. Back come the memories.

Davie's up from London to visit his ma. He can't stop thinking about Red Road. He doesn't keep kestrels. He doesn't even have a pet. He drives one day to Red Road. Doesn't get out of the car but stops outside Thirty-three Petershill Drive which is now the YMCA. That's mine, he says as he, like Ricky, finds his windows on floor six. The veranda where his kestrel and the other birds lived has washing flapping behind the pigeon net. Sheets and towels and pillow cases. Another big family, he presumes, like his own.

Kat drives back to Glasgow on the M77. She loves the view of Glasgow as the motorway crests the edge of the city before it crosses the Clyde. She sees all the high rises and she sees Red Road. She picks out the building that is Ten Red Road and says that's mine. High rises are the bones of a city, she believes, and her own bones were shaped by living there, she knows. It took her years before she lived as long anywhere else.

Jennifer lives in Stirling and makes tablet whenever she's time. It's the longest she's been away from Red Road; the last time she saw her old home was the slow drive-by when she sat in an undertaker's car with James and their families. She plays Irish folk songs, for her father, and keeps herself nice and well-groomed, for her mother. James returns from Leeds from time to time.

Pamela tells Iris that every time she goes by their old house, twenty-four/three in Sixty-three, she looks up and can spot their house easily. There's still the black mark from the fire on the veranda below. That's ours, she always says. She's been clean for eight years. Her ma is as strong as she always was with a house full of weans as it always was.

May sings in the concert party at Alive and Kicking. She's moved from Red Road but she hasn't gone far and she'll never go far. Her second husband was a good man but he died. Her son grew up to be a fine boy – all his pals did from the back slab block. She won't have anything to do with the demolition, won't look as the skin is peeled off her home and the steel left naked underneath. She'll just look out to the audience in the hall of Alive and Kicking and sing until that's gone too.

Jim's already gone, we know that. He didn't have to move from his home of forty-four years, and that will have suited him.

Betty and Douglas, they're gone too. Him, some years back, her not so long ago at all. She drank whisky until the day she died in her tidy living room. The weans stopped coming through her house to the back stairs when they built the add-on stairs. She missed them.

Ermira is in another high rise in another part of the city. She has a son and she's waiting for her own block to be demolished. Perhaps then she'll have a garden like her mother and father. They moved to one of the new builds a few streets along. She meets on a Thursday with other Albanian women, the ones who didn't return to Kosovo when the war was over, many of whom are trained as hairdressers or chefs thanks to her brother-in-law. When she's inside her flat she stands at the window with her son in her arms and looks across the city to Red Road, back to where she started.

Thandie and Mhambi are in a bigger house in Roystonhill. That's mine, she says of her old house when she passes, because she passes frequently for her work. They cook on the braai in their garden. Food tastes so much better on the braai.

Andrea gets her new build with her three bathrooms and neat back lawn. Birnie Court's still standing and she sees it when she hangs her washing out. It reminds her of her twenty-five years in Red Road, up in those structures, far away from the ground she stands on so casually now.

Khadra works as a secretary to support herself through university and thinks constantly about the big questions. She doesn't see her friend any more. Doesn't know if the twins are growing up well. She likes her walk through the city rain to her classes or her office.

Mariam stands on her balcony and watches a man on a mower drive in circles around the field below. She sees her brother playing football with Mustapha and thinks about later, when she will meet up with her friends from school and take the bus into town. She's old enough for that now and sure enough of Glasgow. It's all right here.

Farah is still there too, with her books and her ambition. She watches the dismantling of the far slab block. Men and women taking apart the buildings that she and her parents cling to. Her parents' health still worries her. She didn't get funding for university. Her guidance teacher prepared her for this. So she works as a volunteer instead.

Kamil gives Michael a lift home from a birthday party in Springburn. Snow has fallen on top of old snow and they drive slowly on the empty streets. Let's go by Red Road Michael says because his daughter's birthday is coming up which always reminds him of the time they brought her home from the hospital. Snow on pavements, snow on the ledges around the bottom of the flats. The tyres roll softly over snow. They drive in past Ten Red Road and turn the car where the burger van stands. Barely a light on. A concierge walking with a torch. He sweeps the torch over the windscreen and Kamil and Michael shield their eyes. They drive left onto Red Road and left again down Petershill Drive where the thin blocks stand like silent pines in a forest of snow.

'What's that?' Michael says.

There's a heap in the snow. A bundle of clothes. And a dog circling. The dog stares at the car.

Kamil stops the car and puts on the handbrake. 'Is it a body?' he says. 'Should we get out?'

'He could be dead.'

All the sounds are muffled because of the snow; the click of the doors opening and shutting, the crunch of their footsteps.

'Mind the dog,' Kamil says, because the dog is circling and agitating.

They walk to the bundle in the snow and a man sits up and smiles at them.

'Are you all right, pal?' Michael says.

'Aye, I'm seeing what it's like to lie down in the snow,' the man says.

'So you're not hurt.'

'Hurt? No. I just passed by all this snow and thought I'd lie down for a while.'

His dog licks his face and he puts out a hand and claps it.

'On you go, big fella,' Kamil says and they get back in the car.

The man lies down on his back with his arms wide and his head facing the loaded sky. Kamil and Michael drive away leaving him and his dog peaceful in the snow.

The concierges are still there too. John stamps the snow off his shoes when he returns to the office. He offers George a cup of tea but George already has one that's cold enough for him to drink now. The two men sit in silence watching the CCTV monitors. The night goes on, Red Road sleeping, occasionally twitching awake or tossing and turning – a light on, a car parking, a lone man touching his key fob to the door and coming in from the snow – but mostly sleeping. George and John stay awake and keep watch over the last of its tenants.

Afterword

THE STORIES IN THIS BOOK are largely true. They were told to me by people who lived or worked in the Red Road Flats (some of whom still live and work there). In some instances I've amalgamated characters and invented new ones or altered stories for the sake of the narrative. I wanted to be as truthful as I could to the stories I was told, but I was aware too that I was writing fiction.

I hope that that the stories here chime with the experiences of those who know Red Road and give an insight into Red Road life for those who don't. That was my initial brief when I began working with Glasgow Life: to document the experiences of tenants of the Red Road Flats from the 1960s to the present day. If I'd interviewed a completely different set of people I'm sure I would have had a different book as these are only some of the stories to come out of Red Road. There are plenty more.

THE CONCIERGE

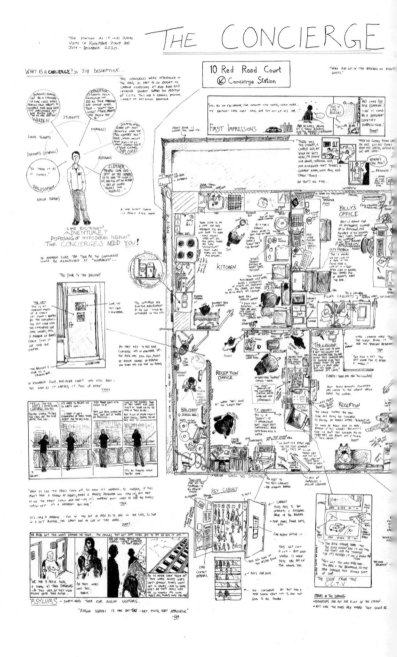

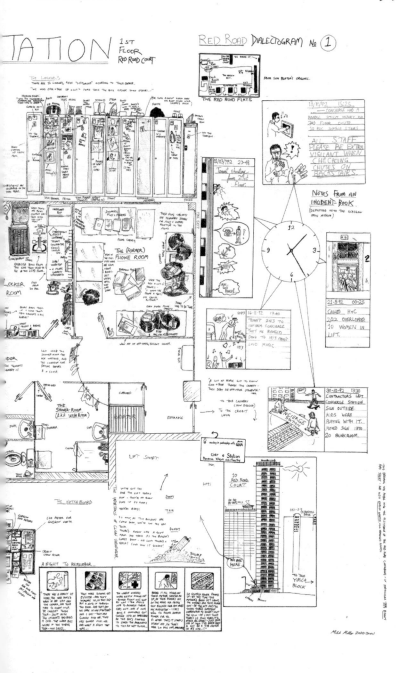

RED ROAD DIALECTOGRAM № 1

Some other books published by **LUATH** PRESS

My Epileptic Lurcher

Des Dillon
ISBN: 978-1906307-74-5 PBK £7.99

That's when I saw them. The paw prints. Halfway along the ceiling they went. Evidence of a dog that could defy gravity.

The incredible story of Bailey, the dog who walked on the ceiling; and Manny, the guy who got kicked out of Alcoholics Anonymous for swearing.

Manny Riley is newly married, with a puppy and a wee flat by the sea, and the BBC are on the verge of greenlighting one of his projects. Everything sounds perfect. But Manny has always been an anger management casualty, and the idyllic village life is turning out to be more League of Gentlemen than The Good Life. The BBC have decided his script needs totally rewritten, the locals are conducting a campaign against his dog, and the village policeman is on the side of the neds. As his marriage suffers under the strain of his constant rages, a strange connection begins to emerge between Manny's temper and the health of his beloved Lurcher.

it's one of the most effortlessly charming books I've read in a long time.
SCOTTISH REVIEW OF BOOKS

It's the kind of book you want to share with people even before you've finished reading it.
THE HERALD

Singin I'm No a Billy He's a Tim

Des Dillon
ISBN: 978-1906307-46-2 PBK £6.99

What happens when you lock up a Celtic fan?

What happens when you lock up a Celtic fan with a Rangers fan?

What happens when you lock up a Celtic fan with a Rangers fan on the day of the Old Firm match?

Des Dillon watches the sparks fly as Billy and Tim clash in a rage of sectarianism and deep-seated hatred. When children have been steeped in bigotry since birth, is it possible for them to change their views?

Join Billy and Tim on their journey of discovery. Are you singing their tune?

Explosive.
EVENING NEWS

The potency of Dillon's writing beats louder than any drum the bigots can bang.
THE IRISH POST

An Experiment in Compassion

Des Dillon
ISBN: 978-1906817-73-2 PBK £8.99

This novel is an experiment in compassion...

Stevie's just out of jail. Newly sober and building a relationship with his son, he's taking control of his own life. But what about his younger brother, Danny?

In this touching and darkly funny story of retribution and forgiveness, Stevie battles against the influences that broke him before, while Danny and his girlfriend spiral further into self-destruction. Can the bond between the two brothers be enough to give them both a fresh start?

Cycles of alcohol abuse affect individuals, families and communities. For each person who tries to break away, there are innumerable pressures forcing them back into familiar patterns. And for those that can't escape, that are fated to make the same choices again and again – can we still feel compassion?

Clydeside: Red, Orange and Green

Ian R. Mitchell
ISBN: 978-1906307-70-7 PBK £9.99

There's more to Clydeside than Glasgow. The River Clyde links west of Scotland communities shaped by a potent mix of Red Clydeside radicalism and Green and Orange religious loyalties.

Ian R. Mitchell takes you on a journey along the River Clyde and shows it's not just about the remnants of shipbuilding, relating stories of conflicts, people and communities. The river rolls from Lanarkshire upriver, once renowned for its coal and steel production, to former centres of textile production such as Paisley and the Vale of Leven, with many other places equally rich in industrial history along its 100 mile course. From Robert Owen's New Lanark utopian experiment to the Little Moscow of the Vale of Leven, here is a working-class history rich in political and industrial innovation.

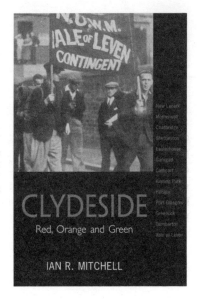

Ian Mitchell's infectious enthusiasm for the places visited in this book leaves the reader with a compelling urge to don walking shoes and retrace his steps.
THE MORNING STAR

This City Now: Glasgow and its working class past

Ian R Mitchell
ISBN: 978-1842820-82-7 PBK £12.99

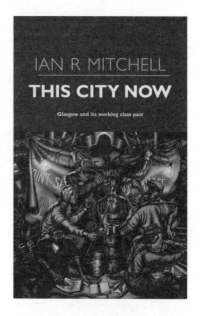

This City Now sets out to retrieve the hidden architectural, cultural and historical riches of some of Glasgow's working-class districts. Many who enjoy the fruits of Glasgow's recent gentrification will be surprised and delighted by the gems which Ian Mitchell has uncovered beyond the usual haunts.

An enthusiastic walker and historian, Mitchell invites us to recapture the social and political history of the working-class in Glasgow, by taking us on a journey from Partick to Rutherglen, and Clydebank to Pollokshaws, revealing the buildings which go unnoticed every day yet are worthy of so much more attention.

Once read and inspired, you will never be able to walk through Glasgow in the same way again.

... both visitors and locals can gain instruction and pleasure from this fine volume... Mitchell is a knowledgeable, witty and affable guide through the streets of the city...
GREEN LEFT WEEKLY

Who Belongs to Glasgow?

Mary Edward
ISBN: 978-1905222-87-2 PBK £9.99

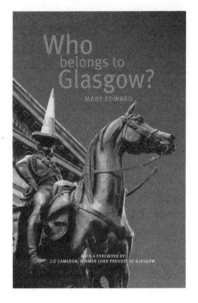

In this insightful second edition, Mary Edward traces the history of immigration to Glasgow over the past 200 years. From Highlanders to exiled Jews and asylum seekers, migrants to Glasgow have infused the city with a truly unique local colour. With penetrating social analysis and an impressive assemblage of historical artefacts, Edward weaves a vivid tapestry of the many peoples and cultures that have created contemporary Glasgow.

The staggering diversity of languages, religions and ethnicities is no new phenomenon in this city on the Clyde. Today's Glaswegians are the children, grandchildren and great-grandchildren of yesterday's emigrants, all of whom have chosen this great Scottish melting pot as their own and all of whom now belong to Glasgow.

Glasgow By the Way, But

John Cairney

ISBN: 978-1906307-10-3 PBK £7.99

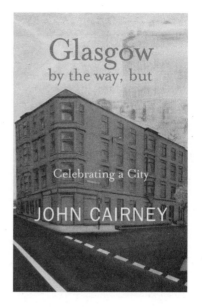

Glasgow to me is the ugly face that launched a thousand quips. If you're born in Glasgow you're born with a sense of humour. It's the only passport you need to get beyond its boundaries. I've gone around the world several times – I don't know if I've held Glasgow in front of me or dragged it behind me – but I've never been far from her in all that time.

JOHN CAIRNEY

In this collection of personal anecdotes, John Cairney takes you on a tour of *his* Glasgow, introducing the people and places that have shaped it. Full of the humour, tension and patter that characterises Scotland's most charismatic city, everyone will be sure to find a part of their own Glasgow reflected in Cairney's honest evocation of his home city. *Glasgow By the Way, But* is the written tribute Glasgow has been waiting for, from one of its most famous sons.

Social Sculpture: The Rise of the Glasgow Art Scene

Sarah Lowndes
ISBN: 978-1906817-59-6 PBK £14.99

Once 'the workshop of the world', in the last 30 years Glasgow has emerged from post-industrial decline to become the UK's main art centre after London, with a reputation for producing innovative and highly acclaimed artists and musicians.

Social Sculpture explains the phenomenon described by the curator Hans Ulrich Obrist as 'The Glasgow Miracle', through detailed analysis of the city's predominantly self-organised and autonomous arts infrastructure and interviews with the people who made it happen.

This fully revised and updated new edition of the first and only book to chart the emergence of the Glasgow art scene contains over 60 original interviews with Glasgow writers, curators, artists and musicians, including Turner Prize winners Douglas Gordon and Richard Wright, Turner Prize nominees Christine Borland and Cathy Wilkes,

Jarman Prize winner Luke Fowler, Becks Futures winner Toby Paterson, curators Francis McKee, Katrina Brown, Will Bradley and Toby Webster, and musicians Stuart Brathwaite (Mogwai), Aidan Moffat (Arab Strap), Sinead Young (Divorce) and Optimo DJ Keith McIvor.

Bunnets n Bowlers: A Clydeside Odyssey

Brian Whittingham
ISBN: 978-1906307-94-3 PBK £8.99

Ach, bit thers nae need tae worry,
ah'll get yi a joab in the yards,
yi'll be fixed up fur life
so yi wull, fixed up fir life

Every ship has a story, and so does every shipbuilder, whether they are bowler hats, the foremen whose job it was to make sure deadlines were met, or bunnets, the skilled artisans that did the graft.

Meet the characters of The Black Squad: Sam Abbott, the knicker knocker from Duntocher; Wild Bill Hickok, the card shark; Irish Pat, the burner who likes his bevvy too much, and many more. They've spent their lives together in John Brown's shipyard sharing in the hilarity and tragedy of their work.

Brian Whittingham started his career in the Clydeside shipyards at just 15 years old when a job in the yards was for life. *Bunnets n Bowlers* follows this Clydeside odyssey, familiar to so many, from smart-arsed apprentice to skilled artisan and celebrates the humour and camaraderie of an ailing profession.

Luath Press Limited
committed to publishing well written books worth reading

LUATH PRESS takes its name from Robert Burns, whose little collie Luath (*Gael.,* swift or nimble) tripped up Jean Armour at a wedding and gave him the chance to speak to the woman who was to be his wife and the abiding love of his life. Burns called one of 'The Twa Dogs' Luath after Cuchullin's hunting dog in Ossian's *Fingal*. Luath Press was established in 1981 in the heart of Burns country, and is now based a few steps up the road from Burns' first lodgings on Edinburgh's Royal Mile.

Luath offers you distinctive writing with a hint of unexpected pleasures.

Most bookshops in the UK, the US, Canada, Australia, New Zealand and parts of Europe either carry our books in stock or can order them for you. To order direct from us, please send a £sterling cheque, postal order, international money order or your credit card details (number, address of cardholder and expiry date) to us at the address below. Please add post and packing as follows: UK – £1.00 per delivery address; overseas surface mail – £2.50 per delivery address; overseas air-mail – £3.50 for the first book to each delivery address, plus £1.00 for each additional book by airmail to the same address. If your order is a gift, we will happily enclose your card or message at no extra charge.

Luath Press Limited
543/2 Castlehill
The Royal Mile
Edinburgh EH1 2ND
Scotland
Telephone: 0131 225 4326 (24 hours)
Fax: 0131 225 4324
email: sales@luath.co.uk
Website: www.luath.co.uk